Final Surrender

Alpha Heroes Yielding to Love Collection

Alison Reid

Final Surrender - Alpha Heroes Yielding to Love Collection

by Alison Reid

This is a work of fiction. Names, characters, businesses, places, events, and incidents are either the products of the author's imagination or used in a fictitious manner. Any resemblance to actual persons, living or dead, or actual events is purely coincidental.

ISBN: 978-1-7644837-3-5

Independently published

Final Surrender

Alpha Heroes Yielding to Love Collection

Strength. Desire. Secrets.

Welcome to **Final Surrender**—a collection of emotionally charged romances where the most guarded men finally yield to love. From sun-soaked ranches to luxurious yachts and unexpected family revelations, these stories follow alpha heroes who learn that true power comes from opening their hearts.

Each novel in this collection is a complete standalone romance, written in the spirit of classic Mills & Boon with a modern edge. You'll find slow-burning tension, irresistible attraction, protective heroes, and women brave enough to make them surrender to love.

Inside these pages, passion ignites, hearts soften, and the men who once resisted discover that some desires cannot be denied. There is no cheating, and every story delivers a guaranteed happily-ever-after.

Whether you're returning to favourite heroes or discovering them for the first time, **Final Surrender** invites you to immerse yourself in a binge-worthy collection where love triumphs over pride, and surrender becomes the ultimate reward.

Enjoy the journey.

Table of Contents

Billionaire Rancher

Alison Reid

A complete standalone romance

Previously published individually

Chapter One

The tyres of Amy Henderson's truck crunched over the gravel shoulder as she crested the final ridge, and there it was— Steamboat Springs, Colorado, spread out below her like a living postcard.

She slowed instinctively, pulling off onto a scenic overlook, her heart thudding in her chest. After everything, after the fear, the nights packed in suitcases, the whispered prayers for courage— she was finally here.

Steamboat Springs nestled between rolling hills and the jagged peaks of the Rockies, the valley a patchwork of meadows, forests, and the winding Yampa River. In the distance, the familiar streak of Fish Creek Falls tumbled down a rocky cliffside, its mist catching the sun.

The town was a patchwork of brick buildings, rustic lodges, and colourful shops, each proudly displaying local pride. It was beautiful, unpretentious, and easy to imagine a life here. But Amy knew that the real solace wouldn't come from the town—it was the isolation she had driven so far to find that would offer her the peace she craved.

A place where maybe — just maybe — she could disappear long enough to find herself again.

Amy gripped the steering wheel tighter, fighting the urge to turn around. She wasn't ready. She would never be ready. But life wasn't waiting for her to be brave. It was happening — messy, raw, and real — whether she wanted it to or not.

She turned back onto the road, the town drawing closer with every mile. She passed a welcome sign —

Steamboat Springs: Come for the Snow, Stay for the Summer

— and gave a small, humourless smile. She wasn't here for the snow or the summer.

She was here for survival. Her reflection in the rearview mirror caught her off guard. She still looked the same — blonde hair pulled into a loose braid, pale blue eyes that seemed too large for her delicate face, skin kissed pink from the endless drive across state lines.

But there was something new now, something heavy in her expression. Guarded. Tired. Hardened. It felt like she had left a part of herself behind, back in the chaos of the city.

The men who passed her in filthy trucks and dusty Jeeps barely registered on her radar. Amy had trained herself not to look too long at any man, not to give them an opening, not to invite anything. Trust was something she no longer handed out freely.

The last time she had trusted a man, it had nearly cost her life.

She forced her thoughts away from the past as she drove through the heart of town. Children raced their bikes along the sidewalks. A farmer's market sprawled across the town square, with stalls overflowing with fresh produce and wildflowers. Couples sipped coffee outside rustic cafés, laughter floating up into the crisp mountain air.

It was painfully normal. And it made her ache in a way she hadn't expected.

Her GPS chimed, directing her toward a small rental cabin just outside the town limits. The road climbed steadily, pine trees thickening along the shoulders, and the houses grew farther apart. Amy exhaled a shaky breath. This was better. The farther from people, the better.

Her new job — the one miracle she could cling to — would start tomorrow. She was stepping in at Steamboat Springs Veterinary Services, taking over for the town's beloved retiring vet, Dr. Henry Harrison.

Amy had agreed to fill the role for six months — maybe longer if she found the courage to stay.

The town needed her. And, though she hated to admit it, she needed them just as much.

So, she packed her two suitcases — and a heart stitched back together with trembling hands — and set out to build a new life.

As she rounded the final bend to her cabin, the mountains rose like ancient guardians on the horizon, their peaks brushed with the last stubborn clinging of snow. A hawk circled overhead, riding the updrafts, free and fierce.

Amy pulled into the narrow gravel driveway and killed the engine. Silence rushed in around her, thick and heavy, broken only by the whisper of wind through the trees.

For a long moment, she sat there, hands resting loosely on the wheel, gathering herself.

This was her chance. Her new beginning.

If the past found her here — if he found her — she would deal with it then.

But for now, Steamboat Springs was hers.

And maybe, just maybe, she could find a way to breathe again.

Amy climbed out of the truck, the door creaking as it swung closed behind her. The late afternoon air was cooler here, scented with pine and something clean and wild she couldn't name. She pulled her sweatshirt tighter around her shoulders, suddenly hyperaware of how alone she was.

She walked up the narrow stone path to the front porch, the weathered boards groaning softly under her boots. A simple digital lockbox hung beside the door, just as the rental agent had promised. Amy punched in the code — 0427, her own birthday — and with a click, the box swung open, revealing a single tarnished key on a red plastic tag.

She held it in her hand for a moment, feeling the small but undeniable shift inside her: This is mine. This is real.

Sliding the key into the lock, she twisted until the door gave way with a reluctant thunk. The cabin's heavy wooden door swung inward, revealing a small, sunlit living space.

Amy stepped inside.

The place smelled faintly of cedar and old stone, like a memory captured in wood and air. The living room was cozy but worn, with a faded leather couch, a coffee table carved from a single slab of tree trunk, and a stone fireplace blackened from years of use. A few pictures hung on the walls — photos of mountains, rivers, and elk grazing in meadows — nothing personal, just generic prints meant to fill empty spaces.

The open-concept kitchen was tucked in one corner, simple and functional: oak cabinets, an ancient but clean white stove, a refrigerator humming quietly in the background. A basket on the counter held a handful of brochures about local attractions — fishing, hiking, ski passes.

Amy dropped her keys on the counter and crossed the room to the hallway, her boots making soft thuds against the worn hardwood floor. She peeked into the bedroom: a queen-sized bed covered with a hand-stitched quilt, flanked by mismatched nightstands. A single window framed a view of the woods, where the trees swayed lazily in the breeze.

The bathroom was small but clean—a porcelain sink, a claw-foot tub with a rusted pipe, and fluffy white towels stacked neatly on a shelf.

It wasn't fancy. It wasn't much.

But it was safe.

And that was everything.

Amy returned to the living room and sank onto the couch with a long exhale. She let her head fall back against the cushions, staring up at the exposed wooden beams that ran across the ceiling. For the first time in months, the tension in her shoulders eased a little.

There would be no fists through walls here.

No shouting in the dead of night.

No hollow apologies, only to be shattered again.

Just space. And silence.

Her stomach rumbled, reminding her she hadn't eaten since breakfast somewhere outside of Denver.

She pushed herself up from the couch, determined to find the box of groceries she had packed, when her phone buzzed sharply in her pocket.

Amy frowned, pulling it free. A local number blinked on the screen.

She hesitated. Instinct prickled at her skin, a whisper of fear rising before she caught herself.

It's just the clinic, she reminded herself. *It's just work.*

She answered on the third ring.

"Hello?"

"Dr. Henderson?" a kind, slightly raspy voice asked.

"Yes, this is Amy."

"Well, hello there, dear," the man said warmly. "This is Dr. Henry Harrison. Thought I'd better call and make sure you made it to town all right. Didn't want you thinking we forgot about you."

A knot of tension loosened in Amy's chest.

"Yes, I'm here. I just got in, actually."

"Good, good." His voice carried the easy, weathered comfort of someone who had spent a lifetime caring for both animals and the people who loved them. "I'm glad. We're mighty lucky to have you, you know. The clinic's been buzzing all week, everyone excited to meet the new doctor."

Amy smiled faintly, the corners of her mouth twitching despite herself.

"I'm looking forward to meeting everyone too," she said. And for once, it wasn't a lie.

"Well, don't you worry about a thing," Dr. Harrison said. "Get some rest tonight. I'll meet you at the clinic first thing in the morning. We'll take it slow; let you settle in."

"Thank you, Dr. Harrison. I appreciate it."

"Henry," he corrected gently. "Around here, we don't stand on ceremony."

Amy laughed under her breath, the sound feeling strange but good.

"Okay, Henry. I'll see you in the morning."

"You take care, Amy," he said, a note of quiet encouragement in his voice. "You're right where you're meant to be."

The call ended, but his words lingered, warming a small, bruised part of her heart.

Maybe, Steamboat Springs could be the beginning of something new.

Amy slipped her phone back into her pocket and wandered to the wide front window of the cabin. Outside, the sun was sinking behind the mountains, painting the sky in strokes of gold, pink, and violet. The air was crisp even in early evening, carrying the faint scent of pine and distant woodsmoke.

She wrapped her arms around herself and stared out at the endless stretch of open land, the snow-tipped peaks standing like quiet sentinels against the sky.

For the first time in months — maybe years — she let herself breathe. Really breathe.

The silence wasn't heavy here. It wasn't filled with dread. It was peaceful.

A fragile tendril of hope unfurled in her chest, cautious but alive.

Maybe this place could be different. Maybe she could be different here too.

This place was a far cry from where she came from — the crowded neighbourhoods and constant noise of Wichita Kansas. There, even the mountains felt distant, walled off by traffic and too many people.

She had driven through the chaos of Denver, watching the city shrink in her rearview mirror like a weight she was finally leaving behind.

Here, in Steamboat Springs, the world felt wider. Safer. Like maybe, just maybe, there was a life waiting for her that didn't hurt to reach for.

Amy pressed her forehead lightly against the glass, whispering a promise only the mountains could hear.

She inhaled deeply, and for the first time in months, the air felt clean, and the silence didn't suffocate. Maybe, just maybe, here, in this quiet place, she could begin to try again.

Chapter Two

Eric Reynolds stepped out of his sleek black SUV, the engine ticking as it cooled in the crisp mountain air. The sprawling acreage of Silver Meadow Ranch stretched before him — acres of rolling pastures framed by the jagged peaks of the Rockies, bathed now in the fiery gold of the setting sun.

He pushed his sunglasses up onto his head, brown eyes narrowing against the light as he scanned the long gravel driveway. A soft breeze stirred the dark hair at his temples. Somewhere in the distance, a few ranch hands moved about, their voices low and easy, but Eric wasn't focused on them.

He was waiting for Patriot, his champion thoroughbred, one of the few living things Eric truly trusted. The horse's victory had been impressive, another million-dollar win — a testament to everything Silver Meadow Ranch was, and more.

This time, at the prestigious Breeders' Invitational in Lexington, a race that had drawn some of the finest bloodstock in the country.

And Patriot had thundered across the finish line with a lead so commanding, the second-place finisher had barely caught a glimpse of his tail.

Another million-dollar purse. Another proof that Silver Meadow Ranch wasn't just a billionaire's vanity project — it was his heart and soul.

Eric rolled his shoulders back, the cut of his navy button-down pulling tight across his broad frame. The years had been good to him, physically at least. He was tall, lean, athletic — the kind of man people still turned to watch. But there was a hardness to him now too, one that hadn't been there before the divorce. Before the betrayal.

He wasn't a fool anymore. He didn't believe in fairy tales, or forever, or promises whispered in the dark.

The low rumble of a trailer pulling up the drive caught his attention. His mouth twitched into a half-smile — rare these days — as the gleaming hauler came into view. The ranch's black and silver logo was emblazoned proudly on the side: a running stallion beneath the words Silver Meadow Ranch.

Eric walked toward the trailer, boots crunching over the gravel, his heart picking up pace. He could already picture Patriot tossing his head, impatient and proud, as if he knew he was the king of everything he surveyed.

And he was.

As the trailer rolled to a stop, the dust kicked up in the fading light. The familiar driver opened the doors, revealing Patriot's powerful form, still pulsing with the energy of his victory.

The horse stepped forward, his dark bay coat gleaming even in the fading light, and he let out a soft, eager nicker upon spotting Eric. There was a knowing in the horse's eyes, a bond that Eric could feel all the way down to his bones.

"Easy, boy," Eric murmured under his breath, his lips curving into a rare, genuine smile. He walked toward the horse, a quiet affection in his eyes that was rarely shared with anyone.

Patriot's ears flicked toward him, and the stallion stretched his neck, his warm breath grazing Eric's chest. Eric reached up, scratching the horse's forehead with a familiar touch, his hand gliding across the glossy surface of Patriot's coat. The horse closed his eyes and leaned into the affection, as if savouring the connection.

"You did it again, huh, buddy?" Eric chuckled softly, his voice low and comforting. "You're something else, Patriot. Just like always."

Behind him, the sound of footsteps approached, boots crunching the gravel with a steady rhythm. Eric turned, and there stood Levi—tall, broad-shouldered, and wearing the weathered expression of someone who had lived a hard life but wouldn't trade it for anything.

Levi had been with Eric since the very beginning. They were more like brothers than employer and employee, having built Silver Meadow Ranch together from the ground up. Levi was the kind of man who knew everything there was to know about running a ranch and a team, and Eric trusted him with the kind of loyalty that came from years of shared hardships.

"Another win for the king, I see," Levi said with a grin, tipping his hat back as he surveyed the horse.

Eric nodded, still giving Patriot a few more scratches. "Million-dollar win. Another one for the books."

Levi grunted, clearly impressed but not one to show too much excitement. "Hell of a horse. You ought to be proud."

Eric gave a half-smile but didn't respond. Instead, he moved to the horse's side, keeping his hand on Patriot's neck as the stallion turned his head toward Levi.

"Want to give him a rub?" Eric offered, stepping aside.

Levi raised an eyebrow but didn't hesitate. He reached up and ran his hand down the side of Patriot's neck, the horse nickering softly in appreciation.

"Not bad," Levi said with a knowing smirk, his eyes flicking between Eric and the horse. "He's got spirit. Just like you, when it counts."

Eric couldn't help but laugh, the sound rough but genuine. "Yeah, maybe too much spirit sometimes. He's a hell of a horse, but he's got a temper."

Levi chuckled and slapped Patriot gently on the shoulder. "Just like his owner, huh?"

Eric's gaze flickered to Levi, his lips twitching into a grin that never quite reached his eyes. "Watch it, Levi. You're treading on thin ice."

Levi's grin widened, but he knew when to let things slide. The bond between Eric and Levi was deep, unspoken, but strong enough that it didn't need words to communicate. After a beat, Levi turned his attention back to the trailer.

"I'll get him settled in the stables," Levi said, his tone shifting to business mode. "Let him cool off a bit. You can handle the press tomorrow, I'm sure."

Eric nodded, his attention still on Patriot as the horse started to walk with Levi, his hooves kicking up dust.

"Thanks, Levi," Eric said quietly, his voice suddenly softer, like a weight had settled on his chest. "I know I can count on you."

Levi looked back over his shoulder, offering Eric a half-smile. "Anytime, boss."

Eric watched them for a moment longer, a strange feeling stirring in his chest. It wasn't often he let down his guard, even for Levi, but there was something about the connection between him and this horse — this part of him — that seemed to pull the veil back just a little. Patriot didn't need words. He didn't need promises. He was simply there, a constant.

Maybe that was the kind of loyalty Eric needed.

He sighed, pushing the thought aside, and turned to head toward the house, ready for the next task. But even as he walked, his mind lingered on something else. Something more.

Eric walked into the house, the heavy wooden door closing softly behind him with a satisfying thud. The familiar scent of cedar and leather filled the air, a comforting reminder of the life he'd built here in Steamboat Springs. He slid off his boots and tossed his keys into a ceramic bowl by the door, then moved through the grand entryway, his footsteps echoing off the polished hardwood floors.

The house was everything he'd ever wanted — modern yet rustic, with a touch of elegance that reminded him of his old life in the city, but with the ruggedness of the ranch. The walls were adorned with local art, paintings of the surrounding mountains and sweeping plains, and there was a giant stone fireplace that dominated the living room, its hearth always ready to welcome him home. The leather furniture was worn, comfortable, but tasteful, and the expansive windows framed the breathtaking view of the valley below and the distant peaks.

He moved through the living room, his mind already drifting toward the shower. The weight of the day clung to him — the dust, the tension in his muscles, the quiet ache of a life reshaped after the divorce three years ago. Each year had brought a new layer of weariness, a steady undercurrent of exhaustion he couldn't quite shake.

The house was quiet, empty except for the staff who were long gone by now. And yet, there was a peace in that. A stark contrast to the suffocating chaos of his past life in the city, in that world of high society and constant noise.

He made his way upstairs to the master suite, the windows in the hallway giving him another spectacular view of the valley. The room itself was a perfect reflection of his new life — simple, uncluttered, yet comfortable. The king-sized bed was made with crisp, dark linens, and a leather armchair sat in the corner, as though waiting for him to unwind after a long day. On the far side of the room, a door opened to the en-suite bathroom.

Eric stepped into the bathroom, the soft, ambient lighting casting a warm glow on the stone walls. The shower, large enough to fit two people, stood in the centre of the room, with glass walls that allowed a panoramic view of the mountains outside. It was his favourite feature of the house, especially in the evenings when the light from the setting sun turned the world outside into an amber haze.

He undressed quickly, tossing his clothes into the laundry hamper, and stepped into the shower. The water hit him in a steady stream, warm and soothing as it cascaded over his body, washing away the sweat of the day and the weight of the past.

As he let the water flow over him, Eric leaned his head against the cool tile and closed his eyes. He hadn't realised how much he'd needed this — the solitude, the quiet, the peace.

When he first moved to Steamboat Springs, it had been to escape. To get away from the toxic world he'd been part of for so long. His marriage to Jessica, the socialite who had promised him everything, had ended in disappointment and bitterness. She had refused to have children; despite the dreams they'd once shared. And when their marriage had unravelled, leaving him with nothing but the cold emptiness of a failed life, Eric had done the only thing he could think of.

He'd walked away.

And coming here — to Silver Meadow Ranch — had been his second chance. Steamboat Springs wasn't just a place on a map. It was a sanctuary. A place where he could build something real, away from the constant pressures of the elite world he'd once inhabited. Where he could breathe without feeling like he was suffocating under the weight of others' expectations.

There were still moments when he thought about the past, about Jessica and the dreams that had been shattered, but they were fleeting. In this town, he didn't need to be anyone but himself. He didn't need to keep up the act or play the part of the charming, successful billionaire. He was just Eric Reynolds — rancher, businessman, and, in his own way, a man who was learning how to trust again.

He tilted his head back beneath the hot stream of water, eyes closed, letting it pound against his face and wash away the tension that had become his constant companion. Steam curled around him, thick and silent, like a shroud he didn't have to explain himself to.

The years had changed him. Hardened him. Made him quieter, colder — cynical in ways he hadn't anticipated. Life had chipped away at the man he used to be, carving out softness and replacing it with sharp edges and silence. Somewhere along the line, he'd stopped reaching for people. He'd built walls so high and thick, not even a whisper could get through. And maybe that was okay. Maybe solitude was safer. Predictable. Clean.

Here, in Steamboat Springs — nestled deep in the mountains, far from the chaos of Denver and the wreckage of his past — he didn't need anyone. The ranch, the horses, the rhythm of the land — it was enough. At least, that's what he told himself.

He hadn't been on a single date since the divorce. Hadn't even considered it. Trusting a woman again? That felt about as likely as snow in July. Jessica had seen to that — unraveling him piece by piece with every lie she'd told, every moment she'd used love like a weapon. He hadn't just lost a marriage — he'd lost faith. In people. In promises. In himself.

He exhaled slowly, water dripping down his face like regret. Maybe this was who he was now — the man who kept his distance, who stayed safe behind caution and quiet. The man who didn't need anyone.

Or at least, didn't want to need anyone ever again.

His reflection stared back at him, eyes dark and serious. But for the first time in years, Eric saw a flicker of something else — something softer. Maybe hope. Maybe the beginning of a new chapter.

He turned off the water, grabbed a towel, and stepped out of the shower, his body warm and relaxed, the weight of the day melting away. As he dried off, he felt an unfamiliar sense of calm settle over him, one that had eluded him for years.

Maybe, finally, he could let go of the past.

Maybe, he could allow himself to hope for something more.

Chapter Three

Amy stood in front of the bathroom mirror, soft morning light bathing her in a muted glow. She studied her reflection with practiced detachment, a habit worn from years of doing this — observing without truly seeing. There was no need to feel anything. No need to dig deeper. It was just another day.

Her blonde hair, shoulder-length and loosely pulled back into a ponytail, framed her face with casual disarray. A few stray strands escaped the elastic, falling carelessly around her forehead. It was deliberately imperfect, not too styled. Polished was a liability. Men noticed polished. And the last thing she needed was attention — not today, not on her first day in a new town, with a new job.

Her fingers grazed the scar at her hairline — a faint, silvery thread barely visible beneath her blonde hair, but ever-present beneath the surface. It had faded over time, softened into a subtle line, almost invisible to anyone who didn't know it was there. But she felt it always — like a whisper from the past, a phantom echo of the night that changed everything.

Darren's hands had left it there. Not just his fists, but his fury. The jagged trace of his rage was stitched into her skin, a cruel souvenir of the night she thought she might die. She had fought back — clawed, kicked, screamed — but every ounce of resistance only made him more vicious. The room had spun with terror; his face contorted in blind anger. When the police finally burst through the door, she had thought it was over. Relief had hit her like oxygen after drowning. But Darren's final, desperate blow had nearly killed her.

The doctors called her survival a miracle. The fracture to her skull should have left her with lasting damage — memory loss, impaired vision, speech problems. Instead, she had walked out of the hospital weeks later, battered but whole. A few metal staples. A long, painful recovery. And the scar.

He was in prison now. Locked away. The sentence had brought justice on paper, but the past wasn't so easily sentenced. She had built a new life — changed her number, moved to a new apartment and now moved to a new town, starting over with nothing but two suitcases and a name she barely recognised as her own. She had left that girl behind.

But the past never stayed gone. It crept in with certain smells, certain shadows, certain silences. It resurfaced when she least expected it — the slam of a door, the echo of a man's voice pitched just wrong, the sight of her own reflection when she forgot how far she'd come.

Still, the scar remained. The only physical evidence of the night that nearly ended her. She sometimes called it her 'gift', though in truth it felt more like a curse. A cruel reminder. But also, maybe, a badge. A mark of everything she'd survived. A symbol that she had not been erased.

The memories stirred now — the screaming, the blood, the blinding pain — but she didn't recoil. She stood straighter. Stronger. She was no longer the woman who froze under the weight of his rage. She wasn't the girl he tried to break.

She had endured. She had rebuilt. She had survived.

And she would never let herself forget it.

Her fingers lingered on the scar, then drifted down to the rest of her reflection. Her eyes — pale blue, sharp, but hard now — had lost the softness they once held. There was nothing left to be vulnerable with. The protective layers had hardened them, and she liked it that way. Her lips, soft and pale, barely parted in the semblance of a smile. She didn't bother with lipstick; there was no need to draw attention to them. All she wanted was to blend in, to slip into the background, unnoticed.

Her skin, olive-toned and clear, didn't require much upkeep, and she was grateful for that. A scattering of freckles across the bridge of her nose was the only hint of her youth, but they were faint, easily overlooked. And that was just how she wanted it — invisible, untouchable, free from anyone's gaze. She was already running from her past; she didn't need it to chase her here.

She dressed quickly, donning the modest outfit she'd chosen the night before. Nothing too bold, nothing too revealing. A pale blue blouse, simple and understated, tucked neatly into a pair of well-worn jeans. She glanced at her reflection, her eyes scanning the ensemble with a flicker of doubt. It was practical, plain — exactly what she wanted. No attention, no questions. She just needed to blend in, and she hoped she'd managed that.

Her heart quickened as she turned from the mirror, taking a steadying breath. First days always brought nerves, and she felt them now. But today felt different. This wasn't just about the job. This was about starting fresh — shedding the weight of the past, leaving Darren's shadow behind, and hoping that for once, maybe she could just be… herself. The person she was now, not the person she used to be.

She pulled on her jacket, smoothing the fabric with a final glance at the mirror. Her reflection, familiar yet distant, stared back at her, and for a brief moment, she wondered if anyone would ever really see her. Not the woman she had been, but the woman she was becoming.

Amy slid into the driver's seat of her old, reliable truck, the worn leather of the seat creaking under her as she adjusted the rearview mirror. The engine roared to life with a smooth hum, the familiar sound settling some of the unease in her chest. She shifted into gear and pulled out of the gravel driveway, steering the truck down the long, dusty road that led into the heart of the small town.

The road stretched out before her, bordered by sprawling fields that gave way to distant hills, the morning sun just beginning to catch the landscape in its golden light. Amy's hands gripped the steering wheel a little tighter, her gaze flicking from the road to the occasional cluster of houses that dotted the way. The town felt like a world apart from the city life she'd left behind — slower, quieter, like something from another time. There was a sense of peace here, almost unnerving in its simplicity. She could almost feel the weight of her past lifting with every mile that took her further from the chaos she'd escaped.

As she neared the town's centre, the landscape began to change. The open spaces gave way to smaller roads, lined with quaint little shops and cozy homes, all nestled against the backdrop of the towering mountains. She followed the main street, the hum of her truck's tyres on the asphalt accompanying her thoughts, until she reached the place she'd come for—the veterinary clinic.

The sign out front swayed lightly in the breeze, a simple but warm illustration of a dog and cat, symbolising the care and compassion waiting inside. It felt like a small, reassuring promise, one that made the weight in her chest ease, just a little.

She put the truck in park, her chest tightening as she stared at the building. This was it. Her first day. Her new life. Taking a deep breath, she shifted the truck into park and turned off the engine, the silence of the truck settling in around her. For a moment, she just sat there, hands resting on the steering wheel, eyes closed, gathering herself.

Finally, with a steadying breath, she opened the door and stepped out onto the pavement. The morning air was cool and fresh, and the cool air, heavy with the scent of pine and earth, filled her lungs, as she adjusted the straps of her bag. Her shoes made a soft tap on the ground as she walked toward the clinic's entrance, each step echoing in her mind.

The door jingled softly as she entered, the warmth of the clinic wrapping around her. She paused, taking in the space — clean and well-kept, with shelves of pet supplies, a waiting area with a few chairs, and a counter where a friendly-faced woman stood. The woman smiled as Amy entered, her expression warm and welcoming.

"You must be Amy," she said with a Southern twang, her eyes sparkling with kindness. "I'm Sally Hayes." She extended a hand. "Welcome to the clinic."

Amy shook her hand, feeling the woman's firm grip and noticing how much older she seemed in person — probably in her mid-forties, with a comfortable, lived-in warmth to her features. Her dark brown hair was pulled back in a loose ponytail, and her scrubs were a bright shade of teal, with a few pet hairs clinging to the fabric.

"Nice to meet you," Amy said, offering a small smile. "I'm excited to be here."

"Well, we're glad to have you. You'll fit right in." Sally motioned toward the hallway behind her. "Dr. Harrison's in his office, if you're ready to meet him."

Amy nodded and followed Sally down the hallway, the walls lined with pictures of various animals — cats, dogs, even a few horses. The smell of disinfectant mixed with the faint, comforting scent of pet shampoo. At the end of the hallway, Sally stopped at a door and knocked lightly before opening it.

Inside, an older man sat behind a desk, scribbling on a notepad. His white hair was thin, his face lined with years of experience, but his eyes were sharp and focused, his posture still strong despite his age. He looked up as Sally knocked, and his lips lifted into a small smile.

"Amy, this is Dr. Henry Harrison," Sally introduced.

"Nice to meet you in person, Dr. Harrison," Amy said, offering a polite smile as she extended her hand.

"Please, call me Henry," he replied, his warm, gravelly voice carrying an easy charm. "Welcome to our little clinic. It's good to have some fresh blood around here. I'm looking forward to my retirement." His eyes twinkled with a mix of kindness and mischief.

Amy chuckled softly, the tension in her shoulders loosening just a bit. "I'm happy to be here."

Henry stood, offering her a firm handshake that was surprisingly gentle, instantly putting her at ease. "It's a small operation, but we do our best. Sally runs the front, and I handle the medical side of things. You'll be taking over in two weeks…"

"Thank you," Amy replied, her voice soft but sincere. She let out a quiet breath, feeling her muscles relax. "I'm looking forward to getting started."

"Well, let's get you settled in," Henry said, gesturing to a chair beside his desk. "I'm sure you've got plenty of questions, but we'll take it slow. One step at a time, and you'll fit right in."

Sally flashed Amy an encouraging smile before slipping out the door, leaving her alone with Henry. Amy took a moment to gather herself, her hands folding neatly in her lap as she mentally steeled herself for the day ahead. The nerves buzzed just beneath her calm exterior, but there was also something else—a small, unanticipated sense of belonging that settled around her like a soft embrace.

Henry gave a slight nod toward the empty seat across from him. "Have a seat," he said, his voice polite, with a thread of warmth beneath it. Amy sat down, her posture straight, hands tucked together as she focused on his words. Henry spoke briefly, outlining some of the key aspects of the clinic and the day ahead.

Amy took a steadying breath, feeling the weight of the day settle on her shoulders. She was here to take over, but right now, she was the one who needed to prove she could manage it.

"Alright, let's get started," she murmured to herself, brushing aside the flutter of nerves that gnawed at the edges of her calm. She squared her shoulders and walked toward the first exam room.

Max, a scruffy terrier with a patchy coat, sat on the exam table, tail wagging in nervous excitement. The woman holding his leash, her face drawn with fatigue and anxiety, barely looked up when Amy entered.

"Hi, I'm Amy," she said with a smile, already moving toward the supplies. "I'll be taking care of Max today. Dr. Harrison will be observing."

The woman nodded quickly, her attention still fixed on Max. "Thank you," she said, but there was a hesitation in her voice — a quiet reservation. Amy could feel it. Some people didn't trust new faces, and that was fine. She wasn't here to win anyone over with small talk; she was here to show she could do the job, take charge, and do it without hesitation.

Amy moved through the exam with focused efficiency, checking Max's temperature first, then his pulse and heart rate. She spoke to him in a soft, reassuring voice, keeping her movements deliberate. Each step felt like a rhythm she knew well — a rhythm she had mastered over time.

Her gaze flickered briefly to Henry, standing by the door, arms crossed, his sharp eyes trained on her every movement. He didn't speak, but his presence was a weight she could feel.

Amy ignored the pressure, keeping her attention on Max as she worked. His vitals were solid — no fever, a steady pulse, healthy gums, and his weight was consistent with his last visit.

"Vitals are normal," Amy reported, turning to Henry. "No fever, pulse is strong. His weight is stable."

Henry grunted in approval, offering nothing more. He stepped forward to examine Max himself, checking the dog's joints and skin for any signs of discomfort.

"You're doing well," he said, his voice low but steady. There was a faint hint of approval in the roughness of his tone, though he still kept things measured, giving only the briefest of murmurs as he examined the dog.

Amy absorbed his praise, letting it pass through her without hesitation. She continued with quiet precision, explaining Max's treatment options for his itchy skin, answering the woman's questions with confidence. By the time they finished, the woman's tension had loosened. She patted Max's head, a small smile pulling at her lips. "Thank you, Amy. Max is in good hands."

Henry didn't immediately approach, but after a few moments, he stepped up beside her as she prepped for the next patient. "Nice work," he said, his voice still low, but now carrying a softening edge that hadn't been there before.

The simplicity of his words settled over Amy like an unexpected warmth. She hadn't expected much from him today — after all, his silence had been as much a test as anything. But now, as his approval lingered, she allowed herself to take it in. It was the first time today she felt seen — not as the new girl, not as someone trying to prove herself, but as someone who had done something well.

She offered him a quick, appreciative nod. "Thanks, Henry. Next one's up."

The hours passed in a blur of patients and cases, each one blending into the next. Amy was in charge now. She guided every exam, explained every procedure, and took the lead in each consultation. Henry observed, taking notes now and then, but never stepping in. His silence was as supportive as his praise had been — steady, unspoken approval that she could feel even without words.

By lunchtime, Amy was drained but determined. Sally popped into the staff room, towel in hand, wiping off her hands as she glanced over at Amy.

"How's it going?" she asked, her smile genuine.

"Good," Amy replied, her voice steady, though the exhaustion was starting to creep in. "Henry's been quiet, so I take that as a good sign."

Sally chuckled, taking a seat. "He doesn't talk much, but if there was a problem, you'd know. Trust me."

Amy smiled, the reassurance washing over her. "That's a relief."

The rest of the day passed with a rhythm Amy was beginning to find natural. With each exam, she grew more confident, more comfortable in her role. Henry never interrupted, only observed, and the weight of his attention felt less like pressure and more like support.

As the day wound to a close, Henry approached her again. He stood beside her for a moment, nodding slowly, his gruff demeanour softened by a quiet respect.

"You've got what it takes," he said, his voice low but filled with a sincerity that cut through the professional detachment. "I'm not worried about my little clinic with you taking over. You'll do just fine here."

Amy felt a surge of quiet pride at his words, her chest lightening for the first time that day. She allowed herself a moment to breathe, to acknowledge that maybe she had done the right thing accepting this new responsibility.

"Thanks, Henry. I appreciate that."

As she packed up her things, ready to leave for the day, she couldn't help but feel a quiet sense of accomplishment. It had been a long day, but a good one. She had proven herself — not just to Henry, but to herself. Tomorrow, she'd do it all again. And this time, she wouldn't be so nervous. She was ready.

Chapter Four

The sun hung high over the open plains as Eric and Levi pulled into the weathered diner on the edge of Steamboat Springs.

It had been a long day—negotiating with ranchers about cattle for Eric's outer fields. Productive, sure, but nothing worked up a man's appetite like a few hours on horseback and ranch business.

Levi hopped down from the truck, stretching against the bright sun. Eric followed, adjusting his worn leather hat.

The bell above the diner door jingled as they stepped inside, the scent of sizzling bacon and fresh coffee wrapping around them like an old friend.

Mrs. Jensen, the owner, stood behind the counter, her apron stained from years of service. She flashed a quick smile as she poured coffee for a regular.

"Well, well, if it isn't Eric and Levi. What'll it be, boys?"

Eric slid onto a stool. "Couple of burgers, Brenda. And fries. Been out buying cattle all morning—need something to fill us up."

Levi nodded, flashing a grin. "Make it two."

"Coming right up," Brenda said, disappearing into the kitchen.

The diner was quiet; the kind of peaceful stillness only small towns could pull off.

Eric leaned back, taking in the familiar sight of checkered floors, cracked red booths, and the dusty jukebox that hadn't worked right in years.

A few minutes later, the door creaked open again.

Larry Benton, the local lawyer, strolled in—crisp white shirt, tie a little too polished for the laid-back crowd.

He offered a nod and slid onto a stool.

"Afternoon, Brenda."

"Afternoon, Larry," she replied warmly.

As Larry ordered, a buzz started around the counter.

"I hear the new vet's taking over for Henry," one of the regulars said.

Another nodded. "Yeah, heard she's sharp. And cute."

Eric raised an eyebrow. "New vet? Didn't know Henry was retiring."

Levi chuckled. "Looks like it. And sounds like she's stirring things up already."

Larry, overhearing, couldn't resist.

"More than just pretty," he said. "Word is, she's damn good at what she does."

Levi swirled his coffee, smirking. "Brains and beauty. Dangerous combination."

Eric shook his head. "You're all just looking for trouble."

The door jingled again.

Henry walked in, Sally close behind him—and with them, a young blonde woman who moved with easy confidence.

"Brenda, this is Amy," Henry said. "Dr. Amy Henderson."

Amy offered a steady handshake and a polite smile. "Nice to meet you."

Eric and Levi exchanged a look.

She wasn't what Eric expected—graceful without being soft, the kind of calm that didn't need announcing.

Levi leaned in with a knowing grin, his voice low enough for only Eric to hear. "They weren't kidding."

Eric didn't respond right away. He kept his gaze fixed on the burger in front of him, pretending to be more interested in the sesame bun than in the woman who had just walked into the room. But the truth was, Levi was right. She wasn't just cute—she was beautiful. Not in the flashy, made-up way that caught attention for a moment and faded just as fast. No, Amy had a quiet kind of beauty, the kind that settled under your skin and stayed there.

As she made her way to the table, laughing softly at something Henry said, Eric caught himself watching the way her blonde hair shimmered in the late afternoon light, how her eyes crinkled when she smiled. She slid into the seat between Henry and Sally with an ease that made her feel like she belonged, like she'd been part of the group forever.

Eric took a bite of his burger, chewing slowly, trying to ignore the flutter in his chest that hadn't been there a minute ago.

It didn't take long before the locals started making their way over, all curious smiles and warm handshakes.

First was Larry.

"Larry Benton," he said, offering his hand. "Welcome to Steamboat Springs, Doc. You'll find we take good care of our own."

Amy smiled easily. "Looking forward to it."

Next came two young cowboys from a corner booth.

One of them—sandy-haired, eager—flashed a grin.

"Cody," he said, shaking her hand. "If you need anything—or anyone—you let me know."

Amy answered with a polite, practiced smile that left no opening.

"That's kind of you, Cody. I'm sure Henry and Sally will keep me plenty busy."

Henry chuckled into his coffee.

Sally gave Amy's hand an approving pat under the counter.

Across the diner, Levi nudged Eric with his elbow.

"Come on," he muttered. "Better say hello before Cody thinks he's got a shot."

Eric hesitated, the weight of indecision tightening his jaw. He was already half-turned toward the door, every instinct urging him to leave. He didn't like the way this woman unsettled him—how her presence stirred things he thought he'd locked away for good. But before he could make his escape, Levi was already crossing the room, that devil-may-care grin plastered across his face, moving with the confidence of a man who never second-guessed a damn thing.

"Afternoon, Doc," Levi drawled as he reached her, tipping his hat in an easy motion that made Amy smile despite herself.

"Levi Carter," he said. "Official welcome committee. If you need a tour guide, I work cheap."

Amy laughed softly, shaking his hand. "Thanks, Levi. I think Henry and Sally have me covered."

Levi clutched his heart in mock offense. "Ah, you wound me."

Beside him, Eric shifted, reluctant.

Levi caught the movement and smirked.

"This here's Eric Reynolds. Owns the Silver Meadow Ranch out west. You'll be seeing a lot of him, Doc."

Eric's nod was polite but brief, his dark eyes steady, unreadable.

"Dr. Henderson," he said, voice low and even.

"Mr. Reynolds," Amy returned, her gaze locking with his for a heartbeat longer than necessary.

Something in the way he looked at her—steady, serious, like he could see more than she meant to show—sent a ripple through her.

She told herself it was nothing.

Levi clapped Eric on the back, making him stiffen slightly.

"Well, we'll let you get back to your lunch. Welcome to Steamboat, Doc."

With a wink from Levi and a brief, unreadable glance from Eric, the two men headed out into the sunshine, the door jingling closed behind them.

Amy exhaled slowly, feeling a heat creep up her neck she stubbornly blamed on the coffee.

Sally leaned in, her voice sly.

"Well, honey, you've been here all of five minutes and already stirred up half the eligible bachelors in town."

Henry chuckled. "Good thing she's got her hands full with work, or we'd have to start takin' numbers."

Amy laughed, shaking her head. "I'm just here to practice medicine, not start a stampede."

Sally winked. "Around here, those two things tend to get tangled up."

Amy turned back to her menu, forcing a smile.

She wasn't here for flirtations or small-town dramas. She knew better than to trust easy smiles and quick conversations. She had a job to do—and no intention of getting distracted.

The first full week without Henry by her side had been a whirlwind.

Amy had handled every call, every emergency, every stubborn rancher on her own—and somehow, she hadn't drowned.

If anything, she found herself thriving.

It was busy—calving calls at dawn, lame horses by midday, the occasional frantic dog owner rushing in at closing time—but rewarding.

The animals trusted her, and slowly, the people did too.

Everywhere she went, she was met with easy smiles and firm handshakes.

Steamboat Springs was the kind of place that remembered your name after meeting you once, that waved from passing trucks, that treated the new vet like she belonged.

By Friday evening, Amy was bone-tired but content.

She locked up the clinic just as the sky turned dusky pink and decided she deserved a quiet evening, and a proper grocery run.

The local supermarket was just down the road—small, friendly, the kind of place where the cashier knew exactly how you liked your eggs.

Amy wandered the aisles, basket swinging from her arm, ticking off a mental list: coffee, eggs, milk, something quick for dinner.

She was studying two different brands of coffee when a familiar voice interrupted her thoughts.

"Doc Henderson," Cody drawled, sauntering up with a crooked grin.

"Didn't figure you for the Friday night grocery run type."

Amy turned, her thoughts momentarily pulled from her shopping list, and flashed Cody a polite smile. "Hey, Cody."

He rocked back on his heels, his casual demeanour at odds with the slight tension she felt creep up her spine. His hand hung loosely by his side, gripping his basket by two fingers, the other resting comfortably at his waist. His grin was easy, but there was something in the way he looked at her that she couldn't ignore.

"Was thinkin'… maybe you'd let me take you out sometime?" He gave a little tilt of his head, as if he didn't have a care in the world. "Show you the real Steamboat. We got a halfway decent steakhouse—I'd even let you pick the dessert."

For a moment, Amy felt the old instinct flare up—the instinct to shut herself off, to put up walls so thick that no one could get close enough to hurt her. She'd been through that before with Darren. His smooth words, his charming smile… and the way he'd slowly chipped away at her trust. It wasn't just the relationship's end that left scars—it was how long it had taken her to realise how toxic it had all been.

She wasn't about to make that mistake again.

Her chest tightened, the weight of the memories pressing against her. She forced herself to stay calm, to push aside the unsettling flicker of fear that crept into her gut. The last thing she wanted was to get involved with someone, especially not someone like

Cody—charming, laid-back, the kind of guy who could slip past a woman's defences without even trying.

Taking a breath, she steadied herself and met his gaze, her smile polite but firmer than kind this time. "That's sweet of you, Cody. But no thanks."

Cody didn't falter. His smile didn't drop, though it turned a little crooked, more amused than anything. He gave a shrug, as if rejection was nothing more than a part of the game.

"No harm in askin', right?" he said with an easy grin. "Guess I'll have to make do with seein' you at the clinic. Maybe I'll bring my dog in for a check-up."

Amy forced herself not to tense, focusing instead on the rhythm of her breathing. He wasn't pushing. He wasn't trying to argue. But the old habits were still there—the ones that told her to stay on alert, to keep her distance. She wasn't going to let herself fall into that trap again.

"Yeah, I'll see you there," she replied, her voice light but resolute.

She could see him heading down the aisle, still humming to himself, oblivious to the quiet storm that had passed through her. She grabbed the coffee off the shelf, her fingers gripping the container a little tighter than necessary. It was a small thing, but it helped centre her, helped her regain the calm that Cody's harmless flirtation had disturbed.

Amy paid for her groceries quickly, the weight of the bags in her hands a small comfort. A reminder that she was in control of her life now, not anyone else. Not Darren. Not Cody. No one.

As she walked out of the supermarket and into the crisp mountain air, Amy felt the weight of the world lighten just a little. The sharpness of the cold, the scent of pine and earth, all of it grounded her. Her breath came out in soft puffs, each one steadying the quiet storm inside her. The familiar thrum of resolve settled back into her chest, firm and unyielding.

She wasn't here for distractions, not for relationships that would end in betrayal, or worse—confusion, manipulation, and the kind of pain that landed her in hospital beds, feeling more broken than she'd ever thought possible.

No, she was here for herself. For her career. For the quiet, hard-earned peace she was starting to feel again after so long. For healing, slow and steady, like the mountain streams that ran beneath the surface of the town.

And for the first time in a long time, that was more than enough.

Chapter Five

It was one in the morning on Saturday when Eric Reynolds was jolted from a deep sleep by a hard knock on his bedroom door. His mind was foggy, still caught in the dreamlike haze of a long, exhausting week. He glanced at the clock on the nightstand, the glowing numbers making his chest tighten. Groaning, he sat up and rubbed his face, trying to shake off the sleep. The knock came again, louder this time.

"Boss!" Levi's voice echoed through the door, urgent and tight. "You need to get up. It's Patriot."

Eric's heart skipped a beat. The mention of his prized racehorse, Patriot, was enough to send a rush of adrenaline through him. "What happened?" he asked, already throwing his legs off the bed and grabbing his jeans from the chair where he'd discarded them earlier.

"He's on the ground, boss. Won't get up. Looks bad. I need you to come."

Eric didn't wait for another word. He yanked on his boots and threw a hoodie over his head, his mind racing with thoughts of what could be wrong. Patriot had been healthy, strong. This couldn't be happening.

By the time he reached the door, Levi was already waiting in the hallway, his face pale in the dim light. He looked like he hadn't slept at all.

"Where is he?" Eric asked, his voice sharp and commanding.

"Stable," Levi replied, his tone strained. "I tried everything, but I can't get him up. He's... he's not himself, boss."

The two men didn't waste another moment. They rushed out of the house, their boots pounding against the dirt as they made their way to the stable. The night air was cold and crisp, biting at their skin, but Eric barely noticed. His focus was entirely on the horse.

When they reached the barn, Eric's stomach dropped. Patriot lay sprawled on the ground, his body twisted awkwardly, his breathing shallow. The racehorse's large brown eyes flickered as he looked up at them, but there was no strength behind it. Panic rose in Eric's chest, but he forced himself to stay calm. He needed to think, to act.

"Levi, call the vet. Now."

Amy's phone buzzed against the nightstand. She didn't need to check—she knew it was an emergency. Her heart skipped a beat as she grabbed it, fingers stiff with adrenaline.

"Dr. Henderson," she said, voice sharp despite the sleep still clouding her mind.

"It's Levi Carter. We've got a problem at Silver Meadow Ranch. One of our horses is down. Won't get up. He's sweating, breathing hard. Patriot needs help now."

Amy's mind cleared. Patriot. Eric Reynolds's prized racehorse. She didn't waste a second. "Keep him calm. Don't let him try to get up. I'm on my way." She hung up, already moving. Boots, jacket, stethoscope. No time to waste.

By the time she reached her truck, the cold night air didn't register. She pushed the vehicle hard, tyres spinning as she raced down the road. The moonlit night stretched on forever, but her focus never wavered — Patriot needed her.

The barn came into view, and she saw Eric standing by the stable door, the weight of the world on his shoulders. She parked and sprinted toward him, boots crunching on gravel.

"Where is he?" she demanded.

"Inside," Eric said, his voice hoarse, and he led the way.

Inside, Patriot lay on the ground, drenched in sweat, his body shuddering with each breath. Amy knelt beside him, her hands checking his vitals—rapid pulse, shallow breaths, a bloated belly. Colic. She cursed under her breath. "Levi, grab the sedatives. We need to stabilise him."

Levi moved quickly, and Eric hovered, anxiety etched on his face. Amy's hands were steady, her mind focused. "I think it's colic," she said. "It's painful. Serious. But we can manage it if we act fast."

Eric's face paled. "Colic?"

Amy nodded. "It's life-threatening, but we can help him if we move quickly."

She prepared the sedative, injecting it into Patriot's muscle. It didn't take long for the tremors to ease and his breathing to steady.

"We need to keep him calm," Amy instructed. "This is just the beginning."

Eric's hand was on Patriot's neck, his voice low and soothing. "You're going to be okay, buddy."

Amy worked quickly, checking the IV line, administering fluids, and monitoring Patriot's condition. His vitals began to stabilise, but Amy stayed focused, never letting up.

Levi's voice was quiet. "Is he going to be okay?"

"It's too soon to say," Amy replied. "We need to keep him stable. Colic can return. If it does, we'll need to act fast again."

Eric nodded, his voice firm. "We'll stay with him. Whatever it takes."

Hours passed. The barn was quiet, save for the steady rhythm of Patriot's breathing. Amy continued to monitor him, her hands moving with practiced precision. Slowly, the bloating in his stomach lessened, the tension in his body easing.

By dawn, Patriot's breathing had deepened, his movements less erratic. Amy sat back, muscles sore from the night's work. The barn, bathed in golden light, felt still and peaceful.

"We're going to make it," Amy murmured.

Eric's gaze lingered on Amy for a moment longer, his eyes filled with gratitude, but Amy felt a flicker of discomfort under the weight of it. She looked away quickly, her pulse quickening, and tried to focus on anything but him. She wasn't here for his praise or gratitude. She was here to save a life.

"You did it, Amy," Eric said, his voice thick with emotion. "He didn't look like he'd make it."

Amy glanced at Patriot, his chest rising and falling steadily now. Relief flooded through her, but it didn't touch the knot of tension coiling in her stomach. "We did it," she replied, her tone clipped, focusing on the horse rather than Eric. She didn't want to acknowledge the intensity in his voice, the way his eyes seemed to search her face, or the way her skin heated under his gaze. She wasn't interested in that.

There were no words to smooth over the unease creeping up her spine, so she chose to remain silent, adjusting her stethoscope absentmindedly, trying to avoid looking at him too much.

The hours had blurred together, and now, with the danger passed, exhaustion set in. She couldn't ignore the weariness any longer, but neither did she want to be the recipient of Eric's lingering attention. She stood up slowly, trying to stretch out the stiffness in her body. The adrenaline that had carried her through the night and day was wearing off, leaving her with an overwhelming need for rest.

"I should go," she said quickly, not waiting for his reply as she started moving toward the door. Her boots scraped against the concrete floor, the sound sharp in the otherwise quiet barn.

Eric didn't move to stop her, but his voice, soft and earnest, stopped her in her tracks. "You've been here all day, Amy. Are you sure you don't want to stay here and rest."

Amy clenched her jaw, refusing to let the warmth of his concern affect her. She wasn't here for him to look after. "I'll be back tomorrow morning. He'll be fine. I've done what I can."

She turned, her hand on the barn door handle, eager to leave the space before her resolve crumbled. She wasn't comfortable being in the spotlight, to receiving this kind of attention. It felt dangerous, unsettling. She had enough of that kind of thing in her life already. She didn't need it from any man.

"Thanks for the offer," she added, her tone cool, "but I'll be fine. Just need to get some sleep."

Eric's voice was quiet now, almost uncertain. "Are you sure? I—"

"I'm sure," she interjected firmly, glancing at him over her shoulder. There was no softness in her eyes. "I'll see you tomorrow."

She didn't wait for him to respond. She pushed open the door, the cool night air hitting her face as she stepped outside. The weight of the day clung to her like a heavy coat, but she couldn't allow herself to relax—not yet. She needed distance. She needed time to forget the way Eric had looked at her, like she had somehow done something more than just her job. It didn't matter how grateful he was or how much admiration he might feel; Amy wasn't interested. She never would be. Not after Darren.

She climbed into her truck, the engine purring to life as she pulled away, heading home to the silence she craved. There would be no emotional entanglements for her—not now, not ever. She couldn't afford that kind of attention. Men were nothing more than a complication. A complication she didn't need.

The road ahead stretched out before her, and for the first time all day, Amy felt the tension in her shoulders ease, if only for a moment. Tomorrow was another day, and the fight for Patriot's life wasn't over yet. But for now, she needed to be alone. No more distractions.

After Amy's truck disappeared into the distance, Eric and Levi stood in the quiet of the barn, the steady rhythm of Patriot's breathing the only sound breaking the stillness. The evening air seemed to carry the weight of unsaid words, and neither man spoke at first, letting the moment settle between them.

Levi was the first to break the silence, his voice low and thoughtful. "You know, she's something else. I don't think I've ever seen anyone work like that."

Eric leaned against the stable wall, arms folded, his gaze lingering on the door Amy had just walked through. But he wasn't seeing the wood or the dust—his mind was chasing her; caught in the quiet storm she'd left behind.

"Yeah," he murmured, almost to himself. "She's... something else."

He paused, a crease forming between his brows.

"She saved Patriot, handled everything like a pro, spent the whole damn day here like she belonged. But still... there's this wall. Like she's here, but only halfway. Like she's holding back something big, and I don't know if it's fear or habit."

He exhaled slowly.

"It's like trying to reach someone through fog."

Levi looked over at him, a small knowing smile tugging at the corner of his mouth. "You like her, don't you? I thought you said you weren't interested."

Eric shifted uncomfortably, rubbing the back of his neck. "Well... I might've changed my mind."

Levi's eyebrow lifted, a smirk playing at his lips. "Yeah, I thought you would. She's the kind of woman who makes it hard to stay indifferent."

Eric met his gaze fully, the exhaustion of the day weighing heavy on his shoulders. "I don't know what it is about her, but there's something. Something I can't quite put my finger on. She's not like anyone I've ever met."

Levi chuckled, crossing his arms over his chest. "Oh, I bet. She's not looking at you for your name or your bank account, huh?"

Eric's gaze darkened, a flicker of irritation passing through him. "Not like that. She's different. She's tough, focused... and she doesn't need anyone's help—least of all mine. She doesn't want my attention, and I respect that. But damn, it's hard to keep my distance when she's so damn... real."

Levi's expression shifted, a more serious tone settling over him. "She's been through something, Eric. You don't act the way she does without a reason. I don't know her story, but I've seen that look before. She's pushing people away. It's not just you—hell, it's everyone. She's not an open book, man. If she's shutting you out, there's a reason."

Eric exhaled sharply, his gaze falling to the floor as he absorbed Levi's words. He'd noticed it, too—the way Amy's eyes flashed with that guarded vulnerability whenever he came too close, the way she recoiled even from simple kindness. The walls she built around herself were impenetrable. "I get it," he murmured, his voice quiet. "I haven't been interested in anyone since the divorce... but she's different."

Levi's eyes softened, a knowing sympathy flickering in them. "I think she'd be worth it. But don't expect her to make it easy, Eric. She's not the type to let anyone in easily."

Eric didn't answer right away, lost in thought. The weight of the barn's silence seemed to echo in his chest. Finally, his voice broke through, quieter now, tinged with something he couldn't quite define. "I'm not giving up on her, Levi. But I'm not going to push her, either. I've got to figure out what she needs before I do anything."

Levi clapped him on the back, a low chuckle escaping him. "Good luck with that, man. Amy's a hell of a lot more complicated than any horse I've ever had to deal with."

Eric smiled faintly, shaking his head. "You don't have to tell me."

They both stood in silence for a moment longer, the stillness of the barn pressing down on them, broken only by Patriot's steady breathing. Eric's mind was a storm of thoughts—his desire to get closer to Amy, the certainty that she wasn't ready for that, and the growing feeling that maybe, just maybe, there was something worth waiting for beneath all her walls.

"I'll stick around," Eric said finally, his voice steady and firm. "I'll wait. I can't rush her, but I'm not going anywhere."

Levi gave him a knowing look before turning back to the horse, a slight smile on his face. "You're in for a hell of a ride, Eric."

Eric nodded silently, his eyes once again on the door Amy had walked through. He knew Levi was right. But for the first time in a very long time, he was beginning to think the wait might be worth it.

Chapter Six

After a peaceful night's sleep and a hearty breakfast, Amy woke early, the crisp morning air brushing her face through the open window of her room. She slipped into her boots and, without much thought, grabbed her keys. The drive back to Silver Meadow Ranch felt different this time, like the world outside was opening up before her, and she was noticing it for the first time. Yesterday, her focus had been solely on Patriot—on the work, the urgency. Today, however, she took in the ranch, its beauty, its vastness.

She pulled into the gravel driveway, the tyres crunching beneath her. Stepping out of her truck, she stood there for a moment, taking it all in.

Silver Meadow Ranch stretched out before her, unlike anything she'd ever seen. The land was tucked neatly into a wide valley, bordered by rolling mountains that framed the property like a natural fortress. Aspen groves shimmered in the early morning light, their golden leaves quivering in the cool breeze. Beyond them, the snow-capped peaks of the Rockies rose majestically, their white crowns gleaming against the clear, early-morning sky.

The landscape seemed endless, a patchwork of vast pastures where tall grasses swayed gently in the wind, dotted with crystal-clear creeks and ponds that caught the sunlight like silver mirrors. It was a place that felt ancient, timeless, untouched by the chaos of the outside world. The kind of place that could calm a restless soul just by looking at it.

Amy's steps faltered as she took it all in—the beauty, the peace. She had been so focused on her work and on Patriot's recovery that she hadn't really taken the time to look at the ranch. Now, with the sunlight casting soft, golden hues over the land, she felt a tug at her heart. There was something undeniably serene about this place, something she hadn't realised she was craving.

She turned her gaze to the ranch house, a sprawling log-and-stone lodge nestled comfortably in the heart of the property. It was a perfect blend of rustic charm and modern elegance, with a wraparound porch that invited you to sit and take in the view for hours. Enormous windows reflected the light, offering a panoramic view of the mountains and the sprawling pastures below. There was something about the place that felt both rooted in history and alive with the spirit of its owners.

Amy could almost feel the weight of the years in the air, as if the house itself had been built with care, each stone placed with purpose, each log telling a story. It was a place that had seen generations of hands shaping it into something special.

With a soft exhale, Amy turned and walked toward the barn. Her boots crunched against the gravel path, the sound steady and reassuring as she made her way toward the large, pristine structure. The barn gleamed in the morning sun, its wooden exterior polished and warm. Inside, the air was heavy with the familiar, comforting smells of hay and leather. The polished wood of the stalls caught the light as she stepped inside. It was a horse lover's dream—a place where each horse had its own space, each stall meticulously cared for.

She paused at Patriot's stall. It was the largest of them all, custom-designed just for him she bet. She ran her hand over the smooth wood of his stall door, her heart warming at the thought of his strength, his spirit.

The barn breathed with life, steeped in the soft, familiar rhythms of the ranch. Horses shifted in their stalls, hooves thudding gently against wood, while the low murmur of cattle drifted in from the outer pastures. Hay rustled as ranch hands moved purposefully through their chores—pitchforks lifting straw, boots scuffing the packed dirt, the occasional sharp whistle to a restless colt.

Beyond the barn, a herd of horses galloped freely across the rolling fields, their glossy coats catching the golden morning light like ribbons of movement. The air carried the mingled scents of earth, hay, and warm animal musk, and overhead, birds called out in sharp, cheerful bursts. The wind danced through the nearby grove, whispering through the leaves like a secret.

Amy paused, soaking it all in. There was a steady hum to this place, a quiet pulse of hard work and freedom that stirred something deep inside her. She glanced toward the trees, narrowing her eyes as she spotted something half-concealed beyond the treeline— an airstrip. She hadn't noticed it before, but now its long, sleek line cut clearly through the landscape.

It was no ordinary landing strip—longer than most she'd ever seen, wide and meticulously maintained, like it was built for more than just hobby flying. Her curiosity stirred. Did Eric Reynolds use it often? Was flying another piece of the puzzle that made up his quiet, complicated world?

There was no denying it—Eric Reynolds had serious money. It was written in every inch of his sprawling ranch, in the bloodlines of the horses he raised, and now in the sight of that private airstrip tucked into the trees like it was no big deal.

But it didn't rattle her. Not really. Amy had never been drawn to wealth. Money never made a man decent or kind—it certainly hadn't saved her from the worst of them. She valued quieter things. Honesty. Safety. Freedom. Her life had been rebuilt on simple moments and small joys, and she protected those fiercely.

Still… Eric made her wonder. Not because of what he had, but because of who he was when he looked at her—like she wasn't broken. Like he saw her and didn't flinch. There was a steadiness in him that unsettled her in a way nothing flashy ever could.

Maybe—there was space in her simple life for something more.

No. Don't go there. You're not here for that.

Men couldn't be trusted. Not with power, not with promises. They took. They controlled. They broke things that didn't belong to them.

Amy folded her arms, forcing the thought away. This wasn't about him. It couldn't be. She had come here for a fresh start—not to lose herself in someone else's world again.

Her attention shifted as she walked a little further, her gaze settling on a small, cozy cabin tucked away just beyond the barn. It was simple, almost hidden from sight by a cluster of trees, and she found herself wondering if that was where Levi lived. The cabin was unassuming but inviting—a quiet retreat, tucked away from the bustle of the ranch.

Amy stopped for a moment, taking it all in—the vastness of the land, the serenity of the place, and the isolation it promised. It was so far removed from the chaos of her life, from the noise of the city. For the first time in a long while, she felt something stir inside her—a sense of peace, of belonging. It was as if the land itself had exhaled, inviting her to slow down, to breathe.

"Morning," a voice broke through the silence, deep and familiar.

Amy jumped, her heart leaping into her throat as she spun around. There stood Eric, leaning casually against the barn door, his arms crossed and a slight smile tugging at his lips.

"Did I startle you?" he asked, his voice a mix of amusement and something else, something softer.

Amy pressed a hand to her chest, still catching her breath. "You could say that," she muttered, still shaken by the unexpected interruption.

Eric chuckled. "I didn't mean to. I saw your truck on the drive."

She nodded, forcing a smile as she glanced toward the barn. "I was just taking a look at the ranch. It's... beautiful out here."

Eric's gaze followed hers, and for a long moment, they stood in silence, both of them taking in the breathtaking beauty of the ranch. The mountains in the distance seemed to stretch endlessly, the golden aspen leaves rustling in the morning breeze. It was peaceful—too peaceful.

"Yeah, it's pretty incredible," Eric said, his voice soft but distant, as though the vastness of the land made him momentarily lost in thought. Then he turned to her, his gaze locking with hers, and for a brief second, she saw something deeper in his eyes, a tenderness that caught her off guard. "Glad you're getting a chance to appreciate it."

Amy nodded, but her heart raced. There was something about the way he looked at her—something she couldn't quite put her finger on. It unsettled her in a way no man ever had before. She didn't want to feel that way, not here, not now. She needed to keep her focus, to remember why she was here. This was about Patriot, not about her feelings or whatever this was with Eric.

"I'm going to check on Patriot," Amy said, her voice a little sharper than she intended. She needed space—distance. It wasn't just the ranch she needed to figure out; it was the work. She had a job here, and that had to come first. With that thought, she turned and strode toward the barn, boots crunching against the gravel as her steps quickened.

The barn was quiet, it's cool, musty air a welcome contrast to the heat of the morning sun. The familiar smell of hay, leather, and freshly cut wood filled her lungs as she moved swiftly through the aisles between the stalls, her mind focused entirely on Patriot. She didn't want to think about anything else—not Eric, not the beauty of the ranch. It was just her and the horse, and she needed to see how he was really doing.

When she reached his stall, she paused for a moment, her breath catching in her throat. Patriot was standing near the back, his head lifted high, ears forward, and his body was noticeably more alert than she expected. His coat gleamed in the soft light filtering through the barn doors—rich and healthy-looking, with no sign of the dullness she had feared after his battle with colic. In fact, his coat seemed almost as vibrant.

As she stepped closer, Amy took in the sight of him with a renewed sense of relief. There was no bloating left in his abdomen, no evidence of distress. His body had begun to regain its normal proportions, and his movements were smoother, more fluid than the last time she'd seen him. He shifted slightly, stretching his neck and flexing his muscles as though to test their strength, a subtle but encouraging sign that he was recovering well.

Amy reached out, her fingers brushing gently against his neck, and she was met with a warmth that reassured her. There was no stiffness in his movements, no sign of lingering pain. He nuzzled her hand with a quiet snort, his breath steady and calm, and the affection in his gaze told her everything she needed to know. He was getting back to his old self—and more quickly than she'd anticipated.

"You're looking good, boy," she murmured, her voice soft as she ran her hand over his sleek coat. It felt warm under her touch, the muscles beneath relaxed and strong. She leaned in, checking his gums and his eyes—everything seemed perfect. There was no sign of the lingering tension that often followed a colic episode. He was standing tall, his posture strong, and she couldn't help but smile at how much better he looked than she'd expected.

Patriot's recovery was nothing short of impressive. His pulse was steady, his temperature normal, and the signs of pain she'd anticipated—especially in his legs—were absent. She gently checked his hooves, testing for any signs of soreness, but there was nothing. He seemed comfortable, content even. If she hadn't known what he'd been through, she might've thought he was just another horse—healthy, calm, and ready to return to training.

Amy stood there for a moment, absorbing the sight of him—a horse on the mend, looking far better than she had hoped for after such a rough ordeal. She exhaled slowly, her heart lightening.

"Well, it looks like we're on the right track," she said quietly to herself, her fingers lingering on his mane. "You're a fighter, Patriot."

She stepped back slowly, her gaze never leaving Patriot. He stood there, his intelligent eyes watching her with a quiet trust, his breathing steady and calm.

Behind her, Eric's voice broke the silence. "Is he okay?"

Amy turned to face him, a small smile tugging at her lips as she nodded. "He's more than okay. He's recovering remarkably well."

As she spoke, Patriot let out a soft nicker and nudged her gently with his nose, pushing against her back. The sudden movement caught her off guard, and she stumbled forward.

In an instant, Eric's arms were around her, steadying her before she could fall. She looked up, meeting his gaze. For a long moment, they just stood there, caught in a kind of stillness. The world seemed to pause, the only sound the soft thrum of their hearts and the quiet rustling of the barn around them.

Amy could feel the warmth of his touch, the strength of his hands on her, and it was as though everything else faded away. She found herself lost in his eyes, the tension between them palpable.

Neither of them moved, neither of them spoke. It was as if time itself had frozen, leaving them suspended in that quiet, weighty moment. The air between them hummed with an unspoken understanding, the connection between them deepening with each passing second.

Amy was the first to break the spell. She pulled away quickly, her hands trembling slightly as she stepped back. "Sorry," she muttered, her voice a little shakier than she intended.

She turned away, her heart pounding in her chest, trying to regain some semblance of control. No, this can't be happening, she thought, the familiar, cold walls of self-protection sliding back into place. I can't afford to get involved with any man. It never ends well.

She focused on steadying her breath, pushing the fluttering in her chest aside, but deep down, she knew it wouldn't be so easy to forget that moment, or the way Eric had made her feel.

Chapter Seven

Eric stood frozen for a beat after Amy pulled away, his hands hovering uselessly in the air as if he could still feel her against him. His mind raced, torn between the surge of desire still burning through him and the steady pull of caution.

The urge to kiss her had been overwhelming—stronger than anything he'd felt in a long time. She'd felt right in his arms, like she belonged there. Her steady breathing, the subtle warmth of her body pressed against his, had calmed something raw inside him, something he hadn't even realised was still bleeding. She melted right through the walls he kept so carefully in place.

But the moment was gone now. Amy had stepped back like the touch had scorched her, retreating not just physically, but emotionally. He saw it—clear as day—the flash of panic in her eyes before she hid it away behind a practiced mask. Fear. Of him?

Eric clenched his jaw, his chest tight as he watched her turn from him. Every instinct screamed to reach out, to pull her back into the safety of his arms, to promise her she had nothing to fear. But he didn't. He couldn't. Not when she was already putting distance between them with every breath.

He exhaled slowly, trying to calm the storm churning inside him. The hunger to kiss her hadn't faded, but something deeper had risen to the surface—a need to understand her, to earn her trust before he even thought about asking for more.

He took a step back, his fists curling at his sides, feeling the absence of her like a physical ache. "It's okay," he said quietly, though nothing about it felt okay. "I shouldn't have..." He trailed off, unsure what words would even matter now.

Amy didn't meet his gaze. Her posture was stiff, her breathing a little too quick, as if she was fighting herself just to stay standing.

He wanted to touch her—wanted it more than he could say—but he stayed rooted, letting her go.

Then her voice, tight and rushed, broke the silence. "I better go."

Before he could react, she turned and headed for the barn door, her boots crunching hard against the gravel. The distance between them widened with every hurried step.

Eric swallowed hard, forcing out the only words he could manage. "Okay. Thanks for everything."

She didn't look back. "No problem. Just doing my job. If anything changes, don't hesitate to call. Have a nice day," she said, the words mechanical, too polite. It was like a wall dropping between them, sealing her safely away.

He watched helplessly as she practically ran to her truck. Moments later, the engine roared to life, and she disappeared down the dirt road, leaving a cloud of dust—and a hollow ache—in her wake.

Eric stood there, staring after her long after the dust had settled.

Levi's voice broke into the silence. "What was that all about? Why'd she take off like someone was chasing her?"

Eric didn't move for a second, still locked in the place Amy had left him. Finally, he let out a rough breath. "Patriot nudged her. She fell into my arms."

Levi barked a laugh. "Good old Patriot. Always looking out for you with the ladies." He gave Eric a teasing shove on the arm.

Eric didn't laugh. His brow furrowed as he replayed the look on Amy's face—the fear, the panic. "Hmm."

Levi narrowed his eyes. "What's wrong?"

Eric turned, meeting his friend's gaze. "She looked terrified. Like she thought I was going to hurt her."

Levi's grin faded, replaced by something more serious. "You sure it wasn't just surprise? Maybe she wasn't expecting you to catch her."

Eric shook his head, frustration tightening his throat. "It wasn't just surprise. It was deeper than that. She looked like she wanted to run."

Levi was quiet for a beat, then said, "Maybe it's not about you at all. Maybe she's been through something. You don't tear down those walls by pushing. You just… wait 'til she's ready to let you in."

Eric stared off toward the empty road, the heavy feeling in his chest refusing to ease.

He wanted to believe he could be patient.

But patience had never felt so damn painful.

Amy gripped the steering wheel tighter as she drove, forcing herself to take slow, steady breaths. Her pulse was still racing, but it was beginning to ease, little by little. She had almost had a full-blown panic attack back there.

All because Eric had caught her.

All because, for a split second, she'd let herself feel something she wasn't ready for.

She hadn't been in a man's arms since Darren—the night everything shattered. The night she barely got away with her life.

The memory hit her hard, sharp and cold, and she blinked rapidly, willing it away. That wasn't fair to Eric. He wasn't Darren. But her body didn't know the difference. Not yet.

Amy cursed under her breath, her hands trembling slightly even now. She hadn't expected that kind of reaction—not from a simple fall, not from a man just trying to help her. But the second Eric's arms had closed around her, her mind had flashed back to that night... the fear, the helplessness.

And Eric had seen it.

He'd looked so confused, so concerned, and she didn't blame him. How could he have known? She barely understood it herself sometimes.

Amy tightened her jaw, blinking hard against the sting in her eyes. She wasn't going to fall apart over this. Not now. Not ever again.

She just needed to keep her distance. Stay professional. Focus on the job. That was the only way to survive.

The only way she knew how.

The Monday morning rush at the clinic had finally died down, leaving Amy a moment to breathe. She leaned against the counter, flipping through a few charts, grateful for the rare quiet. Sally had left for the bank run, promising to be back within the hour, and Amy was alone, savouring the rare calm.

The front door chimed, the sound sharp in the stillness. Amy glanced up, automatically putting on a welcoming smile—then froze when she saw who it was.

Eric.

And he wasn't alone. A black Labrador trotted beside him, tail wagging, tongue lolling happily from the side of its mouth.

For a split second, her heart stumbled, memories of Sunday flickering at the edges of her mind. She forced herself to stand straighter, smoothing her palms over her scrubs.

"Hey," Eric said, his voice easy, almost casual. He wore a baseball cap today, and the corners of his mouth tugged up into a half-smile that did funny things to her stomach. "Hope I'm not catching you at a bad time."

Amy shook her head quickly, stepping around the counter. "No, not at all. Come on in."

The black lab gave a little bark of excitement and pulled on the leash, eager to explore. Amy crouched down, offering her hand. The dog immediately shoved his head against her palm, tail wagging harder.

"And who's this handsome guy?" she asked, her voice softening.

Eric chuckled, the sound low and warm. "This is Boomer. He's been scratching at his ears a lot."

Amy nodded, already slipping into her professional mindset, grateful for the familiar routine. Animals, she could handle. People—especially a man like Eric—were a little trickier.

She straightened and met Eric's eyes. For a moment, something passed between them—unspoken, a flicker of Sunday's memory—but Amy pushed it aside, focusing on Boomer instead.

"Let's get him into an exam room," she said, her voice steady. "We'll take a look."

Eric gave a slight nod and followed her down the hall, Boomer trotting happily between them. Amy could feel Eric's presence at her back, solid and grounding, and despite everything inside her that warned her to stay guarded, she couldn't ignore the tiny thread of warmth curling through her chest.

Just a dog checkup, she told herself.

Nothing more.

Amy ran her hands expertly over Boomer's sides, checking his ears, eyes, and paws. The black lab panted happily, clearly enjoying the attention. After a thorough examination, she stepped back and smiled.

"He's in great shape overall," Amy said, reaching for a treat from the jar on the counter and offering it to Boomer, who took it eagerly with a wag of his tail. "His ear's a bit inflamed—minor infection, nothing serious, but we'll need to start him on drops. Other than that..." She hesitated, then smiled. "He's just a little overweight."

Eric chuckled, rubbing the back of his neck. "Yeah, I figured. Levi spoils him like he's royalty. Table scraps, extra treats, sneaking him half his dinner—it's a full-time buffet."

Amy laughed softly, jotting a few notes in Boomer's chart. "Well, it's nothing a little more exercise and fewer 'bonus snacks' won't fix. He's still young enough to shed it quickly."

They lingered over the topic, discussing Boomer's diet and exercise plan—Amy recommending longer walks and cutting down on people food, Eric promising to deliver the "no more burgers under the table" memo to Levi.

The conversation flowed easily, their banter light, the air between them free of tension for once. Amy found herself smiling without hesitation, the weight on her shoulders easing just a little. Around him, in moments like this, she almost forgot to be guarded.

She was just slipping Boomer's updated health record into a folder when Eric cleared his throat.

"Hey," he said, his voice a little lower, a little more serious. Amy looked up, and their eyes met.

"I just wanted to say thanks… for everything you did for Patriot. I really appreciate it." He hesitated, then added, "I was wondering if I could take you to lunch? As a thank you."

The offer hung in the air between them, simple but carrying a weight Amy wasn't sure how to handle.

Boomer wagged his tail, as if sensing the tension, and Amy dropped her gaze to him for a second, collecting herself before she answered.

She hesitated, searching his face for any hint of pressure. There was none. Just patience. A quiet kind of strength.

Saying yes would mean trusting herself again — trusting that not every touch had to end in hurt.

Amy gave a small, almost nervous smile as she bent down to scratch behind Boomer's ears. "You don't need to do that," she said, keeping her tone light. "I was just doing my job."

Eric's mouth lifted in a half-smile, the kind that made her stomach flip if she let herself notice. "I know you were," he said, voice steady. "But it meant a lot to me. To Patriot too."

Amy stood up, brushing her hands off on her jeans, feeling the weight of his words settle into the quiet space between them. She could hear the sincerity in his voice, and it made it harder to hide behind professionalism.

For a moment, neither of them spoke. Boomer's tail thumped lazily against the floor.

Eric shoved his hands into his pockets, his gaze steady on hers. "It's just lunch, Amy. No strings. I'd just… like to spend a little more time with you. Get to know you outside of all this."

Amy felt her heart start that quick, warning flutter again—but this time, it wasn't fear exactly. It was something warmer, something that scared her for a different reason.

She hesitated, searching his face for any hint of pressure. There was none. Just patience. A quiet kind of strength.

It would be easier to say no. Safer. To retreat behind her walls and pretend she hadn't felt anything when he caught her, when he smiled at her like she was worth waiting for.

But she was tired of being ruled by fear. Tired of letting the past dictate every choice she made.

It wasn't just lunch—it was a step forward. A risk.

She drew in a slow breath, steadying herself against the whirl of doubt and hope tangling inside her.

"Okay," she said, her voice soft but sure. "Lunch sounds nice."

Eric's mouth curved into a real smile then, one that lit up his whole face and made something deep inside her flutter all over again.

"Great," he said, his voice low and rough with something that sounded suspiciously like relief.

Boomer gave a happy bark, and Amy couldn't help the small laugh that escaped her, the tension between them easing just a little.

Maybe it was reckless. Maybe it was foolish.

But for once, Amy let herself believe that maybe—something good could come from taking a chance.

Chapter Eight

Sally bustled back into the clinic a little before noon, jingling her keys and shaking her head. "Bank was a madhouse," she said, dropping her purse onto the counter. "But I'm back now—go ahead and take your break, Amy. You've earned it."

Amy glanced toward the waiting area, where Eric still sat patiently with Boomer sprawled at his feet, tail sweeping lazy arcs across the tile. Her stomach tightened, nerves and something lighter—a cautious kind of excitement—twisting together.

"Thanks, Sally," she said, tugging off her gloves and smoothing her hands down her jeans.

She grabbed her jacket and stepped into the waiting area. Eric rose immediately, an easy smile lighting his face. Boomer wagged harder, picking up on the change in mood.

"You ready?" Eric asked, his voice low, warm.

Amy nodded, feeling that tiny tremor in her chest again. "Yeah. There is a little place down the street. They've got outdoor seating—dogs welcome."

Eric's grin widened. "Sounds perfect."

The afternoon air was bright and crisp, sunlight spilling in golden puddles across the sidewalk. Amy shoved her hands into her jacket pockets as they walked side by side, Boomer happily trotting ahead on his leash, sniffing everything with great enthusiasm.

They didn't rush. There was something about the slow pace, the easy rhythm of their footsteps matching, that soothed the tightness in Amy's chest.

"Boomer looks like he owns the whole town," she said, smiling as the big dog nosed a lamppost proudly.

Eric chuckled. "Wouldn't surprise me. He's a little too used to getting his way."

Amy laughed softly, feeling some of the lingering tension slide from her shoulders.

The café was tucked on a corner just a few blocks from the clinic—Sunny's, the hand-painted sign announced, with a cheerful yellow sun beaming down over a line of cozy tables set along the sidewalk. Half the tables already had dogs lounging beneath them or sprawled across the chairs, bowls of water placed thoughtfully next to each table.

"This okay?" Amy asked, pausing at the little picket fence that framed the outdoor seating.

Eric glanced around, his smile easy. "It's great."

They picked a table near the edge, close enough for a little privacy but still warm in the afternoon sun. Amy dropped into one of the wrought-iron chairs, and Eric quickly looped Boomer's leash around the leg of his own chair, giving the dog enough slack to sprawl comfortably.

A waitress appeared with menus and a wide smile. "Oh, he's welcome on the chairs if you want," she said, nodding at Boomer. "We love our four-legged customers."

Eric raised a brow at Amy, waiting for her call. She grinned and patted the seat beside her.

"Come on, big guy," she said.

Boomer didn't need to be asked twice. With an enthusiastic thump of his tail, he hopped up beside her, settling with his head resting on her lap. Amy laughed, scratching behind his ears.

"I think he likes you," Eric said, his voice low and a little rough.

Amy met his gaze and, for once, didn't look away.

"I like him too," she said, meaning every word—and maybe not just about the dog.

They ordered sandwiches and lemonade, and while they waited, the drinks arrived, cool and sweating in the summer heat.

Amy broke the silence first, twisting the condensation from her glass between her fingers. "So… how long have you lived in Steamboat?"

Eric leaned back in his chair; one arm draped loosely over the back. "Just over three years," he said. "Bought the ranch after my divorce."

Amy blinked, momentarily surprised—though maybe she shouldn't have been. There had always been a quiet heaviness about Eric, the kind of weight you only carried after losing things you thought were yours to keep.

"Oh. You're divorced?" she asked, her voice careful.

"Yeah," Eric said, a flicker of old pain crossing his features before he smoothed it away. "Jessica and I got married young. It… was a mistake."

Amy nodded, sensing there was more beneath the surface. But she didn't press. If anything, she understood the sharp, private places people kept hidden.

"What about you, Amy?" Eric asked, tilting his head slightly. His voice was gentle, inviting.

She tried to deflect, flashing a quick, wry smile. "What about me?"

Eric chuckled, the low, warm sound wrapping around her in a way that made her chest ache. "What brought you to Steamboat?" he asked, his tone easy but persistent, like he genuinely wanted to know.

Amy hesitated, staring down at the rim of her glass. She could offer him the simple answer—the one she gave to acquaintances, to people who didn't matter.

But Eric wasn't just another stranger anymore.

"I guess I needed a fresh start," she said finally, her voice soft but honest. "Things back home… they weren't really working out. Too many bad memories. Too many mistakes I didn't want to keep living next to."

Eric didn't judge. He just nodded, like he understood better than most.

Their food arrived—thick sandwiches stacked with turkey and crisp vegetables—and they ate without rushing, conversation flowing in easy fits and starts, each small exchange weaving an invisible thread between them.

Boomer lifted his head once, thumping his tail against the back of Amy's chair. She reached down to scratch behind his ears, smiling as he leaned into her hand.

"You're easy to like, you know that?" Eric said suddenly, his voice low and certain.

Amy glanced up, startled.

The words weren't flirtatious. They weren't calculated. They were simply true, spoken in a way that made her heart stumble.

"You don't have to say that," she said, half-smiling, half-uncertain.

"I don't say anything I don't mean," Eric said simply.

And somehow, Amy believed him.

Maybe it was the way he looked at her—steady, open, no games—or maybe it was just that something inside her was tired of running from the possibility of something good.

For the first time in a long time, she let herself sit with the warmth of being seen—and didn't flinch away.

After they finished eating, Eric walked Amy back toward the vet clinic, Boomer trotting contentedly at their sides. The afternoon sun slanted low, casting long, soft shadows across the sidewalk.

When they reached the front step, Amy paused, turning to him.

"Thank you for lunch, Eric," she said, her voice quiet but sincere.

He smiled, a real one that crinkled the corners of his eyes. "You're welcome, Amy. I hope we can do it again sometime."

For a beat, she just stood there, feeling the easy weight of his words settle around her.

"I'd like that," she said, surprising herself with how much she meant it.

Eric gave a small nod, a promise without pressure, and then—respecting the fragile trust between them—he simply stepped back, giving her space to go inside when she was ready.

Amy opened the door, her eyes following Eric as he walked away, Boomer trotting happily at his side. She lingered for just a moment, her gaze drawn to the way the afternoon light caught the edges of his form, then she stepped inside, closing the door softly behind her.

For the first time in what felt like forever, the world didn't feel so heavy. It was as if something had shifted, just slightly, a crack in the armour she'd built around herself. She didn't know what it meant yet, but it was a feeling she wasn't ready to push away.

Chapter Nine

The week at the vet clinic had been a whirlwind, the mornings always bustling with appointments, the afternoons a little quieter but no less demanding. By Friday afternoon, Amy was drained—her energy all but spent. She'd just gotten home, a quiet, peaceful moment that felt like an oasis, when her phone rang. She glanced at the screen, silently hoping it wasn't an emergency call. She didn't know if she had the strength for it.

"Hello?" she answered, sinking into the armchair by the window, rubbing her tired eyes.

"Hi, Amy. It's Eric."

The sound of his voice made her sit up straighter, her heart kicking into a faster beat. "Is Patriot okay?" she asked quickly, concern creeping into her words. She hadn't expected to hear from him.

Eric chuckled softly, and she could hear the warmth in his voice. "Yes, yes, he's fine, thanks to you."

Relief washed over her, but she quickly masked it. "Oh, good. What can I do for you?" she asked, trying to keep her tone casual as she settled back into the chair.

There was a slight pause on the other end, and she could almost picture him standing there, uncertainty clouding his words.

"I was hoping I could take you out to dinner tomorrow night," he said, his voice careful, but still undeniably hopeful.

Amy's breath caught in her throat. She wasn't expecting this. She didn't know what to say. Part of her wanted to refuse, to keep things professional, but there was a quiet voice inside her—one that had been growing stronger since their last encounter—that wanted to say yes.

But she wasn't ready to make any decisions. Not yet. The idea of stepping into something new, especially with someone like Eric, felt like too much to handle right now. She wasn't sure if she was ready to trust herself again, let alone trust someone else.

She exhaled slowly, her fingers brushing over the armrest of the chair as she thought about her response. "Ah, I'm not sure, Eric. I'm not... that is, I'm not sure it's a good idea," Amy said, her voice hesitant, though it didn't carry the usual defensive tone she would've expected from herself. No, this was different. She was trying to convince herself, not him. The words hung in the air between them, heavy with the weight of her uncertainty.

Eric was quiet for a moment, and Amy could hear the faint rustling of what she guessed was his jacket. It was the silence that told her he was thinking, weighing his options, just as she was. He wasn't pushing, which, in some ways, made it harder. But that didn't mean he was giving up.

"Why not?" Eric's voice came back, softer now, but still tinged with a note of confusion, maybe even a little vulnerability.

Amy leaned back in her chair, looking out the window at the fading sunlight. She could almost feel the pull of his question, like the warmth of the evening sunlight tugging at her. She knew the answer, but the truth of it was something she wasn't ready to face—at least not out loud. Not yet.

"I'm just… not sure I'm ready to start dating," she admitted, her voice quieter this time. It felt more like a confession than an explanation. The truth was raw, scraping at the edges of her heart, but it was something she couldn't hide. She had to be honest, even if it made her feel exposed, as if she were standing on a precipice. "The last time I trusted someone… well, it didn't end well."

Eric's voice softened immediately, a tenderness that caught her off guard. "Is that why you looked so terrified when Patriot nudged you and you fell into my arms? Did someone hurt you?"

The question hung in the air like a delicate thread, and for a moment, Amy froze. She hadn't expected him to notice the fear in her, the way her body had stiffened when Patriot had knocked her off balance. She hadn't thought anyone would see through the thin veil of composure she'd worn like armour.

Her pulse quickened, her throat tightening as she found herself caught between the desire to tell him everything—the truth of what had happened, the darkness that lingered—and the fear that doing so would make him walk away. Could she really tell him about Darren? Could she risk revealing just how close to death she'd come—how something as simple as being late coming home from work had almost cost her everything?

She swallowed hard, the weight of the memories pressing down on her chest, suffocating her. She thought she had buried them deep enough that they wouldn't resurface, but the truth had a way of rising to the surface, no matter how much she tried to keep it down.

"Are you still there, Amy?" Eric's voice broke through the whirlwind of her thoughts, gentle and patient, pulling her back to the present.

"Yes, I'm here," she replied, her words barely a whisper, thick with the weight of everything she wasn't saying. She could feel the ache in her chest, the tightness that had become a constant companion, as if she were carrying the weight of her silence like a heavy burden.

The silence stretched between them, and for a moment, she wondered if he could sense the storm inside her. Could he hear the fear? The hesitation? Or was he simply being patient, letting her take her time, giving her the space to breathe?

"Amy…" Eric's voice softened even more, a little more vulnerable this time, like he was trying to reach her without pushing too hard. "You don't have to tell me anything you're not ready to. I just want you to know that I would never do anything to hurt you. It's just dinner, nothing more."

Her heart stuttered in her chest at his words. They were simple, yet they carried a weight she hadn't expected. There was something in his voice—a sincerity that reached deep into her, a reassurance that felt almost foreign. Safe. The word echoed in her mind. She hadn't felt safe in so long, not really. Not since Darren.

Back then, safety had been a distant memory, a fleeting illusion. The last time she'd felt truly safe, she'd been a different person—someone who trusted easily, someone who believed that kindness existed without any hidden agenda. But that had been before Darren, before everything had shattered in an instant. She'd built walls around herself, thinking they would keep her from feeling that pain again. But hearing Eric's words, feeling the kindness in them, made her question if she could lower just one of those walls, just a little.

Amy leaned back in her chair, closing her eyes as she took a slow, steady breath, trying to centre herself. The vulnerability felt overwhelming, but so did the longing for something more—something real. She didn't want to be afraid anymore. She didn't want to live in the shadows of the past. Maybe, just maybe, Eric could be the one to show her what it felt like to trust again.

"Okay," she said finally, her voice soft but steady. "Dinner would be nice."

The words felt like a small victory, a step forward, even if it was just a tiny one. But it was something. It was more than she'd allowed herself in a long time. And maybe, just maybe, it was the beginning of something she hadn't dared to hope for.

There was a brief pause on the other end of the line before Eric spoke again, his voice lighter now, warmer. "I'll pick you up tomorrow at seven. I'll make sure it's a dinner you'll enjoy, I promise."

Amy smiled at the warmth in his tone, her heart fluttering ever so slightly. "I'll look forward to it."

As she ended the call, she sat there for a moment, the weight of the conversation still hanging in the air. But for the first time in what felt like forever, she allowed herself to feel something other than fear. There was hope, tentative and fragile, but it was there. And maybe that was enough for now.

Chapter Ten

Amy stood in front of the mirror, taking in her reflection. The soft waves of her blonde hair cascaded over her shoulders, the gentle waves catching the light in a way that made her feel… well, pretty, in a way she hadn't allowed herself to feel in a long time. Her skin was still glowing from the quick shower she'd taken, the minimal makeup she'd chosen to wear just enough to highlight her features without hiding them. A touch of mascara, a swipe of lip gloss, and that was all she needed. She hadn't felt the need to layer on more—it felt good to keep things simple, to feel like herself again.

The navy-blue dress hugged her curves, the fabric smooth and comfortable against her skin, but it flared gently out at the hips, giving it an elegant, almost playful look. It was the perfect balance—feminine, but not too revealing, chic without trying too hard. The colour was striking, and the high heels she'd paired with it were the same deep shade of blue, their subtle height adding just the right amount of grace to her posture. She glanced down at her feet and then back up at her reflection, a quiet sense of satisfaction stirring inside her.

I look good, she thought, the idea feeling both new and comforting. It had been a long time since she'd allowed herself to think that way. It wasn't just the dress, or the makeup—it was the way she felt in this moment, standing here, ready to step outside of her comfort zone. Ready to take a chance.

The clock on the wall showed 6:58 p.m., and her stomach gave a little flutter of nervousness. Just dinner, she reminded herself. She couldn't help but feel a little giddy at the idea of it, though. It wasn't like she hadn't been on dates before—she had. But this… this felt different. With Eric, she felt seen. He didn't rush her, didn't push her for anything more than she was ready to give. That meant something. He respected her boundaries.

But what does it mean for me?

Before she could get lost in that thought, there was a knock at the door. Amy's heart skipped a beat, and she straightened up, taking a deep breath. She could do this. She had to do this.

She opened the door to find Eric standing on the other side, and for a moment, she simply took him in. He looked devastatingly handsome, even more so than she remembered. He wore a well-tailored jacket over a crisp white shirt, the sleeves rolled up just enough to reveal strong forearms—something she had already come to recognise as part of his laid-back yet undeniably confident demeanour. His dark hair was slightly tousled, as if he'd run his fingers through it on the drive over, and the easy, genuine smile he gave her lit up his entire face.

"Wow," he said, his voice low and sincere, his gaze sweeping over her from head to toe in open appreciation. "You look amazing, Amy."

For a brief moment, warmth crept into her cheeks, but she fought the instinct to look away. Instead, she smiled, a little shy but genuine. "Thanks," she said softly. "You're not so bad yourself."

Eric chuckled, a rich, easy sound that made her stomach flutter. "You ready to go?" he asked, his eyes holding hers for a moment longer than necessary.

"Yes," she replied, reaching for her purse. She stepped outside, closing and locking the cabin door behind her with a click that somehow felt louder than usual in the stillness of the evening. Before she could navigate the porch steps herself, Eric was already there, offering his hand without hesitation.

Amy hesitated for the barest second—it's just a hand—before placing her fingers lightly in his. His touch was warm, steady, and utterly unthreatening. He helped her down the steps and opened the passenger door of a sleek black SUV, his movements easy, natural, like he didn't even have to think about being thoughtful.

As she climbed inside and settled into the seat, she caught herself smiling again, a little surprised at how natural it felt.

Eric rounded the hood and slid behind the wheel. The soft purr of the engine filled the quiet as he pulled away from the drive.

Amy glanced over at him. His eyes were on the road, his hands loose but sure on the steering wheel, but somehow, she could feel his awareness of her—like an invisible thread stretched between them, pulling gently, keeping her anchored.

They didn't speak right away, but the silence wasn't uncomfortable. It was something new… something careful, fragile, but full of possibility.

And for the first time in a long time, Amy let herself lean into that feeling, just a little.

The drive into town didn't take long, but Amy found herself memorising little details—the way Eric's profile looked in the soft glow of the dashboard lights, the occasional brush of his hand as he shifted gears, the relaxed way he laughed when he told her about Boomer's latest antics at home.

By the time they pulled into the restaurant's small parking lot, the initial nerves that had coiled in her stomach were starting to unravel.

Eric parked and quickly got out, circling around to open her door before she even had a chance to reach for the handle. He offered his hand again, and this time Amy took it without hesitation, feeling a little stronger for doing so.

The restaurant he'd chosen wasn't flashy or over the top. It was charming, warm—the kind of place where locals gathered on Friday nights, with strings of soft white lights crisscrossing the patio and the scent of grilled steak and herbs drifting in the air.

Inside, the lighting was low and cozy, the tables covered in crisp white linen, each one centred with a small candle flickering inside a mason jar. A hostess greeted them with a smile and led them to a table near a wide window overlooking a small garden, now washed in silver under the moonlight.

Eric pulled out her chair for her and waited until she was seated before taking his own.

Amy smoothed her dress and smiled at him across the table. "This place is beautiful," she said, genuinely touched by the choice.

"I figured something laid-back but nice would be better than crowded and loud." He shrugged modestly. "Didn't seem like you'd enjoy being packed into some noisy bar."

She laughed softly, the sound surprising even herself. "You guessed right."

The waiter arrived, and they ordered—steaks for both of them, though Eric insisted she try the house special mashed potatoes. After the menus were taken away, a gentle hush fell between them again.

Amy twirled the stem of her water glass between her fingers, the candlelight reflecting in the crystal. She didn't feel the same crushing weight she usually did in moments like this. Instead, there was a quiet sense of ease between them, like the early stages of a song where both singers are still finding their harmony, but the melody is already sweet.

Their food arrived, and the conversation shifted into easy banter—stories about Patriot's stubborn streak, Amy's childhood dog who used to steal socks from the laundry, small pieces of life traded back and forth like secret treasures.

And somewhere between the first bite of steak and the second glass of wine, Amy realised something she hadn't dared believe before tonight.

She was enjoying herself.

Really, truly enjoying herself.

And for the first time in a very long time, the walls around her heart didn't feel quite so tall, or quite so impossible to climb.

Chapter Eleven

Eric couldn't believe how relaxed he felt with Amy.

He hadn't been kidding when he said she was easy to like.

She was guarded — that much was clear — but he could tell she was trying.

He decided that if she was ever going to truly open up to him, he'd probably have to do it first.

So, when she asked him to tell her a bit about himself, he drew a breath — the kind that reached deep into his ribs — and answered honestly.

"I grew up in Boston. Old money, old rules. Everything was about appearances—what you wore, who you talked to, who you married. It never really fit me, but…" He shrugged one shoulder. "When you're young, you think you can make it fit. Or you're too damn stubborn to admit you're miserable."

Amy listened silently, her heart tugging for him.

"I married young," Eric continued. "Thought I was in love. She was beautiful, polished, said all the right things. My parents adored her. Said we'd be the next golden couple." His mouth twisted bitterly. "And for a while, we played the part. Perfect smiles at fundraisers, hand in hand at galas. Everyone thought we had it all."

Amy heard the scrape of pain beneath the calm surface of his voice.

"But behind closed doors…" Eric's hands tightened slightly. "She was different. Cruel in ways that didn't leave bruises. Every word, every look was about control. About reminding me that I wasn't enough. That no one would ever want me if I didn't have the Reynolds name or the Reynolds fortune."

Amy's breath caught painfully in her throat.

"And kids…" He shook his head, something raw flickering in his eyes. "She'd promised we'd have a family. Talked about it like it was her dream, too. Then after the wedding, she said she had no intention of being 'tied down.' Said kids would ruin her body, her freedom. That they were… a burden." His voice cracked slightly on the last word.

Amy blinked hard against the sudden sting in her eyes.

"I stayed longer than I should have," Eric said, quieter now. "Told myself I could fix it. That love meant staying, even when it hurt."

He paused, then gave a short, humourless laugh.

"Turns out, she didn't believe in fixing anything. She just believed in getting what she wanted. Affairs. Taking money behind my back for her lovers."

His jaw tightened.

"The final straw was at a charity ball. She humiliated me—publicly. Flirting with someone else right in front of half the city. Smiling like it was a game."

Amy pressed her hand to her mouth, trying to hold in the surge of protective anger.

"I filed for divorce the next morning," Eric said simply. "She fought like hell. Painted me as cold, controlling. Dragged my name through the mud until I finally just... paid her to go away. Took what she wanted and walked."

Silence stretched between them, thick and heavy.

Eric looked at her then — really looked — his eyes raw and unguarded.

"I came out here because I needed something real," he said, voice rough. "Horses, land, sky... they don't lie. They don't care about last names or fortunes. I figured if being alone was the price of peace, I could live with it."

Amy opened her mouth, then closed it again.

There were no easy words to answer pain like that.

Instead, she reached across the table, her fingers hesitating for a fraction of a second before brushing lightly over his hand.

A simple touch. Real.

Eric turned his hand over slowly, curling his fingers around hers with a tenderness so careful it nearly shattered her.

Amy swallowed hard, the lump in her throat threatening to choke her.

"I'm sorry, Eric," she whispered. "I guess I'm not the only one who came to Steamboat to escape their past."

Eric didn't speak. He just held her hand, his thumb brushing over her knuckles, steady and patient.

Amy drew a shaky breath.

"I grew up in Wichita Kansas. My parents... they were everything to me. I was twenty-two when they died in a car accident."

Her voice cracked, but she pushed through.

"No siblings. No close relatives. After that... it was just me."

Eric's hand tightened slightly around hers, anchoring her.

"Not long after they passed, I met Darren. I was so naive. My parents had sheltered me from so much, protected me from the worst parts of the world. Darren seemed charming at first. Sweet. Like he understood what I was going through."

A bitter smile tugged at her lips.

"He didn't. Not really. He manipulated me, little by little. At first, it was just controlling the small things — where I went, who I talked to. Then he lost his job. And that's when the drinking started."

Amy blinked hard, fighting the tears welling in her eyes.

"I had just finished my degree and started working as a vet, putting in long hours. He hated that. Hated that I had a life outside of him. It started with a slap. A backhand when he was drunk. Always followed by tears and apologies. Promises it would never happen again."

Eric stayed silent, but his grip on her hand never faltered.

"I was stupid enough to believe him. I thought I loved him."

Her voice dropped to a whisper.

"But eventually, I started to see the truth. Started pulling away. And he noticed."

Tears spilled freely now, but Amy clung to Eric's hand like a lifeline.

"One Friday night, there was an emergency at the clinic. A dog had been hit by a car. We had to operate, or it would've died. We saved the dog… but when I finally checked my phone, there were ten missed calls from Darren."

She gave a broken laugh.

"I didn't even call him back. I just drove straight home. I should have known."

Her shoulders shook as the memories tumbled out.

"The moment I stepped through the door, I knew. He was waiting for me, furious. Screaming that I was cheating on him. That I was a slut who didn't deserve him."

Her voice trembled.

"He hit me so hard I fell. I probably should've stayed down… but I didn't. I got up. And that made him angrier."

Eric's thumb brushed across her knuckles, grounding her.

"He tore at my clothes, said he was going to teach me a lesson. I fought him. God, I fought so hard."

She shuddered.

"I think the neighbours heard the noise because the police showed up. But before they could get inside, Darren grabbed me by the hair and slammed my head into the bathroom vanity."

Amy reached up, lifting her hair to reveal a scar near her hairline.

Eric's face blanched, horror flashing through him. His stomach twisted violently. He wanted, irrationally, to track Darren down even now — to erase the monster from the world.

"I was in a coma for two weeks," Amy said quietly. "When I woke up… he was already in jail. He took a plea deal. He got three years. That was just over two years ago now."

Eric's jaw clenched. His hand tightened around hers, careful but firm, like he was afraid she might slip away.

"God, Amy," he said finally, his voice rough with emotion. "I'm so damn sorry."

For a long moment, neither of them spoke.

Amy just sat there, feeling the weight of her story settle between them — but for the first time, it didn't feel quite so crushing.

Eric wasn't recoiling.

He wasn't pitying her.

He was simply there. Holding on when she needed it most.

Amy sniffed and gave him a watery smile.

"I guess that's why… I get a little nervous when someone gets too close."

Eric leaned in, his voice low and fierce with sincerity.

"I'm not like him, Amy. I swear to you, I'm not."

She closed her eyes for a moment, letting those words wrap around her battered heart.

Maybe — just maybe — she could start believing it.

Eric sat back a little, his hand still securely wrapped around hers, and offered a faint, reassuring smile.

He understood instinctively that she needed a reprieve — a way to step out of the shadows of her past, even just for a few minutes.

He squeezed her hand gently.

"You know what I think we need right now?" he said, warmth teasing at the edge of his voice.

Amy lifted her head, curiosity flickering in her damp eyes.

"What?"

"Dessert," he declared, the mischief unmistakable now. "Something completely decadent. Something that reminds us there's still sweetness in the world."

Amy's mouth curved, hesitant at first, but undeniably there — a smile.

Eric flagged down the server and ordered without even glancing at the menu, like he had already known what would lift her spirits.

"Two spoons. One giant hot fudge brownie sundae. Extra whipped cream."

Amy blinked, a surprised laugh escaping her lips.

"You like hot fudge brownie sundaes?"

Eric shrugged, grinning like a boy caught sneaking cookies from the jar.

"Who doesn't? Besides, I have it on good authority that calories don't count when you're sharing."

The server winked and disappeared, leaving Amy shaking her head, a real, genuine laugh bubbling up.

It was exactly what she needed — simple, innocent joy.

When the dessert arrived, it was a masterpiece: a warm, gooey brownie drowning in hot fudge, two scoops of vanilla ice cream starting to melt into a delicious puddle, crowned with mountains of whipped cream and a bright cherry on top.

Eric handed her a spoon with a gallant little bow.

"Ladies first."

Amy rolled her eyes but accepted it, digging in and letting the first bite melt on her tongue. It was absurdly rich — the kind of treat that demanded you close your eyes just to savour it properly.

Eric watched her with a lazy smile, then took a bite himself.

"See?" he said around a mouthful. "Healing."

Amy laughed again, lighter this time, easier.

"You might be onto something," she said.

For a while, they shared the sundae in comfortable silence — trading small smiles, playful nudges of their spoons, even mock battles over the biggest brownie chunk.

The heaviness of her story still lingered, yes — but it wasn't the only thing between them now.

There was also laughter.

Trust.

The first fragile threads of something new, something better.

Chapter Twelve

By the time they made a respectable dent in the dessert—though finished was a generous word given its massive size—Amy's cheeks hurt from smiling so much.

The evening had shifted, softened into something she hadn't realised she'd been starving for: normal, easy, safe.

Eric paid the bill with quiet efficiency, refusing to let her even think about arguing, and then they stepped out into the cool night air. The stars were brilliant overhead, scattered like diamonds across a velvet sky, and instinctively, Amy wrapped her arms around herself.

Without a word, Eric shrugged out of his jacket and draped it over her shoulders. The scent of him—something clean and warm, with a hint of soap and pine—wrapped around her, and she was helpless against the sudden flutter in her chest.

"You didn't have to do that," she said softly.

Eric just smiled, that easy, unhurried smile of his that made her feel steadier somehow.

"I know," he said simply. "But I wanted to."

They walked toward his SUV, their steps slow, neither one seeming eager to break the spell the evening had cast. As they reached the passenger side, Eric opened the door for her, but before she climbed in, she hesitated, looking up at him.

"Thank you," she said quietly—not just for dinner, not just for the dessert, but for all of it. For listening. For not looking at her like she was broken. For making her laugh when she thought she'd forgotten how.

Eric seemed to understand. He reached out, brushing a loose strand of hair from her face, his fingers lingering just a moment longer than necessary. His touch was featherlight, but it sent a warmth through her that no jacket could match.

"You're stronger than you think, Amy," he said, his voice low, steady. "And you're not alone. Not anymore."

For a heartbeat, the world stilled around them, and Amy found herself believing him.

She climbed into the SUV, and as he closed the door and circled around to the driver's side, Amy realised something had shifted inside her tonight. A small, fragile part of her—buried deep under years of fear and hurt—was starting to breathe again. It wasn't fully healed, not yet, but it was stirring, stretching toward the light.

When they pulled up to her cabin, Eric was out of the car before she could even reach for the handle. He helped her down carefully, his hand warm and steady in hers, and walked her up the path to her door.

For a moment, they simply stood there, the soft hum of the night surrounding them, stars scattered overhead like silent witnesses.

Amy's heart beat faster—not from fear, but from something that felt achingly close to hope.

Eric's voice was low when he spoke. "Can I kiss you goodnight?"

She looked up at him, at the earnestness in his eyes, the way he held himself so still, giving her all the space she needed to say no.

But she didn't want to say no. Not this time.

She nodded, barely more than a breath, but he saw it.

Eric lifted his hand and cupped her face so gently it made her throat tighten. He gave her time—time to pull away if she needed to—but she didn't move. She couldn't. She didn't want to.

Then he leaned in, his mouth brushing hers in a kiss so tender, so achingly careful, it shattered something inside her. His lips were warm and patient, not demanding, not insistent—just there, offering comfort, offering trust.

Amy melted into him, her hands lightly resting against his chest, grounding herself.

The kiss deepened just slightly, a soft, lingering brush of lips that spoke more than words could: I'm here. You're safe. You're wanted—not for what you can give, but for who you are.

When he finally pulled back, he rested his forehead against hers for a moment, his thumb gently stroking her cheek.

"Goodnight, Amy," he whispered.

"Goodnight, Eric," she whispered back, her voice catching slightly.

As she stepped inside and closed the door, Amy leaned against it, her fingers brushing over her lips.

For the first time in a long, long time, the future didn't feel so terrifying.

It felt possible.

Eric drove through the quiet streets, one hand loose on the wheel, the other resting on his thigh, replaying the night over and over in his mind.

The soft glow of the dashboard lights filled the cab, but all he could really see was her—Amy, standing in the porch light, looking up at him with those guarded, beautiful eyes.

He let out a slow breath, a smile tugging at the corners of his mouth.

That kiss…

God, that kiss.

He'd had his fair share of kisses before—careless ones, urgent ones, ones that were more about distraction than connection—but nothing had ever felt like that. Nothing had ever unravelled him the way one simple, tender kiss from Amy had.

It wasn't just the softness of her lips or the way she had leaned into him.

It was the trust.

The way she had chosen to let him close, even when every part of her probably wanted to run. She had given him a piece of herself tonight, fragile and precious, and he'd felt the weight of that gift in every second their mouths touched.

Eric drummed his fingers lightly against the steering wheel, a quiet energy running through him he didn't know what to do with.

He'd had a great time—better than great.

He hadn't felt this kind of quiet happiness in a long, long time.

And he wasn't ready for it to end.

Not by a long shot.

He wanted more time with her. More conversations. More laughter over shared desserts. More stolen glances across a table and slow walks under the stars.

He wanted Amy.

Not just the easy parts—he wanted all of it. Her past, her fears, her dreams, her strength.

He didn't know exactly what they were starting, but for the first time in years — maybe ever — Eric felt like he was exactly where he was supposed to be.

He turned onto the road that led to his place, the trees arching overhead like a dark tunnel.

The stars above were faint but steady, and he found himself smiling again, a real, unguarded smile.

Yeah, he thought.

This was just the beginning.

And he couldn't wait to see where it led.

Chapter Thirteen

Sunday morning sunlight streamed through the windows of Amy's cozy cabin, casting a golden glow across the small kitchen. She sat at the table, a cup of coffee warming her hands, a plate of scrambled eggs and toast untouched in front of her.

She hadn't stopped smiling since she woke up — last night kept playing in her mind like a favourite song.

Just as she took a sip of coffee, her phone buzzed on the table. Her heart skipped when Eric's name flashed on the screen. She quickly wiped her hands on a napkin and answered, trying not to sound too eager.

"Hello?" she said, her voice soft and a little breathless.

"Good morning, beautiful," Eric's deep voice came through the line, wrapping around her like a warm blanket. "I just… I couldn't wait. I had to tell you — I had an amazing time last night."

Amy smiled, her cheeks flushing with a mixture of happiness and shyness. She tucked a piece of hair behind her ear. "Me too," she admitted quietly. "It was really nice."

"I didn't want the night to end," Eric said, his voice a little rough, like he hadn't slept much either. "That kiss… Amy, I'm not sure I've ever had a kiss knock me sideways like that."

Amy let out a soft laugh, her heart fluttering. "I guess it wasn't just me, then," she teased.

"Not even close." His tone turned playful. "If I hadn't promised myself, I'd behave, I would've begged you to let me stay and kiss you a hundred more times."

She laughed again, lighter than she had in months. Maybe even years.

"I'm glad you didn't," she said, her voice teasing but honest. "I might have said yes… and I'm not ready for that. Yet."

There was a pause — a comfortable silence, full of understanding.

"I know," Eric said quietly. "I'm willing to wait, Amy. However long you need. I just want to spend time with you. Get to know you."

Her chest tightened at the sincerity in his voice. "I'd like that too."

He hesitated, then asked, his voice warm and tentative, "Are you doing anything today? I was thinking… maybe we could go horseback riding at my ranch. No pressure. Just a ride, some fresh air, a little time with the horses."

Amy's smile widened. It sounded easy. Safe. And if she was honest… a little exciting too.

"That sounds really nice, Eric," she said, her voice soft but sure. "What time?"

"Could you come by around noon?"

"Perfect."

"Good," he said, and she could hear the smile in his voice — that effortless way he had of making her feel wanted without making her feel trapped. "I'll see you soon, Amy."

"See you soon," she echoed, reluctant to hang up.

After ending the call, she set the phone down and leaned back in her chair, her heart full and strangely light. For the first time in a long time, she wasn't weighed down by fear or regret.

Today held promise — simple, beautiful promise.

And maybe, just maybe, the future did too.

Amy stood in front of the mirror, tugging lightly at the hem of her plaid shirt. She'd paired it with her favourite faded jeans and worn leather boots — the same ones she hadn't touched since moving to Steamboat. It felt strange pulling them on again, like stepping into a version of herself she thought she'd lost.

Her blonde hair fell in loose waves around her shoulders. No makeup today — just mascara and a swipe of lip balm. She didn't want to hide. Not with Eric. He made her feel like she didn't have to.

Grabbing her denim jacket from the hook by the door, Amy felt a flutter of nerves.

Not fear — not this time.

Something else.

Anticipation. Hope.

On the drive to Eric's ranch, she found herself smiling at the scenery: wide open fields brushed with early spring wildflowers, the distant silhouettes of horses grazing peacefully. The sky was a brilliant, cloudless blue.

For the first time in forever, she felt part of the world again instead of just passing through it.

When she pulled onto the long gravel driveway leading to the ranch house, she spotted Eric waiting near the stables. He wore jeans, a soft grey T-shirt clinging to his broad shoulders, and scuffed boots. He looked so at ease, so at home in his world, that something warm unfurled inside her.

As she stepped out of her truck, Eric walked toward her, a slow, easy smile spreading across his face.

"Hey, you made it," he said, his voice carrying easily across the space between them.

Amy smiled back, tucking a loose strand of hair behind her ear. "I wouldn't miss it."

Eric gestured toward the stables. "Come on. I've got someone I want you to meet."

She followed him, her nerves fading with every step, replaced by something she hadn't allowed herself to feel in a long, long time — belonging.

Inside the stables, the scent of hay and warm leather filled the air, rich with the comforting sounds of horses shifting in their stalls. Sunlight streamed through the open barn doors, spilling golden light across the packed dirt floor.

Eric led her to a stall where a sleek chestnut mare stood, flicking her tail lazily.

"This is Clover," he said, stroking the mare's neck. "She's one of our gentlest horses — steady, good for beginners." He grinned. "I figured we'd take it easy today."

Amy approached Clover with quiet confidence. She ran her hand down the mare's soft muzzle, smiling when Clover nickered in approval.

"She's gorgeous," Amy said. Then, with a teasing glance at Eric, she added, "But you know, you didn't have to bring out the beginner horse."

Eric's brow lifted, amused. "No?"

"No." Amy laughed, light and easy. "I grew up riding. English, Western, a little barrel racing. It's been a while, but I'm definitely not a beginner."

Eric chuckled, a deep, warm sound that sent a ripple through her chest. "Well, look at you, surprising me again." He tipped his hat back and grinned. "In that case, maybe we'll make this a little more interesting."

But even as he said it, he found himself watching her with new eyes — this woman with quiet fire tucked behind her soft smile.

He saddled Clover with quick, efficient ease, and Amy grabbed a helmet without hesitation, adjusting the chin strap like she'd done it a hundred times before. Eric handed her the reins, his hand brushing hers, lingering just a second longer than necessary.

"Ready, cowgirl?" he teased.

Amy flashed a confident smile. "Let's ride."

With practiced grace, she mounted Clover in one fluid motion, settling into the saddle like she belonged there. Eric stood back for a moment, admiration clear in his eyes.

He mounted his own horse — a tall black gelding named Duke — and they set off together, side by side, into the open pastures.

The breeze was cool and fresh, carrying the scent of wildflowers and earth. Amy felt alive, the familiar rhythm of Clover's movement bringing back memories of simpler times. She stole a glance at Eric, who rode beside her with easy skill, his posture relaxed, his hat low over his dark hair.

He looked over at her, smiling wide. "You're a natural."

"Like I said," she teased, "you don't have to go easy on me."

Eric's grin was slow and a little wicked. "Good. Because I was thinking about taking you up the ridge trail. Best view on the whole ranch."

Amy's heart lifted, excitement buzzing through her. "Lead the way, cowboy."

As they trotted across the open fields, the mountains rising in the distance, Amy couldn't help but feel it — the wonder of the moment, the ease between them.

She hadn't just found her footing back in the saddle.

She was finding it in life again, too.

The trail wound upward through groves of aspens and tall pines, sunlight flickering through the leaves. Eric led the way, glancing back now and then, but Amy handled Clover like a pro — natural, sure.

When they crested the final rise, Eric slowed Duke to a stop and dismounted in one fluid motion. Amy followed, swinging down from Clover's back, letting the reins fall loosely as the horses grazed nearby.

She turned — and stopped short.

The view stretched out before them in breathtaking beauty: rolling green pastures unfurling to the horizon, framed by the jagged, snow-capped peaks of the Rockies. A river cut a silver ribbon through the valley below, sparkling under the midday sun.

"It's incredible," she breathed.

Eric watched her, not the view. "Yeah," he said quietly. "It is."

She turned to find him already close, his hat dangling from one hand, his dark hair ruffled by the breeze. His eyes locked on hers, steady and sure, as if memorising everything about her in that moment.

Neither spoke.

Eric stepped closer, his hand rising slowly, giving her time to pull away if she wanted. She didn't. Instead, she leaned into his touch as his fingers brushed lightly along her jawline, tracing the curve of her cheek.

When he kissed her, it wasn't cautious like last night.

It was deeper, fuller — hungry in a way that startled and thrilled her all at once. His mouth captured hers with gentle urgency, pouring all the words he hadn't said into the kiss. Amy responded without hesitation, rising onto her toes, her hands finding his shoulders for balance.

The world disappeared.

There was only Eric — the strong arms wrapping around her, the steady thud of his heart against hers.

When they finally broke apart, breathless and a little dazed, Eric rested his forehead against hers, his smile slow and tender.

"You're trouble, Amy," he whispered, his voice rough with emotion. "The best kind."

She laughed, pure and giddy, a sound she hadn't heard from herself in far too long.

"Good," she whispered back. "Because I think you might be trouble too."

He kissed her again, quick and sweet, before pulling her into his arms, the wind wrapping around them as if the whole world was holding its breath.

For the first time in forever, Amy wasn't afraid of what came next.

She was ready to find out.

Chapter Fourteen

The sun had dipped lower in the sky by the time they returned to the ranch house, long shadows stretching across the porch. Lunch had been simple—sandwiches and lemonade on the back deck—but it felt like the best meal Amy had had in ages. Not because of the food, but because of the easy way Eric talked, the way he listened. The way being around him made her feel…seen.

Now, the moment she'd been trying not to think about had arrived.

Amy stood near her truck, the gravel crunching softly beneath her boots. The air smelled faintly of dust and sweet grass. Eric leaned against one of the porch posts, arms crossed, his expression unreadable but his eyes never leaving her.

"Well," she said, her voice soft, "I should probably get going before the sun dips too low."

He nodded, pushing off the post and walking toward her. "You sure? You could stay a little longer. I could show you the calving barn… or the creek trail."

She smiled gently. "Tempting. But if I don't leave now, I might never leave."

That earned her a slow grin, the kind that made her heart flutter a little too fast. "That doesn't sound like a bad thing."

Amy looked down, then back up. "Today was… more than I expected. In the best way."

Eric stepped closer, close enough that she could feel the heat of him, but he didn't reach for her. He just looked at her, like he was memorising every detail.

"I'm glad you came," he said. "You looked like you belonged out there."

She swallowed. "I felt like I did."

There was a beat of quiet. Then Amy stepped forward and rose onto her toes, pressing a kiss to his cheek — soft, warm, lingering just a moment longer than casual. When she pulled back, her voice was barely above a whisper.

"Thank you."

Eric looked at her for a long moment. Then, gently, he tucked a piece of windblown hair behind her ear. "Come back anytime, Amy. No pressure. Just… when you want to."

"I will," she promised.

With one last look, she opened her truck door and slipped inside. Eric stepped back as the engine started, watching as she drove out of the drive. She gave a small wave through the window, and he returned it, his hand lifting slowly.

Eric stood in the gravel driveway long after Amy's taillights vanished around the bend, the quiet settling in like dusk. A faint breeze stirred the dust at his boots. He exhaled slowly, dragging a hand through his hair.

Footsteps crunched behind him.

"Guess she's not so scared of you after all," Levi said, walking up from the barn, a coil of rope slung over his shoulder and hay clinging to his sleeves.

Eric didn't turn right away. "She's been through a lot."

"She told you?" Levi's voice softened, the teasing edge gone.

"Yeah." Eric nodded once. "And it's not good."

Levi stood beside him now, looking out toward the road as if he could still see her truck. "But she came out here anyway."

"She did." Eric's voice was quiet, full of something heavier than just admiration.

Levi glanced sideways at him. "So… you like her?"

Eric finally looked over, a small, crooked smile tugging at the corner of his mouth. "It's not just that I like her. It's more than that."

Levi let out a low whistle. "Damn. That was fast."

Eric shook his head. "It doesn't feel fast. It feels… like I've known her longer than I have."

They stood there for a beat, the silence comfortable, broken only by the distant whinny of a horse.

"She gonna be okay?" Levi asked.

Eric's jaw flexed. "I think she will be. But I also think she's still figuring out how to believe it."

Levi nodded thoughtfully. "Well… I've seen worse reasons to take things slow."

Eric didn't answer right away. His eyes were still on the road. "I'll wait," he said finally. "As long as she needs."

Levi clapped him on the shoulder. "Then you're already in deep, man."

Eric smiled faintly. "Yeah. I think I am."

Amy gripped the steering wheel with one hand, the other resting loosely in her lap as the road unwound before her. Afternoon sunlight slanted through the windshield, turning the fields to gold, casting long shadows across the hills. But all she could see was him — Eric standing in the driveway, arms crossed over his chest, watching her go with that quiet intensity that had become familiar.

Her heart ached — not the sharp, guarded kind she was used to, but something softer. Yearning. A strange, wonderful ache that made her feel alive again.

She touched her lips, still tender from the kiss on the ridge.

God, what had that been?

It wasn't just attraction — though she'd be lying if she said Eric wasn't completely her type, all strong lines and quiet strength. It was more than that. He'd listened. Really listened. Every moment they'd spent together, he'd noticed things most people missed.

When she told him about her past — the messy truth, the fear, the reason she kept everyone at arm's length — he hadn't flinched. He hadn't looked at her like she was broken.

He'd looked at her like she was still here.

Still fighting. Still worthy.

Amy blinked hard, brushing away the tears that had gathered without her realising. She wasn't used to being seen like that. It scared her — but it made her want to see herself that way too.

She rolled down the window, letting the wind rush in, tousling her hair. The scent of wildflowers drifted in from the roadside. She breathed deep.

Somewhere between the barn and the ridge trail, something had shifted. She wasn't just visiting Eric's world — she'd found something that felt like it could be home. Someday.

Not yet.

But she was closer than she'd been in a long time.

Amy smiled to herself, the kind of smile she hadn't worn in years — soft and real and filled with quiet hope.

Maybe the road ahead wasn't so lonely anymore.

Maybe, just maybe, it was leading her back to something she thought she'd lost.

To someone.

To herself.

Amy leaned against the counter in the back office of the clinic, peeling the wrapper off a granola bar with one hand and flipping through a chart with the other. It had been a steady morning — a limping Border Collie, a cow with mastitis, and a guinea pig with dental issues — and now, with only a few quiet minutes to herself, she was trying to convince her body that trail mix counted as lunch.

Her phone buzzed in the pocket of her scrubs. She expected it to be a client or maybe a reminder, but when she pulled it out and saw Eric Reynolds on the screen, her heart gave a small, traitorous leap.

She answered, trying to sound casual.

"Hey."

"Hey," he said, his voice like warm flannel, slow and easy. "Did I catch you at a bad time?"

She smiled. "Depends. Are you a limping Border Collie or a guinea pig with an attitude?"

There was a low chuckle on the other end. "Neither. Though I'd say I'm at least more charming than a guinea pig."

She laughed, sinking onto the stool beside the filing cabinet. "You might be right."

There was a pause, then his voice softened—still playful but threaded with something more uncertain.

"I was thinking… this Saturday, maybe I could take you somewhere. Just for the night. Separate rooms, no pressure. I just want to show you a place I think you'd really like."

Amy hesitated. An overnight trip felt like a bigger step than she was sure she was ready for. But something in his tone—earnest, careful—chipped away at her doubts. Maybe a leap of faith was exactly what her healing needed.

"Okay," she said quietly, a small nod following the word.

Her smile lingered long after the call ended. Even as she returned to her chart, his voice stayed with her — warm, steady, and full of something she wasn't sure she was ready to name.

But maybe… she was ready to find out.

Amy pulled the truck to a stop, the crunch of gravel beneath the tyres seeming louder than it should have been. Her eyes locked on the sleek, white jet sitting at the far end of the ranch, its polished surface gleaming under the sunlight. It was like something out of a dream—out of her reach, out of her league. She swallowed hard, her fingers tightening on the steering wheel as a familiar knot twisted in her stomach.

She'd never thought of Eric as a man of extravagance—never imagined him in the world of jets and private airstrips. He'd always seemed so down-to-earth, so grounded. And yet here it was, a stark contrast to everything she thought she knew about him.

Her heart raced, and a flutter of panic rose in her chest. Was this the world he truly lived in? A world she didn't belong in. Her boots hit the gravel as she stepped out of the truck, her gaze still caught by the jet, as though it were some kind of symbol—of wealth, of privilege, of everything that separated them.

When had she become someone who needed to be reminded of what she didn't have? She had worked hard for everything she'd built—she wasn't a stranger to sacrifice—but somehow, this felt different. She'd thought she was just visiting Eric's world, dipping a toe into his life. But the jet? That was a whole other thing.

The world of ranching, of horses and hay and quiet, open spaces—that was her world. That was something she understood. But this… this was something she had only seen in movies or on the glossy pages of magazines. It was a life so far removed from hers, a reminder of how out of place she might always feel in his life.

But maybe it wasn't the jet. Maybe it was her. Maybe she wasn't ready to take a step into a world where a private plane could be part of an ordinary day. Maybe she wasn't ready to believe she could be enough for someone like him.

The sound of footsteps drew her out of her thoughts, and she turned to see Eric approaching. Her breath caught in her chest, the ache of uncertainty still gnawing at her. She didn't want to appear small, didn't want to let him see her doubts, but the question lingered: Where did she fit into all of this?

Eric stepped down from the porch, an overnight bag slung casually over his shoulder. He was dressed in jeans and a navy button-down, as comfortable as ever, but he paused the moment he saw her gaze fixed on the plane.

"I didn't mean to spring that on you," he said, walking toward her slowly. "I just… wanted to take you somewhere special."

Amy tore her eyes from the jet and looked at him—really looked. The man who had knelt beside her in a dusty barn, his hands steady as they worked to save Patriot. The man who had taken her riding up to the ridge just to show her the view, like it was something sacred. The man who had laughed with her—not out of politeness, but freely, honestly—as if he hadn't remembered how until she came along.

And yet… he also had a private jet parked beside his horse pastures.

"I guess I just didn't realise…" she started, then stopped, the words catching in her throat.

"What?" he asked, his voice low, careful.

She shrugged, feeling raw. "That maybe I don't fit into your life."

Eric didn't answer right away. He took a step closer, then another, until he was just in front of her. The wind tugged at the hem of her jacket, but he stood steady, unwavering.

"Amy," he said, his tone gentler now. "I didn't bring the jet out to show off. I brought it out because I wanted to spend time with you—somewhere quiet, somewhere that might mean something. I wasn't trying to impress you."

"It's not that I'm impressed," she said softly, her voice barely more than a whisper. "It's that… I'm not sure where I fit in all of this. With you. Maybe this was a mistake."

He reached for her hand, slow and deliberate, giving her the space to pull away. She didn't.

"You fit exactly where you are," he said gently. "With me. And if that ever stops feeling true, you tell me—and I'll do whatever it takes to make it right."

Amy stared at him, heart thudding. She turned to glance back at the jet—sleek and intimidating—and then at him again.

He wasn't flashy. He wasn't arrogant. He was just Eric. And somehow, in this moment, that was enough.

She let out the breath she'd been holding. "Okay," she said quietly. "Where are we going?"

He smiled. "Sedona. You'll love it."

And to her own surprise, she believed him.

Chapter Fifteen

Amy hesitated at the base of the short staircase, her hand resting lightly on the polished railing. The interior of the jet was dimly lit in soft gold tones, a warm contrast to the fading light outside. She took a breath and stepped up.

Inside, the jet was surprisingly understated—elegant without being ostentatious. The interior was sleek, but not showy. Cream-coloured leather seats were arranged in a conversational layout, facing each other across a narrow aisle. The wood trim along the walls and cabinetry was a warm, dark walnut that gave the space a grounded, almost cabin-like feel.

The carpet beneath her boots was a soft grey, thick enough to silence her steps, and the lighting was low and inviting. A built-in console held a small stack of books, a half-finished bottle of water, and a neatly folded flannel blanket—details that spoke more of comfort than wealth. Someone had clearly gone out of their way to make this space feel lived in. Warm. Familiar.

This wasn't some billionaire's cold, high-tech playground. It felt… personal. Intimate, even. Like a place someone brought people who mattered.

Amy turned slowly, taking it in. The air held a faint scent of leather and cedar, and the quiet hum of systems coming online filled the silence.

Eric stepped in behind her. "It's not much," he said, watching her reaction. "But it gets me where I need to go."

Amy looked back at him, eyes soft. "It's more than I ever imagined. But not what I expected."

"How so?" he asked, curious.

She gave him a small smile. "I thought it would feel cold… showy. But it doesn't. It feels like you."

He looked caught off guard by that, then nodded once. "I'll take that as a compliment."

She eased into one of the seats and ran her fingers across the armrest. "It is."

And as the engines began their low, steady rumble, Amy felt something shift inside her—like maybe she was stepping into more than just a jet. Maybe she was stepping into something new entirely.

The soft whir of the jet's engines was a low hum beneath Amy's feet, but her mind was still catching up to what was happening. She glanced at Eric across the cabin—relaxed, one ankle propped casually on his knee, fingers cradling a glass of bourbon like he did it every day.

Maybe he did.

"Sedona?" she asked again, a note of disbelief in her voice.

Eric turned his head toward her, that familiar glint in his eyes. "Yeah. Figured we both could use a change of scenery. And I wanted to show you something."

She folded her hands in her lap, a quiet swirl of nerves and wonder twisting in her chest. "You didn't have to go to all this trouble—"

"I wanted to," he said, his voice low but steady, his gaze locked on hers. "You're the first person—other than Levi—I've ever brought on this jet."

Amy looked out the window as the mountains of Colorado slowly gave way to sweeping desert below. Red cliffs and sun-baked mesas stretched out beneath them, the landscape glowing in the golden light of mid afternoon. She hadn't realised how tightly she'd been wound until this moment—until the world dropped away and all that remained was this bubble in the sky, and him.

They landed smoothly at a private airstrip nestled between crimson ridges. A sleek black SUV was already waiting for them. Eric opened her door, offering his hand, and Amy hesitated only a second before taking it. His fingers were warm—steady.

They drove in comfortable silence until the landscape opened up, revealing a breathtaking overlook where red rock spires stabbed into the sky like ancient monuments. The sun had started to sink low, bathing the cliffs in deep, blazing orange.

"Come on," Eric said, pulling the car off onto a narrow dirt path. They climbed a short way up a trail, and Amy followed him, breath caught in her chest—not from exertion, but from the view.

At the top, a flat outcropping opened up before them. No one else in sight. Just wind, stone, and sky.

Amy stepped to the edge, stunned. "It's beautiful."

Eric moved beside her, quiet. "I thought you'd like it."

She turned to him then, her blonde hair catching the light, eyes soft but unsure. "Why did you bring me here?"

He looked at her—really looked—like he could see past the guarded layers she tried so hard to keep in place. "Because I wanted to give you something you'd never forget," he said quietly. "And because… I can't stop thinking about you, Amy. Even when I try."

Amy's breath caught as Eric's words hung in the air between them. *I can't stop thinking about you, Amy. Even when I try.* The vulnerability in his voice, the raw honesty, hit her like a wave. She had been so careful to keep her heart shielded, to keep him at arm's length. But now, in the face of his admission, she felt the walls she'd carefully constructed start to crumble.

She looked at him—really looked at him—eyes searching, trying to piece together this unexpected truth. The hesitation that had kept her cautious, guarded, now felt small, insignificant. Was it possible? Could she actually trust him, trust this? I want to, she realised. The thought both scared and excited her, as though she was standing on the edge of something deep and unknown.

And then he kissed her.

It was gentle at first, as if he, too, was testing the waters. But there was something in the way his lips moved against hers, in the way he cupped her face like she was something delicate, something precious. Her pulse quickened. The rush of heat flooded through her, replacing the cold distance she'd kept for so long.

She closed her eyes, losing herself in the moment. This is what it feels like to let go, she thought, the realisation settling into her chest like a quiet surrender. The kiss deepened, and she couldn't help herself—her hands found the front of his shirt, gripping it as though she were afraid it would all disappear if she let go.

When they finally pulled apart, her heart was racing, her breath uneven. She felt dizzy, lightheaded with the intensity of it all. He rested his forehead against hers, both of them breathing in the same air, as though their very souls were connected in that single, fleeting moment.

"That was…" she whispered, trying to make sense of the whirlwind of emotions crashing over her.

"Yeah," he murmured, his voice thick with emotion. "It was."

The words didn't need to be said. In that kiss, in the soft, unspoken understanding between them, everything she had feared was laid bare. And yet, in that vulnerability, she felt something else take root—hope. It was terrifying. But it was real.

Amy lowered her gaze, her breath catching. When she looked up again, her voice was a whisper threaded with fear. "You scare me, Eric."

He didn't flinch. "I know," he said. "You scare me too. This… scares me."

Around them, the wind stirred gently, carrying the clean scent of juniper and sun-warmed earth. A hush settled, like even the world had paused to listen.

Amy took a breath—steady, intentional—and reached for his hand. Not from impulse. From choice.

And that was how they watched the sunset: side by side, quietly holding on, two hearts once broken beginning to believe in the light again.

The resort Eric had chosen was nestled against the towering red rock cliffs, its adobe walls painted in warm earth tones that blended seamlessly with the desert. It looked like it had grown from the stone itself—timeless and still. Their casitas were separate but close, a thoughtful detail Eric had made clear when they checked in. No pressure. No expectations. Just space if she needed it.

After a quiet dinner at the on-site restaurant—good food, easy conversation—they'd parted ways with a lingering glance that said more than either of them had spoken aloud.

Now, wrapped in a soft cotton robe, Amy stood on the private terrace outside her room. The night air was cool against her skin, and the sky above stretched endlessly, a deep velvet scattered with stars. She cradled a glass of wine, the quiet pressing in around her—not lonely, exactly, but aware. Aware of how much she wanted to see him again tonight.

Then came a soft knock.

She opened the door to find Eric standing there, freshly showered, his dark hair still damp, dressed down in a simple black henley and jeans. He held two mugs, steam curling from their rims.

"Hot chocolate," he said, a crooked smile playing at his lips. "Figured you might want something sweet."

Amy smiled, warmth blooming in her chest. "You always this thoughtful?"

"No," he said, stepping inside. "Not until you."

They sat side by side on the low terrace wall, the mugs warm between their hands. Silence settled, easy and unforced. The desert hummed around them—crickets chirping, the whisper of wind moving through canyon crevices.

Amy set her mug down and looked out at the stars. "I haven't felt this calm in… years," she said softly. "It feels strange. Like I've forgotten how."

Eric didn't rush to answer. Instead, he reached for her hand, lacing his fingers with hers.

"Maybe we're both remembering," he said.

And in that still, starlit moment, she let herself believe it was possible.

She hesitated. "I want to trust this… you. But I'm scared."

"I don't need all of you at once, Amy." He reached out, gently tucking a strand of hair behind her ear. "Just let me be the one who doesn't hurt you."

The softness in his voice unraveled her. She could feel it happening—the slow, inevitable melting of the walls she'd built so carefully.

She leaned her head against his shoulder, tentative at first, then fully.

"I don't know where this is going," she murmured.

"Neither do I," he said, resting his cheek against her hair. "But I know I don't want it to end."

They stayed like that—wrapped in the quiet, in the stars, in something that felt dangerously close to hope.

Eric shifted slightly, just enough to look down at her. The way her head rested on his shoulder, the soft rise and fall of her breath—he didn't want to move, didn't want to break the spell of the moment. But her eyes lifted to meet his, and in them, he saw it: the same hesitation, the same pull.

"I keep telling myself not to do this," he murmured.

Amy's voice was quiet. "I think you should stop talking."

For a beat, neither moved. Then Eric reached up and cupped her cheek, his thumb brushing a spot just below her scar—a place he knew she still guarded. Her breath caught, but she didn't pull away.

He leaned in slowly, giving her every chance to stop him. But she didn't. Her eyes closed, her lips parted slightly—and then he kissed her.

It wasn't rushed. It wasn't hungry.

It was slow and searching, like a question he didn't know how to ask out loud. She answered him with the softest sigh against his mouth, her hands finding the front of his shirt, gripping lightly, as if she wasn't sure how to hold on.

When they finally pulled apart, her forehead rested against his.

"That was…" she whispered.

"Yeah," he said, just as breathless. "It was."

She smiled—small, tentative, but real.

He tucked a strand of hair behind her ear again, a habit he was quickly forming. "I don't want to screw this up."

"You haven't," she said, her fingers still resting lightly on his chest.

They didn't speak after that. They just sat on the terrace, wrapped in the desert night and the brand-new electricity between them.

The next morning, just as Amy finished getting dressed after her shower, there was a gentle knock at her door.

When she opened it, Eric stood there, freshly shaven and effortlessly handsome, holding two cups of coffee. The morning light caught the steam curling up between them.

She smiled, stepping aside to let him in. "You need to stop this," she teased, taking a cup from his hand. "I'll get too used to you looking after me."

He stepped inside, his eyes warm. "I like looking after you."

They didn't linger long. After a relaxed breakfast on the resort patio—eggs, fresh fruit, and more of that quiet, easy conversation—they packed up and made their way back to the small airstrip. The jet waited, gleaming in the soft desert morning light, its sleek frame somehow less intimidating than it had seemed when she first saw it.

The flight back to Steamboat Springs was quiet and smooth, the private jet humming steadily as it cut through the endless blue sky. Eric sat across from Amy, his arm resting casually along the back of his seat, but his gaze kept finding her—soft, steady, and unreadable.

Amy pretended to be absorbed by the view outside, watching the clouds drift past, but she felt him watching her. Not in a way that unsettled her, but in a way that made her chest tighten with something gentle… and dangerous.

"I'm glad we went," Eric said at last, his voice low and certain.

She turned to him, their eyes meeting across the short distance. Something unspoken passed between them—quiet and charged.

"Me too," she said, the words simple but true.

For the first time in years, she wasn't guarding her heart behind carefully built walls. And that, she realised, might be the most terrifying—and the most hopeful—thing of all.

Chapter Sixteen

The sun hung low over the western ridge, casting a golden wash across the pastures as Eric moved between the kitchen and the back porch. His sleeves were rolled to the elbows, apron dusted with flour, and a bottle of whiskey sat uncorked beside the grill. He glanced at his watch—just after six. She'd said six-thirty.

He found himself replaying their phone call.

"I was thinking… if you're free Friday night, maybe you could come out to the ranch. Just you and me. I'll cook."

"You cook?" Amy had asked, surprised.

"I do, in fact. And don't ask Levi to verify that. He still hasn't forgiven me for the chilli incident of '23."

She'd laughed then — soft and genuine. The sound had stayed with him longer than it should have.

"What's on the menu?"

"Steak. Potatoes. Maybe grilled peaches if I can talk Levi into sacrificing the good whiskey."

She'd hesitated, just for a beat. He could feel it—the weight of whatever it was she still carried. But then came her quiet reply, laced with something that sounded like hope.

"I'd like that. Friday night. I'll be there."

He remembered the breath he'd let out then, as if he'd been holding it without realising. "Good. It's a date."

Now, the steaks were marinating, the potatoes roasting with rosemary and garlic, and a bowl of ripe peaches waited patiently on the counter. He'd even made a salad—though Levi had taken one look at the kale and made a dramatic exit toward the barn, muttering about rabbit food and dignity.

Eric shook his head, smirking to himself as he adjusted the plates on the farmhouse table. It had been a long time since he'd done something like this — really done it. Not a catered event or a last-minute dinner with someone who barely knew the difference between his home and his net worth. This was sixtentional. Simple. Personal.

He wasn't trying to impress Amy with grandeur or flash. There was no linen napkins folded into swans, no staff flitting through the room, no orchestrated perfection. Just a warm meal, a quiet space, and the quiet hope that she might feel something here—

something real. A sense of ease. Of belonging. Like maybe, just maybe, this could feel like her home too if she ever wanted it.

Because he loved her.

He hadn't planned on it, hadn't expected it—but the truth was undeniable now. He loved Amy in a way that felt entirely different from anything he'd ever known. Certainly, nothing like what he'd once called love with Jessica. That, he could now see, had been comfort, habit, maybe even guilt. But this—what he felt for Amy—was deeper. Quieter. Truer.

And he couldn't tell her. Not yet. Not when she was still finding her footing, still unsure. He didn't want to risk scaring her away.

So, he offered her what he could for now: warmth, space, and the silent promise that if she needed a place to land, he'd be right here.

The front door creaked open behind him.

"You missed a spot," Levi called, his voice dry with amusement.

Eric didn't look back. "Thanks for the update."

There was a pause. Then, "You're wearing your nice shirt."

"I know."

Levi came to stand beside him, arms crossed, watching the table like he half expected to see a white-gloved critic emerge from under it. "You're a billionaire," he said flatly. "Why the hell are you cooking?"

Eric straightened one of the forks before answering. "Because I can tell she's not impressed by how much money I have."

Levi snorted. "Not like your ex-wife, then."

Eric's jaw tightened briefly, but he didn't flinch from it. "No," he said. "Amy's nothing like Jessica. Thank God."

Levi studied him for a second, something softer flickering in his eyes. Then, without another word, he clapped Eric on the shoulder and disappeared out the door, boots thudding across the porch.

The house fell quiet again, save for the gentle ticking of the oven and the low hum of the porch fan. Eric exhaled, rolled his sleeves up a little higher, and moved to check the grill.

Ten minutes later, he heard it — the crunch of tyres on gravel. His heart kicked up. He wiped his hands on a towel and stepped onto the porch.

Amy pulled up the long gravel drive, the tyres crunching softly beneath her as the ranch house came into view — and her breath caught.

Eric's home rose out of the landscape like it had grown there, anchored deep into the earth — a sprawling log-and-stone lodge with a wraparound porch, thick cedar beams, and massive windows that glowed gold in the fading light. Flower boxes spilled over with ivy and delicate spring blooms, and two rocking chairs swayed lazily in the breeze.

It was rustic, yes — but not rough. Every detail carried the quiet confidence of intention. The stonework was flawless, the wood polished to a warm sheen, and even the stacked firewood by the door looked like it had been arranged, not just dumped.

Amy cut the engine, her heart fluttering with something she couldn't quite name. Anticipation, maybe. Or nerves. The feeling of stepping into something unfamiliar — and wanting it.

Eric stepped out onto the porch just as she opened her door. He wore a dark button-up shirt, sleeves rolled, jeans and boots. Casual. Effortless. But the way he looked at her — like seeing her settled something in him — sent a quiet heat spiralling through her chest.

"You're right on time," he said, a smile tugging at the corner of his mouth.

Amy smiled back as she crossed the gravel, smoothing a hand over her dress. "I try."

He met her at the steps, taking the bottle of wine from her hands without hesitation. "You didn't have to bring anything."

"I wanted to," she replied with a playful shrug. "I don't know much about wine, but the shopkeeper swore this goes with steak. He looked confident."

Eric laughed, his eyes crinkling at the corners. "Then I'm sold."

He tipped his head toward the door. "Come on in.

She followed him up the steps, nerves fading with each stride. The moment he opened the door and motioned her inside, warmth spilled out, rich with the scent of cedar and something faintly spiced — maybe his cologne, maybe dinner. It was the kind of warmth that settled into her bones, disarming and familiar.

The interior of the lodge was breathtaking. Vaulted ceilings with thick, exposed beams soared overhead. A stone fireplace crackled in the great room, casting shadows over worn leather chairs, wool throws, and rich, earthy rugs. Antler chandeliers glowed above, bathing the space in golden light.

The kitchen, open and tucked beneath a lofted second floor, gleamed with quiet luxury — stainless steel fixtures, a professional-grade range, and smooth stone counters that contrasted beautifully with the hand-carved cabinets.

"You live in a magazine," she said, awed. "Or maybe a dream."

Eric set the wine on the counter and turned toward her, his voice quieter now. "It's just a house," he said. "But… I like it."

"It's beautiful," she said, more softly than she meant to.

His smile deepened, but he didn't say anything — just held her gaze for a moment too long.

"Dinner's almost ready," he said then, gesturing toward the dining room, where candles flickered along a long oak table. "But if you'd like the tour first…"

Amy slipped out of her shoes by the door. "Lead the way."

And as he walked her through the house — pointing out the window seat where he liked to read, the guest suite that overlooked the pastures, the hidden wine cellar behind a panelled wall — she felt something settle in her.

This wasn't just charming. It wasn't just impressive.

Eric Reynolds was wealthier than she'd realised.

But nothing about the way he moved through the space felt performative. It didn't feel like he was showing off.

It felt like he was inviting her in.

Dinner was simple but perfect: marinated steaks, grilled to a tender pink centre and resting beside baby potatoes roasted in garlic, rosemary, and olive oil until their skins blistered crisp. A fresh salad of arugula, cherry tomatoes, and slivers of red onion added brightness, and a bowl of sliced peaches, glistening with a hint of honey, waited for dessert.

Amy sat down, wide-eyed. "Okay," she said, looking from the table to him, "this is… unexpectedly charming. Romantic, even. Should I be suspicious?"

Eric shrugged, smiling as he poured wine into her glass. "I cook. I like good lighting. Doesn't mean I'm dangerous."

She gave him a slow grin. "I didn't say dangerous. I said suspicious. There's a difference."

They ate slowly, talking between bites, letting the conversation meander. Amy told him about her parents and childhood. The candles flickered as they leaned into the stories, hands brushing accidentally as they reached for the salad bowl or wine bottle.

At one point, Amy took a bite of steak and moaned, eyes closing briefly. "This is insane. Why does this taste like something out of a five-star restaurant?"

Eric gave her a modest shrug. "I've had a lot of time to practice. And good food helps with cabin fever."

"How has no woman snapped you up yet?" Amy asked, half-teasing.

His smile faltered, just for a breath. Like her words had landed somewhere tender. He looked away for half a second, then met her eyes again with a quieter kind of smile. "Maybe I was just waiting for someone who appreciates my potatoes."

Amy laughed, but her smile softened. "Well. Mission accomplished."

When dessert came, they stayed at the table, dipping grilled peach slices into honeyed syrup and sharing the bowl without bothering with plates. The candlelight danced between them, casting shadows that felt like secrets and warmth.

As the meal wound down, they lingered, quiet now. Not awkward—just comfortable. The kind of silence that meant neither wanted the evening to end.

Eric leaned forward slightly, his forearms resting on the edge of the table, his voice dropping to a quieter register—lower, more tentative. "I'm glad you came tonight."

Amy looked at him through the warm haze of candlelight, her lashes lowered as her fingers traced slow, absent circles around the rim of her wine glass. Her voice was soft, but steady. "Me too."

For a moment, neither of them moved. The room was hushed but full of unspoken things—desire, uncertainty, the quiet crackle of connection thickening between them like static before a storm.

When the candles burned low, their flames flickering and shrinking to small golden hearts, Eric rose and gathered their empty plates with quiet care. He returned with the wine bottle, refilled their glasses, then nodded toward the living room where the fire still burned, casting a gentle glow across the wood floors.

"Come sit with me," he said, his voice rougher now, threaded with something deeper.

Amy followed him, curling into the corner of the couch as he sat beside her, close but not quite touching. She drew her knees up slightly, one hand cradling her wine, the other resting loosely between them. The silence was companionable but charged. She could feel the heat of him, the awareness of every inch that separated their bodies.

They drank slowly, letting the warmth settle in. Outside, the night was still and velvet-dark, stars hidden behind a hush of clouds. Inside, the fire cast moving shadows that danced across their faces.

Eric took her glass and set both glasses on the coffee table and turned to her. His eyes searched hers, quiet and intense. "Amy…"

She didn't answer, didn't need to. She simply leaned in, and he met her halfway.

The kiss started gentle, exploratory—just the soft press of lips and breath—but quickly deepened. His hand came up to cup her jaw, his thumb brushing the corner of her mouth as if memorising the shape of her. She made a soft sound in the back of her throat and leaned into him, her fingers threading into his hair.

The passion bloomed between them with startling speed, as if the hunger had been waiting for permission. His mouth found hers again, urgent now, his hands moving—her shoulder, her waist, the curve of her spine as she arched into him.

Eric broke the kiss with effort, his breathing ragged. He pressed his forehead to hers, eyes closed, voice hoarse. "Amy… tell me to stop."

Her hands tightened on his shirt, pulling him back to her. She shook her head slowly, her lips brushing his. "I don't want you to stop."

That was all it took. The dam broke.

Eric didn't ask again.

His mouth found hers in a kiss that was deeper now—darker, hungrier. He shifted, guiding her gently beneath him on the couch, the heat between them igniting into something that pulsed and ached. His hands roamed with reverence and need, skimming the shape of her through the soft fabric of her dress, memorising her with his fingertips.

Amy arched into his touch, her breath catching as his lips traced a slow, deliberate path down her throat. Her fingers fumbled with the buttons of his shirt, desperate to feel skin, to close the space between them completely. When she finally pushed the fabric aside and ran her hands over the hard planes of his chest, he let out a low groan that sent shivers down her spine.

"You feel so good," she murmured, her voice unsteady with want.

Eric's mouth curved against her collarbone. "So do you," he said, lifting his head to look at her.

Their eyes locked, and something passed between them—more than lust, more than timing. Something that felt like trust. Like risk. Like falling.

He kissed her again, slow and consuming, as if he had all the time in the world to learn her, to unravel her one soft sigh at a time. His hand slipped beneath the hem of her dress, tracing the bare skin of her thigh with a reverence that made her shiver. She gasped—not from surprise, but from the way it made her feel. Seen. Wanted. Alive.

"I've thought about this," he murmured against her ear, his voice rough with restraint. "Thought about you."

Amy's breath hitched. Her fingers slid into his hair as she whispered against his jaw, "Then stop thinking."

He did.

And she let go.

Chapter Seventeen

Eric kissed her again, deeper this time, until she melted beneath him, pliant and aching. Then, without a word, he rose and scooped her into his arms. Amy clung to him, dress bunched, heart pounding as he carried her up the stairs. The quiet house seemed to hold its breath around them, the only sound the soft creak of floorboards and the faint crackle of the fire downstairs.

His bedroom was warm, the sheets turned down, the space imbued with quiet intimacy. He set her down at the edge of the bed like she was something breakable—but his eyes told a different story. His eyes said he was starving.

She reached for him, and he followed her down, his body settling over hers with exquisite care. He kissed her like she already belonged to him—slowly, achingly, pouring into it everything he hadn't yet found the words to say. Their clothes fell away in silences hotter than speech, until skin met skin, and they found each other in the soft hush of half-light.

His lips trailed along her throat, lingering at the hollow of her collarbone before he took one rosy nipple into his mouth. She gasped his name like a prayer, arching into him. He moved to the other with reverence, like he was learning her—learning what made her sigh, what made her shiver, what she needed without ever asking.

It wasn't rushed.

It wasn't reckless.

It was discovery—every touch, every breath, a new confession. His hands charted her body like a sacred map, learning her curves, her heat, the secret language etched into her skin—one he somehow already knew in his bones.

When he kissed her lower, to the core of her, and worshipped her with his mouth, she shattered around him, crying out in release. He rose up, covering her again, and when he finally entered her, her legs wrapped around him as if to anchor him to this moment—this truth.

And when he moved inside her, it wasn't just bodies meeting. It was something deeper, something soul-deep and staggering. She trembled beneath him as he held her gaze, their breath syncing, their rhythm slow and raw and reverent. His mouth found her neck, his voice rasped her name, and her fingers dug into his shoulders like she was holding on for dear life.

When they came together, it was quiet and blinding, a tidal wave of feeling neither of them could outrun.

Afterward, Eric held her close, his thumb tracing lazy circles along her hip as their heartbeats slowed. He didn't speak. He didn't need to. Everything that mattered had already been said in the way he touched her.

The room quieted to the hum of crickets outside and the faint hiss of embers. Amy lay curled against his chest, one leg tangled with his, her breath soft and steady. His fingers drew slow patterns along her spine, and she thought maybe she'd never felt so safe. Or so known.

But sleep didn't come. Not really.

She didn't know how long they lay like that—just breathing, just holding. But for the first time in a long while, she wasn't bracing for goodbye.

After a while, Eric shifted, propping himself on one elbow to look at her. In the dim light, his expression was soft, searching.

"You're still awake," he said, brushing a strand of hair from her cheek.

Amy nodded, her hand resting over his heart. "So are you."

He kissed her—unhurried, like he had all night to remember her. She kissed him back, deeper this time, the warmth between them sparking again with startling ease.

He rolled over her, their bodies already in sync. Slower now. The kind of intimacy born of knowing each other's need. There was no rush—just long kisses, whispered names, the rediscovery of her curves beneath his hands.

She arched into him, sighing his name into the dark. And this time, when they came together, it was quieter. Softer. The kind of lovemaking that wasn't about urgency—but about choosing. Staying. Holding on.

When they collapsed again, Amy fell asleep with her head on his chest, his arms locked around her, her body still humming with the echo of him.

Dawn spilled gold through the window. Amy stirred first, blinking at the warm light and shifting slightly. She turned her head and found Eric watching her, a sleep-mussed smile on his lips.

"Hey," he said, voice gravelly.

"Hey yourself," she murmured, stretching. Her bare skin brushed his, and his breath caught.

Eric reached for her, fingers skimming down to her waist. "You're trouble, you know that?"

"Am I?" she asked, feigning innocence as her leg slid over his hip.

He growled low in his throat, pulling her under him again. "Mm-hmm. And I'm about to make some very bad decisions before breakfast."

She laughed, then gasped as he kissed her again—slow, but deeper now. Playfulness melting into something hotter.

Morning lovemaking was different. No shadows. No candlelight. Just sunlight and skin, real and raw. She wrapped her arms around his neck, matched his rhythm, breathed his name against his skin.

When they came undone again, sunlight warmed their skin and birdsong filtered through the window. And when they lay tangled in the quiet aftermath, neither said a word.

They didn't need to.

The way he kissed her shoulder before pulling her close said it all.

They weren't circling something unspoken anymore.

They were in it. Completely.

The kitchen glowed with morning light. Amy stood barefoot at the counter in one of Eric's shirts—soft, oversized, and smelling like him—while he flipped pancakes at the stove.

"I could get used to this," she said, stealing a strip of bacon.

Eric raised an eyebrow. "To my shirt or my breakfast?"

"Yes," she said, grinning.

He laughed, warm and deep. The sound of it made her stomach flutter.

They ate at the small table by the window, legs brushing, his hand drifting occasionally to her knee or thigh. The silences were no longer awkward. Just full.

Afterward, he rinsed dishes while she leaned against the counter, sipping coffee. Sunlight hit his profile just right, and something in her ached at the sight.

"Wanna go for a walk?" he asked, drying his hands.

She nodded. "Yeah. I'd love to."

The trail behind Eric's ranch house wove through a small patch of woods, a canopy of spring green arching over them as birdsong echoed through the trees. They didn't talk much—just walked hand in hand, their strides falling into a quiet rhythm.

Amy let herself breathe, really breathe, the fresh air settling something inside her that had been tight for too long.

At one point, he stopped and pulled her to a halt beside a small creek, the water burbling over rocks like laughter. He tugged her close, brushing a kiss to her forehead before resting his chin there. No words, just warmth. Steadiness.

She closed her eyes and leaned into him.

They returned flushed and sticky from the humid air. Eric caught her hand and tugged her upstairs without a word, a smirk playing at his lips.

"We're sweaty," she said with mock protest.

"Exactly," he replied, pulling her into the bathroom. "Shower time."

Steam rose around them as the water poured over their skin. Amy tipped her head back, letting it rush down her face—until she felt his hands at her waist.

She opened her eyes. His gaze was heat and reverence.

He pressed her gently against the wall, one hand cradling her neck as he kissed her— slow, wet, deep. The water rushed around them, but the kiss made everything still.

His hands slid over her with purpose. Hers gripped his hips, dragging him closer.

"You feel like a dream," she whispered.

"Then don't wake up," he murmured, brushing his mouth along her jaw. "Stay with me."

"I'm here," she breathed.

When he lifted her, she wrapped around him instinctively. Their bodies joined with a gasp. This time wasn't gentle—it was consuming. Raw. Real.

The slick heat, the pounding water, the way he moved inside her—it all blurred into one wild ache. She held on. Tipped her head back. Whispered his name like prayer.

And when they broke apart, trembling, gasping, she was still wrapped around him. Heart to heart.

He pressed his forehead to hers. "Still trouble."

She smiled. "You like trouble."

He laughed, then kissed her again — slow and lingering. Like a promise.

Wrapped in towels, they ended up on the bed. Amy sat towelling her hair, droplets glistening on her shoulders. Eric sat beside her, pulling on a T-shirt.

They sat in silence. The kind that buzzed with contentment.

Eventually, Amy turned toward him. "This feels… different."

He looked at her, brow furrowed. "Different good or… complicated?"

"Both, maybe?" she admitted. "I just don't want this to be some perfect weekend that doesn't survive the real world."

He brushed a strand of hair from her cheek. "It's not just a weekend to me. You know that, right?"

She nodded slowly. "I do. I just… I think I'm scared. Of messing this up. Of wanting too much."

His jaw flexed. He took her hand. "Amy, I spent a long time convincing myself I was better off alone. But then you walked in, and now… I can't imagine life without you."

Her eyes shone. Her chest ached.

"That sounds dangerously close to a declaration."

He smiled, small and unsure. "I'm not great at this part. But I know how I feel. And I'm not going anywhere—unless you ask me to."

She leaned in, pressing her forehead to his. "I don't want you to go."

He exhaled quietly, kissed her gently. Their joined hands rested between them.

And this time, when she looked at him, she didn't just see the man she'd fallen into bed with.

She saw the man she had falling in love with.

"So," she said softly, "what do we do now?"

Eric smiled. "We make coffee. We eat leftover pancakes. We take it one day at a time."

She nodded, her heart full. "That, I can do."

Chapter Eighteen

The next two weeks were a whirlwind—sweet, dizzying, impossible to pin down. Time slipped through Amy's fingers like river water, fast, warm, and gone before she could hold on.

She and Eric spent every spare moment together, trading between her cozy little cabin and his sprawling ranch house like they were playing house in two different worlds. Some nights he fell asleep beside her in her queen bed, legs tangled, arm draped across her stomach, the scent of pine and laundry soap in the air. Other nights she woke wrapped in his sheets, sunlight pouring in through wide windows, the sound of horses outside grounding her in a life that wasn't hers—but felt like it could be.

He'd make her coffee in the morning—strong, just how she liked it—and she'd cook him dinner in the evenings, barefoot in his kitchen, humming along to the radio while he leaned in the doorway, watching her like she was the most interesting thing in the room.

They rode horses at dusk, walked along the creek with their fingers laced, shared kisses that started slow and turned hungry in the dark. They talked about books and music and old regrets. They made love like it was the only thing tethering them to the earth.

Amy knew she had falling—fallen hard—but she tried not to name it. Tried not to hold it up to the light. Because if she did, it might break.

Love scared the hell out of her.

Not the feeling itself—it was beautiful, terrifying, consuming—but the after. The what-comes-next. The shift in gravity that happened when something too-good-to-keep slipped out of your hands.

So, she didn't talk about the future. Not yet.

Instead, she lived in the moments:

Eric pulling her onto his lap on the porch swing.

Eric kissing her temple as she chopped vegetables.

Eric whispering her name against her shoulder in the middle of the night.

And she let herself believe, for now, that this might be enough.

But in the quiet spaces between laughter and skin, a whisper of fear lingered. What if this ended the way everything else did? What if the timing shifted, or life pulled them apart?

Still, when he smiled at her like that—like she was the only woman in the world—she chose not to ask the questions.

She chose him.

Again and again, for fourteen days of stolen mornings and tangled nights.

And in those days, something soft and unshakable took root.

Love. Wild, quiet, unstoppable.

Whether she was ready for it or not.

On Wednesday morning, just before Amy left Eric's ranch for the vet clinic, he drew her into his arms with quiet tenderness.

"There's something I need to tell you," he said, his voice lower than usual. "This weekend, Levi and I are hauling Patriot to Tulsa. There's a race series starting. Big one."

Amy nodded slowly. "How long will you be gone?"

"Week, give or take. Depending on how Patriot runs."

She tried to keep her smile easy, casual. "Well, I'll miss you."

Eric's eyes held hers, steady and warm. "I'll really miss you, Amy."

There was a softness to the way he said it—no teasing, no guard. Just truth.

Amy's breath caught for a second before she masked it with a small shrug. "You'll be too busy winning trophies to think about me."

He shook his head. "Don't think that's possible."

The quiet between them stretched, not awkward but full—full of everything they hadn't said yet. He rubbed his thumb along the back of her hand.

"I've been away from a lot of things in my life," he murmured. "Never missed any of 'em much. But I already know this is gonna feel different."

Amy looked down at their joined hands, then up at him again. "You better come back in one piece, Reynolds."

His smile deepened. "I will. You'll be here waiting?"

She didn't answer right away. Then, quietly, "Yeah. I'll be here."

And in that shared silence, they both felt it—the ache of distance that hadn't even started yet.

Saturday morning sunlight spilled across the ranch, painting the horse trailer in a soft golden hue. Amy stood beside it, one hand resting against the cool metal as Patriot snorted softly from inside, ready for the long haul to Tulsa.

Levi strolled up, his boots crunching on gravel. With an easy grin, he tipped his hat. "See you later, Doc. I'll look after your man."

Amy smiled and reached up to kiss his cheek. "Thank you, Levi."

Eric chuckled from behind her. "Should I be jealous?"

Levi threw him a wink as he climbed into the driver's seat. "I wish."

As the truck engine rumbled to life, Eric stepped close and drew Amy into his arms. "I'll miss you," he said, brushing a soft kiss against her lips.

Amy wrapped her arms tightly around his waist, pressing herself into his chest like she could imprint the moment into memory. "I'll miss you more," she whispered.

Eric kissed her long and slow, savouring the moment before reluctantly pulling away. With one last glance, he climbed into his black SUV and fell in line behind the large horse trailer, which rumbled forward, the ranch's black and silver logo gleaming proudly on its side—a running stallion beneath bold letters that read Silver Meadow Ranch.

And Amy knew she would miss him—more deeply, more achingly—than Eric could possibly realise.

Amy kept herself busy. She cleaned everything that could be scrubbed, swept, or dusted—twice. She read the same paragraph in her novel three times before giving up and reaching for another. Anything to keep her mind from drifting to Eric—his voice, his touch, the warmth in his eyes when he looked at her like she mattered.

Sunday afternoon, her phone rang. Her heart leapt the moment she saw his name.

"Hey, beautiful," Eric's deep voice wrapped around her like a hug. "We made it to Tulsa. Patriot's settled in. I just… I miss you."

Her chest tightened. "I miss you too. So much."

They talked for a few minutes—light, easy conversation—but when the call ended, the silence felt louder than ever.

The cabin was peaceful that weekend, the kind of quiet that usually soothed her. But Sunday night, as darkness settled, it shifted into something heavier.

A knock at the door jolted her from the couch.

She wasn't expecting anyone.

She opened the door—and her breath caught in her throat.

Darren.

His presence hit her like a punch to the chest. Taller than she remembered. Older, harder. But it was him. The man who had once loved her—and hurt her.

Her voice barely worked. "What... what are you doing here?"

Terror crept through her body like ice in her veins. She took a step back, instinctively.

"You're not supposed to be here," she whispered, her fingers twitching near the doorframe.

Amy's pulse thundered in her ears. "You're not supposed to be here," she repeated, firmer this time. "You're supposed to be in jail—"

Darren's expression darkened. "I just got out, I'm on parole." He stepped forward, forcing her back into the cabin. The door swung shut behind him with a final, chilling click.

Amy's heart pounded as she backed away, inching toward her phone on the kitchen counter. "Get out, Darren. I'll call the police—"

"You won't get the chance."

In one quick, terrifying movement, he lunged. Amy screamed, twisting away, her fingers brushing the phone—before he grabbed her wrist and yanked her backward. She kicked and struggled, but he was stronger, meaner, and frighteningly determined.

"Don't make me hurt you," he snarled, clamping a hand over her mouth. "You owe me, Amy. After everything you did—running off, replacing me."

Tears streamed down her cheeks as he dragged her toward the door, his grip bruising. She fought, trying to remember the self-defence moves she'd learned, but panic clouded her thoughts.

Outside, the cabin was cloaked in night. No one saw him shove her into the back of a pickup truck she didn't recognise. Duct tape silenced her. Rope burned against her wrists. The last thing she saw before he slammed the door was the porch light flickering behind her, glowing uselessly in the dark.

And then they were gone.

Into the night.

Into silence.

And Amy didn't know if anyone would find her in time.

Chapter Nineteen

By Monday afternoon, Patriot had completed his first run in Tulsa. Eric stood near the paddock, phone to his ear, a small smile tugging at his lips as he waited for Amy to pick up.

It rang. Once. Twice. Then again. No answer.

Then her voicemail clicked on: "Hey, it's Amy. Leave a message and I'll get back to you."

He chuckled softly. "Hey, sweetheart. Just wanted to hear your voice. Patriot did great. I'll call later."

He didn't think much of it.

But when Tuesday came and went—two more calls, both going straight to voicemail—something in his chest began to tighten.

Amy was busy sometimes, sure. But not this busy. And she always called back.

By Wednesday morning, the silence had settled into his bones. He stood outside the stables, phone pressed to his ear once more, heart thudding harder with every unanswered ring.

This time, he didn't call Amy.

He called the clinic.

"Steamboat Springs Veterinary Services, this is Sally."

"Hi Sally, it's Eric Reynolds. I've been trying to get a hold of Amy since Monday," he said, keeping his voice casual, though his gut was churning. "Is she in today?"

There was a pause on the other end. A pause that sent a jolt of dread straight through him.

"Oh, Eric… you don't know?"

His stomach dropped. "Know what?"

Sally's voice trembled. "Amy's missing. She didn't show up for work Monday morning. Her cabin door was wide open. Her phone's there, her truck, too. She has just… disappeared."

Eric went cold.

"What?" he whispered, already reaching for his keys. "Why the hell didn't anyone call me?"

"We thought maybe she went to Tulsa with you. Or… or took time off. But when she didn't answer, and the sheriff came by… Eric, something's wrong."

Eric didn't even respond. He was already running.

Eric sprinted across the stable yard, gravel crunching beneath his boots, his heart pounding harder with every step. He spotted Levi near the feed shed, unloading hay off the back of a flatbed.

"Levi!" Eric called out, breathless.

Levi turned, instantly alert at the look on Eric's face. "What's wrong?"

"I'm leaving. Now."

Levi dropped the hay bale, instantly on alert. "Why? What's happened?"

Eric's voice was tight, barely controlled. "Amy's missing."

Levi froze. "Missing? What do you mean, missing?"

Eric dragged a hand through his hair, pacing in a tight, frantic circle. "She never showed up for work Monday. Her truck, her phone—they're still at the cabin. Sally just told me. No one's seen or heard from her since Sunday night."

Levi's face went pale. "Jesus."

"I knew something was wrong. I just didn't want to admit it." Eric muttered, voice rough. "She always calls back. Always."

"What do you want to do?" Levi asked, voice low but steady.

Eric didn't hesitate. "Can you load up Patriot and bring him home?"

Levi frowned. "What about the race meet?"

"I don't give a damn about the race, Levi. Amy's missing. She's all that matters."

Something shifted in Levi's expression—concern, loyalty, and understanding all rolled into one. "I'll get Patriot home safe. Don't worry about a thing. You go find your girl."

Eric nodded, jaw tight. "Thanks."

Without another word, Levi turned and headed toward the stables to load the horse for the long drive back. Eric was already striding toward his SUV, keys clenched in his fist.

No one said it, but they both knew—Eric Reynolds wouldn't walk away from a high-stakes meet unless it was life or death. And this was worse. This was Amy.

Whoever had taken her had a three-day head start. And Eric couldn't shake the thought that something terrible had already happened.

As he peeled out of the dusty lot, his hand tightened on the steering wheel. Twelve hours to Steamboat Springs. Anything could happen in that time.

He hit dial.

"Sheriff Harding," came the voice on the other end.

"Tom, it's Eric Reynolds."

"Eric." The sheriff's voice was tense. "Figured we'd be hearing from you."

Eric's voice cracked with frustration. "Why the hell didn't anyone call me? I had to hear it from Sally."

There was a beat of silence. "We don't have proof she was taken. She could've left on her own."

"Don't give me that," Eric snapped. "You think she just walked out, left everything behind? You know her history. Her ex?"

Tom's voice turned grim. "Yeah. We pulled his file—Darren Kane. Released two weeks ago. His parole officer hasn't heard from him since last check-in."

Eric's jaw clenched. "He nearly killed her."

"We know," Tom said quietly. "We got the full report after Sally called it in. That man put her in the hospital, Eric. And now he's vanished."

"Then why the hell are we still talking?"

"We've got a BOLO out for parole violation, but without direct evidence—"

"He took her," Eric growled, voice low and shaking. "You and I both know it. And if anything's happened to her…"

He let the words hang, dark and dangerous.

Tom exhaled. "We went through her cabin. Her phone, her purse, her truck keys—all still there. No signs of a struggle, but the door was wide open when Sally stopped by Monday morning. She never showed up for her shift. Henry's covering at the clinic until…"

"She's coming back, Tom." Eric's voice cut like steel. "You hear me? She's coming back."

Tom didn't argue. "We'll do everything we can."

Eric pressed harder on the gas, gravel spitting beneath his tyres. "Not good enough. I'm going to do everything I can."

"We'll find her," Tom said firmly.

But Eric's voice cut through, low and ragged. "Not we. Me. I'm going to find her."

He paused, breath shaking. "And God help him if he's laid a hand on her."

Eric ended the call, his pulse pounding in his ears. He didn't waste a second—he dialled another number from memory; one he hadn't used in years.

It rang once. Twice.

Then: "John Sawyer."

"John, it's Eric Reynolds."

There was a beat of silence, then a familiar voice, cool and composed. "Eric. Been a while."

"Too long," Eric said, his voice tight. "But I need your help."

"Tell me where."

"Steamboat Springs, Colorado. I need you here as soon as you can get on a plane. A woman's missing—someone I care about."

"You always did call me when things turned to hell," John said dryly. But his voice softened. "What's her name?"

"Her name's Amy. She didn't leave on her own."

John's tone sharpened. "You think she was taken?"

"I know she was. By her ex—Darren Kane. He's out on parole and off the radar. The sheriff's doing what he can, but it's not enough. I need someone who doesn't play by the damn rulebook."

"I'm on it," John said without hesitation. "Text me everything you have—dates, names, locations, photos. I'll book a flight tonight and bring my gear."

"Thank you." Eric's voice cracked again, but this time with relief. "I owe you."

"You already paid me once, remember?" John said. "This one's personal. We'll find her."

Eric stared out at the empty highway, the sun beginning to sink beyond the horizon. His fingers flexed on the wheel.

"She's not just someone I care about." He swallowed hard. "She's the life I am supposed to have."

Chapter Twenty

The barn was cold and damp. Mildew clung to the air, thick and relentless. A single drop of water plinked from the rafters, echoing like a ticking clock. Amy stirred on the thin, stained mattress, the coarse fabric biting at her skin. Her wrists screamed beneath the coarse rope that bound them behind her back, raw from hours—maybe days—of struggling.

Her head throbbed. Whether from the blow Darren had struck or the dread eating away at her chest, she didn't know. Time had unraveled — night blurred into day, sleep into panic. All she had was the crack of light beneath the barn doors to mark the hours, and even that had dimmed.

Her mind replayed it over and over: the knock on her cabin door, the stillness in the air just before she opened it... and his face.

Darren.

Taller, thinner, but his eyes hadn't changed. Cold. Possessive. Empty.

She'd barely breathed before everything went black.

Now, lying in the dark, her muscles cramped and her mouth dry, Amy fought to stay focused. She twisted her hands again, hunting for slack in the rope, but it only carved deeper into her skin. A quiet gasp escaped her lips, and she froze—listening.

There. Footsteps. Slow. Measured. Boots scraping against the ground outside.

The barn door rattled, hinges groaning. A moment later, it creaked open. Light spilled across the dirt floor like a blade, and Darren stepped inside.

His silhouette was backlit, but as he moved forward, a single bare bulb overhead flickered to life, revealing the familiar, twisted smile she hadn't seen in years.

"Well, there you are," he said, voice soft, almost affectionate. "Still as pretty as ever."

He walked toward her, his boots thudding against the old crumbling concrete. Amy's stomach turned with each step.

Darren crouched beside her, eyes roaming her face with a disturbing sort of nostalgia. "Hey, baby," he murmured. "I've missed you."

Amy clenched her jaw, refusing to speak. Refusing to give him the power of her voice.

His smile twitched. "Still got that fire in you, huh? That's what I loved. You always had a little fight."

He reached out. She flinched violently. He let his fingers graze a lock of her hair anyway, like he owned her.

"You don't need to be afraid," he said. "I didn't bring you here to hurt you. I just want to talk. We never got closure. You left like none of it mattered. Like I didn't matter."

Her breath hissed out between clenched teeth. "You think this is closure? Tying me up in a goddamn barn?"

Darren's face darkened. "Don't say it like that. I loved you. I still do. We had something real—something you don't just throw away because things got rough."

"Rough?" Amy snapped. "You broke my ribs, Darren. You made me afraid to breathe in my own home. Then you nearly killed me."

He stood abruptly, eyes flashing. "Don't twist it. I lost my temper. But I paid for that— I went to prison, didn't I? I paid."

Amy forced herself upright, legs curled beneath her. "Then why are you here? Why not leave me alone?"

He turned away, running a hand through his greasy hair, pacing a few steps. "I just come here to see if you were okay. Because thenI heard about you and that ranch guy. Eric Reynolds. Rich, clean-cut cowboy playing house with my girl. Like I didn't exist."

"You don't exist anymore," she said, voice steel. "Not in my life."

He turned slowly, and his smile was gone now. His eyes flat.

"I'm giving you a chance," he said quietly. "To remember who you really are. Before all this ranch and romance crap. Before you turned into someone else."

Amy's blood ran cold. She felt it then—not just the danger, but the delusion. He truly believed this was love. That this was right.

"If you won't listen to me," he said, moving toward her again, slower this time, "then I'll make sure there's nowhere else to run. No one to run to."

Amy stared up at him, defiant even as terror wrapped its claws around her spine. Her lips parted in a whisper.

"Eric will find me."

Darren's jaw ticked, his nostrils flaring as his smile vanished like a snuffed-out flame, and something colder settled behind his eyes. He leaned in, close enough that Amy could smell the stale coffee on his breath, the sweat clinging to his clothes.

"Not if I find him first," he whispered, menace curling around every word like smoke.

Outside, a crow cawed—sharp, jarring—cutting through the oppressive stillness like a warning shot.

Amy's breath caught. Her pulse rocketed. "Don't you go near him!" Her voice cracked, rising in panic. "Darren, if you touch him—"

He crouched again, eyes gleaming with something wild and unhinged. "You're worried about him?" he said, tone laced with disbelief. "You're lying here, tied up in the middle of nowhere, and you're worried about your fancy cowboy?"

"You leave him alone," she gasped, panic clawing up her throat. "He has nothing to do with this!"

"Oh, but he does," Darren hissed, the mask slipping completely now. "He's the reason you changed. The reason you think you're too good for me now. I saw the pictures— on Facebook. You looked… happy."

Amy's heart thudded violently.

"You're mine, baby," Darren said, his voice dropping to a whisper again. "You always were. And if I can't have you the way I want—no one else will."

He stood abruptly, pacing the length of the barn like a predator in a cage, then turned back toward her, face flushed, breathing ragged.

"I'm giving you time," he said, like he was offering mercy instead of madness. "Time to remember who you really are. Before he twisted you into something fake."

Amy shook her head, shaking from adrenaline. "You never loved me. You only ever wanted to own me."

He stared at her for a long moment, and when he spoke again, his voice was eerily calm.

"I do love you. That's why I brought you here. To fix us. But if he comes sniffing around—"

He trailed off, smiled faintly, and mimed a gun with his fingers.

"Let's just hope he's smart enough to stay away."

Amy's stomach rolled. Her wrists burned as she twisted against the rope again, ignoring the sting, the blood, the fear.

Eric don't come alone. Please. Come fast—but come prepared.

Chapter Twenty-One

By the time Eric turned into the long gravel drive leading into Silver Meadow Ranch, his body was on autopilot. The SUV's headlights cut through the darkness, casting long, eerie shadows across the familiar fence posts and skeletal trees. It was nearly eleven. He had been driving for over twelve hours straight; muscles locked with tension and eyes gritty with exhaustion. The sky was moonless, and the land stretched out black and quiet, as if holding its breath.

He killed the engine and sat still, gripping the wheel like it was the only thing tethering him to earth. Every inch of him ached. But none of it compared to the ache in his chest—the raw, splitting pain that hadn't let up since finding out Amy had vanished.

John had called somewhere around Colorado Springs, said he'd be at the ranch by eight. They would head out at first light. But that meant Eric had to force himself to rest now—to close his eyes, even if only for a few hours. He didn't want to. Everything in him screamed to get back in the car, to comb the mountains and roads and forgotten barns by moonlight if he had to. But if he passed out at the wheel or missed something critical out of sheer exhaustion, he wouldn't be any help to her.

He owed her more than that.

Inside the house, everything was still. The place was clean, orderly—Amy's touch lingered even in her absence. Her scarf was still draped over the back of the kitchen chair, and her boots sat by the door like she might walk in any second, cheeks pink from the cold, laughing at something he'd said.

Eric swallowed hard, his throat tight with exhaustion and fear. He undressed slowly, movements heavy, as if every piece of clothing weighed a hundred pounds. Stepping into the shower, he welcomed the rush of hot water, but it did nothing to ease the cold dread coiled in his chest. The last time he stood here, Amy had been with him—her laughter echoing off the walls, her body warm against his. They had made love before he left for Tulsa, tangled in steam and whispered promises. Now, he braced his hands against the tiled wall, bowing his head as the spray beat against the back of his neck. It couldn't wash away the image burned into his mind—Amy, bound... frightened... alone. And he wasn't there to protect her.

God, Amy... where are you?

He dried off quickly, pulled on a pair of sweats, and lay down on the bed they had shared so many nights. But it felt empty now. Hollow. As if the room itself missed her.

The mattress groaned beneath him as he stared up at the ceiling, his arms behind his head, jaw clenched so tightly it ached. Sleep didn't come easy. It never did when your heart was walking around outside your chest.

He hated the helplessness. He'd spent the last three years of his life fixing things—broken fences, sick cattle, busted trucks, even his own damn pride. But this? This was beyond his reach. It was like being caught in a storm you couldn't see, just the sound of her voice echoing in the back of his mind, calling for him.

He turned on his side, eyes burning.

He thought he knew love once. Thought he had it all figured out with Jessica. His ex-wife. Their life had been polished and proper—country club events, designer smiles, the kind of relationship that looked perfect on paper. His parents adored her. Pushed him toward her. Said they'd be the golden couple, the future of the Reynolds name. And for a while, he believed them.

But now, with distance and clarity, he saw it for what it was. A carefully curated illusion. What he had with Jessica wasn't love. It was infatuation, dressed up in designer clothes and promises that never reached the heart. It looked good in photos. It played well in public. But behind closed doors, it was hollow.

Amy was the truth he never knew he needed.

Amy… she was different.

With Amy, everything felt raw. Real. Like the first breath after drowning. She saw straight through him—the pain, the pride, the past—and loved him anyway.

She hadn't said the words, not yet. But he felt them in the quiet way she reached for his hand, in the way her walls lowered just enough to let him in.

And he loved her. God, he loved her so much it felt like his bones might splinter from the weight of it.

It wasn't just a feeling. It was a knowing. A truth so deep it rooted itself in his marrow. The kind of love that didn't vanish when someone walked out of the room. It stayed. It haunted. It ached.

He rolled over and pressed his face into her pillow, breathing her in. Her scent was faint now—lavender and something warm, like sunshine and hay. It hit him like a ghost of a summer day, wrapping around him until he couldn't breathe. But it was still there. Just enough to make his throat close.

He would find her.

No matter how far, no matter how long it took. He would bring her home.

And he'd never let her go again.

Sleep didn't come easily. After hours of tossing, turning, and listening to the empty house breathe around him.

Eric had barely slept.

He'd drifted off sometime around four, a restless doze that brought no peace—only fragmented dreams of Amy calling out for him, her voice lost in the wind. When he finally woke, it was just past six. The sky outside his bedroom window had barely begun to lighten, the faint blush of dawn casting long shadows over the Silver Meadow landscape.

By seven, he was dressed, boots laced, and a thermos of black coffee in hand. He stood on the porch, scanning the horizon, the stillness of the ranch almost unbearable in its silence. This place—his refuge—felt hollow without her. They'd only been official for four weeks, but Eric already knew—Amy was it for him. The one. The kind of love that didn't creep in slowly, but struck hard and deep, like lightning in a dry field.

Now, every inch of Silver Meadow Ranch echoed with her absence. The porch swing where she'd sat bathed in golden evening light. The kitchen where she'd danced barefoot, humming along to old country songs while eggs sizzled on the stove. The barn where she fed his horses with quiet confidence, like she'd always belonged there.

Now she was gone. Taken. And every second that passed felt like another mile between them—each one harder to close than the last.

At seven fifty-two, he heard the crunch of tyres on gravel.

John rolled to a stop in front of the house, a plume of dust rising behind the rental truck like smoke from a fuse. Eric was down the porch steps before the engine had even sputtered off.

John stepped out, boots hitting the gravel with a crunch. He wore worn jeans, a weathered canvas jacket, and his old Stetson pulled low over eyes that were sharp and serious. His face was carved with worry, and there was no trace of his usual easy grin.

"How was the flight?" Eric asked, his voice low and hoarse.

"Bumpy," John said. "But I've had worse. You ready?"

Eric gave a tight nod, his jaw clenched. "Didn't sleep much."

John studied him for a beat. "Didn't figure you would."

They stepped into the house. John set a large map of the area on the kitchen table and pulled out a set of highlighters and a notebook. Eric poured him coffee without asking.

"Okay, I ran a deep dive on Darren Kane. Guy's a real piece of work. He put Amy through hell—her last hospital visit, the doctors said she was lucky to survive. He took a plea deal, served three years, got out early for 'good behaviour.' Supposed to be reporting to a parole officer in Wichita Kansas, but he's gone dark."

Eric's jaw tensed. "Skipped town?"

"Yeah. My team pulled some CCTV footage—caught him buying a burner phone at a gas station outside Pueblo. We managed to trace it, but it hasn't pinged since yesterday."

Eric's eyes locked onto John's. "Where was the last ping?"

John hesitated, then answered quietly. "Steamboat."

Eric stepped back like the words had landed a punch. "I knew it," he said, voice tight. "He's taken her."

"I know you're worried," John said, his voice steady. "But this is a good thing—it means he hasn't taken her out of the county or across state lines. That gives us a fighting chance. We're going to find her."

Eric's throat tightened, his fists flexing at his sides. "But will we find her in time—before he hurts her?"

John didn't answer immediately. His silence said more than words could.

Instead, he turned his attention back to the map spread across the kitchen table. "If he's got her stashed somewhere, he's using an old structure. We're talking barns, hunting shacks, off-grid cabins. Places no one checks anymore."

Eric leaned over the map, eyes darting across every road, ridge, and shadowed stretch of forest. "How wide are we casting the net?"

"Fifty-mile radius for now," John replied. "I've got a couple of retired deputies starting a sweep from the south. You and I will head northwest. I brought drones and thermal gear. If we find anything—tracks, disturbed brush—we'll scan it immediately."

Eric gave a tight nod, his pulse hammering in his ears. "And if we find him?"

"We're ready," John said, cool and certain. "But our focus is Amy. We don't go in guns blazing unless we have to. We get her out safe. That's the mission."

Eric's jaw clenched. "She's strong. But if he's laid a hand on her—"

"He'll answer for it," John said, his voice low with quiet fury. "But we stay sharp. Emotion gets people killed."

Eric took a deep breath, forcing calm into his veins. "Alright. We start near the old train depot. There's a line of cabins out there—some haven't seen a soul in years."

John marked the area on the map. "That's our first stop. But before we hit the field, we check in with the sheriff. See what intel he's got."

They moved to the truck, running through a final check of gear—first aid kits, weapons, drones, flashlights, thermal goggles, extra batteries, bottled water, protein bars. Everything they might need for a long day in the field.

Eric slid into the passenger seat; the map folded beside him. John started the engine, gravel crunching under the tyres as they rolled out.

They were done waiting. Now, they were hunting. And God help the man who stood in their way.

Chapter Twenty-Two

Eric and John pulled into the gravel lot outside the sheriff's office just after eight. The morning sun was beginning to climb over the hills, casting long shadows across the cracked pavement. The building was modest—weathered stone, a single rusting flagpole, and a wooden sign that had seen better days.

Sheriff Tom Harding was waiting for them just inside, arms crossed over his chest, a cup of lukewarm coffee in hand. He straightened when he saw Eric.

"Knew it wouldn't be long before I saw you," Tom said, his voice low and laced with familiarity.

Eric gave a tight nod. "Tom. This is John Sawyer—private investigator. John, meet Sheriff Harding."

The two men shook hands, both firm grips and steady eyes.

"We came to see if there's been any news," Eric said. "Anything at all you can share."

Tom exhaled slowly, the lines around his eyes deepening. "I wish I had something, Eric. Truth is… it's like she vanished into thin air."

Eric's jaw worked as he looked past the sheriff, gaze distant. "She didn't just vanish. Someone took her."

Tom nodded solemnly. "I don't doubt it. We've been working every angle—checking traffic cams, canvassing the area, even called in favours from state patrol. But so far, nothing's stuck."

John stepped forward. "Any signs of Darren Kane?"

Tom's eyes narrowed slightly. "I've got people looking into him. We've got an APB out, but it's quiet. Too quiet. My gut says he's here—somewhere close. Lying low."

Eric's hands curled into fists at his sides. "Then we flush him out."

Tom gave him a long look. "Just don't do anything that'll get you locked up before we find her. I get it, Eric. I do. But I need you sharp."

"I'm sharp enough," Eric said. His voice was steel.

John pulled out the map. "We're starting northwest—old cabins near the train depot. You have any local intel on abandoned structures in that area?"

Tom nodded slowly. "Yeah. A couple hunting lodges, an old ranger station, maybe a shut-down mine out that way. I'll get you a list."

As Tom moved to his desk, Eric turned to the window, staring out at the sleepy town he now called home.

Amy was out there. Somewhere.

And they were running out of time.

The first site was a crumbling hunting lodge about twelve miles north of the old train depot. The roof had partially caved in. Eric stepped over a broken threshold, the scent of rot and animal musk clinging to the air.

"Empty," John called from the back room, his flashlight beam slicing through cobwebs and dust.

Eric swept the main room, checking every corner, every creak in the floorboards. He paused by an overturned chair, half-hoping for a sign—any sign—that someone had been here recently. But the place was still. Abandoned. Forgotten.

Like every other damn place, they'd seen that morning.

They hit a dozen locations by mid-afternoon—barns collapsed in on themselves, one-room shacks littered with raccoon droppings, a boarded-up ranger station with nothing but rusted tools and a bird's nest in the rafters.

By four o'clock, Eric's muscles burned, his boots were caked with mud, and frustration throbbed in his temples like a second heartbeat.

John parked the truck at the edge of a clearing near a run-down cabin barely visible through the trees. "Last one for the day," he said, glancing at the fading light. "We'll lose visibility soon."

Eric climbed out without a word. The cold mountain air bit at his skin, but he welcomed it. Anything to keep the rising panic at bay.

The cabin was small—log-built, single story, the front door hanging crooked on its hinges. Eric approached first, pushing the door open with his shoulder. The hinges groaned.

Inside, it was dark and damp, the floor sagging in the centre. A rusted cot sat in the corner beneath a cracked window, and a pile of empty beer cans littered the hearth.

John scanned the room with his flashlight. "Animals, squatters maybe. But no sign of Amy. No personal items, no fresh footprints."

Eric moved to the cot and crouched, running a hand over the dust-caked blanket. It disintegrated under his touch. "She hasn't been here," he said quietly.

They checked the surrounding woods, just in case—nothing but elk tracks and fallen branches.

By the time they returned to the truck, the sun had slipped behind the ridge, throwing the valley into deep blue shadow. Eric leaned against the hood, head bowed, breathing hard.

"I thought we'd find something," he murmured. "Anything."

John didn't respond right away. He opened the cooler in the backseat and handed Eric a bottle of water. "You're chasing ghosts your first day out," he said calmly. "This isn't over, not even close."

Eric didn't take the water. "What if we're always one step behind him?"

John's voice was low, steady. "Then we keep walking until we catch up."

Eric nodded slowly, his jaw tight, a muscle ticking beneath the stubble. His eyes swept the horizon one more time, the tree line fading into shadows as twilight settled over the valley.

Amy was out there.

Somewhere in the silence, in the cold, in the dark.

And he wasn't stopping—not now, not ever—until he brought her home.

They drove back to Silver Meadow Ranch in near silence, the weight of the day pressing down like lead. Over a quiet dinner of reheated stew and black coffee, they mapped out their next moves—areas they hadn't covered, terrain to prioritise, contact lists to revisit.

By the time the clock struck ten, they had a strategy.

John took the guest room down the hall. Eric returned to the master bedroom, where the bed still held the ghost of Amy's warmth. He lay down fully clothed, her pillow cradled in his arms.

Sleep didn't come easy. But tomorrow, they'd hit the ground running.

Tomorrow, the hunt continued.

The barn was silent except for the creaking of old wood and the occasional rustle of a rat in the hayloft.

Amy lay curled on a thin, stained mattress on the splintered floorboards. Her wrist was raw from the rope looped through a rusted ring bolted into the beam. The cold bit through her jeans, settling deep in her bones.

She didn't know how many days it had been—four, maybe five—but each one bled into the next like a slow, suffocating fog.

Her mouth was dry. Her head throbbed. And still, the only thing sharper than her fear was her anger.

He'd dragged her here like a trophy that didn't know how to behave.

Amy glared at the sliver of moonlight peeking through the warped wooden slats, her jaw clenched tight. She wasn't going to cry. Not again.

Eric's face kept flickering through her mind—his steady eyes, that roughened voice that always softened when he spoke to her. She pictured him out there now, searching, calling her name into the trees.

He had to be looking. He had to be.

The barn door groaned open.

Her heart jumped to her throat, hope flaring for one impossible second—before it was crushed.

Darren stepped inside, silhouetted against the night.

He had a paper bag in one hand, a water bottle in the other and a smug smile on his face. "Brought you something to eat and drink," he said, setting the bag down like he was doing her a favour.

When she didn't move, he raised an eyebrow—then remembered. Her hands were still tied.

"Oh right," he murmured, uncapping the bottle. "Guess that means I'm playing nurse, too."

He held it to her lips, and she drank—grudgingly at first, then with a thirst she couldn't hide. His gaze never left her face, and there was something almost tender in the way he tilted the bottle, careful not to spill a drop.

"You're welcome," he said, that grin still tugging at the corners of his mouth.

Amy didn't answer. She just stared at him, hate pulsing like a heartbeat.

"You'll see, Amy," he went on, crouching beside her. "You'll understand. I'm the one who's always been there. Not him."

"Go to hell."

He grinned like she'd just told him a joke. "Still got that fire in you. That's what I love about you."

She recoiled as he reached to brush a strand of hair from her face.

He pulled back with a small shake of his head. "You know, I've been thinking… Maybe it's time your boyfriend learned what it feels like to lose something."

Amy froze.

"What did you just say?"

Darren stood slowly, cracking his neck. "It's time to pay Eric a visit."

"No!" Her voice came out raw and panicked. She scrambled to her knees, straining against the tie. "You stay away from him! Do you hear me? Don't you go near him!"

But Darren was already walking toward the door, his tone calm, casual, chilling.

"See you soon, Amy."

The barn door slammed shut behind him, the echo rattling through the rafters like a warning. Darkness swallowed her whole, thick and suffocating.

Amy pressed her forehead to her knees, trembling.

God, please…

Her lips moved in a whisper, the prayer torn from the raw edges of her heart.

Please protect Eric. Keep him safe from Darren. He doesn't know what's coming—he doesn't know what he's capable of.

A tear slid down her cheek.

He's the only man I've ever loved… the only one I ever will. Please don't let him pay the price for my mistake.

Her voice cracked as she choked back a sob.

"Please, Eric," she whispered into the dark. "Be safe."

Chapter Twenty-Three

The patrol cruiser rolled slowly along the winding road just outside of town. It was mid-morning, the sun climbing higher behind a thin veil of clouds, casting long, sleepy shadows over the fields. Sheriff Tom Harding nursed a cup of lukewarm coffee from a battered travel mug, his eyes scanning the horizon while the radio crackled with static and the occasional dispatch chatter.

Deputy Carla Reyes sat beside him, one hand resting on the wheel, the other near her holster.

"Looks like a quiet day," she said, glancing out at the empty fields. "Feels too quiet."

Tom grunted. "Quiet's never just quiet around here. It's the kind that waits to bite."

As if on cue, an old, beat-up pickup truck appeared over the crest of the hill—faded blue, rust eating through the edges, one headlight cracked, and the passenger-side taillight swinging by a wire like a broken limb. The truck wobbled as it hit a pothole, then lumbered toward town like it was held together by nothing but spite and luck.

Carla narrowed her eyes. "You seeing what I'm seeing?"

"Yeah," Tom said, setting his coffee in the holder and flipping on the cruiser's lights. Red and blue strobes lit up the truck's rear. "Broken light, drifting lane. Let's go say hello."

The pickup hesitated for a breath, then pulled onto the gravel shoulder with a groan of brakes.

Tom stepped out just as the driver's door creaked open. A tall, wiry man climbed out, dressed in jeans and a stained grey hoodie. He moved with the cocky slouch of someone who'd spent too much time slipping past the law—and just enough time thinking he was smarter than it.

The moment the man turned toward the flashing lights, Tom's breath caught.

He knew that face.

"Darren Kane," he said, his voice flat and cold.

Darren offered a faint, crooked smile. "Sheriff. What seems to be the problem? I wasn't doing anything illegal."

Tom's hand dropped to his belt. "Step away from the truck. Hands where I can see them."

Carla flanked him, her stance sharp and focused. "Now."

Darren raised his hands slowly, still smirking. "C'mon now, I'm just drivin' through. Ain't broken any laws."

Tom stepped forward, cuffs in hand. "Where's Amy Henderson?"

For the briefest second, something flickered in Darren's expression—hesitation, maybe fear. Then it was gone.

"I haven't seen Amy."

"That's funny," Tom said, tightening the cuffs with a sharp click, "because half the damn town's been looking for her. And you, Darren Kane, are exactly where I figured you'd show up."

Darren tensed under Tom's grip but didn't resist. "You got no proof, Sheriff."

"Maybe not yet," Tom muttered, pulling him toward the cruiser, "but I think your truck's about to get really interesting."

He turned to Carla. "Hold him."

Tom moved to the pickup, opened the driver's door, and began searching the cab. Fast food wrappers, a dirty thermos, a worn-out road map. Then he checked under the seat—and froze.

A handgun.

Unregistered, by the look of it.

Next to it, folded neatly, was a piece of paper.

Tom unfolded it, his stomach tightening as he read the handwritten address:

Eric Reynolds

Silver Meadow Ranch

142 Mill Creek Road

Steamboat Springs

His blood went cold.

He turned back toward the cruiser, face grim. "We've got a problem."

Carla straightened. "What is it?"

Tom held up the paper. "Eric's address. In his truck. And a gun under the seat."

Darren laughed softly, leaning against the car door like this was all just some misunderstanding.

But Tom's eyes were steel.

"Let's take him in," he said. "And put out a call to Eric Reynolds. I want eyes on him now."

Carla nodded sharply, already reaching for her radio.

The morning was no longer quiet.

It had started to bite.

The sunlight slanted through the broken windows of the old mill, casting long bars of gold across the dusty floor. John pushed open a door that groaned on its hinges, revealing another empty room filled with collapsed crates and the smell of mildew.

"Nothing," he muttered, wiping sweat from his brow. "Just more rot."

Eric didn't answer. He was pacing slowly through what used to be an office, the walls still bearing yellowed calendar pages from twenty years ago. He opened a rusted filing cabinet, then slammed it shut in frustration.

His phone buzzed in his pocket. He pulled it out, the screen lighting up with Sheriff Harding.

"Eric Reynolds," he said, straightening up.

"Eric, it's Tom Harding," came the sheriff's steady voice.

"Yes, Sheriff," Eric replied quickly, nerves snapping taut.

"We just arrested Darren Kane."

Eric froze. "What?" His voice rang out too loud in the empty space, drawing John's attention. "Was Amy with him?"

"No," Tom said. "He says he hasn't seen Amy since their 'misunderstanding' before he went to prison."

Eric's jaw clenched. "He nearly killed her—and he calls that a misunderstanding?"

There was a pause on the line—just enough for Eric to hear the weight in Tom's voice.

"That's what he's saying. He's a real piece of work. We found a gun in his truck… and your address written on a piece of paper."

Eric's heart skipped a beat. "My address?"

"Yeah. Folded up, tucked under the seat. He was heading your way, Eric."

John stepped closer, hearing enough to catch the tension in Eric's face.

"You think he was coming after me?" Eric asked, voice low and tight.

"I think it's a damn good possibility," Tom replied.

Eric didn't hesitate. "I'm coming in."

"Eric, wait—" But the line went dead.

He shoved the phone into his pocket, jaw clenched.

John stepped forward, brow furrowed. "What was that about?"

Eric's hand was still wrapped around the phone like he might crush it. "They got Darren."

"Holy hell." John's voice dropped. "Was Amy—?"

"Still missing." Eric's eyes flared with restrained fury. "But he had a gun in the truck. And a piece of paper with my address on it. Folded. Tucked under the seat."

John swore under his breath, the weight of it sinking in fast.

They exchanged a look. No more questions. No more wasting time.

Without a word, they climbed into the truck, gravel spitting beneath the tyres as they peeled out. The road back to the station stretched ahead, and with every mile, Eric's grip on the wheel tightened like he was holding back a storm.

The sheriff's office door banged open, the sound cracking through the station like thunder. Eric stormed in, breath ragged, eyes wild with fury. Deputy Reyes had just stepped into the hallway, her hand firm on Darren Kane's arm as she guided him toward the holding cells.

Eric didn't stop to think.

In two long strides, he crossed the lobby, and before anyone could react, he had Darren by the collar and slammed him against the wall.

"Where is she, you bastard?" Eric shouted, his voice rough with rage.

Darren winced from the impact but barely flinched otherwise. He looked at Eric with a slow, curling smirk, unbothered by the fury in his face.

"Ah," he drawled, lips twisted. "You must be Eric."

Tom burst out of the side office, boots thudding hard on the tile. "Eric! Back off—now!"

But Eric didn't move. His hands fisted tighter in Darren's shirt, shaking him hard. "Where is she?"

Darren's eyes glittered with a sick kind of satisfaction. "She said she never wanted to see you again," he sneered. "She was never yours, mister money bags. She only ever wanted me."

"You son of a bitch," Eric growled, surging forward. "I'll kill you."

Darren laughed—low and cold. "You'll never find her. She doesn't want to be found. Not by you, especially."

Eric's fist shot up, rage boiling over—but Tom was faster. He wedged himself between them, grabbing Eric's arm in a steel grip and shoving him back.

"Enough!" Tom snapped, voice like a whip. "You lay a hand on him, I swear to God, I'll cuff you myself."

Eric's chest heaved, fury pulsing through every vein. He didn't look away from Darren, who was still smirking like the devil with a secret. Tom's voice cut through again, quieter but sharper.

"Don't give him what he wants."

Eric's entire body trembled—not from fear, but from the terrible, helpless fury coiled in his gut.

Darren just chuckled under his breath. "You think money can buy love. It can't. Amy doesn't care about money. She chose me. She always will."

Tom turned to Deputy Reyes. "Get him in the cell. Now."

As Darren was dragged away, still smiling, Eric stood frozen in the hallway, his jaw clenched so tight it ached. Tom looked at him, his voice quieter now, but no less firm.

"You're no good to her like this," he said. "We're going to find her, but not like this."

Eric didn't answer. He couldn't. All he could see was Amy—alone, scared, and somewhere out there, beyond his reach.

Chapter Twenty-Four

The sun was starting to sink, casting long shadows across the parking lot. Heat shimmered off the asphalt, but Eric didn't feel it. He stood with his hands braced on the hood of John's rental truck, head bowed, breathing hard like he'd just run a mile.

John leaned against the passenger door, arms folded, watching him with quiet concern.

"Eric," he said finally, his voice low but steady. "You've got to get a grip."

Eric didn't look up. "He knows where she is. I saw it in his eyes. He was enjoying every damn second of that."

"I know," John said calmly. "And we'll get it out of him. But right now, you losing your head is helping him. Not Amy."

Eric slammed a palm against the hood, metal ringing out across the lot. "He was coming for me. He had my address and a gun. You don't write that down unless you plan to use it."

John stepped closer, his voice dropping. "Yeah. But he's behind bars now. Which means the pressure is off him. And that's the problem."

Eric finally looked up, his eyes rimmed with fury and desperation.

"No one's watching for her now," John said, voice low but sharp. "They think it's over. They think locking Darren up means the case is closed. But Amy's still out there. Still missing. And he's the only one who knows where."

Eric's jaw clenched. "You think she's still alive?"

John hesitated, his gaze drifting toward the dusky horizon. The silence stretched, taut and painful.

"I think if she is," he said quietly, "we're running out of time."

The weight of it settled between them, heavy and unspoken.

John exhaled, stepping in closer. "We've got to stay ahead of this. Go where the cops won't. Backwoods cabins, old hunting shacks, anywhere he wouldn't want law enforcement poking around. People he trusted, even loosely."

Eric gave a slow, tense nod, the wildfire in his chest beginning to burn into something sharper — focus.

"We start where he was coming from," John added. "He was headed into town when they grabbed him. That means he was leaving somewhere—and that somewhere could be where she is."

Eric stood straighter, the storm inside him no longer out of control—just dangerous and aimed in the right direction.

"If she's out there," he said, voice like steel, "I'm bringing her home."

John clapped a firm hand on his shoulder. "Then let's get moving. Before she disappears for good."

They climbed into the truck. The engine rumbled to life as the fading sun lit their path, two men chasing the last thread of hope that anyone was still looking for Amy.

The truck rumbled up the long gravel drive toward Silver Meadow Ranch, headlights sweeping across the darkening fields. The sun had slipped below the horizon, painting streaks of copper and violet across the sky. First came the silhouette of the barn, then the house, warm light glowing in the windows.

Levi stood at the paddock fence, one hand resting on the top rail. He turned as the truck approached, his figure still and shadowed. Behind him, Patriot—the tall, muscular bay stallion—paced within the enclosure, ears flicking toward the engine's hum. He'd just returned from Tulsa the morning before, still brimming with restless energy.

As the truck rolled to a stop, Levi stepped forward. "Any news?" he called, voice low and tense.

Eric slammed the door shut, meeting his eyes. "They got Darren. Brought him in this morning."

Levi's brow lifted—hope flickering in the dim light. "And Amy?"

Eric's jaw tightened. "He won't talk. Just plays games. Says he hasn't seen her."

Levi swore under his breath and turned away, fists clenched. "Bloody hell."

John came around the front of the truck, boots crunching over gravel. "They found a loaded gun under his seat. And a piece of paper with Eric's address with it."

Levi turned sharply. "He was coming here?"

"Looks that way," Eric muttered. "Which means he's definitely seen her. Maybe worse. And now, everyone thinks it's over. The cops got their guy—they've moved on."

Behind them, Patriot let out a restless snort, pawing at the dirt like he sensed the tension rolling off the men.

Eric cast a glance toward the stallion and exhaled. "We're not done. We've got a new plan. We check every place Darren might've holed up. Off-grid spots. Cabins. Anyone who owed him favours."

"I'm in," Levi said without hesitation. "Whatever you need. She's family."

Eric gave a nod. "We start first light. Tonight, we map it out."

Levi looked back toward the paddock. Patriot had stilled, standing near the fence like a sentinel. Watching.

"Then we leave at dawn," Levi said. "One way or another, we bring her home."

Eric's voice was low, but solid. "We have to."

And he would. He couldn't let himself think of the alternative. The idea of her being hurt, of losing her, was more than his mind could bear. He had to be the one to save her.

The dinner plates were cleared, coffee poured, and the last of the cornbread sat untouched in the centre of the table. A county map lay spread across the kitchen table, covered in red ink and hand-scribbled notes. The faint hum of a radio played in the background, but none of them were listening.

Eric leaned over the map, tapping a pen against a dense stretch of forest near the southern county line. "There's an old hunting cabin out here. Last time I heard, it hadn't been used in years. Could've fallen off the radar."

John nodded, jotting it down. "That's three tonight. We'll start marking them off. He was heading from that direction when they picked him up. That narrows the routes he could've taken."

Levi had been quiet, leaning back in his chair. Then he sat forward, folding his arms on the table. "I've got an idea. Not sure it'll work—but it's worth a shot."

Eric looked up quickly. "Please. Any suggestion is welcome."

Levi's gaze moved between them. "Darren won't talk to cops, right? He gets off on the power play. But what if I went into the holding cells? Posed as another prisoner. Got close. He might open up."

Eric blinked. "You mean go undercover?"

"Exactly," Levi said. "Something small. Drunk and disorderly, maybe. Act like I've got my own woman troubles. Guys like Darren love to brag when they think they've found a kindred spirit."

John tilted his head, considering. "You know… that could work. He might not give us a location, but even a name or some detail—we could follow it."

Eric looked between them, that flicker of hope finally catching fire. "You think he'll fall for it?"

Levi shrugged. "He just needs to think I'm the kind of guy who'd understand. That's all it takes."

John nodded. "We'll run it by Sheriff Tom in the morning. Quietly. Make sure only the right people know."

Eric's voice was quiet, but steady. "Do it. If there's even the slightest chance it leads to her—we take it."

Levi gave a sharp nod. "If Tom signs off, I'll go in tomorrow."

The three of them leaned over the map again, eyes scanning roads, trails, and forgotten places. The silence wasn't heavy anymore. It buzzed with purpose—movement. A plan was taking shape. And with it, the first fragile thread of something none of them had dared let themselves feel.

Hope.

The barn was dark, the only light seeping in through the cracks in the weather-warped boards. Dust floated in the air, catching slivers of moonlight like ash. Amy lay slumped against a wooden beam, wrists raw and aching from the rope, her limbs heavy with exhaustion. Her throat was dry—painfully so. She hadn't had water in nearly twenty-four hours. Maybe more. It was getting hard to keep track.

Her head lolled forward, then jerked back up. Don't sleep. If she fell asleep again, she might not wake up. Not this time.

She shifted slightly, the coarse rope biting into her skin. The thin mattress felt like concrete beneath her, but sweat clung to her skin, a sickly sheen that came and went in waves. Dizziness pulsed behind her eyes, and every now and then, her vision blurred completely.

The last time she'd seen Darren was yesterday morning—or was it the day before? He'd come in without a word, dropped a bag of something near her, unopened, untouched. Gave her a drink from a water bottle. Then he'd said it—casual, almost amused.

'It's time to pay Eric a visit.'

And he'd left.

Amy had waited for hours afterward, breath locked in her lungs, heart pounding so loudly she was sure it would echo through the walls. She'd stared at the door, willing it not to open again. Willing him to never come back.

Please, God. Let Eric be safe.

She closed her eyes now, a hot tear slipping down her cheek. She wasn't praying for herself anymore. She hadn't in a while. Her body felt weak, like something separate from her. Something slipping away.

But Eric—he was everything good that had ever happened to her. The thought of him being hurt because of her was worse than any pain Darren had caused. Her fingers twitched uselessly behind her back, the ropes unmoving.

Her lips parted. "Eric," she whispered, voice barely audible. "Please be okay…"

A distant sound caught her attention. A creak of wood? A breeze? Her head lifted sluggishly, her pulse surging with the faintest hope. But the silence returned just as quickly, thick, heavy, and smothering.

The barn swallowed her whole again.

Her gaze drifted upward to the rafters, where dust swirled like fading stars in the thin moonlight. She imagined him there—Eric—storming through the door, voice low and fierce, eyes full of that relentless fire she loved so much.

He'll find me, she told herself.

Even as her body sagged, even as darkness crept at the edges of her vision, Amy clung to that one fragile truth.

Eric will find me.

She had to believe he was coming for her. He had to be.

Chapter Twenty-Five

The morning sun hadn't yet burned off the fog that clung low to the ground as John, Eric, and Levi stepped into the small-town sheriff's office. The scent of stale coffee and paperwork hung in the air, familiar and oddly grounding. Fluorescent lights buzzed softly overhead, casting a pale glow across the scuffed linoleum floor.

Sheriff Tom Harding looked up from his desk as they entered, his weathered face already etched with the exhaustion of a man who hadn't slept much. He stood when he saw them, brow furrowing. "You boys got something?"

Eric nodded tightly. "We do. And we need your help to pull it off."

Tom gestured to the chairs across from his desk. "Let's hear it."

Levi stepped forward, folding his arms across his chest. "I want to go in. Into the holding cells. Pretend to be a drunk or a guy in trouble. Just enough to get thrown in with Darren. If he thinks I'm just another screw-up, he might talk."

Tom leaned back slowly, his gaze narrowing. "You're talking about an undercover op. In my jail. Without backup. You do realise what kind of mess that could turn into?"

John spoke before Levi could. "We know it's risky. But he's not talking to anyone official. He gets off on control. He wants to be the smartest man in the room. We give him a new room. One where he thinks he's got the upper hand."

Tom looked to Eric. "You back this?"

Eric's voice was low, firm. "If it gets him to tell us where he's got Amy, I back it."

Tom exhaled, rubbing a hand down his jaw. "Jesus. You're asking me to fake an arrest, falsify a booking, and risk a civilian getting face-to-face with a known psychopath. You boys sure this is the best move?"

Levi didn't blink. "I'm not a civilian. I've done worse for less. You just need to make it look good. Public drunk, maybe a bar fight. Something no one would question."

Tom looked between them, then turned and closed his office door.

"When did you boys get so damn persuasive?" he muttered. He stepped back to his desk and sat, steepling his fingers. "Alright. I'll authorise it—but this doesn't leave this room. If anyone else catches wind—press, deputies, Darren himself—it's over."

Eric's jaw flexed. "We understand."

Tom turned to Levi. "You're sure you can sell this?"

Levi's mouth curled into something between a smirk and a scowl. "You get me in the cell; I'll handle the rest."

Tom reached for a pad of paper, scribbling down a name. "There's a bar just outside town—Murphy's. No cameras. No questions. You go in around six tonight, pick a fight with one of my guys. He'll book you and slide you into the cell next to Darren. You've got twelve hours max. After that, we pull you out."

John leaned forward. "That enough time?"

Levi nodded once. "It'll have to be."

Tom looked at all three men, his expression hard. "If he even suspects something's off, he'll shut down. Or worse—he'll lie just to send you in the wrong direction."

Eric's voice was quiet. "We don't have time to do this the clean way. She's still out there. I can feel it."

Tom looked at him long and hard, then finally nodded. "Alright. Tonight, it is. I'll brief Deputy Crane—he'll be the one to throw you in."

Levi stood, pushing back his chair. "Thanks, Sheriff. For trusting us."

Tom didn't smile. "Don't make me regret it."

Eric held out a hand, gripping the sheriff's forearm tight. "We won't."

The sheriff didn't answer. Just gave a single sharp nod.

As the three men left the office and stepped into the morning light, the weight of the plan settled over them.

"Tonight," Levi said. "Let's end this."

Eric's eyes were steel. "Let's bring her home."

After another long day combing the woods and calling her name into silence, John and Eric pulled up outside Murphy's Bar. The sun had sunk behind the hills, but neither man had noticed. Their clothes were dirty, their faces drawn, their hope hanging by threads.

Eric turned to Levi in the back seat, his voice low but thick with emotion.

"Thanks for doing this."

Levi met his eyes without hesitation. "I'd do anything for you—and for Amy."

Eric nodded, jaw tight, and watched as Levi stepped out and shut the door behind him.

John shifted in the driver's seat, watching too. "Let's hope to God this works."

Levi didn't look back.

The bar was already alive with noise and the kind of trouble that simmered just beneath laughter. Murphy's reeked of beer and sweat, of long nights and worse regrets.

Neon signs buzzed over the bar, casting sickly pinks and greens across the walls and faces of the regulars. Levi stood just inside the door for a beat, letting it all wash over him.

Then he moved.

Slouched shoulders. Unsteady feet. A dead-eyed glaze over sharp, calculating eyes. He pushed through a crowd by the jukebox like he had a score to settle and nothing to lose.

By the time he reached Deputy Crane—planted near the bar like a loaded trap—his performance was flawless.

Crane turned at the exact moment Levi knocked the soda out of his hand.

"You got a problem?" Levi snarled, too loud.

Crane didn't answer.

Levi shoved him. "Say something, you smug bastard."

The bar quieted.

Crane grabbed Levi, shoved him hard against the wall, and twisted his arm behind his back. The cuffs clicked shut a little too tight.

"Let's go," Crane muttered. "You're under arrest for being a damn idiot."

Levi didn't resist. Just grinned, like the whole thing amused him.

Levi sat on the hard bench inside the cell, the bars cold against his spine. The adrenaline had long since burned off, leaving only the hum of the fluorescent lights overhead, the occasional creak of old pipes, and the soft, steady breathing from the cell across the aisle.

Then—movement.

Darren stepped from the shadows like a spider testing the edges of its web. His pale eyes gleamed in the dim light, sharp and unreadable, but locked on Levi with something close to amusement.

"You're new," Darren said, voice smooth as oil. "What'd you do?"

Levi slouched, rubbing a fake bruise on his jaw. "Bar fight. Guy said I touched his girl. I didn't. She touched me. Guess it didn't matter."

Darren chuckled, low and dry. "It rarely does."

Silence settled between them.

"You drink a lot?" Darren asked eventually, almost like he was asking the weather.

"Most nights," Levi muttered. "Beats thinking."

Darren stepped closer to the bars. Shadows slid over his face. "And what is it you don't want to think about?"

Levi hesitated just long enough. Then, his voice cracked with just enough feeling to sell it: "My wife. No matter what I do for her, it's never enough. She doesn't appreciate anything."

Darren tilted his head, birdlike. "That why you drink?"

Levi gave a bitter nod. "That's why I fight."

A slow smile twisted Darren's lips. "You're not like the rest of them."

Levi met his gaze, calm and guarded. "Neither are you."

A beat of silence. Darren reclined on his cot, folding his arms behind his head, eyes on the ceiling.

"My girl," he said after a while. "Pretty. Smart. Thought she was too good for me. Thought she'd be better off with some rich cowboy."

Levi's tone stayed flat. "Ungrateful?"

Darren smiled faintly. "Let's just say… not anymore."

Levi kept his reaction locked down. "How'd you manage that? Some days I wish my wife would either stop whining or just… disappear."

Darren's gaze sharpened. "That's easy done."

Levi shrugged. "Yeah? Got any ideas?"

Instead of answering, Darren leaned in. "What's your wife's name?"

Levi didn't flinch. "Emily."

A smirk. "Mine's Amy."

Then, quieter, almost like a prayer: "Maybe they'll find her. Or maybe… they'll just find what's left."

Levi's pulse spiked. He couldn't show it. He leaned forward, voice just a whisper. "You got rid of her? How?"

Darren stared at him for a long moment—measuring. Then he spoke, soft and deliberate. "You're asking the wrong questions."

"What should I be asking?"

"If she's alive… she's somewhere no one's looking. Somewhere so ordinary, no one even thinks to check."

Levi gave a small, humourless laugh. "Man, you're lucky. I wouldn't even know where to take someone."

Darren grinned wider. "That's your first mistake."

Levi let the silence stretch, then said, "So where'd you put her?"

Darren eyed him sidelong. "Why do you care?"

"I told you. I need ideas. If you pulled it off, and they haven't found her yet… that's genius."

Darren narrowed his eyes. "You sound real curious for a guy who's just angry at his wife."

"Curious ain't a crime," Levi said with a shrug.

Another pause.

Then Darren leaned forward, conspiratorial, the whisper of a secret thick in the air. "She's not far."

Levi raised an eyebrow. "No?"

"She's in a barn." Darren's voice held pride now. "Old one. Used to keep horses there. Real quiet. Back in the woods past Fish Creek."

Levi fought the spike of panic. "A barn? Damn."

"No one thinks to check barns," Darren said, grinning. "Too close. Too normal. That's what makes it perfect."

"And if they find her?" Levi asked, his voice tight.

Darren's smile didn't waver. "She'll wish they hadn't."

The words hung like smoke in the air.

"You ever think she didn't deserve it?" Levi asked, barely above a whisper.

Darren didn't even blink. "I know she did. She left me. Ungrateful bitch."

Levi let his head fall back against the wall, quiet now, cold and still on the outside.

Inside, his heart raced. He needed to get out. Fast.

Twenty minutes passed.

Then Levi stood, banging a fist on the bars. "Hey!" he shouted, loud and urgent. "I haven't made my call yet!"

He kept yelling until the deputy came stomping down the corridor.

Time was running out. Amy could be alive—or dying—inside that barn.

And Levi had just been handed their only lead.

He just prayed it wasn't too late.

Chapter Twenty-Six

The buzz of the fluorescent lights overhead felt sharper now—the kind of sound that crawled under your skin after too long without sleep.

Levi stood just outside the holding cells, jaw tight, shoulders braced under the weight of what he'd just heard. His knuckles were scraped raw from where he'd hit the wall—part of the act, but it still stung.

Sheriff Tom Harding unlocked the final security door and motioned him through. "You alright?" he asked, voice gruff but not unkind.

Levi didn't answer. Not until he stepped into the main office and saw John and Eric standing, waiting. Both of them straightened the second they saw him.

Levi's eyes locked onto Eric. "He talked."

Eric stepped forward, pale with barely contained hope. "Where?"

Levi turned to the sheriff, voice clipped. "There's an old barn. Abandoned horse property just past Fish Creek. That's where he said she is."

Tom swore under his breath, already moving to his desk and pulling a map from the drawer. "You sure?"

Levi nodded. "He's proud of it. Said no one would think to check somewhere that close. Called it perfect."

John leaned over the map, scanning the terrain. "There're a dozen properties near Fish Creek. Any more detail?"

"Just a barn. Quiet. Used to keep horses. That's all he gave me—but he was sure we wouldn't find her in time."

Eric was already grabbing his jacket. "Then we prove him wrong."

Tom slapped the map flat. "Here," he said, tapping the top edge. "Murphy family used to own this spread. Horses, hay storage. No one's lived there in years, but it's still standing. That's your best bet."

Levi's voice dropped low. "He said... if they found her, she'd wish they hadn't. We need to go. Now."

Eric looked at him—something fierce and grateful in his eyes. "You did good, Levi. You gave us a chance."

Levi's jaw tightened. "Let's hope it's enough."

Tom was already on the radio, voice sharp and commanding. "All available units, converge on the Murphy barn near Fish Creek. Code red. Possible hostage on site. EMTs on standby. Move now."

John snatched the keys from the desk. "Let's go."

They were halfway out the door when Tom called after them.

"Boys—" His voice cut through the rush. "You find her, you bring her home. Alive."

Eric turned back, voice low and tight. "That's the only option."

Then they were gone, boots pounding down the steps, urgency rolling off them like heat.

The truck skidded to a halt in a cloud of gravel and dust, headlights piercing through the thick woods that choked the property. The barn loomed ahead, old, silent, and wrong.

Eric was out before the engine finished dying, flashlight in hand, breath fast and sharp in the cold night air.

John slammed his door. "I'll take the back. Watch yourself."

Eric nodded once and ran for the main entrance. The rusted doors groaned open under his shove, loud enough to echo.

The barn swallowed him whole.

It was pitch black. The beam from his flashlight wavered with the tremble in his hand.

The smell hit first—mildew, urine, and underneath it, something metallic.

His boots crunched across dirt and glass. The light swept over cobwebs, splintered rafters, broken tools. Nothing that mattered.

"Amy!" His voice echoed. No answer. Just the sound of his breath and his heart slamming against his ribs.

Then—he turned.

Near the far wall, tucked deep in shadow.

A shape.

Slumped. Bound to a wooden support beam. A filthy, threadbare mattress beneath her.

Eric ran. He dropped to his knees beside her, hands shaking as he cupped her face.

Her skin was ice-cold.

"Amy," he choked. "God—Amy, please be okay."

No response.

Then—

Her eyelids fluttered. A faint breath shuddered past her lips. Her head tilted just enough to find him.

"Eric…?" Her voice was cracked and brittle, barely more than a breath. "Thank God… you're okay."

The words hit him like a blow to the chest. Even now—half-conscious, barely clinging on—she was worried about him.

Relief broke over him, hard and aching.

"I've got you," he whispered, brushing the damp hair from her forehead. "I'm here, sweetheart. You're safe now. I found you."

Red and blue lights lit up the barn walls as EMTs poured in, boots thudding, voices sharp and urgent. John called for a stretcher. Cleared the path.

Eric stayed with her. Held her hand. Never let go.

"You held on," he whispered. "You're so damn strong."

Amy's eyes drifted closed again.

But this time—it wasn't from fear.

Because she knew he was there.

Sounds floated in and out.

Like echoes underwater.

A siren—far, then close. Then gone again.

Flashes of light stung behind her eyelids. Red. White. Red. White.

A storm she couldn't escape.

Everything hurt. Her skin, her ribs, her throat. Even her teeth.

She tried to move. Couldn't. Something tugged at her wrist. Tape? Pain? She couldn't tell.

Her eyelids cracked open. Blurred ceiling. Fluorescent lights.

A man's face hovered. EMT. Beard. Focused.

"She's crashing," someone said. "BP's bottoming. Get another line in."

Crashing?

No. She wasn't crashing. Just… tired.

So tired.

A sharp sting in her arm made her flinch. Pressure followed. More shouting. She drifted again.

Then—

A voice.

Not the EMT.

Eric.

"I'm right here, Amy. I'm not going anywhere."

Warmth curled through her, faint but real. Like a thread pulling her back.

She turned her head—or tried to. Her lips cracked when she moved them.

"Eric…?"

"I've got you," he said, hand wrapping around hers. "I'm right here."

Safe.

She could feel it this time.

"Cold," she murmured. "So… cold."

Someone tugged a blanket up higher. A hiss of warm air touched her face. Her lungs loosened. Breathing got easier.

Her eyes slid closed.

Eric's voice was close now, right near her ear.

"You're going to make it. I swear to God, Amy. Just hold on."

She wanted to tell him she believed him.

That she'd held on—for him.

But her body was already sinking again, heavy with exhaustion.

This time, she didn't fight it.

Because he was still holding her hand.

And that was enough.

Chapter Twenty-Seven

The antiseptic sting burned Eric's eyes, though he hadn't blinked in minutes. He sat hunched forward on the edge of a plastic chair, elbows on his knees, Amy's blood still drying on his shirt sleeves. His hands were clenched together so tightly they'd started to go numb, but he didn't notice.

Levi sat to his right, silent. The older man's jaw worked every so often like he wanted to say something but couldn't figure out how to start. On Eric's other side, John paced slow, wide loops across the tile floor, his boots echoing in the too-quiet room.

The clock on the wall was broken—stuck at 3:14. It hadn't moved in hours, or so he thought. Just like Amy. That felt cruel.

A nurse had taken Amy back almost three hours ago. The doctor had come out once—only once—to ask questions. Her name, any medical history. If she had allergies. Then she disappeared behind the double doors, leaving Eric with nothing but the image of Amy's limp body on the stretcher, her face pale and sunken, her wrists torn raw where the ropes had bitten through skin.

He squeezed his eyes shut. He couldn't get the picture out of his head: how light she felt when he carried her, like bones wrapped in paper. How her lips barely moved when she whispered his name.

"She's strong," Levi finally said. His voice was low, hoarse. "She made it five days. That's not luck—that's her."

Eric didn't respond. Couldn't. His throat burned from holding everything in.

John stopped pacing, folded his arms. "They're doing everything they can. You know that, right?"

Eric nodded once, barely. "They said she was dehydrated. Severely." His voice cracked. "She hadn't had water in days. No food. And those rope burns—God, John, they were down to the flesh."

John exhaled, his face tight with anger. "I saw. Bastard's gonna pay for every second of that."

Levi leaned forward, elbows on his knees now too. "She kept herself alive. However, she could. She made it because she knew someone would come."

Eric rubbed his hands over his face. "She was worried about me. When I found her... she said she was glad I was okay. Not even thinking about herself. Just me." He dropped his hands. "What kind of person does that after what she's been through?"

John answered quietly, "Someone who loves you."

The doors finally swung open. All three of them stood at once.

A woman in scrubs stepped into the waiting room. Mid-forties, tired eyes, her surgical mask pulled down around her neck. "Mr. Reynolds?"

Eric took one step forward. "That's me."

"She's stable," the doctor said. "She's still very weak, but she's conscious and responsive."

Eric nearly folded with relief. He had to grip the back of the chair to keep standing.

The doctor continued, her tone professional but kind. "She's malnourished and dehydrated. Her vitals were unstable when she arrived—blood pressure dangerously low, core temperature dropping from exposure. We're rehydrating her with IV fluids and started her on antibiotics for the infection in her wrists. We'll monitor for signs of shock, but so far, she's fighting."

Eric swallowed hard. "Her wrists... are they—?"

"We cleaned and dressed them. They'll scar, but we don't believe there's tendon damage. She may need physical therapy and time to heal, physically and emotionally. But she made it. That in itself is extraordinary."

"Can I see her?"

The doctor nodded. "She's been asking for you. She's exhausted, but I think seeing you will do her more good than rest at this point."

Eric didn't wait. He moved the moment she nodded, Levi and John's voices fading like background noise.

He didn't know what he was going to say when he walked in. All he knew was that she was alive—and he was going to make damn sure she stayed that way.

The hallway stretched longer than it should have, each step echoing like a heartbeat in Eric's ears. His legs felt heavy, like they didn't quite belong to him anymore. The doctor stopped at the last room on the left and gave him a gentle nod before slipping away, leaving him alone in front of the door.

He hesitated.

Only for a second.

Then he pushed it open and stepped inside.

The room was dim, the only light coming from a small lamp near the bed. Machines beeped softly in the background, their rhythm steady and reassuring. A plastic bag of fluid hung from a metal stand, dripping steadily into the IV line that disappeared beneath the thin blanket.

Amy lay motionless on the hospital bed; her face turned slightly toward the wall. Her skin was pale, lips cracked, dark shadows beneath her eyes. Her hair was tangled and damp, clinging to her temple, and her wrists—both bandaged thickly—rested lightly on the blanket.

Eric's breath caught in his throat.

She looked so small.

So fragile.

He moved closer, careful not to make noise, like anything too loud might shatter the thin thread holding her here. He sat down in the chair beside her bed and reached for her hand, gently lacing his fingers through hers.

She stirred.

Her eyelids fluttered, then opened slowly, as if just waking from a long, heavy sleep. Her gaze was unfocused at first, until it found his face.

"Eric," she whispered, the word barely sound.

He smiled through the ache in his chest. "Hey, sweetheart. I'm right here."

Tears welled in her eyes, slipping down her temple in silence. "You found me."

"Of course I did." He leaned forward, brushing his thumb over her cheek. "Nothing was going to stop me."

Her throat worked around a dry swallow. "You look tired."

That broke him a little. He laughed, soft and hoarse. "You've been tied to a post for five days, and you're worried about how I look?"

Amy tried to smile. It almost made it. "I love you."

Eric bowed his head, holding her hand tighter, his voice trembling. "I love you too. More than I ever thought I could."

She blinked slowly. Her breathing was shallow but even.

"I was scared," she whispered.

"I know," he said. "But you're safe now. You're safe, and you're not alone."

"I knew you'd come…" she whispered.

She closed her eyes again, but her hand stayed curled in his. He stayed like that for a long time—his fingers wrapped around hers, his presence a quiet promise that he wasn't going anywhere.

Not now.

Not ever.

The holding cells were quiet, lit by the low hum of fluorescent lights that gave everything a cold, sterile glow. Sheriff Tom Harding stood just outside the reinforced door, arms crossed, jaw set. He glanced at Eric, who was pacing in tight, controlled circles like a predator waiting to strike.

"You sure you want to do this?" Tom asked, his voice low.

Eric stopped. "I don't want to. I need to."

The sheriff studied him for a long second, then gave a short nod and unlocked the door. "Five minutes. Don't touch him."

"I won't need to," Eric muttered as he stepped through.

The heavy door clicked shut behind him, sealing him inside with the man who had haunted his nightmares for five straight days.

Darren Kane sat on the other side of the bars, hands cuffed, ankles shackled, a smug tilt to his mouth. His eyes lifted lazily, landing on Eric like a mosquito sizing up its next bite.

"Well, well," Darren drawled. "Look who finally showed up."

Eric didn't rise to the bait. He stepped closer, hands in his jacket pockets, expression unreadable—except for the fire in his eyes.

"We found her," he said flatly.

Darren's smile faltered. "How."

"Because we're smarter than you. She's alive. She's safe. You didn't break her."

The smugness returned in a flash, thin and brittle. "Maybe not, but she'll come back to me."

Eric stepped in until only the bars separated them. "No. You will never see her again. You don't get to win."

Darren's expression twisted into something ugly. "She begged. You know that? I didn't even have to lay a hand on her to make her scream."

Eric's eyes sharpened, his voice low and steady. "We both know that's not true. Amy would never beg you."

For the first time, Darren faltered. His smugness cracked, just for a beat.

Eric stepped closer, calm and composed. "You'll spend the rest of your life behind bars. That smart mouth won't mean much when you're the one shackled and forgotten."

Darren sneered, desperate to regain control. "You think this is over? It's never over. She'll never stop looking over her shoulder."

Eric leaned in, his voice sharp and cutting, like a blade. "No. You will. From a six-by-eight box where no one knows your name, and no one cares if you rot."

Darren lunged against the cuffs, teeth bared. "She'll never forget me."

Eric smiled, cold and razor-sharp. "You're right. She'll remember that she survived you. And that I got to stand here and tell you—you lost."

"Bastard," Darren spat.

Eric took one last step, lowering his voice to a whisper meant only for Darren's ears. "I'm a very wealthy man. And if you ever get near her again—if you so much as breathe in our direction—you'll vanish. No one will even think to look for you."

Before Darren could speak, the door creaked open behind Eric.

"Time's up," Sheriff Harding said.

Eric backed away, never taking his eyes off the man in the cell.

"She's going to heal," he said, voice ringing with quiet promise. "She's going to laugh again. Love again. And you? You're going to rot in here, forgotten. Alone."

Then he turned and walked out, not sparing Darren a second glance.

Tom gave him a look of quiet respect as they stepped into the hall. "He got under your skin?"

"Not anymore," Eric said, his voice hard. "He doesn't get to live in my head. Or hers."

Tom nodded. "Good man."

Eric exhaled, long and slow. And for the first time since Amy disappeared, his lungs felt full.

Chapter Twenty-Eight

The room was still and dim, the hush of machines weaving a quiet rhythm into the air. The IV line tugged lightly at Amy's arm when she stirred, and for a moment, she wasn't sure if she was awake or still floating in that strange, soft place between sleep and memory.

Then she felt it—warmth.

Not from the blanket or the fluid dripping steadily into her veins, but from a hand wrapped gently around hers. Large, callused fingers threaded through hers, unmoving but firm, like even in sleep he couldn't let go.

Her eyes fluttered open.

Eric's head rested on the edge of the mattress, turned slightly toward her. His dark hair was tousled, his brow relaxed in sleep, lashes casting faint shadows on his cheek. The side of his face pressed against their joined hands, his breath slow and even. His other hand was curled in toward his chest, like some part of him still hadn't stopped guarding her.

Amy blinked slowly, the ache in her chest not from fear this time—but from the sheer, overwhelming weight of love.

He was still here.

Her fingers tightened around his. Only slightly. Barely enough to make contact.

But it was enough.

Eric stirred. His eyes opened slowly, blinking as if surfacing from deep water. When he focused on her face, a breath escaped him—shaky, disbelieving.

"Amy," he said, voice raw and quiet.

She managed a small, tired smile. "You drooled on the sheet."

He huffed out a laugh, choked with relief. "Worth it."

He sat up, brushing a hand through his hair, and leaned closer, his thumb brushing softly over the back of hers. His eyes were red-rimmed, exhausted, but full of something else now—something steady and bright.

"I didn't want you to wake up alone," he said.

"I didn't," she whispered. "I woke up holding you."

His throat worked, emotion tightening his jaw. "You scared me. I didn't know if... I thought maybe—"

"I'm here," she said softly. "You found me."

Eric leaned forward, pressing a kiss to her knuckles. "I never stop trying."

Tears welled in her eyes. She didn't fight them this time.

He shifted slightly, laying his hand gently on her bandaged wrist. "Does it hurt?"

"Not like it did," she said. "They will get better."

Eric bowed his head over her hand again, holding it like it was the most precious thing in the world. "I'm never letting you go again."

"You won't have to," Amy whispered. "I'm holding on this time too."

A soft knock tapped against the doorframe, and Eric turned, not letting go of her hand.

Levi stepped inside first, a tentative smile pulling at his face. Behind him was a man Amy didn't recognise—tall, broad-shouldered, with the kind of stillness that came from long experience with chaos. His expression was unreadable, but his eyes were kind.

"Hey, Doc" Levi said gently. "We wanted to see how you're doing."

Eric gave a small nod, glancing down at Amy. "Are you up for a few visitors?"

Amy's fingers tightened faintly around his. "As long as they don't mind me looking like I got dragged through a hedge."

Levi gave a low laugh. "You look better than you did when we found you, I'll say that much."

Amy's eyes shifted to the man beside him.

Eric noticed. "This is John Sawyer," he said. "He's an old friend—private detective."

John stepped forward with a quiet nod. "Ma'am. It's good to see you awake."

Amy tried to smile. "I'd shake your hand, but mine are kind of out of commission for a little while."

John's mouth curved, just slightly. "No worries. You just focus on healing."

Eric glanced between the two men, then looked back at her, something unspoken in his eyes. "They both helped find you, Amy. I couldn't have done it alone."

Levi pulled a chair closer to the bed and sat carefully; his usual cocky grin muted under the weight of the moment. "You scared the hell out of us."

Amy blinked slowly, her lips parted, trying to put pieces together through the haze. "How… how did you find me?"

Eric exhaled and looked down at their joined hands. "We didn't have much to go on. But Levi—" he paused, his voice tight with something deeper than pride "—he went into the holding cell with Darren. Alone. Got him talking."

Amy's brows lifted slightly. "You… went in there?"

Levi nodded, his expression turning serious. "It wasn't exactly pleasant, but I pushed the right buttons, asked the right questions."

She looked back at Eric, eyes shining. "You all saved me."

Eric cupped her cheek, brushing his thumb across her skin. "There was never a second where we weren't trying. Not one."

Amy looked between the three men—each so different, each carrying the weight of what they'd done to bring her back. Her heart ached, not from pain this time, but from gratitude.

"I don't know how to thank you," she whispered.

"You don't have to," John said quietly. "You're here. That's enough."

Levi cleared his throat, eyes flicking toward the IV stand. "And you've got some impressive fight in you. Don't let Eric take all the credit."

Amy managed a smile. "Don't worry. I won't."

Eric laughed softly, shaking his head, then leaned down and kissed her forehead.

"I love you," he said, low and certain. "And you're safe now. That's all that matters."

She let her eyes fall closed for a moment, the warmth of his lips on her skin, the sound of familiar voices in the room, the steady hum of machines—it all grounded her.

Then, slowly, she opened her eyes and turned toward Levi and John. "I know you've already done so much, but can I ask one more favour?"

Both men straightened slightly. "Anything," they said in unison.

She looked at Eric, then back to them. "Take him home. Make him rest."

Eric opened his mouth. "I don't want—"

"No," she cut in gently but firmly. "You look dead on your feet. Please. I'd feel so much better knowing you were taking care of yourself now that I'm safe."

Levi rose from his chair with a quiet huff. "Come on, man. You heard the Doc."

Eric hesitated, torn, his grip on her hand lingering.

"I'll be back," he said softly.

"Not today," she replied, her voice tender but resolute.

Their eyes held for a long moment before he finally leaned down and kissed her again.

"I love you," he whispered.

"I know," she whispered back, watching him go, knowing it was love that had brought her back—and love that would heal them both.

The hospital's sliding doors whispered shut behind them, silencing the steady beeps and hushed voices that had been the soundtrack of their lives. Outside, the late morning air was crisp, laced with the scent of freshly cut grass drifting in from the surrounding grounds. Spring had arrived, Eric realised distantly—quiet and indifferent—while he'd been buried too deep in fear to notice.

Eric and Levi turned to John, who stood with his hands in his coat pockets, already glancing toward the street.

Eric reached out, shaking his hand. "Thanks for everything, John. We couldn't have done it without you."

John offered a short, modest nod. "You don't have to thank me. You've got a good one in there." He tilted his head back toward the hospital entrance.

Eric's chest tightened, but his voice was steady. "I know."

John's mouth lifted slightly, and then he gave them both a final nod. "Take care of her. And get some sleep—both of you."

With that, he turned and headed down the walkway, his figure growing smaller against the lengthening shadows.

Levi glanced at Eric. "He's not wrong."

Eric's gaze lingered on the hospital doors a moment longer. "No. He's not."

Levi shoved his hands into the pockets of his jacket and let out a long breath. "Jesus," he muttered. "I was so glad to see her sitting up in that bed."

Eric didn't answer right away. His hands stayed clenched at his sides, like letting go of Amy had drained the last of his strength. He stood still, staring at nothing, until Levi gave him a gentle nudge with his shoulder.

"She's okay, man."

Eric finally exhaled and rubbed both hands over his face. "I know. I know she is. I just… I didn't let myself believe it until I saw her open her eyes."

Levi's voice dropped, quiet and steady. "You were the one who never stopped. Even when it got dark."

Eric gave a bitter laugh. "It was dark. I've never been that afraid in my life."

They walked slowly down the sidewalk, neither in a rush to leave the hospital grounds. The tension had started to bleed out of Eric's frame, but exhaustion clung to him like a second skin.

"Thanks for going in that cell," Eric said after a beat. "I will never forget what you did."

Levi shrugged. "It was for her. For you." He glanced over. "I know what it would've done to you if we hadn't found her."

Eric's jaw tightened. "It would've destroyed me."

Silence stretched between them as they reached the edge of the lot. A bench sat beneath a sprawling oak tree, half in shadow. Eric lowered himself onto it like gravity had doubled.

Levi stood for a second, then sat beside him. "You should go home. Sleep in a bed. Shower. Eat something that doesn't come from a vending machine."

Eric gave a hollow chuckle. "Sounds like luxury."

"You earned it."

Eric tilted his head back, eyes closed. "She told me not to come back today."

Levi smirked. "Yeah, she kind of ordered you, Doc-style."

"She always thinks of other people before herself."

Levi's voice gentled. "She wasn't wrong, though. You need to rest. You're no good to her if you fall apart."

Eric was quiet for a long time. Then, finally, he nodded. "I'll go. Just for tonight."

Levi stood and held out a hand. "I'll drive. And if you argue, I'll drug you and throw you in the back seat."

Eric managed a smile—small but real. He handed Levi the car keys and stood. "You're a terrible nurse."

"I aim to please."

They walked toward the car, quiet again, but a stillness settled between them—a kind that didn't press down but lifted.

Chapter Twenty-Nine

The soft shuffle of footsteps outside the hospital room pulled Amy from a light doze. She turned her head just as the door eased open, and there he was—Eric, freshly showered, dressed in clean clothes, his hair damp and pushed back like he'd finally slept. The dark circles under his eyes had faded, and though he still carried the weight of the last five days, something in his posture had shifted. Calmer. Steadier.

Amy smiled. "You clean up nice."

Eric let out a quiet breath of laughter and crossed the room to her bedside. "You're one to talk. You look like hell," he teased gently, but his voice cracked with affection. "And still the most beautiful thing I've ever seen."

She rolled her eyes, but the smile stayed. "Smooth."

"I try." He pulled the chair closer and sat beside her, reaching for her hand without hesitation. Her fingers curled around his, slow but sure.

"You look better," she said softly.

"I feel better. Knowing you're okay." He gave her hand a careful squeeze. "How are you feeling?"

"Weirdly… good," she said, surprised at herself. "Still weak. Still sore. But not… broken. And the doctor said I'm on track. They took the IV out this morning."

Eric exhaled with visible relief, but she could tell he'd been holding his breath since walking through the door.

"Oh—and Sally and Henry stopped by," Amy added. "They brought flowers. Told me Henry is covering for me at the clinic until I'm ready to come back."

Eric's eyebrows lifted. "They came here?"

She nodded. "Didn't stay long. Sally cried, Henry didn't know what to do with his hands, but it meant a lot." Her voice softened. "They're good people."

He smiled. "Yeah. They are. I'll have to thank them."

"You do that." Amy shifted slightly in the bed, winced, and settled again. "Doctor says I'll be here at least two more days. They want to monitor the infection in my wrists, make sure I can keep fluid down."

Eric nodded. "Whatever you need. I'm not going anywhere."

A comfortable silence stretched between them. Amy's gaze drifted to their joined hands, then up to his face. "I dreamt you didn't make it," she whispered. "That I came out of it, and you were gone."

Eric leaned in, forehead nearly touching hers. "I'm right here, Amy. And I'm not leaving. Not now. Not ever."

Her throat tightened, but she smiled through it. "Good. Because I've got a long list of things I want to do. Starting with eating something that's not clear broth."

He laughed, warm and real this time. "I'll see what I can do."

For the first time since everything fell apart, the air felt light. Fragile, maybe—but full of possibility.

A gentle knock came at the door just before it opened, and Dr. Jensen stepped inside, clipboard in hand and a kind smile on her face.

"Good morning," she greeted, her tone warm and reassuring. "How are we feeling today, Amy?"

Amy sat up a little straighter in the hospital bed, her face pale but more animated than the day before. "Better," she said honestly. "Still tired, but I don't feel like I'm floating anymore."

"That's a good sign." Dr. Jensen glanced at the monitors briefly, then nodded. "Your vitals have stabilised overnight. The infection in your wrists is still something we're watching, but the antibiotics are doing their job. I see the nurse took your IV out."

Eric stood beside the bed, quiet but attentive, his hand resting lightly on the bedrail. Amy glanced at him before turning back to the doctor.

"So," Amy ventured, cautious hope in her voice, "does that mean I can… move around a little?"

Dr. Jensen smiled. "Actually, yes. If you're feeling up to it, I'd like you to try standing and maybe take a short walk. Just down the hall and back. We'll monitor how your body handles it."

Amy perked up, relief and nerves colliding in her chest. "And… can I shower?"

Dr. Jensen chuckled. "You're not the first patient to ask that." She nodded. "Yes—but only if someone's with you. You're still weak, and your blood pressure could drop. You need support, especially standing that long."

Amy's gaze slid back to Eric, who was already nodding.

"I'll help," he said gently. "Whatever she needs."

"Good," Dr. Jensen replied. "Take it slow and call the nurse if anything feels off." She gave Amy's shoulder a light touch. "You're doing well. Better than expected, honestly."

"Thanks," Amy said softly.

The doctor left them alone again, and the room felt suddenly larger.

Eric looked at her, the corners of his mouth twitching up. "So… walk first or shower?"

Amy laughed—a small, raw sound that surprised them both. "Walk. I want to earn the shower."

He reached for her hand. "Then let's get you moving, champ."

"Don't call me champ."

"I absolutely will."

The hallway seemed impossibly long.

Amy stood in the doorway of her hospital room, one hand gripping the door frame, the other curled loosely around Eric's arm. Her legs trembled beneath her hospital gown, muscles weak from days without movement. But her eyes were determined.

Eric stayed close, his body steady and strong beside hers. "You sure you're ready?"

She nodded. "I've never been surer of anything."

They stepped out together, her bare feet touching cool tile. Each step was slow, deliberate, the ache in her limbs sharp but manageable. The walk wasn't long—twenty feet down the corridor, then back—but by the halfway mark, Amy was breathing hard, her grip on his arm tightening.

"You're doing great," Eric murmured. "Just a little further."

She managed a weak smile. "Feels like a marathon."

They made it back to the doorway, and Eric helped her into the chair by the bed. She leaned back, breath shaky but triumphant.

"I earned that shower," she said.

Eric grinned. "You definitely did."

He moved around the room, gathering the things she'd need—towels, clean hospital gown, a washcloth. When he knelt beside her to begin unwrapping the thick bandages from her wrists, his hands stilled.

Her skin was raw and scabbed, the wounds deep, angry red around the edges. Some areas were beginning to heal, but others were still open, layered with gauze and ointment.

Eric swallowed hard.

"Eric…" Amy said gently, watching the pain gather in his eyes.

He blinked and kept working, quieter now, his jaw locked tight.

She reached out, resting her uninjured fingers lightly against his forearm. "I know it's hard to look at."

He met her eyes then — full of guilt, helplessness, fury he didn't have anywhere to put.

Amy's voice softened but didn't waver. "But I'm going to heal. I am healing."

He nodded, throat too tight for words.

Amy reached up, brushing her fingers along his cheek. "I won't let him win, Eric. You can't either."

That cracked something in him. He closed his eyes briefly, pressing her hand to his face. Then he nodded again—firmer this time.

"I won't," he said quietly. "Not ever."

She gave him a small, tired smile. "Good. Now help me up. I'm not doing this shower thing alone."

He helped her to her feet, steadying her with gentle hands as they made their way to the bathroom—her body broken, yes, but her spirit slowly rising, step by step.

Steam curled around the edges of the bathroom mirror, softening the sterile lines of the hospital walls. The water ran warm, just shy of hot, misting the air with comfort.

Eric stood just outside the shower stall, giving her as much privacy as the situation allowed. He held a clean towel in one hand, his back rigid, every muscle taut with focus and restraint.

Amy stepped carefully onto the non-slip mat; her hospital gown already draped over a nearby hook. Her body ached in a hundred quiet ways—shoulders sore, knees unsteady, wrists throbbing dully under the fresh gauze—but the water felt like salvation. It poured over her like rain after a drought, washing away layers of memory she didn't want to carry anymore.

She stayed under the spray for a long time, her eyes closed, hands braced against the tiled wall. When she finally turned off the water, she was shaking—not from weakness this time, but from something heavier. The water had washed away the grime, but not all of the shadows.

"I'm done," she called softly.

Eric moved, eyes downcast until he reached her side. He held the towel open, and she stepped into it, letting him wrap her up like something precious. His hands were gentle, reverent almost, like touching her was an honour he didn't take lightly.

He dried her hair with slow, careful strokes, not speaking, just being present. When he knelt to pat her calves and feet dry, he hesitated—then lifted her wrist with both hands and began to redress the wound with a clean bandage.

Amy watched him as he worked, his brow furrowed, his throat tight with emotion he didn't voice.

"I know this isn't easy," she said quietly, "but I need you to see me like this. I need you to know I'm not broken."

His gaze met hers, raw and searching. "You're not," he said fiercely. "You never were."

She leaned into him, resting her forehead against his. "I need your strength right now. But I'm going to find my own again too."

He nodded, his voice low and steady. "I'll be here every step."

When she was dressed again, hair damp and clean, bandages fresh, and a warmth returned to her cheeks that hadn't been there in days, he helped her back to the bed.

But something had changed. Not just in her.

In both of them.

They weren't surviving anymore.

They were beginning to heal.

Chapter Thirty

Amy stood at the kitchen sink, watching the late afternoon light spill across the countertop like liquid gold. The world beyond the window was quiet—peaceful in a way that felt almost foreign. Birds chirped lazily in the trees, the Eric's beloved pet Boomer barking—probably at a rabbit or maybe Levi, and wind chimes clinked softly on the porch. It was a small, ordinary moment. But for Amy, it felt extraordinary.

She flexed her fingers slightly. The fresh bandages were gone now, replaced with light gauze and healing skin. The angry red wounds were fading, the ache duller each day. Two weeks had passed since she'd left the hospital, and though her body had mostly recovered, the nights were still hard.

She heard the soft thud of footsteps behind her before arms wrapped gently around her waist.

"You okay?" Eric's voice was low, close to her ear.

Amy nodded, leaning back into his chest. "Yeah. Just… thinking."

He pressed a kiss to her temple. "Dangerous hobby."

She gave a soft laugh and tilted her head toward him. "You insisted I come here. I'm just trying to make myself useful."

"You being here is useful," he said simply, his hands settling on her hips. "You breathing, smiling—even when it's only a little—that's more than enough for me."

Amy turned in his arms, resting her hands lightly against his chest. "I haven't exactly been a ray of sunshine."

"You've been through hell. And you're still standing." His eyes were steady on hers. "You don't have to perform for me, Amy. Just be."

She exhaled slowly and leaned her forehead against his chest. "The dreams are getting better."

"I know." His fingers brushed soothing circles along her back. "You haven't screamed in three nights."

She winced. "I'm sorry."

"Don't be." He tipped her chin up, so she had to look at him. "I meant what I said. Every time you wake up, I'll be there. I don't care how long it takes. I'm not going anywhere."

Her eyes softened. "You say that like it's easy."

"It's not," he admitted. "But it's right."

There was a pause—quiet and warm—before she spoke again.

"I keep hearing his voice in those dreams," she whispered. "When he said he was going to find you… I still feel that panic in my chest sometimes. Like I'm back there. Powerless."

Eric's jaw tightened, but he didn't speak right away. Instead, he pulled her closer, letting her feel the solid weight of him, the safety in his embrace.

"He can't touch you anymore," he said firmly. "He's behind bars. Kidnapping, assault, attempted manslaughter—the charges stacked up fast. And with his record, he's not walking free again anytime soon."

Amy nodded slowly, pressing her cheek to his shirt. "It should make me feel better."

"It will," he said gently. "It just takes time. You're safe now, Amy. I swear to you."

She let those words settle inside her, deeper than they had before. Safe. Not just physically, but emotionally. Here, in this house—with Eric—she wasn't surviving anymore. She was healing.

"I don't know what I would've done if you hadn't found me," she said softly.

"You would've made it," he whispered. "But I'm damn glad I did."

She looked up at him, something quiet and fierce shining in her eyes. "So am I."

They stood like that for a long moment—wrapped in the hush of a safe home, in a life slowly beginning again.

They hadn't made love since the kidnapping.

But Amy was done being fragile.

Eric had been patient, attentive, gentle in ways that both soothed and frustrated her. He never pushed, never even hinted. Instead, he held her when the nightmares came, made her coffee in the mornings, kissed her forehead like she was made of porcelain.

But Amy was done being breakable.

Yes, she was still healing. Yes, there were moments when the fear returned like a ghost. But tonight, that wasn't what she felt.

Tonight, she missed him.

Not just his presence or his steady warmth in bed beside her, but him—the man she had fallen in love with. The man who knew how to touch her, kiss her, understand her. She wanted all of him, and more than that—she needed to feel like she still belonged to herself, not just the part of her that had survived, but the part that desired, that loved, that craved.

So, she had a plan.

Eric was in the shower, steam curling beneath the bathroom door, and she took a steadying breath as she stood at the edge of the bed. Her fingers trembled slightly—not with fear, but anticipation—as she slipped out of her clothes and reached for the silky robe he always said drove him crazy.

She lit the candle on the nightstand. Just one. Enough to cast a soft, golden glow across the room.

When the water stopped and she heard the creak of the bathroom door opening, Amy moved to the centre of the bed and sat on her knees, the robe falling open just enough to reveal her bare skin underneath. Her heart pounded, but she held steady.

Eric walked in, towel slung low on his hips, his hair damp and unruly. He froze when he saw her.

"Amy."

She smiled slowly. "Hey."

His eyes darkened. "You look…"

"Ready," she said softly, cutting him off. "For us. I want you, Eric. I need you."

He crossed the room in two long strides but didn't touch her. His hands hovered just shy of her skin, eyes searching hers with worry. "Are you sure?"

"I've never been surer of anything," she whispered, reaching for his hand and guiding it to her cheek. "You've taken such good care of me… but this is part of my healing too. Let me have this. Let me have you."

His throat worked as he swallowed hard. "God, Amy…"

Then he kissed her—slow, reverent, almost disbelieving at first. But when she sighed into his mouth and slid her hands up his chest, something shifted. The restraint he'd held onto so tightly began to unravel.

And finally, they came together—not out of urgency or to forget the pain, but because love had waited patiently… and now, it was ready to be remembered.

Eric's hands moved to her waist, tentative at first, like he was still afraid she might shatter beneath his touch. But Amy leaned into him, her lips brushing against his with soft insistence, her fingers curling into the damp towel around his hips.

"You're not going to break me," she whispered, her voice warm against his mouth. "You bring me back to life."

That was all it took.

His restraint unraveled completely, and he kissed her like a man who'd been holding his breath for weeks. Deep, searching, reverent. His hands slid over her hips, then up her back, pulling her closer until there was nothing between them but shared breath and heat.

He untied the robe slowly, reverently, parting the fabric like it was sacred. When it fell away from her shoulders, he didn't stare—he looked. His gaze swept over every inch of her like he was memorising the places she'd fought to reclaim. His fingers traced the healed edges of the wounds on her wrists, brushing the gauze that still protected the most fragile areas. She didn't flinch. She held his gaze.

"I love you," he said, voice raw. "You are so damn strong. So beautiful. And I love you more than I know how to say."

Amy cupped his face in both hands. "Then show me."

Eric kissed her again, deeper this time, his hands finally exploring the way she remembered. He laid her gently back on the bed, his body warm and solid above hers. There was no rush—only reverence. Every touch felt like a vow. Every kiss like a promise.

He worshipped her—slowly, with aching tenderness—his lips tracing a path down her collarbone, across her chest, to the hollow just above her heart. Amy arched into him, her breath catching as the fire she'd been holding back surged forward.

Her hands found his back, her nails grazing lightly down his spine. "I've missed this," she breathed. "I've missed you."

Eric looked up at her, his voice thick. "You never lost me. I've been right here."

He moved with her then, their bodies finding the rhythm they'd once known, but this time it was different—deeper. Quieter. Not frantic or urgent, but full of emotion. The kind that builds in your chest until it breaks you open.

Amy clung to him as they moved together, her breath soft gasps against his shoulder. The weight of what they'd survived filled every sigh, every whisper, every heartbeat. And when the moment came—when the pleasure crested and spilled over—it wasn't just release.

It was relief.

When it was over, Eric held her close, his hand gently stroking her hair, his breathing slowly returning to steady.

Amy nestled her head beneath his chin, her voice barely above a breath. "That… felt incredible."

Eric brushed a kiss to her temple, his hand gently stroking her back. "That's exactly what you are."

They stayed that way for a long time—wrapped in each other, in warmth and wonder, in the quiet intimacy of two people who had weathered the storm and found solace in each other. The silence between them wasn't empty—it was full. Of love. Of healing. Of unspoken promises.

Then, softly, Eric spoke. "Amy?"

She lifted her head, meeting his gaze. "Yes?"

"I love you. You know that don't you?"

A smile touched her lips, warm and certain. "I do. And I love you."

He held her gaze, his voice low and full of emotion. "After my divorce, I didn't think I'd ever find someone like you. Someone I could love with everything I am… someone who loves me just as deeply. You've changed everything, Amy."

He drew in a breath, steadying himself as the words finally rose to the surface—words that had been living in his heart, waiting for the right moment. "Amy, will you marry me?"

Her heart skipped, not from fear, but from the sheer, overwhelming beauty of what he'd just asked. She searched his eyes—those steady, unwavering eyes that had seen her at her lowest and loved her anyway—and she found her answer waiting there, unshakable.

"You've brought a kind of happiness into my life I never believed I'd ever have," she whispered, emotion catching in her throat. "Yes, Eric. I will marry you."

He pulled her into his arms, holding her as if the world had finally made sense. And in that quiet room, where healing had begun and love had quietly taken root, the future opened wide in front of them—bright, full of promise, and completely theirs.

Epilogue

Amy stood on the wraparound porch of the sprawling ranch house, her arms folded loosely as she watched the dust plume rise behind the truck rolling down the long driveway. The sun was beginning to dip behind the trees, casting golden light across the fields—soft and familiar.

Eric was home.

He and Levi had been gone for a week, traveling to a race meet with Patriot. Another win—his third straight. She'd caught the broadcast online and seen the thrill in Eric's eyes when Patriot crossed the finish line. Someone had mentioned a purse—maybe a million, maybe two. Amy hadn't asked. She didn't care about the money. As long as Eric was happy, as long as he came home to her, that was enough.

This past week at the vet clinic had been a blur of patients, emergencies, and paperwork. They'd finally hired another vet to help ease the load, and it was already making a difference. Still, the days had been long, and the nights even longer.

Eric didn't like her working those late hours. He said he understood, said he trusted her judgment—but she knew. Even if he never said it aloud, she could see it in the way he watched the clock when she was gone too long, or the way he pulled her just a little closer at night. He didn't have to say the word kidnapping. It hung in the air between them sometimes, unspoken but deeply felt.

She didn't mind his protectiveness. Not anymore. She knew now that it wasn't about control—it was about love. Raw, fierce, unshakable love. And in the quiet weeks after she'd come back to the ranch, she'd learned just how much her absence had cost him.

There were nights he still woke up reaching for her, his breath caught in his throat. And on those nights, she'd press her forehead to his and whisper, "I'm here. I'm safe. You found me." That was all he needed.

They were married two weeks after he proposed.

They stood beneath a canopy of wildflowers in the pasture behind the barn, surrounded by close friends and the open Colorado sky. No ballgown, no chandeliers, no ballroom full of guests. Just them.

Eric had worried she might regret not having the big white wedding. But she'd taken his face in her hands and told him, "I don't need a thousand people or a string quartet. I just want to be Mrs. Amy Reynolds. I want you. That's it."

That had been nine months ago.

Nine months of laughter and late-night dances in the kitchen. Of sunrise trail rides and quiet evenings on the porch swing. Of shared glances across dinner tables and whispered promises beneath warm sheets.

Nine months of absolute bliss.

She heard the engine cut off, a truck door slam shut, followed by Levi's voice—low and easy, probably teasing Eric like always. Amy smiled, her heart beating a little faster as footsteps crunched across the gravel.

Then he was there.

Eric rounded the corner, boots dusty, face tired, his ball cap pulled low over eyes that still lit up the second they landed on her.

"Amy," he breathed, like just seeing her was a relief.

She didn't wait. She stepped off the porch and into his arms, and everything else faded— money, races, busy clinics, even the memories that still sometimes haunted her dreams.

"You're home," she whispered.

His arms tightened around her. "Yeah, baby. I am."

"I missed you."

He kissed her, slow and sure. "I missed you more."

Amy pulled back just enough to see his face, her fingers brushing against the scruff along his jaw. Her eyes searched his, tender and hesitant. "I haven't been feeling very well this week."

Immediately, Eric's expression shifted — concern flooding his features. "Are you okay? Have you been to the doctor?"

Her fingers trailed lightly over the front of his shirt, tracing lazy circles across the fabric stretched over his chest.

"Yes," she said softly. "I went yesterday."

"Well… are you okay?" His voice dropped, tense now, every muscle in his body drawn tight.

Amy didn't answer right away. Her gaze dropped to her hand on his chest, then lifted again. "We need to talk about something."

Eric's hands slid to her waist, holding her steady, his brows drawn tight with worry. "Amy, you're scaring me."

She bit her lip, her voice barely above a whisper. "I'm a little scared too… because I'm pregnant."

For a long heartbeat, Eric just stared at her. No words. No movement. Just the wind stirring around them, and his dark eyes searching hers.

Then, slowly, a smile broke over his face—wide and disbelieving at first, then brighter, fuller, until it lit him up like a Christmas tree. "We're going to have a baby?"

Amy nodded, a grin spreading across her face, tears pricking the corners of her eyes.

"Amy. Seriously?" he asked again, as if needing to hear it twice just to believe it.

She laughed. "Seriously."

With a joyful laugh of his own, Eric scooped her into his arms and spun her around, holding her close against his chest. Her laughter rang out across the porch as he set her back down gently.

His hands cupped her face, thumbs brushing her cheeks, eyes locked on hers with a look so full of love it made her heart ache.

Then he kissed her—deeply, passionately, like he was pouring every ounce of joy and love and awe into that moment.

"God, I love you," he whispered against her lips.

"I love you too," Amy murmured, her eyes shining.

He kissed her again, slower this time, savouring it, letting the moment sink deep into his bones.

Then suddenly, with a burst of joy he couldn't contain, Eric spun around, threw his arms wide to the open sky, and shouted at the top of his lungs, "We're having a baby!"

His voice echoed across the pasture, startling a few birds into flight and sending the horses at the fence tossing their heads.

Amy laughed, her hand pressed over her heart, watching the man she loved more than anything lose himself in happiness.

Eric turned back to her, eyes damp, smile still wide. "We're having a baby," he repeated, this time softer, like he still couldn't believe it.

Levi walked up, grinning as he approached them. "Congratulations," he said. "I think the whole county just heard the news."

Eric didn't even flinch. "I don't care," he said proudly, reaching for Amy again. "Because we're having a baby."

Amy looked up at him, her heart full. She nodded, her voice barely above a whisper as she stepped into his arms once more. "Yes, we are."

The End

The Billionaire's Bargain

Alison Reid

A complete standalone romance

Previously published individually

Chapter One

Willow Taylor had always believed in order—clean lines, neat endings, stories that wrapped themselves up just right. Maybe it was the editor in her. Or maybe it was what happened when you lost your parents young: you chased stability like a ship seeking shore, hoping structure could make up for the parts of life that felt wildly out of your control.

The soft clang of the subway echoed through the tunnel as she gripped the overhead bar, her favourite leather tote nestled against her side like armour. It was still early morning in Manhattan, but already, the day had its teeth in her. She was running five minutes late, which in Willow's world felt like a minor catastrophe.

Her long brown hair—still damp from her rushed shower—curled softly down the back of her beige wool coat. She checked her reflection in the train's window: minimal makeup, delicate gold earrings, clear blue eyes that always gave away too much. She exhaled slowly and glanced down at her phone just as it buzzed in her palm.

A text from Dennis blinked at the top of the screen:

Don't forget our dinner with the partners tonight. 7pm. Sharp. Wear that navy dress— they liked it last time.

Willow's thumb hovered over the keyboard, her brain supplying a dozen possible responses—Sure, Got it, Can't wait. But none of them felt right. With a sigh, she slipped the phone back into her bag, letting the moment pass.

She'd worn that navy dress four weeks ago when Dennis had introduced her to his firm's senior partners as "the woman I might marry." It had been said with a smile, but it hadn't landed like a compliment. It had felt like a line from a pitch deck. Like she was a bullet point in a larger plan.

Still, Dennis wasn't a bad man. He was responsible. Smart. Predictable.

And once, predictability had felt like safety.

When she stepped out of the station, the city greeted her in a rush of light and noise. Morning sun spilled between the buildings like golden syrup, warming the pavement and tinting the glassy skyline with possibility. Taxis honked. A vendor called out prices for bagels. Somewhere, a saxophonist played Autumn Leaves just out of tune.

Willow let the noise anchor her. New York was messy and loud and unapologetically alive. It didn't ask for order—it just was. That was what she loved most about it.

Tucked between a florist and a vintage bookstore, the narrow brick building that housed Bright Press looked almost shy compared to the looming office towers nearby. But inside, the scent of old paper and freshly brewed coffee mingled in the air like a secret handshake.

"Morning, Willow!" chirped Grace from behind the reception desk. Her voice was already two lattes into the day. "You're glowing today—hot date last night?"

Willow laughed as she unwound her scarf and slipped off her coat. "Hardly. Dennis and I had dinner. He made a spreadsheet for our potential wedding timeline. Very romantic."

Grace blinked. "A spreadsheet?"

Willow nodded, completely deadpan. "Colour-coded. Orange for catering deadlines. Blue for fertility windows. I think green meant… bridesmaid dress fittings?"

Grace gasped. "Tell me you're joking."

"I wish I was."

They both dissolved into quiet giggles, their laughter softening the fluorescent light and early hour. This was what Willow cherished about Bright Press—not just the books, but the people who still believed in stories, even if their own weren't perfect.

Grace leaned in, lowering her voice. "When are you going to get rid of him, Willow? You're gorgeous, smart, kind. You could have any man you wanted."

Willow's smile faltered. "I care about Dennis."

Grace tilted her head. "But do you love him?"

Willow hesitated. It was the question she never let herself sit with too long. Because deep down, she already knew the answer.

Before she could respond, the office phone rang, slicing the air like a judge's gavel. Grace straightened with practiced cheer. "Bright Press, this is Grace speaking…"

Willow gave her a grateful smile and moved past the reception desk, her heels clicking softly against the wood floor. She wove through the bullpen—a maze of desks, half-empty coffee mugs, and stacked manuscripts—offering quiet nods and warm greetings to her coworkers.

Her desk was nestled in the corner near a tall, crooked ficus that she'd rescued from the break room. A cork board hung above it, pinned with author quotes, postcards from her travels, and a few old rejection letters she kept not out of spite but to remind herself how far she'd come.

She sat, logging into her computer as the familiar flood of emails welcomed her: submission queries, author edits, print schedule updates. It was comforting chaos—structured chaos. And in it, she came alive.

The quiet shaping of stories. The magic of line edits. The whispered possibility that maybe, just maybe, the next manuscript in her queue might be the one.

And yet… lately, something inside her had begun to ache. Not loudly. Just a steady, persistent tug in the space between her ribs.

It wasn't that she disliked her life. She liked it just fine. Her job was meaningful, her apartment was cozy, her routines were well-oiled. She met deadlines. She replied to texts. She smiled at the right moments.

But fine wasn't thrilling.

It wasn't the kind of life that made your chest ache with joy or your breath catch with wonder.

She wasn't sure if she truly loved Dennis. They kissed. They held hands. They made plans. But whenever things edged toward intimacy, she pulled back. He didn't press her. He was understanding. Patient. Courteous.

But his affection often felt like an obligation, a polite gesture wrapped in expectation. He had never asked why she hesitated, never wondered aloud if she was afraid or uncertain. He had never asked if she was a virgin. Maybe he assumed. Maybe he didn't care. Maybe, like everything else, it was just part of the timeline.

Sometimes she stared too long out the window, watching the city pulse below like it held an answer she couldn't reach.

Sometimes a song on the radio would wreck her, and she wouldn't know why.

Sometimes she dreamed of her mother's laughter—bright, unpredictable, always just ahead of the world—and woke up with wet cheeks and the hollow ache of missing something too long gone.

Willow shook herself and refocused on her screen. Deadlines didn't care about melancholy. An author was waiting. A manuscript needed polishing. And her life—her tidy, well-kept, mostly pleasant life—was still exactly where she'd left it.

At least for now.

That morning, sunlight spilled across Willow's desk in thin golden stripes, warming the stack of manuscripts beside her elbow. She was halfway through a charming middle-grade novel about a brave girl who befriended a fox in the Arctic tundra. The prose was whimsical, the pacing tight, and she found herself smiling more than once as she scribbled notes in the margin. It was the kind of story that reminded her why she'd chosen this career—to be part of something that could make a child believe in magic.

Then her phone buzzed.

She ignored it at first, assuming it was Dennis checking in with another "just thinking of you" text or a link to an article titled Why Couples Who Plan Early Stay Together Longer. But the phone buzzed again—more insistent this time, the vibration rattling faintly against the side of her bag.

Willow sighed and fished it out, planning to silence it.

Her smile vanished.

Two missed calls from Lily.

Her half-sister.

Willow stared at the screen, her stomach knotting.

Lily.

Blonde, impulsive, wild. The kind of girl who wore eyeliner to breakfast and treated rules like optional suggestions for the unimaginative. They shared a father, but not a childhood. Lily had been born of an affair—one that shattered Willow's family like a grenade tossed into a glass house.

Her father had strayed when Willow was just a baby. But the truth didn't come out until much later—until Willow was ten and Lily was eight. It wasn't just a betrayal. It had a name. A face. A daughter.

Lily.

At twelve, Lily moved to Italy with her mother—a striking, unpredictable painter who spoke in poetry and never fully acknowledged the wreckage she'd left behind. Willow remained in New York, grounded by a mother who carried the weight of betrayal like a second skin, even as she tried to forgive, to rebuild.

Then, when Willow was eighteen, the fault lines split wide open.

Her parents, tentatively trying to reconcile, were in the car together when the accident happened. Her mother died on impact. Her father survived for a week before he succumbed to his injuries.

In the years since, Lily had drifted in and out of Willow's life like a breeze through an open window—sometimes warm, sometimes a storm. Their relationship was complicated. Tentative. A tangle of shared blood, pain, and cautious affection.

The phone buzzed again.

A text from Lily.

Please. I need you. It's bad. I'm in Rome. I'm in jail.

Willow's heart stopped for a full beat.

Jail?

She read it twice, then a third time. The words didn't change, but her understanding of them did.

Jail. Lily. Rome.

The manuscript in her lap slipped to the floor, forgotten.

She stood abruptly, the room around her suddenly too bright, too sharp.

Grace glanced up from reception. "Everything okay?"

Willow opened her mouth, but no words came out at first.

She looked back down at the phone, at the glowing screen, at the desperate little message from the half-sister who was always a mess—but never this much of one.

"I... I have to make a call," Willow managed, her voice shaky. "Something's happened."

She didn't know what she'd find in Rome, only that Lily needed her.

And that—for better or worse—Willow couldn't look away.

The last she'd heard, Lily was working as a financial assistant for some Italian luxury conglomerate. Something about private jets and wealthy men who wore too much cologne.

A chill ran down Willow's spine as she called her back immediately.

"Willow?" Lily's voice cracked through the static. "I—I messed up. I didn't mean to. But I didn't have a choice—"

"Lily, slow down. Where are you exactly?"

"I'm at the police station in Rome. Please… I didn't steal it. I just—I borrowed it. I was going to put it back. But they found out, and the boss—he's pressing charges."

"What boss? Who are you talking about?"

"Luca Lombardi."

The name hit her like a thunderclap.

Luca Lombardi.

Even Willow had heard of him—the Luca Lombardi. Billionaire tycoon. CEO of Lombardi International. One of those names that whispered through headlines and financial reports like mythology. Ruthless. Brilliant. Impossibly rich. The kind of man who had entire skyscrapers with his name in gold and the kind of power that could crush people like ants… and never even look down to see them.

Her breath caught.

What had Lily gotten herself into?

Willow pressed the phone harder to her ear. "Okay. I'm coming."

There was a pause on the other end of the line. "Wait—you don't have to—"

"I do," Willow said firmly. "I'll see you when I get there. Just hang on. I'm coming."

She hung up, already reaching for her laptop.

The rest of the day passed in a blur, each minute melting into the next as if time itself couldn't decide whether to pause or sprint. Willow moved like someone underwater—quiet, disoriented, suspended between worlds.

Her boss at Bright Press, a middle-aged woman named Beverly with sharp glasses and a surprisingly soft heart, called her into the glass-walled office around noon. Manuscripts and coffee mugs were pushed to the edges of the desk like afterthoughts.

Beverly adjusted her frames and peered at Willow with concern. "You've never taken more than a day off," she said slowly. "Are you sure this isn't something the embassy or a lawyer could handle?"

Willow's throat tightened. "It's my sister."

That was all she said. All she needed to say.

Beverly's eyes softened. With a reluctant sigh, she scribbled her initials on the leave request. "Take what you need. Just… come back in one piece, okay?"

Willow nodded, offering a fragile smile before hurrying out.

The earliest flight to Rome she could find was at 5:00 a.m. the next morning—an ungodly hour for a life-altering journey. She booked it with trembling fingers, the confirmation screen blinking back at her like a dare. Rome. Jail. Lily. Luca Lombardi. The words didn't even sound real together, as if her life had suddenly been handed to someone else's screenwriter.

She sat on her bed afterward, unmoving, her laptop still open beside her. A fog rolled in behind her eyes. Shock. Disbelief. Maybe something darker. She was going. She had to go. But the weight of what waited for her there sat heavy on her chest, like an anchor pressed into her sternum.

She needed to tell Dennis.

Their dinner plans still loomed— "7 p.m. sharp," he had said, in that clipped, matter-of-fact voice he used to schedule dentist appointments and dry-cleaning pickups. But this dinner was more than that. He'd arranged for her to meet two of his law partners and their wives. Another stepping stone in their carefully calibrated relationship. A handshake away from engagement. A smile away from permanence.

For a long time, Willow just sat on the edge of her bed, phone in hand, thumb hovering over his name. She could cancel. She could text a breezy excuse and curl up under her blanket with a pint of gelato and the ache building behind her ribs.

But that wasn't who she was.

She believed in facing things. In honesty, even when it hurt.

She stood, shedding the haze of indecision like a second skin, and headed for the shower. The hot water poured over her in soothing sheets, but her mind raced. By the time she stepped out, towel-wrapped and still dripping, she felt clearer, even if the knot in her chest remained.

She opened her closet, eyeing the dresses like choices in a story she no longer wanted to tell. The navy one hung front and centre—Dennis's favourite. He'd called it "safe and classic," the same way he once described mutual funds.

The Instead, she reached past it.

The red one.

She rarely wore it. It dipped slightly at the neckline, hugged her waist, and had just enough swing to remind her she was allowed to take up space. Not for Dennis. Not for approval. For her.

Tonight, she didn't want to be "classic" or "safe." She wanted to be real. Unapologetically herself—even if that self was messy, uncertain, and terrified.

When Dennis arrived—right on time, not a minute early or late—she saw it. That flicker in his eyes. A brief pause as he scanned her outfit: surprise, then recalibration.

"You look… different," he said, leaning in to kiss her cheek. "Good different."

Willow smiled, tight and unreadable. "We need to talk."

His brow lifted, annoyed before it was curious. "Before dinner?"

"I'm going to Rome," she said.

He blinked. "What do you mean you're going to Rome?"

"My sister's in trouble," she said gently. "She's in jail. I leave tomorrow morning."

His expression faltered like a puzzle missing a corner. "You're joking."

Willow shook her head. "I wouldn't joke about this. She called me today. She's terrified, Dennis. She needs me."

Dennis exhaled, his composure returning like armour. "And you're just… dropping everything? Flying across the world on a whim?"

"It's not a whim," she said evenly. "It's Lily."

A faint scoff escaped him, almost too soft to catch. "What exactly do you think you can do?"

"I don't know," she admitted, voice rising. "But I can't sit here and do nothing."

The silence between them stretched taut, a rope between two cliffs. He glanced at his watch, recalculated his priorities.

"We'll talk about this after dinner," he said finally. "We're already late."

She almost said no. The word nearly burst from her mouth like an overdue truth. But instead, she nodded. Still her. Still loyal. Still trying.

Dinner was elegant and tedious.

At the candlelit restaurant, she slipped into her role with practiced ease—smiling, laughing, engaging. She answered questions about her job, asked the right ones in return. She charmed the wives, impressed the partners. Willow knew how to make people like her. It was a skill born of needing to be liked when love felt too distant to hope for.

Dennis sat beside her, glowing with approval like a man proud of a well-executed acquisition. She was polished. Presentable. His.

But she wasn't there.

Her mind kept drifting—to Rome, to Lily's trembling voice, to a man she hadn't even met yet but already resented: Luca Lombardi. Her chest ached with questions she couldn't yet ask.

When they returned to her apartment, the evening's veneer cracked. Dennis stepped inside behind her, but the warmth had drained from his smile.

"I don't get it," he said, pacing just slightly, his tone tight. "You and I are building something here, Willow. You said you wanted stability. Marriage. A life."

"I do," she said, her voice low but steady. "But that life doesn't mean turning my back on my sister when she's scared and alone."

He stopped. Faced her. "This is exactly the kind of chaos I've always tried to protect you from."

The words hit like a cold slap. Protect you from.

Willow stared at him, something inside her—small and quiet—shifting. She saw him clearly now. Not cruel. Not even unkind. But structured. Conditional. He loved the idea of her, the idea of their life. But not the real woman beneath the timelines and tidy smiles.

She drew in a breath.

"Dennis," she said, almost gently. "You should go. I have a suitcase to pack."

He didn't move.

She walked to the door and opened it.

"I'll call you when I land."

For a moment, he just stood there. Then, without a word, he stepped past her and out the door, the scent of his cologne trailing behind like a signature on a contract she was no longer interested in signing.

Willow closed the door and leaned against it, the silence folding around her like wings.

And then—for the first time in a long, long time—she exhaled.

Not with fear. Not with guilt.

But with something rare and rising.

Freedom. Uncertain. Unfamiliar.

But hers.

Chapter Two

Rome sprawled beneath his office like a living masterpiece—ancient stone and golden light, a tangle of history and humanity that pulsed with energy even in the heat of late afternoon. From the thirty-eighth floor of the Lombardi International tower, the city looked almost still, frozen in time under the weight of centuries. But inside Luca Lombardi's office, time was something else entirely—measured not in history, but in precision, power, and control.

Sunlight spilled through the floor-to-ceiling glass that framed the room like a cinematic lens, washing the sleek marble floors in molten gold. The Vatican's dome shimmered in the distance, just visible past the curve of his shoulder. He didn't glance at it. He didn't need to. He'd memorised this view years ago.

Luca sat behind a custom-built desk of black walnut and brushed steel—minimalist and commanding, like everything else in the space. The interior was masculine, clean, intentional. Grey stone walls. Sharp angles. A single abstract painting in deep crimson, its bold strokes hinting at chaos barely restrained. Every piece of furniture had been chosen not for comfort, but for message.

The man behind the desk wore that same message. Navy suit, tailored within a millimetre of perfection. White shirt, collar open, throat bare. He never wore ties unless a board demanded it or a funeral required it. Power didn't need a noose.

He leaned back in his chair, legs crossed at the knee, posture deceptively relaxed—like a lion lounging in the sun, knowing full well it still ruled the savannah.

Across from him, the company lawyer shifted in a high-backed leather chair, the kind that subtly discouraged long visits. He adjusted his glasses, clearing his throat as he dared to speak again.

"She siphoned the funds into a ghost account," the lawyer repeated, though his tone was careful now, cautious. "Used a shell company registered in Naples. It took time to trace, but we confirmed her access credentials. Lily Taylor. Twenty-two. American. Junior financial assistant, hired nine months ago."

Luca's eyes flicked toward him. Deep brown, intense, unreadable. Eyes like espresso—dark, bitter, impossible to look away from. They narrowed slightly.

"She was clever enough to cover her tracks. For a while," the lawyer added, as if reluctant to admit the thief's skill.

"But not clever enough," Luca said, his voice smooth and flat, a blade sheathed in velvet.

"No," the lawyer said quickly. "She made a mistake transferring the funds back. Got sloppy. We locked the transaction and called in the police before she could move it again."

"Good." Luca didn't blink. "File the charges. Make it public."

The lawyer hesitated. "She's… young. She claimed she was going to repay it."

Luca's jaw tightened, but his voice remained calm. "She's also a thief. People like her assume men like me won't notice when a few thousand go missing. But if I let her get away with it, I teach everyone that weakness is tolerated. That I don't see everything." He paused. "I do."

He rose to his full height—six foot three, and every inch of it carved by discipline. The subtle stretch of fabric over his shoulders reminded the room that beneath the suits and the charm lived a man forged in steel. His workouts were relentless: sunrise runs through Rome's quiet streets, punishing weight sessions, sparring in a private gym beneath his penthouse. He didn't train for vanity. He trained for control. Over his body. Over his mind. Over everything.

"She'll spend a few days in a jail cell," he said, tone colder now. "Let that sink in. Then maybe she'll realise actions have consequences."

He turned to the windows, arms folded across his chest, gaze sweeping the horizon as if it belonged to him. In many ways, it did. Rome had bent to his will, just like every city before it. Paris. London. New York. Empire by empire, deal by deal, he had built his kingdom.

"Anything else?" he asked without turning.

The lawyer stood, fumbling with his briefcase. "Just one thing. Her sister called the police station—apparently flying in from New York today."

Luca stilled. "Her sister?"

"Yes. Willow Taylor. She's not listed anywhere on the company's records. She doesn't work for us."

The name lingered in the space between them. Willow.

There was something in it. A softness. A subtle melody that didn't belong in this world of steel and balance sheets. His brow lifted, just slightly.

"Let me know when she arrives," he said, eyes still on the city.

"Of course."

The door clicked shut behind the lawyer. Silence fell again.

Luca walked slowly to the bar cart near the built-in shelves—crystal decanters, untouched whiskey, a single bottle of champagne from a deal closed years ago. He poured himself a glass of still water and dropped in a lemon slice, the rind curling like a ribbon in the ice.

He sipped slowly. His chest was tight, but not from stress. Not really. Something else. A restlessness. A gnawing sense that victory had stopped tasting like anything at all.

The water slid down cool and bitter. He set the glass aside and ran a hand through his hair, still slightly damp from his morning workout. He'd stayed too long today. Too long in the office. Too long in Rome. Too long playing the role of the man who had it all.

Every day was the same. New contracts. Bigger margins. The illusion of forward motion. And yet, behind every win was a strange emptiness. The sharper the success, the hollower it rang.

His last relationship had ended with a text message and a shrug. A supermodel. Beautiful, poised, a goddess on red carpets—but vapid beneath the surface. The moment the cameras were off, the conversation died. No spark. No curiosity. Just airbrushed boredom.

Luca wasn't looking for love. That was a lie people told themselves before they got hurt. He'd believed in it once—young and reckless, convinced that passion could be trusted. Jessica had burned that belief out of him the night he found her tangled in silk sheets with his best friend.

He hadn't raised his voice. Hadn't asked for an explanation. He'd turned around, walked out, and sealed that door behind him. Permanently.

Now he didn't do trust. He didn't do vulnerability.

He did control.

And still… some part of him—hidden, distant—ached for something real. Not love. He didn't need love.

He needed interest. Challenge. Someone who could surprise him. Someone who didn't care about the suits or the money or the headlines. Someone with questions. Fire. A mind that moved like a blade.

But he never met women like that. He met socialites and heiresses. Women who smiled on cue and gasped at his jet. Women who asked if he'd ever dated royalty, as though that were the prize.

He had. And no, it hadn't been interesting.

He was bored. And boredom was dangerous. Boredom made men reckless. Boredom made kings burn down their own kingdoms just to feel something.

He glanced down at the glowing screen of his tablet, stock numbers ticking upward. Another win. Another zero added to the bottom line.

And yet, for the first time in weeks, something flickered. Something unnameable.

The sister of a thief. A woman named Willow.

A complication. A nuisance.

But possibly… something more.

Something different.

Something interesting.

And Luca Lombardi, ruthless billionaire, master of control, felt the faintest curl of anticipation stir in his chest.

He turned back to the window, Rome glittering beneath him like a challenge waiting to be answered.

He picked up his phone and typed a quick message to his assistant, his fingers moving with practiced precision.

Lily Taylor's sister is arriving this afternoon. Arrange a car. I want to meet her. Also— get me everything we can find on her. Quietly.

He hit send, then set the phone down and leaned back in his leather chair, his gaze drawn to the floor-to-ceiling windows behind his desk. The sun was beginning its descent behind the Roman skyline, washing the city in molten gold. Shadows lengthened across the marble floor, dark and elegant, like brushstrokes on a canvas.

Something about this afternoon tugged at him. A quiet, inexplicable pull in his chest.

She was just a sister, coming to clean up a mess.

And yet…

For the first time in a long while, Luca Lombardi didn't feel bored.

Three hours later, the door to Luca Lombardi's office opened with a soft, deliberate click.

He didn't look up.

No one reached this floor without a reason—and only one man entered without knocking.

"Matteo," Luca said coolly, reclining slightly in his chair.

His chief investigator, Matteo Ricci, stepped into the expansive space, a leather portfolio tucked under one arm and the faintest flicker of intrigue in his eyes.

"She landed," Matteo said, laying the folder on Luca's desk with precision. "Willow Rose Taylor."

Luca finally shifted his gaze. "Let's hear it."

Matteo opened the portfolio, revealing a dossier and a single photograph clipped to the top.

"Twenty-four. Lives in New York City. Editorial assistant at a boutique publishing house—Bright Press. NYU graduate, English literature. No criminal record, no debt. Keeps to herself. No tabloid history, no socialite connections. She's… clean."

Luca raised an eyebrow. "That's rare."

"There's more." Matteo's voice took on a thoughtful edge. "Parents died in a car crash when she was eighteen. She raised herself from that point on. Quiet life. Steady job. Minimal contact with Lily over the years—seems their relationship is strained. Different mothers. Lily moved to Rome with her mother when she was still young."

Luca's fingers drummed once on the armrest as Matteo slid the photograph across the desk.

Willow.

She wasn't like the women Luca was used to—no designer heels, no practiced pout, no red-carpet poise. In the photo, she stood outside the airport with a battered suitcase at her side, waiting for a taxi. Her brown hair was twisted into a loose bun, a few strands escaping to frame her face with effortless grace. There was nothing posed about her— no awareness of the camera, no performance. Her gaze was fixed on something in the distance, calm and unguarded. And yet, there was something arresting about her— something real.

Unaware of her quiet, striking effect.

She looked real. Untouched by artifice. Beautiful in a way that wasn't performed but lived.

"She's booked at the Hotel Eden," Matteo added, tapping the itinerary inside the folder. "Her flight touched down at 1:07 p.m. at Fiumicino. She's headed straight to the jail where her sister's being held. Your driver is downstairs, ready to take you there."

Luca didn't respond immediately. His eyes were still on the photograph of Willow Taylor, his expression unreadable. After a beat, he closed the folder with a soft, definitive snap.

"Thank you, Matteo. That'll be all."

The door whispered shut behind his investigator, returning the office to its usual hush—but the stillness was deceptive.

Because inside Luca Lombardi, something had shifted.

He didn't know exactly what he'd expected from Lily Taylor's sister. A tearful sibling desperate to bargain? A shallow socialite trying to leverage sympathy? Someone forgettable?

Instead, he'd gotten her.

A woman who didn't seem to belong in his world of sleek suits and sharper lies—yet somehow, just from a photograph, had managed to unsettle his focus. There was no artifice to her. No self-conscious effort to impress. She hadn't posed for the camera.

She hadn't needed to.

She didn't scream for attention.

She commanded it.

Quietly. Naturally. Without trying.

And that alone was enough to pull her out of the blurred parade of women he couldn't remember and place her squarely in the centre of his attention.

Willow Taylor wasn't what he expected.

And for the first time in a very long while, Luca wasn't thinking about mergers, profits, or power plays. He wasn't calculating his next move—he was simply curious.

Intrigued.

And if he was honest with himself... a little excited.

He shrugged on his tailored jacket, checked his watch, and headed for the elevator.

Whatever waited for him at that jail—negotiation, confrontation, or something else entirely—he was ready.

Because something in his gut said this wouldn't be a typical meeting.

And he wouldn't be walking away the same man.

Chapter Three

The wheels of the plane touched down on the tarmac with a soft jolt, and Willow Taylor gripped the armrest tighter than she meant to. The captain's voice crackled overhead in Italian first, then English, announcing their arrival at Leonardo da Vinci International Airport. Fiumicino.

Rome.

Her stomach twisted with nerves and jet lag.

Willow hadn't slept on the flight. Not really. She'd drifted in and out between turbulence and half-finished thoughts—her mind looping endlessly through Lily's voice on the phone, the terror in it, the shame.

'I—I messed up. I didn't mean to. But I didn't have a choice—'

The seatbelt light dinged off, and the cabin filled with the rustling sound of travellers rising, reaching, stretching. Willow stood and grabbed her carry-on from the overhead bin, her body moving on autopilot even as her heart pounded with the enormity of what she was walking into.

Customs was a blur. The officer barely glanced at her passport. A stamp. A nod. Next.

Outside baggage claim, the chaos of arrivals swirled around her in a cacophony of languages and motion—families reuniting, taxi drivers calling out, luggage wheels clattering over tile. The air was warm, fragrant with espresso and car fumes and something faintly floral that clung to the Roman breeze.

Willow spotted her suitcase—battered navy blue, a leftover from her college days—on the carousel and heaved it off with both hands. She paused for a moment, hugging it to her chest, trying to ground herself.

This was real. This was happening.

She had crossed an ocean to fix something that might not be fixable.

With a deep breath, she moved toward the exit. Her plan was simple: get to the jail, see Lily, and try to understand what in God's name had actually happened.

Outside, the Rome sun was blinding—late afternoon light that turned the concrete golden and made everything feel like a film set. Her phone buzzed to life, catching up on missed texts from Dennis, each more frustrated than the last.

Willow, this isn't your responsibility.

You shouldn't be throwing your life away for her.

Call me when you come to your senses.

She silenced the phone without responding.

Not now.

She spotted the official taxi line and made her way toward it, suitcase bumping behind her. The man at the front of the queue gave her a courteous nod and opened the door of the next cab.

"Stazione di polizia?" she asked hesitantly, then clarified, "The jail. Where… detainees are held?"

The driver raised an eyebrow but nodded. "Carcere. Sì. Address?"

Willow fumbled for the crumpled sheet of paper she'd scribbled on back in New York—name of the police precinct, address, and Lily's case number. She handed it over, and the driver gave a short, approving grunt.

"Bene. We go."

The taxi pulled away from the curb and merged into the chaotic ballet of Roman traffic—Vespas zipping past, horns beeping not in anger but in rhythm, like punctuation. Ancient ruins blurred past her window, tucked between modern storefronts and winding alleyways. Rome was everything at once: chaotic and elegant, old, and defiant.

And somewhere in this wild, beautiful city… her sister was sitting in a jail cell.

Willow pressed her forehead against the cool glass of the window and closed her eyes for a moment, letting the hum of the cab soothe her. She didn't know what Lily had done. Not really. The story didn't add up. Embezzling money from a billionaire? It sounded like something out of a bad crime novel. But the fear in Lily's voice had been real. The regret.

Of course, Willow had to come.

Not because she had the answers. Not because she had any real plan.

But because family was family.

And no matter how messy or broken or strained that bond had become… she couldn't leave her sister to face this alone.

The taxi slowed in front of a squat, grey building flanked by a tall iron gate and uniformed guards. It wasn't what Willow expected—less like a prison, more like an office complex that had lost its soul. Still, the tension that gripped her spine said it loud and clear: this was real.

"Here," the driver said, glancing in the rearview mirror. "Carcere."

Willow nodded, forcing her voice through the knot in her throat. "Grazie."

She handed the driver a crumple of euros without counting, too distracted to care about the exchange rate. The moment she stepped out, the Roman afternoon hit her like a wall—hot, dry, and blinding.

Her suitcase landed with a dull thud on the pavement. She grabbed the handle and hauled it up the stone steps, each one heavier than the last.

A uniformed guard at the entrance raised a hand, blocking her path.

"Name and reason for visit," he said in crisp English, his tone efficient but not unkind.

"Willow Taylor. I'm here to see my sister, Lily Taylor. She was arrested yesterday."

He looked her up and down—white t-shirt, black jeans, hair in a messy twist, not exactly dressed for international negotiations—and took her passport from her hand. After a moment of scanning, he nodded.

"One moment."

Willow stood awkwardly near the entrance as he disappeared through a metal door. The minutes dragged. Her palms were sweating. Her heart thundered.

Finally, the door buzzed open again. "Follow me." Handing her passport back to her.

She stepped inside and was met by the harsh echo of her own footsteps on tile. The fluorescent lights were too bright. The walls were too white. Everything smelled faintly of bleach and worry.

They led her to a small visitation room—stark, with a plastic partition and a single chair on each side. A phone receiver hung on the wall.

"Wait here."

She left her suitcase against the wall and sat, nerves rattling in her chest like loose change. What would she even say? What did one say to a sister who'd been arrested for stealing from a billionaire?

The door on the opposite side opened.

And there was Lily.

Willow's breath caught.

She looked smaller than she remembered. Pale. Her usually perfectly styled blonde hair was pulled into a limp ponytail. No makeup. No smirk. Her clothes—standard-issue grey—hung on her like defeat.

But it was the look in her eyes that gutted Willow the most.

Ashamed. Scared. Like a child who'd broken something she couldn't fix.

Lily stepped forward, slowly, and picked up the phone. Willow mirrored her, the cold plastic receiver pressed to her ear.

"Willow," Lily said softly, her voice cracking.

Willow swallowed hard. "Hey."

Tears welled in Lily's eyes, and she looked down. "I didn't think you'd come."

"Of course I came," Willow said, voice firm despite the lump in her throat. "You're my sister."

Lily let out a shaky breath. "I didn't know who else to call. I was so stupid. I thought— I thought I could fix it before anyone noticed."

Willow leaned in, her voice low but firm. "Just tell me the truth. What happened, Lily?"

Lily's gaze dropped to her lap, fingers twisting in the hem of her thin cotton shirt. "It was… complicated. I got behind on rent, and there were bills—things just got out of hand."

Willow frowned. "That doesn't explain stealing from your boss. From Luca Lombardi."

The name landed heavy between them.

Lily flinched. "I know who he is."

"Then you know how serious this is," Willow said, struggling to keep her voice even. "Why didn't you come to me? I would've helped."

Lily hesitated, her jaw tightening before she finally whispered, "Because I didn't think you would."

Willow blinked. "What? Why?"

"Because of Mom," Lily said bitterly. "Because her affair broke up your family. Because I'm the reason your parents split and everything fell apart. I figured… if I asked for help, you'd just say no."

Willow's breath caught in her throat. She hadn't expected that.

The air between them thickened with everything they'd never said—the years of distance, the awkward holidays, the resentment neither of them had dared to name.

Willow swallowed hard. "You should've asked anyway."

Lily's voice cracked. "I was ashamed, Will."

Willow sat back, the ache behind her ribs tightening. "What exactly is he threatening?"

"Prison. There's already a lawyer. Charges are being filed," Lily said. "He's not bluffing."

Willow closed her eyes for a second, then nodded. "Okay. I'll try to talk to him."

Lily's head snapped up. "What?"

"I'll go to his office tomorrow. I don't have an appointment, but I'll find a way. I'll ask him to reconsider."

"You can't," Lily said, panic creeping into her voice. "He's not the kind of man you just walk up to. He's cold. Untouchable."

Willow's jaw set. "Then it's time someone tried anyway."

For a long beat, Lily just stared at her. And then, behind the exhaustion and shame, a flicker of something else—hope.

Willow caught the door as it swung behind her and held it tight.

Because she hadn't flown across the ocean to give up.

And she wasn't leaving Rome without fighting for her sister.

The sun had dipped lower in the sky, gilding the rooftops of Rome in molten amber as Willow descended the cracked stone steps of the jail, each one echoing faintly in the heavy summer air. Her suitcase bumped behind her with every uneven slab, its small wheels clicking like a metronome to her fatigue. The heat clung to her skin, sticky and relentless, and her sensible black flats—chosen for practicality over style—offered no relief to her aching feet.

Her muscles throbbed from the long flight and hours of tense waiting. She hadn't eaten since New York. Her mouth was dry, her temples throbbed, and a headache bloomed just behind her eyes. All she wanted was to reach the hotel, peel off the travel-stiff clothes, take a long shower, and maybe—just maybe—let herself break for a moment. A minute of tears. That was all she'd allow.

She was halfway to the curb, blinking against the late sun, when a shadow separated from the others on the sidewalk. A man in a sharply tailored charcoal suit stepped into her path, his posture erect, his features unreadable behind designer sunglasses. His Italian accent wrapped around each syllable like velvet over steel.

"Miss Willow Taylor?"

She froze, the sound of her name tightening the grip on her suitcase handle. Her heart gave a small kick.

"Yes?" she said, guarded and wary.

The man offered a nod, formal and restrained. "Mr. Lombardi would like a word."

Willow blinked. Her breath snagged on the name. "Luca Lombardi?"

It tasted strange on her tongue—heavy and immediate, like the name of a storm she hadn't expected to encounter so soon. She had only just begun to form a strategy, barely mapped out the beginning of a plan for tomorrow. Now he was summoning her like she was already a piece in his game.

Her eyes flicked to the street—and that's when she saw it.

A limousine waited at the curb, long and black and gleaming like onyx in the sun. Its windows were tinted to near opacity, and the vehicle hummed softly with restrained power, ready to glide away on command.

The suited man stepped aside and gestured toward it with quiet precision.

Willow hesitated, the air thick with a thousand warnings. This was not how it was supposed to happen. She had planned to be composed, prepared, armed with facts and a speech—tomorrow. Not ambushed on the street, not sweaty and jet-lagged and emotionally frayed.

But then the back door of the limo opened.

And there he was.

Luca Lombardi.

He sat like a man born to dominance, one leg crossed loosely over the other, exuding a lazy kind of control that made it clear he never needed to demand authority—it bent to him on instinct. He wore a navy suit that clung to his broad frame like it had been sewn onto him, the open collar of his white shirt revealing a glimpse of tanned skin and smooth confidence. A shadow of stubble framed his sharp jaw, and his dark hair was slicked back with effortless precision.

But it was his eyes that arrested her—cool, commanding, unflinching. The eyes of a man who missed nothing.

"Miss Taylor," he said, his voice smooth and low, laced with unspoken power. "You've had a long day."

Willow stared, breath caught in her throat. "You were watching me?"

He offered the barest shrug. "I like to be informed."

"Of what? Strangers coming to plead for their criminal siblings?"

A ghost of a smile touched his mouth, more calculation than amusement. "Something like that."

The heat on her skin suddenly had nothing to do with the sun. She took a step closer, eyes narrowed. "What do you want?"

"To offer you a ride to your hotel," he said smoothly. "Rome can be… overwhelming to navigate in the afternoon traffic. Especially for someone new. Please." He gestured toward the leather seat across from him with a kind of elegant finality.

Her eyes flicked to the driver's seat. The man in the suit lingered nearby, watching silently, still, and unreadable.

Her gut twisted in knots. Every instinct told her to run, to say no, to hold on to what little control she had left. But another part of her—rational, tired, and painfully aware of what was at stake—knew she couldn't afford to offend him. Not now. Not when Lily's future hung in the balance.

She exhaled, almost shaky, and gave a slight nod.

The driver took her suitcase without a word and loaded it into the boot. Willow smoothed the front of her wrinkled t-shirt, squared her shoulders, and stepped forward.

The door shut behind her with a soft, almost ominous click. The outside world vanished, muffled by the thick doors and luxury silence. Inside, the air was cool, perfumed faintly with leather and something citrusy and clean. Minimalist. Impeccable. Intimidating.

Luca watched her like he was already solving her, like she was a puzzle he'd decided would amuse him for an afternoon.

"You're not what I expected," he said, his voice deceptively calm.

"Good," Willow replied, chin lifting. "Because I didn't come here to impress you."

His eyes didn't waver. They scanned her—carefully, methodically—from the stubborn angle of her chin to the flyaway strand of hair clinging to her cheek. Then down to her hands, clenched too tightly in her lap. When he leaned forward slightly, resting his forearms on his knees, the air seemed to shrink between them.

She sat up straighter in response. She could feel his attention like heat on her skin—steady, penetrating, not unkind but wholly unapologetic. A dare. A warning.

Luca's lips curved—slow, deliberate. A smile that could dismantle defences, or destroy lives, depending on how it was used.

"No. I can see that."

The limousine pulled smoothly into traffic, melting into the golden chaos of Rome.

And somewhere beneath her ribs, Willow felt it—that quiet, unmistakable shift in the air.

The game had begun.

But this time, she wasn't entirely sure whose move it was.

Chapter Four

Luca hadn't planned to meet her today.

He was going to wait.

The strategy had been simple: let her simmer in the reality of her sister's mess, let the weight of consequence settle like ash. Then, tomorrow—when desperation had softened her edges—his assistant would schedule a meeting on his terms. His office, his rules, his terrain. Controlled, deliberate, every advantage leaning quietly in his favour.

That had been the plan.

But then he saw her.

Through the tinted window of the limo, Luca Lombardi sat like a king in exile—detached, unreadable. His gaze drifted lazily across the stone façade of the Roman jail. And then it caught. Fixed. Unmoving.

A lone figure stood on the sidewalk, suitcase by her side. Shoulders taut with fatigue. Head high with quiet defiance.

Willow Taylor.

She didn't look like anyone who usually crossed his path.

No designer heels, no curated elegance, no scent that announced itself five feet in advance. Just a plain white T-shirt, black jeans faded at the seams, and flats worn so thin they may as well have walked across continents. Her strawberry-blonde hair was twisted into a knot, loose strands escaping with a stubbornness that resisted polish.

It should have looked careless.

It didn't.

It looked like temptation—dressed in defiance.

He leaned forward, just slightly, watching from the shadows. No fanfare to her presence. No performative femininity. Just quiet strength wrapped in exhaustion and resolve. Something in his gut shifted.

Damn.

He gave the order to let her in before he knew why.

By the time the door opened, and she stepped inside, he'd already slipped back into his role: cold, unreadable, powerful. He would keep this clinical. Detached. Let her squirm. Let her understand the distance between them.

But then—she spoke.

No fear. No tremor. No sugary charm.

Just steel.

It surprised him.

Worse—it stirred something far more inconvenient.

She sat across from him, knees drawn close, hands clasped in her lap. But her chin was up. Her gaze locked with his—not defiant, but honest. Unflinching.

Luca let his eyes drift, slow and deliberate. A study masquerading as indifference. Cataloging her.

Her skin hadn't dulled from travel. Her cheeks carried a faint flush—heat? nerves? fire? Her lips were full, unsmiling. The kind that made a man wonder what it would take to make them curve. To see if the steel in her voice would soften when she smiled.

He shouldn't be noticing these things.

She was a complication. A mess to clean up. A sister of a thief.

And yet…

There was something about her. A magnetic stillness. She didn't try to be beautiful— she was. Not in the curated, strategic way the women in his world were. Willow Taylor didn't care what she looked like when the sun hit her hair. Or worse—she knew and didn't give a damn.

That, he realised, made her more dangerous than any heiress he'd ever seduced.

Because he didn't know what she wanted.

And he hated not knowing.

He shifted, the whisper of his Brioni suit filling the silence. A calculated movement. Most women fidgeted under his gaze. Blushed. Looked away.

Willow didn't flinch.

She was clearly tired—the slump of her shoulders, the slight tremor in her fingers—but she held herself with a grace that wasn't performative. It was survival. It was earned.

And she was sitting in his car.

He had invited her in to test her.

Now he wasn't sure who was being tested.

Willow felt his gaze.

Not a glance. Not the distracted flicker most men gave before returning to their phones or their egos.

This was different.

It was razor-sharp. Surgical.

And it made her skin prickle.

She straightened instinctively, spine stiff against the butter-soft leather. Hands folded tight in her lap so he wouldn't see them shake. Her suitcase had vanished, her hair was falling loose, her shoes had lost their colour to travel and Rome's chaotic streets.

But none of it mattered.

She met his gaze, unwavering.

If he expected her to shrink, to plead, he'd be disappointed.

And yet—she wasn't sure he was disappointed.

His stare lingered. On her face. Her mouth. The slope of her neck where one stubborn curl had slipped free. Not lustful. Not crude. Just… focused. Intimate in a way that felt like a quiet threat.

Like he was peeling her apart without touching her.

Her breath caught. She lifted her chin a fraction higher.

Then, calmly:

'I didn't come here to impress you.'

His smile was slow. Not kind. Not cruel. The kind of smile a man gave when he stumbled across something unexpected—and wasn't sure whether to destroy it or treasure it.

Willow's heart stuttered.

This wasn't supposed to happen.

She wasn't supposed to feel anything. Not this flicker of awareness, not the curl of uncertainty in her stomach. She was here for Lily. To stay grounded. Rational. Immune.

But Luca Lombardi didn't seem like a man anyone stayed immune to.

He didn't try to be magnetic.

He just was.

His power was quiet, ingrained, woven into every breath. Dangerous not because it shouted—but because it didn't have to.

There was something behind his eyes. Not passion. Not yet.

A warning.

A temptation.

A threat.

Maybe all three.

She looked away. Watched Rome blur by the window. Watched golden light slant over ancient buildings and strangers on Vespas who had no idea her world was shifting.

But she still felt it.

The shift.

Something had begun.

And she wasn't ready.

Not for him.

Not for this.

Not for how much she didn't want to stop it.

Inside the car, the silence stretched.

Rome blazed golden outside—reckless, beautiful, alive.

But in the limo, it was too still. Breathless.

Until Luca spoke.

His voice was low. Measured.

"Have you been to Rome before?"

She turned slowly. That wasn't the question she'd expected.

"No."

A beat. "First time."

He nodded, storing the information away.

"A shame. You arrived under unfortunate circumstances."

She exhaled a dry sound. Half a laugh.

"That's one way to put it."

His gaze remained fixed. Still studying. Still dissecting.

"Most people come for the history. The art. The food."

A hint of amusement touched his mouth.

"Not the jails."

Willow's jaw tightened.

"It wasn't on my bucket list."

The amusement deepened. Not mockery—interest. He liked being surprised. And she had surprised him.

He leaned in slightly. The movement subtle. But the air shifted again.

"And yet here you are. Marching into a city you've never seen, defending a sister you barely speak to, sitting across from a man you know almost nothing about."

His tone wasn't mocking. Just… curious.

Willow met his gaze.

"I know enough."

He tilted his head.

"Do you?"

The question slithered under her skin.

She looked away before he could see too much.

"I know you can drop the charges. That's enough for now."

A beat of silence.

Then, soft:

"You have courage, Miss Taylor. I admire that."

She turned back to him.

"You say that like it surprises you."

Something flickered in his eyes. Brief. Human.

Then he said it—quiet, almost to himself.

"It does."

The limo turned. Rome softened around them.

Willow folded her arms. She needed something to hold.

"You don't know me."

Luca didn't argue.

He just said:

"No. But I'd like to."

And that—God help her—was the problem.

Because part of her wanted that, too.

And that was the most dangerous thing of all.

The limousine pulled to a smooth stop in front of Hotel Eden, its elegant façade glowing under the golden Roman twilight. Willow looked up through the tinted window at the marble entrance, the polished doormen in white gloves, the cascade of flowers climbing the stone walls.

Her stomach fluttered. This wasn't just a hotel—it was a statement.

The door opened, and Luca stepped out first, effortlessly commanding the space without even trying. He turned back and offered a hand.

Willow hesitated.

But her legs were stiff, and her pride had taken enough hits for one day. She took his hand.

His fingers were warm and sure around hers, and the contact sent a pulse of something unwanted—something inconvenient—through her chest. He released her almost as soon as she was on her feet, stepping aside as the concierge approached, already smiling.

"Signor Lombardi," the man said with a deferential nod. "Benvenuto. Sempre un piacere."

"Grazie, Carlo," Luca replied easily. "Miss Taylor is checking in."

The concierge turned his attention to Willow, who was still adjusting to the whiplash—from detention centres to a Roman dream.

"Your name, signorina?"

"Willow Taylor," she said slowly, stepping forward to the desk. "I have a reservation. I booked a standard—"

Before she could finish, the concierge glanced at the computer screen and then smiled wider.

"Ah, sì. You have been upgraded to a deluxe suite, with city view and terrace. Courtesy of Mr. Lombardi."

Willow blinked. "I didn't... I didn't request that."

"No need. It is our pleasure," he said smoothly. "There will be no additional charge."

Luca said nothing, but the faint curve of his mouth told her everything—he had arranged it without asking. Without even blinking.

Willow turned to him. "That wasn't necessary."

"I know," Luca said, unbothered. "But I don't like the idea of you sleeping next to an ice machine."

"That's not—" she started, but the concierge was already gesturing toward the bellhop, who arrived to whisk her suitcase away with practiced elegance.

"It is done," Luca said. "Enjoy the view."

Willow followed the bellhop reluctantly, feeling the weight of his presence behind her as they stepped into the glittering lobby—marble floors, chandeliers like constellations, hushed voices, and quiet wealth humming in the air.

At the elevator, she turned.

"You do this for all the women whose sisters steal from you?" she asked quietly.

Luca's eyes met hers—cool on the surface, but with that same flicker underneath. The one she was starting to recognise. Interest. Heat. A flicker of something he hadn't meant her to see.

"No," he said quietly. "Only the ones who surprise me."

Willow's breath caught.

Before she could summon a reply, the elevator chimed softly behind her. The bellhop gave a polite gesture, holding the doors.

Luca stepped back, giving her space, but not distance.

"I'll be in touch tomorrow morning," he said. "We'll talk."

She nodded, her voice barely above a whisper. "Thank you."

Their eyes held for a beat longer than necessary—then the doors slid shut between them.

Inside the mirrored elevator, Willow exhaled, pressing her back to the wall as if the glass could steady her.

Her heart was racing. Unreasonably so.

She wasn't sure what startled her more.

That she was standing in one of the most luxurious hotels in Rome…or that some part of her—deep and dangerously curious—didn't want to leave.

Chapter Five

He didn't look back.

Not as the elevator doors slid shut behind him.

Not as her eyes clung to his, wide with questions she didn't dare ask.

Luca kept his back straight, spine rigid with the discipline of a man who'd taught himself long ago never to hesitate. His face was unreadable—deliberately neutral. Controlled.

The concierge offered a polite "Buona sera," and Luca returned the faintest nod. The bellhop lingered just a moment longer, waiting for a cue, a command—anything. But there was nothing. Not from him.

Because Luca Lombardi said nothing.

And yet, his pulse was louder than it should've been.

It echoed behind his ribs, steady but undeniable, like the warning beat of something beginning to slip through his grip.

He stepped through the gilded revolving doors of Hotel Eden and into the soft embrace of Roman twilight. The air was warm, tinged with jasmine and the fading gold of another Mediterranean sunset. Somewhere nearby, church bells chimed the hour. A breeze caught the hem of his suit jacket as cars hummed past in murmurs of luxury and motion.

But Luca barely registered them.

Because this wasn't how it was supposed to go.

This was meant to be a clean exchange—intimidation, softened by civility. Show her the edges of his world. Remind her who held the power. Press just enough to make her fold. That had been the plan.

But then she spoke.

With that calm, steel voice that didn't waver.

Then she met his gaze like she wasn't afraid of him. Like she wouldn't ever be.

Then she surprised him.

Again.

He reached the edge of the piazza, his polished shoes clicking against the stone as his driver stepped forward, holding the door of the sleek black car open. Luca paused, one hand braced against the doorframe, his jaw clenched tight as the city shimmered in the distance behind tinted glass.

This should be simple.

It wasn't.

Willow Taylor wasn't beautiful in the way women usually were in his world—polished, posed, rehearsed. She was something else.

She was real.

Painfully, achingly real.

There was no façade. No performance. Just a kind of bruised loyalty that echoed in every word she spoke, in the way her voice softened when she talked about her sister, even through her anger. A weariness that hadn't dulled her strength.

And that mouth—

Soft and unsmiling, even when she clearly wanted to bite back.

He had seen it tighten as she fought to stay composed. Had seen the way she folded her hands in her lap, knuckles white, willing herself not to react.

He shouldn't have said what he did. He knew that.

'No. But I'd like to.'

It had slipped out before he could stop it. A rare truth, spoken in a moment he wasn't supposed to feel anything.

But damn it, he meant it.

Luca finally ducked into the back seat and shut the door behind him. The city moved on around him—alive, elegant, uncaring. But inside the car, the air was different now. Close. Still.

He didn't speak as the driver pulled away. Didn't reach for his phone or glance at his watch.

Because his mind was still inside the hotel lobby.

With her.

In that elevator.

With the girl who hadn't flinched.

With the girl who made his carefully constructed detachment feel like glass under pressure.

Willow Taylor.

With trembling hands.

And unshakable eyes.

And just like that—

She wasn't a complication anymore.

She was a problem.

A beautiful, inconvenient, unforgettable problem.

The suite was bigger than her entire apartment.

Willow stood frozen just inside the doorway, her suitcase abandoned near the velvet bench, the bellhop's words still echoing at the edges of her mind: "If you need anything, simply call."

Anything.

She didn't even know what that meant in a place like this. Not really.

The room looked like something out of a dream—an impossibly elegant dream stitched together in soft golds and muted creams. Marble accents glowed under hidden lighting, and a chandelier shimmered overhead like a constellation made just for her. It was beautiful. It was surreal.

It was not hers.

She took a tentative step forward, the plush carpet muffling her movements like a secret, and glanced around at the impossible luxury. The bed was the size of a small continent. A tray of chocolate-covered strawberries rested beside a glass bottle of sparkling water and a folded welcome card embossed with gold script.

It all felt absurd.

Then she saw the windows—floor-to-ceiling, framing a breathtaking view of the Eternal City, bathed in the lavender hush of early evening. She moved instinctively toward them, slipping off her shoes without thinking, her bare feet sinking into the carpet as she opened the glass doors to the terrace.

And then she froze again.

Rome stretched out before her like a masterpiece—warm terracotta rooftops, winding cobbled streets, ancient domes catching the last of the sun like cupped hands. The scent of blooming bougainvillea floated up on the breeze, mingling with the faintest trace of incense and motor oil. Somewhere in the distance, a bell tolled, slow and solemn, marking the passage of time in a city older than belief.

She wrapped her arms around herself and exhaled slowly.

She shouldn't be here.

Not in this suite. Not in this hotel. Not on a private terrace overlooking a city she'd only ever dreamed of visiting while scrimping to pay rent and utility bills. And certainly not thinking about him.

But Luca Lombardi lingered.

In the scent of his cologne still haunting the air. In the echo of his voice—velvet-wrapped steel, laced with something she didn't want to name.

'Only the ones who surprise me.'

Her heart fluttered. Again. Traitorous. Uninvited.

She turned from the view and stepped back inside, needing solid ground, needing space that didn't smell like temptation, wealth, and confusion. But even the bathroom was palatial—a spa masquerading as a washroom. Gold fixtures. A soaking tub large enough to swim laps in. Thick robes hung like clouds, ready to swallow her whole.

Willow sat gingerly on the edge of the bed and pressed the heels of her palms into her eyes.

This was a trap.

A beautiful, luxurious, intoxicating trap—designed to lower her defences, to make her forget why she was here. To make her feel... special.

But she wasn't special.

She was just a girl trying to fix her sister's mess. A girl with no business catching the attention of someone like Luca. No business feeling anything about him at all.

And yet—when he looked at her like that…

She let out a shaky breath and lay back, staring at the intricately painted ceiling as if it might offer clarity. The sheets were impossibly soft, almost sinfully so. Nothing in her life had ever felt this gentle. This welcoming.

And it scared her.

He'd said he'd be in touch tomorrow.

Willow closed her eyes.

Tomorrow felt too soon.

But also… not soon enough.

She sat on the edge of the enormous bed; her fingers curled around her phone like it might bite. The suite had gone dim, now lit only by the amber glow of a bedside lamp. Outside, Rome shimmered with possibility and music and wine-soaked conversation.

Inside, she felt impossibly small.

She stared at Dennis's name on the screen for a long time. Her almost-fiancé. Her safe place. Her plan.

Her future, theoretically.

She pressed the call button.

It rang twice.

Then—

"Willow?" His voice was brisk. Clipped. The faint sound of keys clicking in the background, a printer whirring. She could picture him perfectly: in his condo, sleeves rolled up, leaning over spreadsheets with surgical focus.

"Hey," she said softly. "Did I catch you at a bad time?"

"Well, I didn't expect to hear from you so soon," Dennis replied, not unkind, but not exactly warm. "Are you alright?"

"I'm okay," she said, though the words didn't feel entirely true. "I just… needed to hear a familiar voice."

A pause. Then, "Where are you staying?"

Willow glanced around the suite, as if speaking the truth aloud might anchor her. "Hotel Eden. It's… really beautiful."

Dennis gave a low whistle. "That's a five-star place. How on earth did you afford that?"

She hesitated. "I have savings. Luca Lombardi arranged a suite though."

A longer pause.

"The billionaire you're negotiating with. The one pressing charges?"

"He's not—well, yes. But it's not like that. He just wanted to talk. I think he wanted to see if I was serious about helping Lily."

Dennis sighed, the sound loud in her ear. "And you agreed to stay in a hotel suite he paid for?"

"It wasn't like I had a choice," she said, sharper than she intended. "I can't afford to offend him. And when someone that powerful says, 'you're staying here,' it doesn't feel like a suggestion."

"You should've called me."

"I'm calling you now."

"But after the fact," he said. "Willow, you flew across the world to defend your screw-up sister, and now you're being hosted by the man she stole from. Do you hear how insane that sounds?"

Willow flinched. "She's still my sister."

"I know," he said, voice cooling again. "But this whole thing is dangerous. You don't know this man. You don't owe Lily your sanity—or your safety."

There it was.

The line in the sand.

"I didn't call to argue," Willow said, quieter now. "I just wanted to talk. To feel... grounded."

A beat.

Then Dennis said, "Well, you can't expect me not to worry when you throw yourself into something like this without a plan. Are you at least keeping your distance from him?"

Her silence was answer enough.

"Willow."

"He hasn't done anything," she said quickly. "He's been... respectful."

Dennis exhaled again. Sharper this time. "Right. The criminal mastermind is being respectful. Look, just get through the week and come home, okay? We'll figure this out together. Like we planned."

Like we planned.

The words sat like stones in her chest. Predictable. Practical. Safe.

But not warm. Not what she needed tonight.

"I'll call you tomorrow," she murmured.

"Good. Please do."

He hung up first.

Willow stared at the phone for a long time, its screen dark and silent in her hand. Then she lay back against the mountain of pillows, the city lights brushing faint gold across the ceiling.

And she wondered why she felt lonelier now than before she made the call.

Sunlight spilled through the sheer curtains, golden and soft, casting long shadows across the marble floor. The air smelled faintly of jasmine and citrus—leftover traces from the bouquet sitting on the glass-topped table near the window.

Willow rubbed her eyes as she padded barefoot across the suite, still wrapped in the hotel's impossibly plush robe. A soft knock had roused her moments ago. When she opened the door, no one was there—just the flowers.

White peonies, creamy garden roses, and sprigs of fresh eucalyptus. Tasteful. Understated. Elegant.

Tucked between the blooms was a small cream-coloured envelope.

She opened it carefully.

The note inside was handwritten in an elegant, steady scrawl.

A car will pick you up at 10 a.m. – L.

No greeting. No explanation. No signature beyond the single initial.

Willow stared at the note for a long moment; her heart ticking faster than it should have.

She glanced at the clock. 8:17.

"Of course," she muttered, setting the note down with a soft thud. He wasn't going to ask. He was going to orchestrate.

Still… she found herself stepping closer to the flowers, fingertips brushing a soft petal. They smelled divine.

A part of her wanted to be annoyed. Another part—deeper, quieter—was unsettled by how easily Luca Lombardi had slipped into the cracks of her carefully maintained defences.

She looked out over the terrace, where Rome stretched wide and golden beneath the morning sun. The view was staggering—rooftops and domes and bell towers basking in the hush of early day.

She wrapped her arms around herself, still holding the note.

10 a.m.

Not a question.

An invitation disguised as a command.

And the part that startled her the most?

She was already wondering what she should wear.

At exactly 10a.m., the sleek black car pulled up to the curb in front of Hotel Eden.

Willow stepped outside, dressed simply—white sundress, her hair pulled into a loose braid. She hadn't planned to look like anything in particular. But somehow, she still found herself checking her reflection before she left the suite.

The driver opened the door with a polite nod.

"Miss Taylor."

She slid inside, gripping her purse a little tighter than necessary.

"Where are we going?" she asked.

The driver smiled faintly in the rearview mirror. "Signor Lombardi asked that I not spoil the surprise."

Of course he did.

The car glided through the Roman streets, weaving past piazzas and narrow alleys, past open-air cafés, and corner vendors. Willow craned her neck, trying to guess—but the turns didn't lead to the business district. Or the jail. Or anywhere remotely official.

Twenty minutes later, the black car turned off the main road and crept down a narrow, cobbled lane shaded by olive trees. Willow leaned toward the window, curiosity prickling her skin. The neighbourhood had a quiet charm—old stone walls, ivy-covered arches, and that worn, romantic feel only centuries of history could give.

They pulled up to a modest iron gate nestled between tall hedges. No grand entrance. No doorman. Just an unassuming archway, nearly hidden by cascading bougainvillea.

The driver got out and walked around to open her door. With a nod, he stepped ahead, unlocking the gate and holding it open. "This way, signorina."

Willow stepped out, her heels crunching softly on the gravel path. As she passed through the gate, the noise of the street fell away like a curtain had been drawn.

Beyond it lay a hidden garden.

And it was breathtaking.

Completely enclosed by stone walls and lush greenery, it felt like a secret tucked inside the heart of Rome. Bougainvillea spilled from the walls in magenta waves, and lemon trees stood like sentinels, their golden fruit glowing against the glossy leaves. Soft ivy crept up the aged stone columns that framed a vine-covered pergola. Beneath it, a single table had been set with white linen and sparkling crystal—like something out of a magazine, too beautiful to be real. A full breakfast spread was arranged across the table: croissants dusted with sugar, fresh berries, cheeses, cured meats, still-warm bread, and a carafe of orange juice catching the morning light.

And seated at the table, legs crossed and newspaper in hand, was Luca.

Casually elegant in a crisp white shirt, sleeves rolled to the elbows, sunglasses resting on the table beside his espresso cup. Like he belonged there. Like he belonged everywhere.

Willow blinked. "Seriously?"

He looked up, folding the paper with smooth, deliberate precision before setting it aside with a faint smile.

"I thought we could talk somewhere more civilised than a boardroom."

She raised an eyebrow. "This is your idea of civilised?"

"I don't believe in bad coffee and fluorescent lights," he said, rising from his seat with effortless grace. "Please—sit."

Willow stepped cautiously onto the flagstone terrace, eyes scanning the space like it might suddenly shift into something more reasonable. It didn't. The setting was too romantic. Too curated. Too… intimate.

Her voice was wary. "I thought this was a business conversation."

Luca stepped behind her and pulled out her chair. "Everything's a conversation. Some just taste better with fresh fruit and Italian sun."

She hesitated. It would have been easier if he'd brought her to an office with cold air-conditioning and legal pads. Instead, she found herself inhaling the scent of lemon blossoms and warm pastry, her stomach rumbling in betrayal.

Still, she sat—slowly—and met his gaze across the table. "This isn't necessary."

"I know," he said easily, pouring her a glass of orange juice. The carafe clinked softly against the rim. "But I find people are more honest when they feel… at ease."

Willow studied him. He was calm. Controlled. But something about his expression was watchful, calculating beneath the charm.

"And you think this will put me at ease?" she asked, arching a brow.

Luca didn't answer right away.

Instead, he took a moment to look at her—really look. As if trying to read past her words, past the polished armour she'd wrapped herself in. Then, slowly, he smiled. Not the arrogant grin she'd seen in photos, but something quieter. Almost thoughtful.

"No. But I hoped it might distract you long enough to forget your guard."

Willow's breath caught.

Just for a second.

The sun filtered through the pergola above them, casting delicate shadows across the linen. Somewhere in the distance, a church bell chimed.

She reached for her fork and stabbed a piece of melon. "You're going to need better strategy than lemon trees and pastries."

Luca leaned back in his chair, his eyes glinting in the dappled light. Amused. Undeterred.

"Challenge accepted."

Chapter Six

She wore a simple white sundress—and it ruined him.

No silk, no heels, no dramatic entrance. Just soft cotton that moved with the breeze, bare shoulders that caught the sunlight like porcelain, and that braid—loose, imperfect, trailing down her back like a line he wanted to follow with his hands. She hadn't even tried, and yet the effect was devastating.

There was no makeup, no glittering accessories, no effort to impress.

But she walked into the garden like she belonged in it.

Her beauty didn't shout. It didn't perform. It simply was. It radiated from her like heat from the sun—quiet, constant, inescapable. Her skin was kissed by sunlight, a natural glow that made highlighters and filters look ridiculous. And that braid… God help him, he hadn't thought a braid could undo him, but here he was, unable to tear his gaze away, barely remembering the speech he'd spent half the night rehearsing.

She looked even more beautiful than she had yesterday.

Not in the polished, red-carpet sense he was used to. Not in the sleek, styled way women usually presented themselves around him—sharp tailoring, bold lips, the soft weaponry of curated seduction.

Willow Taylor was something else entirely.

Unvarnished. Unapologetic.

Real.

And that made her dangerous in a way he hadn't accounted for.

Luca took a sip of coffee—bitter, scalding—more to anchor himself than for the taste. His fingers curled around the porcelain cup, eyes drifting around the garden like he could steady himself with ivy and sunshine alone. He'd chosen this place on instinct— Villa Serata, one of his quiet properties tucked into the hills above Trastevere. He almost never brought anyone here. It wasn't on any client itinerary. No press photos. No charity galas. No entourage.

Just climbing ivy, lemon trees, and stillness.

His assistant had looked at him like he'd lost his mind when he rejected every typical venue—the glass-walled conference room at Lombardi Capital, the rooftop at the Palazzo Aurelio, the executive lounge that reeked of money and control.

But this wasn't a negotiation he wanted under fluorescent lights.

He didn't want her thinking of him as a billionaire, or a CEO, or the man holding her sister's future like a coin between his fingers.

He wanted her to see something else.

Something more honest. More human.

Something he wasn't even sure existed anymore—but if it did, it lived here, in this walled garden, in the filtered sun and weathered stone.

The garden had been restored years ago by an old friend of his mother's—an artist who believed nature needed only gentle guidance to become divine. Every stone path and flowering vine had been placed with quiet intention. The place was meant to feel hidden. Sacred. A breath of calm in a city that never slept.

Yet today, it didn't feel like than a sanctuary.

It felt like a gamble.

Because she was sitting across from him now—unassuming, quietly luminous, her fingers curled around a glass of orange juice, sunlight tangled in her hair like strands of gold.

And he suddenly couldn't remember why he ever thought this would be simple.

Willow set down her glass, the light catching in the amber liquid. Her eyes, clear and unreadable, lifted to his.

"Why here?" she asked quietly. "This doesn't feel like a man trying to make a bargain. It feels like a man trying to impress a woman."

There it was. Direct. No hesitation. No flirtation in her tone—just curiosity, laced with caution.

Luca's jaw flexed slightly. She wasn't wrong. But she wasn't entirely right, either.

"I didn't want to meet you in my office," he said, his voice low. "I know what that place does to people. The glass walls. The pressure. The sense that everything's being watched or measured."

She tilted her head slightly, listening.

"I wanted you to see me without the title," he added, watching her reaction. "Not Luca Lombardi, CEO, but just… Luca. The man who drinks too much espresso. The man who still remembers how this garden looked before it was restored. The man who…" He stopped himself, not finishing the sentence. It was already more than he intended to give.

Willow looked around slowly, taking in the ivy, the crumbling stone archway blooming with wild roses, the breeze dancing through lemon trees. It was beautiful. Effortlessly so.

"You could've had this conversation anywhere," she said softly. "But you brought me here."

"I did." His gaze lingered on her. "Because I hoped this place might make it harder to lie. For both of us."

A beat passed. Long enough for a bird to chirp nearby. Long enough for something unspoken to settle between them.

"I'm not here to lie," she said finally. "I'm here for my sister."

"I know." He leaned forward slightly, the playful glint in his eyes tempered now by something deeper. "But you're also here as yourself. And I find… I'd rather talk to that woman."

Her expression shifted, almost imperceptibly. A flicker of surprise. Maybe even a flicker of something else.

She looked away first.

And Luca, for once, didn't feel triumphant about it.

Willow reached for a croissant, tore off a piece, and said without looking at him, "So you're telling me this isn't a performance."

Luca raised a brow. "Pardon?"

She popped the bite into her mouth, chewed thoughtfully, then glanced at him with deliberate calm. "You brought me to a hidden garden at a villa most locals don't even know exists. There's antique silver on the table, pressed linen, citrus trees strategically placed to catch the breeze… and you're telling me you just wanted a more honest conversation?"

A slow smile tugged at his mouth. "You think this was staged?"

"I think you're a man who doesn't make a move without calculating the outcome." She reached for her juice, eyes still on him. "So no, I don't believe this is just about fresh air and fruit."

Luca sat back in his chair, arms folding. Damn. She was sharp.

"I underestimated you," he murmured, not hiding the admiration in his voice.

"Most people do," she said, sipping her juice. "And that usually works out well for me."

He chuckled softly, shaking his head. "I didn't peg you for ruthless."

"I'm not." She set the glass down, her gaze steady. "But I'm not naive either. You say you wanted to talk without titles or pressure—but you're still the man who holds my sister's fate in his hands. That hasn't changed, no matter how beautiful the setting."

Luca's smile faded, just slightly. She wasn't wrong. And she wasn't afraid to say it.

"But here's what I haven't figured out," Willow continued, voice quieter now. "If this is just about testing me—seeing how far I'll go to clean up Lily's mess—why go to this much trouble? Why not scare me into backing off? Why..." Her gaze flicked to his. "Why make it comfortable for me?"

Luca didn't answer right away. He watched her as the morning sun kissed her shoulders, her braid falling slightly loose, the white sundress glowing against her skin.

There were many ways he could answer.

But none of them felt like the truth.

Finally, he leaned forward again and said simply, "Because I wanted to."

Willow blinked, caught off guard for just a moment.

He let the silence stretch between them.

She stared at him for a moment, incredulous. "So that's your whole strategy now? Surprise and citrus?"

Luca laughed—a real one this time. Low and warm.

"Like I said," he said, lifting his glass toward her in a toast, "challenge accepted."

Willow met his gaze for a heartbeat longer than necessary.

Then she clinked her glass softly against his.

"Game on, Mr. Lombardi."

The clink of their glasses faded into the soft rustle of leaves. A breeze stirred the lemon trees, carrying the faintest hint of something floral—lavender, maybe. Willow leaned back in her chair, the edge of a smile still ghosting her lips, but Luca could see it— beneath her calm, the sharp alertness of someone ready for battle.

He took another sip of espresso, then set the cup down with care. "You asked why I'm making this... comfortable for you."

She arched a brow. "You said it's because you wanted to."

"I did," he said quietly. "But that's not the whole reason."

Willow tilted her head, curiosity flickering behind her eyes. He could almost see her cataloguing every word, ready to unpack it later.

Luca glanced toward the garden wall before returning his gaze to hers. "Your sister didn't just steal from the company, Willow. She came to me first. Personally."

Willow straightened in her chair. "What?"

"She asked for a loan," Luca said. "Said it was for something urgent—medical bills. She was nervous, desperate, but not dishonest. At least, not at first."

Willow's breath caught. "She never mentioned that."

"She didn't want a handout. She offered to work it off—said she'd do anything." He paused. "I turned her down."

A heavy silence fell over the table. Willow blinked at him, stunned. "Why?"

"Because I thought she was lying. I've had people fabricate sob stories before to get money from me. She didn't have paperwork. No proof. Just trembling hands and a sad smile. And I... didn't believe her."

He looked down at his hands, steepling his fingers.

"A week later, the money disappeared. A perfect digital trail—sloppy, almost as if she wanted to get caught. That's when I realised it wasn't just theft. It was punishment."

Willow stared at him, stunned into silence.

"I didn't know who the surgery was for," he said, voice low, almost regretful. "But I believe now she wasn't lying. Not entirely. I backed her into a corner, and she did what people do when they feel trapped—she found a way out. Even if it meant crossing a line."

Willow dropped her gaze to her lap, her fingers curling slightly. "She never mentioned anything about medical bills. She told me it was rent... overdue payments. Just life piling up."

The truth settled between them like dust after a storm—quiet, fine, impossible to ignore.

Willow looked up, her gaze steady despite the flicker of doubt behind it. "She's only twenty-two, Mr. Lombardi."

"Call me Luca," he said, his voice low, almost distracted.

He didn't answer immediately. Instead, he watched her in silence, his expression unreadable. As if he were trying to peel back her words, to separate the plea from the person making it. To decide whether this was strategy—or sincerity.

"She's young," Willow continued, her voice soft but clear. "And impulsive. She's made mistakes, more than I can defend. But she's not beyond saving."

A breeze rustled the vines above them, casting shifting patterns of light across the tablecloth. Luca's expression didn't change, but something in his eyes shifted—just slightly.

"She stole from me," he said, not harshly, but as a reminder. A fact. "She created fake invoices. Funnelled money. Lied to my team's faces."

"I know," Willow said, her fingers tightening around her napkin. "And she should face the consequences. But not a prison sentence. Not something that will ruin the rest of her life."

He studied her, quiet.

"She wasn't trying to hurt you," she said. "She wasn't thinking of you at all, and that's part of the problem. She panicked. But if you give her a second chance… if you drop the charges… I swear I'll make sure she doesn't waste it."

Her voice wavered at the end, not from weakness, but from the weight of it all. The stakes. The trust she was placing in both her sister—and him.

Luca leaned back in his chair, letting the silence expand between them like a held breath.

"And what about you?" he asked at last, voice measured.

Willow's brows drew together. "What about me?"

"You're asking me to spare your sister," he said slowly, deliberately, "to show mercy after she lied, stole, and put my company—my people—at risk. That kind of leniency comes with a cost. Are you prepared for that?"

Her breath caught, just barely. But she didn't look away.

"I didn't come here looking for favours," she said, her voice steady. "I came to make it right. For her. For you. Whatever that looks like."

Luca studied her. The vulnerability in her eyes. The defiance in her spine. The quiet conviction in her voice that didn't ask—it offered.

She wasn't begging.

She was standing her ground.

And something inside him shifted. A crack in the armour he'd worn so long it had begun to feel like skin.

He wasn't sure what surprised him more—her courage or the fact that it mattered.

She had no idea what it would cost. And yet… she was here.

Willing.

Present.

Complicated.

Luca looked at her—really looked—and knew, with a clarity that unsettled him: he didn't want her to disappear at the end of the week.

He wanted more time.

Because Willow Taylor didn't just intrigue him.

She disarmed him.

And that, more than anything, made her dangerous.

She sat across from him in that simple white dress, the morning light kissing her bare shoulders, and Luca couldn't decide if she was unaware—or devastatingly aware—of the effect she had on him. There was no artifice in her posture, no flirtation in her gaze. She didn't lean forward, didn't angle her body to seduce. She simply was. Present. Steady.

Not performing.

Not manipulating.

Real.

And it terrified him more than any boardroom betrayal ever had.

He'd stared down hostile takeovers and watched grown men flinch under pressure. But this—this woman, this quiet intensity—unsettled something deeper. She wasn't like the women who moved in his world, all polished elegance and social calculus. She wasn't playing the long game or angling for a payoff.

She was simply here.

And that made everything more complicated.

Luca exhaled slowly, a quiet breath meant to anchor him, his fingers tapping once on the arm of his chair as if grounding himself in the present moment.

"Spend a week with me on my yacht," he said, his voice low, deliberate. "And I'll drop all charges."

Willow stared at him.

The air changed.

For a moment, she didn't move. The breeze stirred the hem of her dress like a breath across silk. A bird sang somewhere overhead, light, and sharp—and still, the world seemed to hold its breath.

"I beg your pardon?" she said finally.

"You heard me."

"You want to barter my sister's freedom—for my time?"

"I want to know the kind of woman who would cross an ocean to fix a mess she didn't make," he said, his gaze steady. "Who walks into a lion's den without flinching. Who tells the truth even when it doesn't serve her."

Her eyes narrowed, sharp as glass. "And you think you'll figure that out in seven days?"

"I intend to try."

She placed her napkin down on the table with quiet precision. Each movement was measured—elegant, restrained. "You're serious."

"Completely."

"And if I say no?"

"Then your sister faces trial," Luca said, standing as if to meet her on even ground. "And I go back to believing the world is exactly as cold and transactional as I've always known it to be."

She sat there, stunned.

The garden, the sunlight, the crisp linen and carefully arranged citrus trees—it all felt surreal, like a scene painted too perfectly to be trusted. Her heart knocked against her ribs in protest, as if it sensed something she hadn't yet named.

Then, soft—almost to herself—she said, "Dennis wouldn't like that."

Luca heard it.

"Who is Dennis?" he asked, tone calm, but with an edge that hadn't been there a moment ago.

Willow hesitated. "My..."

She almost said it. Fiancé. The word hovered, suspended on the tip of her tongue. But something—uncertainty, guilt, the realisation that it didn't quite fit—stopped her.

"…My boyfriend."

Of course.

Of course she had someone.

A woman like her—so grounded, so luminous—would never go unnoticed. Someone would've seen her worth. Claimed her. Protected her.

Luca nodded once, slowly, like he was logging a footnote in a contract. A minor detail. A point of reference.

But something in his chest pulled tighter.

"What does Dennis do?" he asked, too casually.

"He's… a lawyer."

His mouth curved. Just a touch. Of course he was.

Polished. Predictable. The kind of man who wore cufflinks and used words like "acceptable risk." Someone who lived by prenups and long-term strategy. Someone who'd never gamble—never offer something raw or uncontained.

Safe. Dependable.

Boring.

Luca leaned forward slightly, eyes gleaming under the dappled light. "And does your lawyer boyfriend know you're here making bargains with the man your sister stole from?"

Willow hesitated. "He told me not to come."

His smile sharpened, cool and precise. "Wise man."

But even as he said it, a part of him hoped Dennis was exactly what he sounded like: forgettable.

She tilted her head then, studying him as if trying to see beyond the offer. "Why your yacht? What would this week entail exactly?"

Luca didn't look away. He met her gaze head-on.

"Time," he said simply. "Undivided. No lawyers. No assistants. No press releases or polite lies. Just you and me. Seven days."

She folded her arms, sceptical. "Doing what? Sipping champagne while you interrogate me in designer swimwear?"

His smile deepened, lazy and unrepentant. "Only if you insist."

She didn't laugh.

He hadn't expected her to.

Willow Taylor was cautious. Sharp. Not immune to charm, perhaps—but not ruled by it either. Still, he saw the flicker in her eyes. The curiosity.

That was something.

"The yacht is private," he said, his tone shifting, softening just enough. "No interruptions. I want to understand who I'm really dealing with. And I want you to understand me."

She paused, weighing his words.

"That sounds less like a bargain," she said slowly, "and more like a test."

"Call it what you like," Luca replied. His voice dropped. "But if you want to save your sister, it starts with trust."

She looked at him, searching for a catch. For fine print. For the moment, the mask slipped.

And for the first time since she'd walked into his world, he realised—he didn't know what she was going to say.

Her gaze didn't flinch. "You're not expecting me to sleep with you, are you?"

His smile curved again—slow, deliberate, unapologetic. "Only if you insist."

"I won't."

The silence that followed was tight. Heavy.

Like glass stretched too thin.

Luca studied her, equal parts amused and impressed. "Noted."

Willow drew in a breath, slow and careful. "I'll need to think about it."

He leaned back in his chair, one hand drumming lightly on the carved wood armrest. "You have twenty-four hours. After that, the offer expires."

She nodded once. "I understand."

She rose, graceful as ever, but he didn't miss the flicker of hesitation in her eyes before she turned. It wasn't fear. It was calculation.

She wasn't overwhelmed.

She was assessing risk.

And that, Luca thought as he watched her walk away, made her far more dangerous than he'd ever anticipated.

Chapter Seven

The soft hum of the luxury car barely registered as Willow sat rigid in the back seat, staring out the tinted window at the winding streets of Rome. The cobblestones gleamed faintly under the afternoon sun, and the city moved around her in a blur of vespas, tourists, and ancient stone. But none of it touched her.

All she could hear was his voice.

'Spend a week with me on my yacht, and I'll drop all charges.'

The words echoed in her mind, looping like a haunting refrain she couldn't silence. It sounded like something out of one of the romance novels she edited back home—outlandish, intoxicating, threaded with danger. A beautiful woman. A powerful man. A proposition that bordered on the unthinkable.

But this wasn't fiction. This was real. This was Lily's life hanging in the balance.

Her hands lay clenched in her lap, nails biting into her skin through white-knuckled fists. The car's leather seat offered no comfort. Nothing did.

She'd walked into Luca Lombardi's villa expecting arrogance. Coldness. Indifference. And in a way, he'd delivered. But there was something else there, too. A sharpness beneath the charm. Something calculated, yes—but also curious. He'd studied her like she was a puzzle he couldn't quite solve. And that unsettled her more than she wanted to admit.

If she said no, Lily might go to prison. That was the reality. But if she said yes…

Her breath caught.

A week alone with him. On a yacht. Out at sea, with no escape but trust. The thought sent heat rising to her face—and not entirely from fear. Luca wasn't dangerous in the obvious way. He didn't threaten or raise his voice. He didn't need to. His danger was quieter. Subtler. It was in the way he looked at her—like he saw something underneath the polished surface she tried so hard to maintain. Like he wanted to unravel her, and worse… like he could.

You're not that girl, she reminded herself. She was careful. She planned. She worked hard, lived modestly, said no when things didn't make sense. She had a steady boyfriend, a normal life, a timeline she and Dennis had carefully laid out.

But Dennis hadn't been in that sunlit garden. He hadn't watched Luca lean back in his chair, calm as a king, making her feel as if the outcome was already written.

And maybe it was.

Her phone felt heavy in her hand as she pulled it from her bag. She stared at the screen for a long moment before finally pressing call.

He picked up on the third ring.

"Hey, babe. How's Lily?"

His voice—so familiar, so reasonable—stabbed her with guilt.

"She's okay. Scared. But she's hanging in there." She paused, swallowing the dread in her throat. "I talked to Luca Lombardi."

A beat of silence. "And?"

"He made an offer." Her voice was soft. Careful. "He said he'll drop all the charges… if I agree to spend a week with him. On his yacht."

The silence stretched, longer this time.

"A week?" Dennis said slowly. "What does that mean— 'spend a week with him'? Like… in what way?"

"He didn't say anything inappropriate," she said quickly. "He made it clear—no expectations. Just… my company. It's like a trade. A bargain."

"A bargain?" His tone sharpened. "Willow, that's insane. You can't be serious."

"I am serious," she said, her voice cracking. "I'm not saying I've agreed. But I don't know what else to do. He's not bluffing, Dennis. Lily could go to prison. This might be the only way."

Another pause. Then a low scoff. "So, what—you're just going to play escort for a billionaire to save your sister?"

The words hit like a slap.

"That's not fair."

"No, what's not fair is you even considering this. What does he really want, Willow? No man makes an offer like that for 'conversation and sunshine.'"

"I know how it sounds," she whispered. "But I can't let Lily go to jail. I can't. Not if there's something I can do."

"You are doing something. You're there. You're calling lawyers, trying to help her. But this—this is crossing a line."

"I haven't agreed," she said again, more firmly this time. "But I needed to tell you. You deserve to know."

He didn't answer right away. The silence between them now felt weighted, strained.

"I can't believe we're even having this conversation," Dennis said finally. "You seriously think this is an option?"

"I don't want it to be," she said, the words trembling out of her. "But I don't see another way."

There was a long, slow exhale on the other end.

"You need to think long and hard about what you're risking here, Willow. Because this—this changes everything."

She closed her eyes, nodding even though he couldn't see. "I know," she whispered. "Believe me… I know."

Luca stepped into the lobby of the boutique Roman hotel with his usual quiet confidence, every movement deliberate, practiced. But beneath the smooth exterior— beneath the custom Brioni suit and polished leather shoes—was a storm of emotion he couldn't quite rein in.

It had been twenty-four hours since he'd made the offer.

An audacious offer. One that would make most people laugh, or slap him, or both. But desperation made people listen. And he'd seen something in Willow's eyes when he said it. Not just shock or indignation. Something deeper. A flicker of possibility. A door, cracked just enough for him to step through—if he dared.

The concierge recognised him at once, offering a respectful nod and a murmured "Buongiorno, Signor Lombardi."

Luca barely returned the gesture. His focus was ahead—on the elevator, on the fourth floor, on her.

As the doors closed around him, he caught a glimpse of himself in the mirrored walls. Impeccable. Cold. Detached.

Except… he wasn't.

His jaw was tight. His pulse thrummed under his skin. She had gotten under it, somehow—this sweet, defiant woman with storm-coloured eyes and a backbone stronger than most men he knew.

What if she says no?

The thought settled like a stone in his gut.

She had every reason to refuse. She was principled, rational. Loyal. But yesterday, when she'd looked at him across the table, her spine straight and voice trembling... there had been something else in her expression. Not just fear for her sister. Curiosity. And maybe—God help him—a little temptation.

The elevator dinged softly.

He stepped out, his Italian loafers silent against the plush hallway carpet. Room 407. He didn't hesitate.

A sharp knock. Then a beat of silence. Then the door opened.

And everything in him stilled.

Willow stood in the doorway, barefoot and flushed from the shower. Her legs were bare, golden skin leading up to soft denim shorts that hugged her hips with infuriating precision. A white cotton crop top clung to her form, revealing a delicate strip of smooth, pale skin at her waist. Her damp hair fell around her shoulders in soft waves, and her eyes—those eyes—were wide and unreadable.

Luca blinked. Once.

She was—Cristo. She was stunning. Effortlessly, achingly beautiful.

Her legs were longer than he'd imagined. Her skin glowed in the soft morning light, and her bare feet made her look vulnerable. Real. Somehow even more dangerous.

He cleared his throat, voice low. "Do you always answer the door looking like that?"

Her brow arched, but a glint of dry amusement softened the question's edge. "I wasn't expecting anyone."

The corner of his mouth lifted. "I did say twenty-four hours."

She hesitated. Just a breath. Then stepped aside in quiet invitation.

Luca entered. The air inside smelled faintly of jasmine and citrus—her. Not perfume, exactly. More like shampoo. Something simple. Intimate.

He took in the suite—tasteful, sun-drenched, with a view of terracotta rooftops and distant domes. And then he looked back at her, always back to her.

"Do you like your room?" he asked.

She nodded. "I do. Thank you. It's beautiful… and the view is to die for. Coffee?"

"Yes, please."

Willow led him through the sitting room and out onto the balcony. A breeze caught the hem of her shorts, tugging playfully. She didn't seem to notice, or maybe she did and didn't care. There was a casual confidence in her that made his chest tighten.

She poured from a French press, hands steady. No cream. No sugar. He liked that.

He took the mug with a quiet "Thank you."

She leaned against the railing, arms folded, eyes on the city sprawled out below. Her voice, when it came, was calm—but steel lay beneath it.

"You're asking a lot. For me to go with you for a week… It's not a simple decision. I'm risking my relationship with Dennis. He's not thrilled I'm even considering it."

Luca took a sip of coffee, his gaze never leaving her. "I can imagine. If you were mine, I'd lock you up."

She turned sharply, her eyes sharp and startled. "Excuse me?"

A slow smile curved his lips, unapologetic. "Not literally. I just mean… I wouldn't let you out of my sight."

She shook her head, a flush rising in her cheeks. "That's not exactly reassuring, Luca."

He tilted his head slightly, eyes narrowing. "I didn't come here to reassure you. I came for your answer."

There it was. The line drawn in the sand.

Willow went still, the moment stretching between them like a held breath.

"And what if I say no?" she asked quietly.

His voice was low, firm. "Then I'll press charges against Lily."

She flinched, just barely. But she didn't look away.

"And if I say yes?"

Luca stepped forward, his voice softer now. "Then we spend the week together. No expectations. Just time. Honesty."

She searched his face, as though trying to peel back the layers of charm and find something real beneath. He let her look.

"Say yes, Willow."

The breeze caught a strand of her hair, and she tucked it behind her ear with a hand that trembled slightly. Her silence stretched, taut and dangerous.

Finally, she whispered, "Okay."

His brow lifted. "Okay?"

She turned to face him fully. "I'll go with you. One week. That's it."

Relief and triumph collided in his chest. He hadn't realised how much he'd needed to hear those words until now.

"You won't regret it," he said, the promise curling at the edge of his voice like smoke.

"I might," she replied flatly. "But I'm doing this for Lily."

He stepped closer—close enough that she could feel his heat, smell the coffee and subtle spice of his cologne. "Is that the only reason?"

Willow didn't answer. Her gaze flicked away, unreadable.

She turned back to the table and poured herself another cup of coffee. This time, her hand shook just enough to betray the storm inside.

Luca didn't press.

"My driver will pick you up tomorrow morning," he said.

She glanced at him over her shoulder. "Separate rooms."

"Of course," he said smoothly. "Unless you change your mind."

Her eyebrow arched. "Don't count on it."

Luca just smiled. He set his mug down on the table and nodded once. "Tomorrow."

Then he turned and walked out, the soft click of the door the only sound behind him.

Willow stood frozen on the terrace, the sun warming her skin but not her nerves.

What the hell am I doing?

The question echoed in her chest like thunder.

Her coffee had gone cold. Her thoughts tangled and frayed.

She walked back inside and sat heavily on the edge of the bed, reaching for her phone. Her thumb hovered over Dennis's contact for a long moment before she pressed call.

He picked up on the second ring.

"Willow?" His voice was cool, controlled. Tense.

She swallowed. "Hey. I… I talked to Luca."

A beat of silence. Then, "And?"

"I'm going," she said softly. "One week. On the yacht. After that, he'll drop the charges."

The pause was longer this time. When Dennis spoke again, his voice had changed—harder, colder.

"You're actually doing it."

She stood, walking toward the window. "Dennis, it's not like I have a choice. Lily—"

"Lily stole from him, Willow. And you're selling yourself to clean up her mess."

She flinched. "It's not like that."

"Isn't it?" he snapped. "You're going to play house with some billionaire playboy on his boat, and I'm supposed to just be okay with that?"

"I set boundaries. Separate cabins. No—"

"Oh, well, that makes everything better," he cut in bitterly. "You honestly think he's going to respect boundaries? That man's entire reputation is built on breaking them."

She pressed a hand to her forehead. "I need to do this. You don't have to agree, but I need your support."

A long breath hissed through the line. "You want my support while you go sail off into the sunset with another man?"

Her throat tightened. "It's one week."

Another pause. Then, finally, quietly:

"I hope she's worth it."

The line went dead.

Willow stared at the screen in her hand, heart thudding, the silence in the room suddenly deafening.

She sank onto the edge of the bed again, numb.

She'd made her choice.

And now, there was no going back.

Luca stepped out of Willow's hotel room, the soft click of the door closing behind him sounded far too loud in the hushed hallway. The quiet pressed in around him, but he didn't move. Not at first. He stood still, hand still resting on the doorknob, as if part of him wasn't entirely ready to walk away.

As if something vital had just shifted—and he wasn't sure if he'd won or lost.

She'd said yes.

Relief curled low in his gut, slow and heavy—but it wasn't the clean, satisfying kind he was used to. No rush of triumph. No smug satisfaction. Just a dull throb of something tighter, more complicated, coiling beneath his ribs.

This wasn't supposed to feel like a victory.

He exhaled hard and ran a hand down his face, dragging it across his jaw before shoving it into his pocket. His feet finally started moving, each step toward the lift feeling heavier than the last. Her voice still rang in his head, calm but resolute.

'I'll go with you.'

Not because she wanted to.

Because she felt she had to.

That truth gnawed at him more than he liked to admit.

He stopped at the elevator and pressed the call button, watching the light above flicker down toward his floor. In the gleaming metal doors, his reflection stared back—crisp suit, composed stance, but his eyes were shadowed. Tight around the edges.

For a man who usually got everything he wanted, he looked like hell.

Tired. Frustrated.

And something else he didn't dare name.

He hadn't expected her to agree. Not really.

Willow Taylor didn't strike him as the type to be swayed by luxury or seduced by pressure. She was practical. Principled. She'd got into his limousine with fire in her spine and challenge in her gaze, despite the fact that he could've crushed her case with a single phone call.

That was what had intrigued him from the beginning—her strength. Her unwillingness to yield. She was the kind of woman who didn't beg, didn't break. Even when cornered, she'd stared him down like she dared him to underestimate her.

And now?

Now she was his.

For a week.

But not in the way he wanted.

Not freely. Not truly.

The elevator arrived with a muted chime, the doors sliding open like a breath being held. He stepped inside, jaw tight, and jabbed the ground floor button harder than necessary. The doors closed, trapping him in with his thoughts.

He hated Dennis.

The bland, polished, perfectly timed boyfriend who couldn't see past Willow's calm demeanour to the wildfire simmering underneath. Who probably scheduled affection the same way he planned business dinners. A man like that didn't deserve her.

Not even close.

But worse than Dennis was the voice inside Luca's own head whispering what he didn't want to hear.

If she had any other option—any real way out—she wouldn't be coming.

She wasn't doing this for him.

She was doing it for Lily.

The elevator glided down, floor by floor, but the pressure in Luca's chest didn't ease. He could feel the clock ticking already, seconds slipping through his grasp like water. He hated that, too—the sense of time running out before anything had even begun.

When the lift opened into the lobby, he strode through it with purposeful steps. The concierge greeted him again, but Luca didn't bother responding. He pushed through the glass doors and stepped out into the Roman morning.

The sunlight hit him full on—sharp, golden, immediate.

But it didn't warm him.

Not where it counted.

He crossed the pavement to the waiting car, the driver already holding the door open. Luca slid inside without a word, the door shutting behind him like a vault sealing closed.

One week.

That was all he had. Seven days to change the way she saw him. To tilt the balance of power. To turn something transactional into something real.

To make her want him—not out of obligation, not out of desperation, but because she couldn't help it.

And that terrified him more than it should have.

Because Luca Lombardi didn't chase. He didn't need to.

Until now.

He leaned back in the seat, eyes closing for a brief second.

Let the countdown begin.

Chapter Eight

Willow stood on the curb outside her hotel, clutching the handle of her single suitcase like it was an anchor. The Roman morning wrapped around her with soft golden light, the kind that made the old buildings glow and the cobblestones shimmer. The air was already warming, thick with the promise of another sweltering summer day, but she barely felt it.

A sleek black car glided up to the curb like a shadow, silent and gleaming. The driver stepped out the moment it stopped, dressed in a perfectly pressed suit, posture crisp, his presence as polished as the car he drove.

"Miss Taylor?" he asked politely, voice smooth and accented.

She nodded, her voice coming out quieter than she expected. "That's me."

With practiced efficiency, he took her suitcase and opened the back door. Willow slid into the leather interior with a quiet breath, trying not to fidget as the cool scent of citrus and luxury surrounded her. The door closed with a hushed thunk, sealing her in.

They didn't speak during the drive. She was grateful for the silence. Her mind was already too loud, filled with questions she couldn't answer and emotions she hadn't yet named. Her fingers twisted in her lap as the city passed outside the window—ancient stone, crumbling fountains, flashes of bougainvillea. Beauty that should've calmed her. It didn't.

What am I doing?

A week on a yacht with a billionaire who exuded charm like cologne and wielded power like a sword.

A week with a man who'd made a bargain that felt more like a trap.

Except… he wasn't entirely a stranger anymore.

And she wasn't being forced. Not exactly.

She was choosing this. Choosing him. Even if part of her still wasn't sure why.

When the car turned off the main road and onto a narrower street lined with high hedges, she leaned forward instinctively, trying to see where they were headed. Then the hedges parted—and her breath caught.

"Wait," she whispered, not meaning to say it aloud.

The yacht was massive.

No, not just massive. It was monumental—a gleaming, floating palace moored at the edge of the marina. Its white hull shone like marble in the sunlight, sleek and graceful, with curves that spoke of elegance and power. Crew members in white polos and navy shorts moved with fluid precision across the deck, adjusting ropes, checking instruments, preparing for departure like it was a choreographed ballet.

It didn't look real.

The car rolled to a smooth stop at the edge of the dock, just steps from the gangway.

The driver got out and opened her door. Willow didn't move.

She just stared.

It was the kind of yacht you saw in films. The kind that hosted royalty and billionaires, scandalous affairs, and champagne-fuelled parties. Not twenty-four-year-old women with one suitcase, a fractured life, and no idea how to navigate any of this.

She climbed out slowly, her sandals tapping against the dock, the breeze immediately tangling a few strands of hair around her face. She lifted her chin, eyes wide as she took it all in.

She didn't belong here. Not in this world of polished chrome and silent wealth. She wasn't glamorous or powerful or particularly brave.

But she was here.

And then she saw him.

Luca.

He stood at the top of the gangway, poised like he belonged to the yacht—or maybe it belonged to him. He wore tailored navy slacks and a crisp white shirt with the sleeves rolled casually to his elbows. The sun bathed him in warm gold, glinting off the angles of his face. He didn't wave. Didn't smile. Just watched her.

And in that stillness, something shifted.

Because for the first time, she felt seen. Not assessed. Not judged. Not pitied. Seen.

Willow swallowed against the flutter in her throat and forced herself forward. Her legs were shaky, but she kept walking. The driver rolled her suitcase behind her and handed it off to a waiting steward. Willow's fingers brushed the polished rail as she reached the start of the gangway, and she paused.

One step—and the world behind her would shrink away.

One step—and the bargain she'd made would become real.

She took a breath.

And crossed.

As soon as her foot touched the deck, the yacht seemed to wake. The engines rumbled beneath her feet with a deep, steady thrum. Lines were being untied. Orders called. Crew moving like clockwork around her.

Luca gave a nod to the captain, and everything shifted into motion.

But Willow barely noticed. She walked slowly along the deck, her hand drifting over the cool metal railing. The city was slipping away behind them, the skyline already beginning to fade as the yacht moved toward open water.

The sea stretched out before her, impossibly blue and endless, sparkling like scattered diamonds beneath the morning sun. Gulls called overhead, their wings sharp against the sky. A breeze kissed her skin, rich with salt and possibility.

Everywhere she looked, there was beauty—curved white loungers under umbrellas, glassy surfaces that reflected light like mirrors. But it was the vastness of the horizon that held her. That freedom.

She had never seen anything like this. Never felt anything like this.

Small. And alive.

Luca didn't say a word. He stayed a few steps behind her, hands in his pockets, eyes on her—not like he was waiting for her to be impressed, but like he was curious. Like he couldn't quite look away.

There was something about her, he thought. The way she took it all in, not with awe or greed but with quiet reverence, like it was a gift she hadn't asked for and wasn't sure she could keep.

She turned and caught him watching.

"What?" she asked, brushing wind-blown hair from her face with a self-conscious laugh.

He shrugged, a rare softness in the curve of his mouth. "You're not what I expected."

She arched a brow. "And that's a good thing?"

He tilted his head slightly, his eyes lingering. "It's the only thing."

Her smile faltered, not from doubt—but from the heat in his voice, the quiet intensity behind the words. He meant more than he said. She could feel it.

Willow turned away before she forgot how to breathe.

They were almost past the last buoy, the Roman coastline now little more than a watercolour behind them, when her phone buzzed in her bag.

She froze. Reality tugging at the hem of her dress.

Pulling it out, she glanced at the screen.

Dennis.

A new message.

She opened it.

If you get on that boat with Luca Lombardi, we're done. You can't play house with a billionaire like some kind of hooker and expect me to wait. Don't bother calling me when you come to your senses.

The words hit like ice water.

Her smile faded. Her throat tightened, as if the message had lodged itself there like a splinter.

She turned slightly, angling her body away from Luca, clutching the phone as though the pressure of her fingers might somehow hold her together.

Luca noticed immediately. The warmth in his expression cooled, his eyes narrowing slightly with concern.

"Willow?" he asked, stepping toward her, voice low.

She didn't answer right away. She shook her head and blinked quickly, trying to clear the tears rising against her will. Her chest tightened as the bitter familiarity of doubt and shame began to creep in.

"May I?" Luca asked gently, nodding toward the phone still gripped in her hand.

She hesitated. For a second, she wanted to say no. To keep that pain private, locked behind her ribs. But something in his voice—his steadiness, his restraint—unlocked her fingers.

Silently, she handed the phone over.

Luca read the message without a word. His jaw tightened as his eyes moved across the screen. Once. Then again. He exhaled through his nose, slow and sharp, and locked the screen before glancing up at her.

"He sent this to hurt you," he said flatly.

Willow nodded, barely able to speak. "I know."

"You didn't do anything wrong."

"I know that too," she whispered. But her voice cracked halfway through, unravelling her composure.

Luca hesitated, then slid the phone smoothly into his pocket.

She blinked, confused. "You're keeping my phone?"

"For now," he said, calm but unyielding. "Just until we're past the last bit of land. After that, you can have it back. Or throw it into the sea. Either works."

A laugh slipped out of her—thin, watery, but real. She wiped under her eyes with her fingertips, brushing away the tears before they could fall.

"Come," he said, and his hand lightly touched her elbow, warm and steady. "Let me show you something beautiful."

Still shaken, Willow let him guide her away. Dennis's message echoed faintly in her mind like a bruise, but with every step across the polished deck, the sting began to soften. The sea air wrapped around her like a balm—briny, sun-warmed, endlessly free.

Luca led her up a sleek staircase to the upper deck. It unfolded before her like a hidden sanctuary—open to the sky, edged with glass railings and lined with ivory cushions. A light breeze danced through the space, stirring the corners of white umbrellas and making the teak flooring glow beneath the sun.

But it wasn't the yacht's elegance that stole her breath.

It was the view.

The ocean surrounded them now—vast, glittering, without borders. The land had slipped behind them, now just a blur on the horizon. The wake fanned out behind the yacht in soft, silver ribbons, trailing into infinity.

Willow moved closer to the railing, eyes wide with wonder. She pressed her palms to the smooth glass and whispered, "It's like the world just... falls away."

Beside her, Luca stood quietly, hands resting on the edge of the rail, eyes on the endless blue. "That's why I come out here. No meetings. No voices. Just this."

She turned her head to look at him. "And you want to share it with me?"

He met her gaze without flinching. "Yes."

There was no flirtation in his voice, no agenda. Just a quiet truth. And something inside her shifted—like a locked door cracking open just enough to let in light.

She looked back out over the water, the horizon wide and merciful. The breeze caught her hair, lifting it from her shoulders, as if even the wind wanted to carry away what had hurt her.

"It's beautiful," she murmured.

"So are you," he said, without pause.

Willow turned to him, caught off guard by the directness of it.

He didn't look away. "You didn't deserve that message. You didn't deserve a man who would try to shame you for saving your sister."

Her eyes burned again—but this time, it wasn't sorrow. It was gratitude. The kind that rose from being seen. Truly seen.

"I don't know what this week will be," Luca added softly, "but I promise you—no games. No cruelty. You'll be safe here."

Willow took a deep breath, the promise echoing through her in a place that had known too much uncertainty.

"Okay," she said.

They stood together in silence, surrounded by sky and sea—two people with bruised hearts and a horizon full of possibility.

A low hum rumbled beneath their feet as the yacht picked up speed, slicing through the waves with graceful power. The deck shifted gently beneath her, and Willow stumbled, her hand flying out to steady herself on the back of a lounge chair.

Behind her, Luca let out a soft chuckle—low and warm.

She turned toward him, lips parting to speak, but paused.

He was leaning against the railing, arms folded, watching her with that maddening half-smile. His dark hair was tousled by the wind, and the sun lit him like a painting—his cheekbones sharp, his brown eyes gleaming.

And for the first time that day, Willow didn't feel overwhelmed.

She felt... something beginning.

"Careful," he said smoothly. "She moves like a woman who knows her power."

Willow raised an eyebrow. "The yacht or you?"

Luca grinned. "Both."

She rolled her eyes and turned back toward the water, trying to hide the reluctant tug of amusement at her lips. The spray from the waves misted the air now, cool and briny and deliciously wild. The front of the yacht split the blue with confidence, sending white foam dancing up the sides.

"You're smiling," Luca said behind her.

"No, I'm not."

"You are," he insisted, stepping closer. "You're trying not to, but it's there."

Willow shook her head, hair flying in the wind. "I'm just enjoying the view."

He leaned closer. "You mean me?"

That earned him a quick glance, sharp and unimpressed. "You're very sure of yourself, aren't you?"

"Only when I'm right."

She huffed, walking toward the edge of the deck as the yacht picked up even more speed. The wind caught the loose ends of her sundress, plastering it gently against her legs.

"You'll get used to her," Luca called over the wind. "Takes a little time to find your sea legs."

"I think I'll be fine," she said—just before the yacht gave another sudden lurch. She lost her footing and squeaked as her body tipped sideways—

—only to land in strong arms.

Luca had crossed the space between them in seconds, catching her against his chest.

For a moment, the world tilted again, but not from the waves.

Willow blinked up at him, breath shallow, her hands pressed against the crisp linen of his shirt. She could feel the steady beat of his heart beneath her palm.

"Still fine?" he asked, voice low.

"I—" she started, but her voice caught.

He didn't move. He didn't have to.

His closeness was a heat she couldn't ignore, and his eyes held hers like a challenge.

Then, with surprising gentleness, he helped her upright and stepped back.

"No harm done," he said, his tone light but his gaze lingering.

Willow cleared her throat and smoothed her dress. "Don't get used to catching me."

"I wouldn't dream of it," Luca replied with a wink. "Unless you fall for me again."

She shot him a glare that didn't quite land.

And Luca smiled to himself as he turned away—because for the first time since she boarded his yacht, her wariness had slipped... just a little.

The sun had begun its lazy descent, casting a warm golden glow over the sea as the yacht cruised steadily into open water. On the aft deck, a small table had been set for two—white linen, polished silverware, and a centrepiece of fresh flowers that swayed slightly with the breeze.

Willow stepped out hesitantly, her soft blue sundress fluttering against her legs. The air smelled of salt and citrus, and somewhere in the background, faint Italian jazz played from hidden speakers.

Luca stood at the table already, hands in his pockets, watching her approach with an appreciative smile. He'd changed into a navy linen shirt, sleeves rolled to the elbows, collar open just enough to hint at a tan line and the kind of confidence that didn't require effort.

"You clean up well," he said, pulling out her chair.

Willow sat without meeting his gaze. "I wasn't aware this was a formal dinner."

"It's not." He took his seat across from her. "But I thought you deserved something beautiful after the day you've had."

Her eyes lifted then, cautious but curious. "You mean being blackmailed into coming aboard your yacht?"

A grin tugged at the corners of his mouth. "I prefer to call it... strategic persuasion."

She didn't smile, but she didn't look away either.

A steward appeared quietly with the first course—chilled melon wrapped in prosciutto, drizzled with balsamic glaze. Willow thanked him softly and picked up her fork.

They ate in a quiet rhythm at first, the tension between them like a third presence at the table—simmering but unspoken.

"I hope you're comfortable," Luca said eventually. "Your cabin has everything you might need, but if you're missing anything—"

"I'll manage," she said, a bit too quickly. Then, more gently, "It's… all very beautiful. Overwhelming, but beautiful."

"Most people would be impressed."

"I'm not most people."

He chuckled. "So, I've gathered."

Willow sipped her sparkling water and took in the ocean beyond them. "I didn't come here to be impressed, Luca."

"No," he said, his voice low, "you came to protect your sister. I admire that."

That startled her. He wasn't teasing now. The look in his eyes had shifted—less smug, more… sincere.

"You don't know anything about me," she said softly.

"I know enough." He leaned forward slightly. "You had every reason to walk away. And yet, here you are. That tells me something."

Willow felt heat rise to her cheeks but held his gaze. "It doesn't mean I trust you."

Luca shrugged with a slow smile. "Trust is earned. I have six days left to try."

She gave a faint, dry laugh. "Is that what this dinner is? Part of the seduction?"

"No," he said. Then, after a pause: "But it doesn't hurt."

She blinked, caught between offence and amusement.

Dessert arrived before she could answer—a simple panna cotta topped with fresh berries and a hint of mint. Willow tasted it, letting the cool sweetness distract her from the way Luca watched her with such relentless curiosity.

When they were finished, he stood and extended a hand.

She stared at it warily. "What now?"

"A walk on deck," he said, eyes glinting. "Or are you afraid of what might happen under the stars?"

"I'm not afraid of you," she said, rising without taking his hand.

"Good," Luca replied smoothly, falling in step beside her. "Because I'm only getting started."

The sky stretched out above them in an endless, velvet canvas. Stars blinked into life one by one, their reflections glittering on the inky water. The yacht moved smoothly through the sea, a gentle hum beneath their feet as Willow and Luca strolled along the upper deck.

A warm breeze tousled her hair, and she tucked a strand behind her ear, eyes fixed on the horizon. Luca walked beside her in silence for a moment, his hands loosely in his pockets, gaze drifting to her when he thought she wasn't looking.

"Are you always this quiet after dinner?" he asked, his voice low and unhurried.

She glanced at him sideways. "Only when I'm processing a blackmail bargain."

He grinned. "You know, I'm starting to think you enjoy giving me a hard time."

"It's not hard," she said dryly.

He laughed under his breath, but then his tone shifted. "You didn't have to come, you know. Most people would've run."

"I'm not most people," she said again, softer this time.

"No," he agreed. "You're not."

They reached the railing, and she leaned against it, staring out at the endless water. For a moment, neither of them spoke. The breeze lifted the hem of her dress slightly, and Luca turned to her, his expression more curious than flirtatious now.

"What do you do, back home?" he asked. "When you're not flying across the world to clean up someone else's mess?"

She hesitated, then said, "I work in publishing. Small firm. Mostly indie authors and niche markets. Not glamorous, but... I like it."

"Books," he mused. "You seem like someone who reads a lot."

She nodded. "They're safe. Predictable. When things fall apart, I can still open a book and know how it'll end."

He studied her face. "And yet here you are—in the middle of something that has no predictable ending."

Willow looked away, her throat tightening slightly. "I didn't come here for adventure. I came for Lily."

"You could have just called a lawyer."

"I did. He couldn't fix it."

"And you think I can?" Luca's voice was quiet now, not teasing.

Willow met his eyes. "I think you're the one who broke it. So yes—I think you're the only one who can."

They stood in silence again, the sound of the ocean the only thing between them.

"You're loyal," he said finally. "Fiercely so."

She tilted her head. "Is that a bad thing?"

"No," he said. "But it's dangerous. The world doesn't always repay loyalty with kindness."

She let out a quiet breath. "I've figured that out."

He stepped closer—not too close, but enough that she could feel the heat of his presence.

"I'm not your enemy, Willow."

"You're not my friend, either."

"No," he said, eyes dark in the moonlight. "But I could be. If you let me."

Her heart skipped once. She looked away again, unwilling to let him see that he was getting to her.

"Let's just get through this week," she said, pushing away from the rail. "That's the bargain, right?"

Luca nodded slowly. "Right."

But as he watched her walk away, her hair catching the starlight, he wondered if this week would be enough.

Chapter Nine

Willow was stretched out on a lounger near the upper deck rail, a paperback resting on her chest, though she hadn't turned a page in ten minutes. The rhythm of the waves beneath the yacht had lulled her into a peaceful haze. The wind played with the ends of her hair as the sun bathed her skin in golden light.

"Enjoying yourself?" Luca's voice came from above her.

She tilted her head back to find him descending the steps from the helm, shirtless this time, in navy swim trunks and aviator sunglasses that should have made him look ridiculous—but didn't.

"I was," she said, squinting up at him. "Until I remembered I agreed to spend a week with a man who doesn't know what personal space means."

He chuckled. "That's rich, considering you're currently lounging on my deck."

She arched an eyebrow. "It's technically your yacht, not your deck."

He ignored the quip and leaned one hand on the railing beside her. "We'll be anchoring soon. There's a cove coming up—a small, secluded spot I like. Crystal-clear water, soft sand, no paparazzi."

She sat up a little, curiosity flaring. "Sounds suspiciously like paradise."

"It is." He pushed his sunglasses up, letting her see his eyes—warm and glinting with mischief. "I thought we could go for a swim. Unless, of course, you're afraid to see me shirtless."

Willow rolled her eyes. "You're already shirtless."

"Exactly. I'm just trying to ease you into the experience."

She snorted despite herself. "And what if I don't feel like swimming?"

"Then you'll sit on the beach and pretend not to watch me," he said smoothly, straightening up. "But I should warn you—I'm very hard to ignore."

Willow crossed her arms. "You're not used to being told no, are you?"

"I'm not used to women pretending they don't want to say yes."

She gave him a flat look, but her lips twitched, betraying the amusement she was trying to hide.

"I'll think about it," she said, swinging her legs off the lounger.

"That's all I ask," he replied with a grin, then turned and strolled back up the steps.

Willow watched him go, then sighed and looked out at the horizon, where the jagged silhouette of a rocky cove was just beginning to come into view.

She wasn't sure what she'd expected when she agreed to this… but it hadn't been this strange, glittering blur of teasing smiles and emotional undercurrents.

And definitely not secluded coves.

She stood and went to find her swimsuit—just in case.

The yacht dropped anchor in a crescent-shaped cove that looked like it had been carved out of a dream. The cliffs rose steeply on either side, dramatic and ancient, their rocky faces softened by the warm Mediterranean sun. Below them, the beach unfurled like a ribbon of powdered sugar—untouched, pristine. The water shimmered in impossible shades of turquoise, gently lapping the shore like it had all the time in the world.

Willow stood at the railing, towel in hand, her hair lifted by the sea breeze, her eyes wide with quiet awe.

"It's beautiful," she breathed, almost to herself.

"Told you."

Luca's voice came from beside her, casual but pleased. He held a pair of flippers in one hand and two snorkelling masks in the other, his sunglasses pushed up into his thick dark hair. "No tourists. No phones. No Dennis."

She turned toward him with a sharp look but said nothing. A sliver of amusement played at the corners of her lips, quickly smoothed away.

Below, the yacht's crew had already lowered a small, motorised tender into the water. The vessel bobbed gently beside the swim platform. Luca gestured toward it and extended his hand gallantly. "Ladies first."

Willow arched an eyebrow, ignored his hand entirely, and climbed down the narrow ladder herself with practiced grace. Luca chuckled and followed her down, unoffended.

Once seated side by side in the tender, he gave her an exaggerated once-over. "You're going to wear that?" he asked, gesturing toward her oversized white cover-up, wide-brimmed straw hat, and comically large sunglasses.

"I like sun protection," she said primly, pulling her hat lower as if to emphasise the point.

"You look like a glamorous librarian on safari."

She fought a smile and tilted her head. "Better than looking like a man who Googled 'how to seduce a woman on a boat.'"

His laugh was low and unbothered, roughened by sun and salt. "Touché."

The ride to the beach took only minutes, the tender slicing cleanly through the glassy sea. The scent of salt and pine drifted on the wind, mingling with something faintly floral carried from the cliffs. As soon as they neared the shallows, Luca jumped out, water spraying up around his calves. Then he turned and, before she could climb out herself, swept her up by the waist.

Willow yelped, instinctively clutching his shoulders. "You're infuriating," she snapped, though her voice caught with the shock of contact. Her body had betrayed her—heat unfurling in her chest, tingling at the edges of her skin.

"And yet," he murmured, not releasing her immediately, "you're still here."

She stepped back the moment her feet touched the sand, reclaiming her space and her balance. "Only because I don't want my sister in prison. Let's not rewrite history."

Luca bowed with a hand over his heart, all theatrical charm. "Understood. You're here under protest. I'll try to keep my charm at a minimum."

"You could try silence," she offered helpfully.

But her mouth twitched with the effort it took not to smile.

She dropped her towel and slid the cover-up off her shoulders in one smooth motion. Beneath, she wore a sleek navy one-piece with a low, elegant back and high-cut hips— modest in design but maddening in effect. Sunlight caught the sheen of her skin, turning the line of her collarbone to gold.

Luca's gaze lingered a fraction too long. He cleared his throat, his voice a little rougher now. "Eyes up here, Lombardi."

He grinned, unrepentant. "I was just admiring your bravery. Swimming with sharks can be dangerous."

Willow walked into the water without hesitation, the sea biting at her ankles before softening into a pleasant chill. "I'm not afraid of sharks."

"No?" he said, following her in, the waves lapping gently around their legs. "Then what are you afraid of, Willow?"

She paused, water now up to her waist, then turned toward him. The sunlight danced on the surface between them, casting rippling shadows on their skin.

"People who think they already know the answer."

That stopped him cold.

The air between them stilled, taut and quiet. Then Willow dipped beneath the water with a graceful kick, leaving Luca alone in the sunlight.

They swam for a while in friendly quiet. The water was clear as glass, revealing smooth pebbles, darting fish, and swaying strands of sea grass far below. They dove, floated, splashed—not quite children, but not burdened adults either. At one point, a curious silver fish darted past Willow's stomach, and she laughed—bright, breathless, surprised by joy. Luca, floating nearby, turned toward her instinctively, drawn by the sound.

He smiled—not his usual charming, carefully curated smile. A real one. Unpolished. Unplanned.

Later, they floated side by side, the sun warming their faces, silence resting easy between them. The sea cradled them gently, like it understood the weight they both carried and chose, just for this moment, to carry it for them.

"You're different when you're not trying so hard to hate me," Luca said quietly.

She glanced sideways. "You're different when you're not trying so hard to seduce me."

They drifted a moment longer, the rhythm of the water soft and steady.

"Maybe," Luca said at last, voice low, "we're both better when we're not trying so hard."

Willow didn't respond. But the faint smile that tugged at her lips lingered, soft and unguarded.

They swam a little more, but the mood had shifted. Less teasing, less tension. Just the hush of the sea, the sunlight on their skin, and a fragile peace blooming like sea foam between them—light and fleeting, but unmistakably real.

When they finally stepped out of the water, dripping and breathless, a surprise awaited them on the sand.

A large blanket had been spread out beneath a striped umbrella, and lunch was already laid out—chilled lemonade in glass tumblers beaded with condensation, fresh caprese salad, warm focaccia, olives, grilled shrimp, and slices of juicy melon. Someone had even thought to bring an ice bucket with a bottle of sparkling water.

Willow blinked. "You had this planned?"

Luca grinned. "I may have mentioned a preference for lunch not served on deck chairs."

She raised a brow, but sat carefully on the blanket, wrapping her towel around her waist. "How very civilised of you."

"I contain multitudes," he said, settling beside her.

They ate in companionable silence for a few minutes, the only sounds the waves lapping against the shore and the occasional call of seabirds above. The sun was warm, the food delicious, and for the first time since she'd stepped onto his yacht, Willow felt… at ease.

She popped a grape into her mouth and let out a content sigh. "Okay, this is officially the nicest hostage situation I've ever experienced."

Luca let out a low laugh. "You know, for someone allegedly being blackmailed, you're adapting remarkably well."

She looked over at him, the breeze lifting her damp hair. "I'm choosing not to panic. It's a coping strategy."

"I approve." He reclined back on his elbows. "Although I have to say, you're not what I expected."

Willow glanced at him warily. "And what did you expect?"

"A thief's sister. Someone shallow, loud, dramatic. Instead…" His gaze swept over her, lingering for a beat too long. "You're… warm. Witty. Stubborn as hell."

"And you're a smug billionaire with a god complex," she shot back, but there was no venom in her tone.

He smiled. "Guilty."

They laughed, and this time it was easy. Unforced.

Willow reached for a slice of melon and bit into it thoughtfully. "You don't laugh like that very often, do you?"

Luca turned to her, slightly caught off guard. "No," he admitted after a moment. "Not anymore."

She nodded, as if she'd already guessed. "You should."

Their eyes met, the air suddenly still between them. There was something about the way she said it—simple, sincere—that disarmed him.

He broke the moment first, reaching for the lemonade. "Careful, Willow. Keep being this charming and I'll think you actually like me."

She smirked. "Let's not get ahead of ourselves."

But she didn't look away.

And neither did he.

The sun dipped low on the horizon as the tender boat glided smoothly over the rippling water. The cove behind them faded into twilight, and ahead, the yacht stood like a glowing palace, its lights twinkling in the gathering dusk.

Willow wrapped her arms around herself, the sea breeze cooler now against her damp skin. The day had been almost… too perfect. It unsettled her, how easily she'd laughed, how naturally her guard had dropped. She wasn't sure if it was the salt air or Luca's charm—maybe both—but she felt different. Off-balance.

Luca sat beside her, quiet for once, his gaze focused on the fading coastline. He hadn't tried to flirt again, hadn't pushed. That unnerved her more than his teasing ever had.

As the tender pulled alongside the yacht, crew members moved swiftly, helping them aboard. The deck lights bathed everything in soft gold, and the scent of lemon oil and sea lingered in the air.

Luca turned to her as they stepped back onto the main deck. "Dinner will be in an hour. Unless you'd like something sooner."

"No," she said quickly, brushing damp strands of hair from her face. "An hour's fine."

He nodded but didn't move. "Did you enjoy today?"

She hesitated, then met his eyes. "Yes. More than I wanted to."

That pulled a slow smile from him, the kind that made her stomach tighten. "Good."

Willow started toward her cabin, but his voice stopped her.

"Willow."

She turned halfway.

"Nothing about this has to be pretend," he said, voice lower now. "You're here because you chose to be. Whatever happens… I won't force anything."

That, somehow, was worse than a flirtation. The sincerity of it. The way it made her feel like the walls she'd spent years building were dissolving grain by grain under his gaze.

She nodded once, almost imperceptibly, and disappeared down the corridor.

Luca watched her go, hands loose at his sides, then exhaled slowly and turned to face the open sea.

The dining table was set on the upper deck beneath a canopy of stars. Candles flickered in the warm night breeze, casting golden light over gleaming silverware and crystal glasses. The sea stretched out around them, endless and still, the yacht gently rocking like a lullaby.

Willow approached slowly, her damp hair curling softly around her shoulders, sundress fluttering in the warm breeze. She paused when she saw Luca already seated, leaning back in his chair with a glass of wine in hand, dressed in an open-collared white shirt and linen trousers. He looked infuriatingly at ease.

"You look nice," he said with a smirk, standing to pull out her chair.

"I was going to say the same," she replied cautiously, sliding into her seat without meeting his eyes.

A steward poured her wine and then stepped away as a light antipasto course was placed in front of them. Willow picked at marinated olives and grilled artichoke hearts, conscious of the way Luca watched her—not hungrily, but thoughtfully. Like he was studying her.

"You were quiet after we returned," he said after a moment.

She glanced up, surprised by his gentler tone. "Just tired, I guess. It was a long day."

"But not a bad one," he prompted.

She gave a half-smile. "Not bad."

They ate in easy silence for a while, the sound of the ocean mingling with the soft classical music playing from hidden speakers.

Midway through the second course—grilled sea bass with lemon and capers—Luca leaned forward slightly.

"Tomorrow," he said, "we'll be stopping at a small village just up the coast. It's a favourite of mine. Off the tourist path. Quiet. Beautiful."

Willow arched an eyebrow. "What's the catch?"

"No catch," he said, lips twitching. "Unless you count charming locals and ancient cobblestone streets as a trap."

She hesitated, then nodded. "Okay. That actually sounds… nice."

"I thought it might. There's a market in the morning. You might find something worth taking home."

Willow stabbed at her fish, not looking up. "This already feels like something I won't be able to explain back home."

"You don't need to explain it," Luca said quietly. "Just live it while you can."

That caught her off guard. She looked up, and for a second, the playboy mask was gone. His expression was open, sincere. Almost wistful.

Willow set down her fork. "You're making this harder."

He leaned back with a small smile. "Good. You're not supposed to be comfortable around me."

"Mission accomplished," she muttered, but there was no heat behind the words.

They finished their meal slowly; the mood suspended between something intimate and something cautious. As dessert arrived—tiny cups of espresso and panna cotta with wild berries—Willow found herself relaxing again, lulled by the night, the wine, and Luca's unexpected restraint.

And when he didn't press her for more, didn't reach for her hand or try to tempt her under the stars, it unsettled her more than any kiss would have.

Because she'd started to wonder if she wanted him to.

Chapter Ten

The yacht anchored just beyond the curve of a secluded cove, and a smaller tender carried Luca and Willow to shore as the early morning sun gilded the horizon. The village ahead looked like something out of a postcard—stone buildings clinging to the hillside, their shutters painted in faded blues and greens, bougainvillea tumbling down the walls. Narrow cobblestone streets twisted upward toward a quiet piazza, and the scent of espresso and fresh bread filled the air.

Willow stepped onto the weathered dock with wide eyes, her sandals clicking softly as she took in the surroundings.

"It's like something out of a dream," she murmured.

"It's better than a dream," Luca replied, helping her up the short steps. "This place is real. Untouched."

He led her into the heart of the village where a small market was already bustling with early risers. Stalls brimmed with sun-warmed tomatoes, fresh herbs, wheels of cheese, and handwoven baskets. Locals greeted each other in lyrical Italian, and the entire square seemed to pulse with a slow, peaceful rhythm.

As they passed a bakery, a white-haired man with kind eyes and a deep tan stepped out from the doorway. He blinked at Luca, then broke into a broad, gap-toothed grin.

"Luca Lombardi!" the man exclaimed in accented English, stepping forward and clapping him warmly on the shoulder. "Still too handsome for your own good, eh?"

Luca chuckled and shook his hand. "Ciao, Pietro. You're the one who doesn't age."

Pietro waved him off. Then his sharp eyes flicked to Willow and widened. "And who is this bella ragazza?"

Willow flushed instantly.

Luca glanced at her, a slow smile playing at his lips. "This is Willow."

Pietro looked between them, clearly delighted. "Willow," he said, drawing out the name as if tasting it. "Ah, like the tree. Gentle and strong. Bellissima."

Willow laughed softly, charmed despite herself. "Thank you. It's lovely to meet you."

Pietro beamed. "Any woman who can make him smile like that must be very special."

Luca coughed, clearly amused. "Pietro, please."

"What? I'm old, not blind," Pietro said, winking at Willow. "You take her to the market. Show her the real treasures. But don't let her leave without trying Rosa's olive bread—it's almost as famous as your reputation, eh?"

Willow looked at Luca with a lifted brow. "That sounds like a story I need to hear."

"Later," Luca said dryly, tugging her gently toward the stalls. "Much, much later."

As they walked away, Willow glanced back and caught Pietro giving Luca a thumbs-up and an exaggerated wink. She shook her head, half-laughing.

"You've got fans in every port, don't you?"

Luca's hand brushed lightly against the small of her back. "Only the charming ones."

Willow didn't respond—but she didn't step away, either.

The sun climbed higher as Luca and Willow wandered through the bustling market. Brightly coloured awnings flapped in the breeze, shading stalls filled with fresh produce, woven scarves, handmade ceramics, and delicate jewellery. Willow moved from booth to booth like a child in a candy store, her fingers trailing over carved olive wood bowls and sun-bleached postcards.

She picked up a hand-painted tile, turning it over with interest. "It's all so beautiful here. I feel like I've stepped into another world."

Luca stood close, watching her more than the market. "This place has a way of reminding people what life can feel like. Slower. Simpler."

She glanced at him, arching a brow. "And yet you live on a yacht surrounded by staff and luxury."

He grinned. "I didn't say I practice simplicity. I only said I appreciate it."

Willow shook her head, smiling. "Of course you did."

They paused near a cart piled with fresh peaches and lemons. The vendor handed Willow a slice of juicy fig on a toothpick. She tasted it, eyes widening.

"Wow," she murmured. "It's like honey and sunshine had a baby."

Luca chuckled. "That's a new one."

A few steps later, they came upon a gelato cart with gleaming silver bins and a cheerful man behind the counter.

"Cioccolato e fragola," Luca said to the vendor, then turned to Willow. "Unless you'd prefer something tamer?"

Willow put her hands on her hips. "I'm not tame."

His smile deepened. "No. You're not."

He paid for two cones and handed her one. The chocolate and strawberry were rich and creamy, the perfect balance of indulgence and sweetness. They found a low stone wall near the fountain in the piazza and sat side by side.

Willow licked her gelato, then caught a smear of chocolate on her lip. Before she could wipe it, Luca reached out and gently swiped it away with his thumb. His touch was fleeting but warm, and it made her breath catch.

"You're a mess," he said lightly, but there was something behind his voice. A note of tension. Of curiosity.

She tilted her head at him. "And you're too smooth."

"Is that a complaint?"

She grinned. "Maybe."

They sat in comfortable silence, the laughter of children echoing through the square, the scent of espresso lingering in the air. Willow turned her cone upside down and pretended to inspect it seriously.

"I think yours is bigger," she said.

Luca raised an eyebrow. "Are we really comparing cone size now?"

"Only because you're clearly compensating for something."

He let out a low laugh. "You're dangerous when you're relaxed."

She licked her gelato with exaggerated slowness, shooting him a mock-innocent look. "You have no idea."

His smile faded just a little, his gaze deepening. "I'm starting to."

Willow's heart gave a strange little twist. She looked away quickly, but the air between them had changed—warmer now, charged with something unspoken.

She stood, brushing non-existent crumbs from her dress. "Come on, Lombardi. Let's see if we can find that olive bread Pietro was so dramatic about."

Luca followed, eyes lingering on her with open admiration. "Lead the way, bella ragazza. But fair warning—I'm not done with you yet."

Willow laughed over her shoulder. And for the first time in days, it was real and easy.

They followed the winding cobblestone alleyways, Luca confidently leading the way with Willow just a step behind, until the scent of baking bread and rosemary drifted toward them on the breeze. Around the corner, a small stone bakery stood nestled between two flowering balconies. A hand-painted sign above the door read Pane di Rosa.

Inside, the warmth hit them immediately—along with the mouthwatering aroma of fresh bread. Behind the wooden counter stood an older woman in a flour-dusted apron, her silver hair twisted into a loose bun, eyes sharp as ever.

"Luca!" she cried, wiping her hands on her apron and coming around the counter.

"Ciao, Rosa!" Luca greeted, opening his arms.

She embraced him fiercely, then stepped back and looked him over with a knowing smirk. "Still as handsome as ever. Still not married, I assume?"

Luca chuckled. "Not quite."

Rosa turned her eyes to Willow and immediately softened. "Ah… ma chi è questa bella creatura?" she asked, eyes twinkling.

"This is Willow," Luca said, watching the exchange with amusement. "She has excellent taste in gelato and a questionable opinion of me."

Willow held out her hand, smiling. "It's lovely to meet you."

Rosa ignored the hand and pulled her into a warm embrace instead. "Bellissima! Look at those eyes! And such lovely manners." She stepped back and wagged a finger at Luca. "Don't mess this one up. You never bring anyone here."

Luca raised a brow but said nothing.

Rosa returned to the counter and pulled a warm loaf of olive bread from a basket, tearing off two generous pieces and handing them over.

"Still warm," she said proudly. "My own olives, pressed just this season."

Willow took a bite and let out a soft moan of appreciation. "Oh my god. This is unreal."

"Told you," Luca said, watching her with a half-smile.

Rosa beamed. "She appreciates good bread. She's a keeper." Then, to Willow: "You tell me if he starts acting like a fool. I'll sort him out."

"I'll keep that in mind," Willow said with a laugh.

Rosa winked at her. "Good girl."

They stayed a while longer, nibbling on bread and sipping espresso from tiny ceramic cups. Willow found herself charmed by the warmth of the woman, the small-town intimacy of the moment. It was so far from her life back home, from her worries about Lily, from the cold logic of Dennis's world.

And Luca—here in this place, with these people—seemed softer. Real.

As they left the bakery, arms full of warm bread wrapped in paper, Rosa called after them from the doorway. "Don't let her go, Luca! You'll never do better!"

Luca turned to Willow, smiling. "She's rarely wrong."

Willow shook her head, trying to hide her blush. "That remains to be seen."

But her smile lingered all the way back through the square.

By the time they returned to the yacht, the sun had dipped low on the horizon, draping the sea in a veil of molten gold. The water shimmered like liquid fire, casting dancing reflections against the hull as if the world itself had been set aglow just for them.

Willow stepped aboard slowly, her sandals brushing the teak deck, a soft smile still clinging to her lips. The charm of the village lingered on her like the scent of sun-warmed flowers and fresh-baked bread. She could still hear the echo of laughter from the children playing near the fountain, the strains of accordion music from a shaded café, the way Rosa had pressed that last piece of olive bread into her hand with a wink.

Her cheeks were still flushed from the warmth of the day—and perhaps from something more. Her eyes sparkled with the quiet afterglow of genuine delight, the kind that came from unexpected joy.

One of the stewards had already taken the small bundle of treasures she'd gathered: a woven bracelet in coral and sea-foam green from a cheerful vendor at the market, a tiny glass jar of local honey with a handwritten label, and that precious bit of Rosa's bread, lovingly wrapped in brown paper and tied with twine. They were small things, but meaningful—tangible proof of a day that had felt, impossibly, like something out of someone else's life. A simpler one. A sweeter one.

But as the engines hummed to life and the yacht began to pull away from the shore, slicing gracefully through the gilded waves, something in Willow's posture shifted. She paused at the top of the stairs leading down to the main deck, her hand drifting to the back of her neck as if trying to massage away the weight that had returned.

Luca, a few paces behind her, noticed the change immediately. Her shoulders, once relaxed and carefree, were now slightly hunched. The sun caught in her hair, highlighting strands of gold and copper as the wind lifted them gently.

"Tired?" he asked softly.

"A little," she admitted, offering a faint smile. It didn't quite reach her eyes. "It was a perfect day." And yet something about the motion of the yacht, the cooling air, the realisation that the sun was setting—on more than just the day—left her subdued.

He reached out instinctively, a hand half-raised to her back in support, but she waved him off gently, a polite refusal laced with hesitation. Then she turned to descend the steps.

At that same moment, the yacht shifted slightly with the pull of the current—a subtle movement, but enough.

Willow's heel caught on the top stair.

She gasped as her balance slipped, arms flailing slightly as she tipped forward.

"Willow!"

Luca moved faster than thought. In a single stride, he was there, arms wrapping tightly around her waist just as she would have fallen. His grip was firm, protective, grounding.

Her hands clutched at his shoulders, fingers curling into the soft linen of his shirt. Her breath came in a sharp intake, her chest pressed against his, rising and falling in sync with the rush of adrenaline.

The moment stilled. Neither of them moved.

Willow stared up at him, wide-eyed and breathless, heart pounding in her chest—not only from the sudden scare, but from the way he held her. The way he looked at her.

His hand remained splayed against the small of her back, thumb brushing just slightly against the curve of her waist, as if he didn't trust the world enough to let her go. His face was close, the shadow of his jaw grazing the sunlight. His scent—clean and warm, touched by sea salt and something uniquely him—washed over her.

"Are you okay?" he asked, voice low and rougher than usual, like it had scraped against something raw.

She gave a small nod, her throat too tight to speak. Everything about him felt too close, too real. The warmth of his hands, the steadiness of his breath, the way his eyes weren't looking at her—they were looking at her lips.

Willow swallowed hard. "I didn't mean—"

But the words never finished.

Because Luca kissed her.

It wasn't tentative. It was sure, full of purpose—like a decision he'd already made a hundred times but had only just allowed himself to act on. His hand came up to cradle the side of her face, fingers curving around her jaw with reverent pressure as his mouth claimed hers.

The kiss was heat and certainty and years of restraint unravelling in a single, breath-stealing moment.

Her thoughts scattered like petals in a storm.

Willow's breath hitched, and her hands instinctively found his chest—broad, solid, warm beneath the soft cotton of his shirt. Her palms flattened against him as if to steady herself, but instead, she found herself drawn closer. Her fingers slid upward, exploring the strength in his shoulders, the tension in his neck, before tangling in the thick, dark waves of his hair.

And when she kissed him back, it wasn't careful. It was hungry. Needy.

His other arm wrapped around her waist, pulling her flush against him, her thighs brushing his. She gasped into his mouth when his tongue teased hers, coaxing a soft, involuntary moan from her throat that made him groan low in response.

The sound vibrated through her, sparking something primal and electric.

Her body responded before her mind could catch up—arching into him, her legs shifting to make space, her grip tightening in his hair as the kiss deepened, darkened. There was fire in the way he kissed her, yes—but also a kind of aching gentleness. A tenderness that made her feel cherished, not just wanted.

One of his hands slid down, skimming her ribcage, her hip, resting possessively at the small of her back. He kissed her like he was trying to memorise the shape of her mouth, the breathless little sounds she made, the way her body trembled slightly beneath his touch.

And she let him. God, she let him.

When they finally broke apart, it wasn't out of hesitation. It was survival. They needed air.

Willow's chest heaved with ragged breath, lips parted and swollen, her eyes wide with wonder and disbelief. Luca's hand was still on her back, fingers curling slightly as if reluctant to let go. His forehead rested against hers for a long, silent moment, their breaths mingling, hearts pounding in perfect sync.

"Dio," he whispered, voice hoarse. "I didn't plan that."

Willow blinked up at him, lips tingling, heart racing. "Neither did I."

They stood like that for a moment, the sea whispering around them, the sky darkening.

And somewhere between danger and desire, a line had been crossed.

Neither of them seemed eager to step back.

The silence that followed crackled with the weight of what had just happened. Luca's hand lingered at her back, his touch still burning through the thin fabric of her dress. Willow's lips tingled, her heartbeat erratic, and yet—it wasn't just the kiss that left her breathless. It was the meaning behind it. The way he looked at her. Like she wasn't part of a bargain. Like she was the only thing that mattered.

And that scared her more than anything.

"I—" Her voice was barely audible. She took a half step back, just enough to slip out of his hold. "I need a moment."

Luca's brows drew together slightly, but he didn't stop her. "Willow…"

She shook her head gently, already turning away. "Please."

She didn't wait for his response. She couldn't. Her sandals clicked softly against the polished deck as she moved toward her cabin, the Mediterranean breeze wrapping around her like a question she couldn't yet answer.

Once inside, she shut the door behind her and leaned against it, pressing a trembling hand to her lips. Her fingers brushed where he'd kissed her—where she'd kissed him back—and the heat of it was still there. Too vivid. Too real.

Her breath came in shallow waves as she crossed to the small porthole window and stared out into the night. The moon cast a silver path across the dark sea, calm and endless. She wished she felt the same.

But inside her, a storm was brewing.

This wasn't part of the plan. She came for Lily. Not to fall under the spell of a man who should have been the enemy. A man who saw through her too easily. Who touched her like she was fragile and kissed her like he already knew she wasn't.

Willow hugged her arms around herself and closed her eyes. She could still feel him. Still taste the lingering espresso on his tongue, the salt on his skin, the way his hands had steadied her like he'd never let her fall.

And the worst part?

She wasn't sure she wanted him to.

Chapter Eleven

The early morning sun spilled gold across the deck, warming the polished wood beneath Luca's bare feet. Light danced on the gentle ripples of the sea, the horizon blurring where the sky kissed the water in soft shades of pearl and blue. A breeze stirred the linen of his shirt, but he barely felt it. Normally, this was his favourite part of the day—the quiet stillness before the world intruded, before people spoke and phones rang, and complications reared their heads.

But today, silence felt heavy.

He couldn't focus. Not on the view. Not on the perfect weather. Not even on the espresso cooling beside him, untouched. His mind refused to settle, replaying every second of the night before on a loop.

He hadn't slept much.

Luca ran a hand through his hair and exhaled slowly, jaw tightening as his eyes drifted toward the closed cabin door at the far end of the corridor. Hers.

She hadn't come out last night. Not for dinner. Not even when he'd gently knocked, murmuring her name—just once, careful not to pressure her. He'd lingered by the door longer than he'd meant to, hoping for any sound, any sign. But there'd been nothing. No footsteps. No soft voice. No breath.

Just silence.

And now... now he didn't know where they stood.

The kiss hadn't been planned. It had ambushed him as much as her. When she'd slipped on the stairs, when he'd caught her and held her against him, the fear of her falling had crashed headfirst into the longing he'd buried beneath charm and bravado.

Her sapphire-blue eyes had met his—wide, startled, inches from his own—and something inside him had snapped. All the walls he'd so carefully built between them, the cynical reminders that this was temporary, strategic, controlled... had crumbled like sand under a tide.

And she had kissed him back.

God, she'd kissed him back—with fire and urgency and something dangerously close to wanting. Not out of obligation. Not out of gratitude. But real, aching want.

And then she'd fled. Torn herself from his arms like she'd touched a live wire. Vanished into her cabin and closed the door, leaving only the echo of her footsteps and the ghost of her lips on his.

Luca clenched his jaw, staring out at the open sea as if it might give him an answer. He didn't regret kissing her. Not for a second. Every part of it had felt… right. Real. But what gnawed at him now, what twisted in his chest like an anchor, was the fear that maybe he'd pushed too far. Moved too fast. Maybe he should've waited. Let her choose the moment. Let her come to him.

Because Willow wasn't like the others.

She wasn't dazzled by his wealth or flattered by his name. She didn't melt under expensive wine or fall for rehearsed smiles. She saw through him—straight through—with eyes that read past the charm and the persona, eyes that left him feeling more exposed than he'd ever allowed himself to be.

She was stubborn. Fiercely selfless. Disarmingly sincere.

And that kiss…

That kiss hadn't felt like a mistake.

It had felt like the beginning of something.

Something dangerous. Something exhilarating. Something real.

And that terrified him almost as much as it thrilled him.

But maybe she didn't feel the same.

Maybe it had only been a slip. A fluke. A heat-of-the-moment lapse she now regretted.

Luca rubbed a hand across the back of his neck, then down his jaw, frustration rising beneath the surface of his carefully controlled exterior. He was used to control. Used to knowing where he stood. But Willow made the ground shift beneath him—and he was beginning to realise he didn't want it to stop.

What he wanted—what he was beginning to need—was Willow.

Not just for a kiss. Not for a fleeting week on a luxury yacht.

But for something longer.

He didn't do forever.

But he could do longer.

And that thought… that hope… scared him in a way nothing else had in years.

Luca picked up the espresso cup and took a sip, even though it had gone cold.

Behind him, a door creaked faintly.

Luca's head snapped around, his pulse skipping before he could control it.

Willow stepped out onto the deck, sunlight catching in her loose hair. She wore a simple sundress, the hem brushing her knees, and her eyes were bright—open, cheerful—as if nothing at all had happened the night before.

"Good morning," she said lightly, her voice breezy and warm. "I was wondering where the coffee was hiding."

He blinked. "Morning."

She moved past him, the scent of citrus and ocean clinging to her skin. No hesitation. No lingering awkwardness. Not even a flicker of tension.

"I hope I didn't sleep too late," she added, reaching for the carafe and pouring herself a cup like they did this every day. "I think I needed it after all the walking yesterday."

Luca stared at her, momentarily thrown by the calm in her expression, so at odds with the storm of thoughts in his own mind.

"You slept well?" he asked carefully.

She took a sip, then nodded. "Like a rock."

He almost laughed. Almost.

Willow glanced at him over the rim of her mug. "Why are you looking at me like that?"

"I—" He caught himself, smile tugging faintly at his mouth. "No reason."

"Hmm." Her eyes sparkled. "You look like someone who had far too much espresso and not enough sleep."

Luca folded his arms, watching her as she moved to the railing, gazing out at the sea. Everything in her body language was composed, unbothered. And yet, beneath the surface… was it an act?

She hadn't forgotten the kiss. He was sure of it. You didn't kiss someone like that— didn't melt into them and breathe them in—only to wake up and feel nothing.

But if Willow was flustered, she wasn't showing it.

She was giving him… space. Or maybe she was building a wall.

"I thought we'd dock again this afternoon," he said, walking over to join her. "There's a place I think you'd like. Small bay, hardly anyone ever goes there. Quiet. Private."

She turned to look at him, lips curling into a soft, measured smile. "Sounds lovely."

He met her gaze. "Willow…"

"Yes?"

There it was. A flicker. A hesitation in her eyes—gone in an instant, but it was there.

He wanted to press. Wanted to ask if she was all right if she was pretending. If the kiss had shaken her as much as it had shaken him.

But she was smiling again, taking another sip of coffee, the sea breeze tugging at her hair like nothing had changed.

So, neither of them said what lingered between them—unspoken, undeniable. But it was there. Refusing to vanish.

And it wasn't going anywhere.

The yacht slowed as it glided into the small, secluded bay. The water was a deep, shimmering turquoise, calm and clear enough to see the rippling sand beneath. Steep cliffs framed the inlet, lush with wild greenery, and the only sound was the rhythmic splash of waves against the hull.

Willow stepped onto the lower deck barefoot, her dress fluttering in the soft breeze. She stared out in quiet awe.

"This place is beautiful," she murmured.

Luca, standing beside her, watched her more than the scenery. "I thought you'd like it."

A small launch boat had been prepared to take them closer to shore. No bustling towns, no other boats—just the gentle hush of nature and the scent of salt in the air.

They explored the cove slowly, walking along the narrow stretch of untouched sand. Willow dipped her toes into the water, gasping at its coolness, and laughed when a tiny wave chased her ankles.

"Is this what you do when you're not intimidating boardrooms and terrorising your staff?" she teased, glancing over her shoulder.

"Only the lucky ones get to see this side of me," Luca replied, dryly amused.

They sat on a weathered rock, sharing a few bites of the snacks brought from the yacht. There was something simple about it. Peaceful. Uncomplicated—at least for a while.

But by the time they returned to the yacht, the sky had shifted.

The sun had dipped behind a layer of fast-moving clouds, casting a strange, dull light over the water. The wind had picked up too, lifting Willow's hair off her shoulders and tugging at the corners of the tablecloth on the upper deck.

She paused, glancing toward the horizon.

"Looks like weather's coming in," she said softly.

Luca followed her gaze. The sea, once glassy, had darkened—now a steel-blue under the encroaching clouds. In the distance, thunder rolled faintly, muffled but unmistakable.

"I'll speak to the captain," he said. "We'll reroute if we have to."

Willow nodded, but she lingered, her arms folding around herself as the breeze grew cooler. The mood had changed—the light-heartedness of the day giving way to something quieter, tenser.

Luca returned moments later. "It should pass us by. Nothing serious, just a summer squall. But we'll stay cautious."

She offered him a smile, faint but steady. "You're good at pretending not to be worried."

"And you're good at pretending yesterday never happened," he said, before he could stop himself.

The wind whistled between them. Willow's smile faded, and her eyes met his—steady, unreadable.

"We'll talk," she said. "Just… not yet."

And then she turned and walked inside, her footsteps quiet against the deck as the first distant raindrops began to fall.

The wind howled louder now, whistling through the rigging and rattling the yacht's windows. The sky had turned a menacing charcoal, and the sea was no longer calm— it rolled beneath them in great, restless swells, tilting the vessel with each pass. Rain came down in heavy sheets, lashing the decks and soaking anything not under cover.

Willow stood frozen near the sliding glass doors of the main salon, watching the chaos outside with wide eyes. The earlier confidence she'd shown had dissolved, her arms wrapped tightly around herself as thunder cracked like a whip across the sky.

"We've hit rougher waters than expected," Luca said, entering behind her. His voice was calm, but his eyes searched her face. "The captain assures me we're safe. Just a storm cell passing through."

She didn't respond. Her fingers tightened on her arms, her body rigid.

"Willow?" he said more gently.

"I—I don't like this," she admitted in a quiet voice. "I've never been on a boat in a storm before. It feels like… like it's too much. Like we could tip over."

Lightning split the sky, casting a stark flash across her pale face. A heartbeat later, thunder cracked overhead—loud and sudden—making her flinch.

Luca moved closer. "We won't tip over. She's built for this. Stabilisers, reinforced hull. Everything's under control."

But she didn't look convinced. Her breathing had quickened, and when the yacht tilted suddenly, her hand flew out, grabbing the back of the couch for balance.

"I don't want to go below deck," she said, voice barely above a whisper.

He stepped beside her, lowering his voice. "Then you stay here. With me."

Her eyes flicked to his, searching—reassurance, maybe—and whatever she found made her nod.

Luca reached for a throw blanket draped over the nearby armchair and gently wrapped it around her shoulders. Then, without a word, he guided her toward the couch and sat beside her, keeping a respectful distance but close enough that his presence could steady her.

Outside, the storm raged on, rain slamming against the windows and wind howling like a living thing.

But inside, there was a fragile calm. Willow sat tucked under the blanket, her knees drawn up slightly, Luca beside her, watching her more than the storm.

"I didn't peg you for the nervous type," Luca said softly—not teasing, just curious.

Willow's eyes stayed fixed on the rain streaking the glass, her voice quiet. "It's not just the storm."

He waited, giving her space.

"My parents died in a car accident," she said finally. "It was raining. I was eighteen." Her hands tightened around the blanket. "The roads were slick, visibility was bad. I was waiting for them to come home, and they never did."

Luca's expression shifted—no longer just concerned, but something deeper. Understanding. Regret.

She gave a small, hollow laugh. "I guess storms have never felt the same since."

He didn't speak right away. Then, gently, "That's not something you just… get over."

"No," she whispered. "You just learn to carry it differently."

Luca was silent for a moment, watching her with something raw and unguarded in his gaze. Then, slowly, he shifted closer on the couch.

"Come here," he said gently, extending his arm in quiet invitation.

Willow hesitated—but only for a heartbeat. Then she moved, wordlessly, curling into his side. His arm wrapped around her shoulders, strong and sure, anchoring her as the yacht swayed gently beneath them.

He held her close, the rhythm of his heartbeat steady against her cheek. No words were needed—just warmth and closeness, the unspoken understanding between two people who had both lost and learned to guard their hearts.

Her breath softened, her body relaxing by degrees as the storm raged outside but not within. Luca rested his cheek against her hair, closing his eyes for a moment.

Neither of them moved.

And for the first time in a long while, Willow felt safe.

The rain tapped rhythmically against the windows, a low, steady drumbeat that echoed the soft rise and fall of Willow's breath.

Luca looked down at her, surprised to realise she'd fallen asleep.

Her head rested against his chest, one hand curled loosely near his collarbone, her lashes casting delicate shadows on her cheeks. In sleep, she looked even younger. Vulnerable. Unarmoured. The faint crease of worry that so often lived between her brows had smoothed out, and her lips parted slightly with each even breath.

He didn't move. Didn't dare.

Something tightened in his chest—a strange pull he didn't recognise or maybe didn't want to name.

He could still feel the echo of her earlier words. The storm. Her parents. The fear she rarely let show. And yet she'd trusted him enough to fall asleep in his arms.

Luca tightened his hold just slightly, his hand brushing slowly along her back, protective and quiet. Outside, lightning flashed, illuminating the sky, but inside the room, all was still.

He let his eyes close, not to sleep—but to savour this unexpected peace.

Because for the first time since Willow Taylor had walked into his world, Luca Lombardi didn't feel alone.

Willow stirred slowly, warmth cocooning her, the rhythmic thump of a heartbeat beneath her cheek.

It took her a moment to remember where she was.

The soft hum of the yacht. The faint patter of rain easing into silence. The steady rise and fall of Luca's chest beneath her. She blinked, disoriented, then lifted her head slightly—and froze.

Luca was asleep.

His arm was still wrapped around her, holding her gently but securely. His head was tilted back against the cushions, his dark lashes fanned against his cheekbones, his features softened in sleep. In that moment, he didn't look like the arrogant billionaire she'd first faced in his sleek black limousine. He looked human. Tired. A little bit undone.

Willow's breath caught.

She didn't move, didn't speak. Just… watched him.

The storm had passed. The yacht rocked gently, cradled by quiet waves, but inside her, a different storm churned.

How had this happened?

She had come on this trip with walls in place, with boundaries firm and clear. Yet here she was, wrapped in his arms, her heart betraying her with its fluttering rhythm. She studied the curve of his mouth, the relaxed lines of his brow, and felt a tug low in her chest she didn't want to name.

Carefully, slowly, she shifted—just enough to see his face more fully. He murmured something in his sleep, something in Italian she didn't understand, and the sound of it sent a shiver down her spine.

Willow closed her eyes for a beat, forcing herself to breathe.

This wasn't supposed to happen. She wasn't supposed to feel… this.

But as Luca held her in sleep like she was something precious, something worth keeping, she realised the line she'd drawn between them had blurred a long time ago.

And deep down, she wasn't sure she wanted to go back.

He woke when she was looking at him.

Luca's eyes blinked open slowly, still hazy with sleep, and for a moment he simply stared at her. Disoriented, maybe. Or surprised to find her still in his arms.

Her face was close—too close—and when full awareness settled in, his gaze dropped to her mouth before climbing back to her eyes. The air between them tightened.

Neither of them spoke.

Willow's breath caught. Her heart thudded against her ribs like it had been waiting for this exact moment—silent, intimate, and full of all the things they hadn't said. She should've looked away. Should've laughed, or made a joke, or said something—anything—to ease the tension.

But she didn't.

And when Luca reached up to tuck a strand of hair behind her ear, his fingers didn't fall away. They lingered, tracing a line down her jaw with a tenderness that made her skin prickle.

"You stayed," he murmured, his voice thick with something quieter than surprise. Something closer to hope.

Willow swallowed. "So did you."

The silence between them shifted—no longer heavy but charged. Electric. Her breath came shallow as his hand cupped her cheek, slow and reverent, thumb brushing along her cheekbone.

Her lips parted, just slightly, and that was all it took to break the spell.

She bolted upright, pulling away as if the couch had suddenly caught fire beneath her.

"Sorry," she said quickly, her voice breathless and too bright. "I didn't mean to fall asleep on you."

Luca cleared his throat, dragging a hand through his hair. He was sitting up now; gaze fixed on some vague point across the room.

"It's okay," he said, voice rougher than usual. "You looked… peaceful."

She gave a tight nod, crossing her arms to still the tremble in her hands.

But inside, nothing felt peaceful. Not anymore.

Chapter Twelve

Luca watched her disappear down the stairs to her cabin, the soft sway of her dress brushing against her legs, the faint scent of citrus and sea still lingering in the air.

He wanted to follow her. Wanted to press her back against the wall and kiss her like he'd been thinking about since the moment she stepped onto his yacht. Wanted her—completely, wholly, maddeningly more with each passing hour.

But he didn't move.

Instead, he stayed rooted where he was, jaw tight, heart hammering like a man on the edge of something he wasn't sure he could handle. Every time she looked at him with those wide, searching sapphire eyes, every time she smiled like she didn't know she was breaking down his walls… it undid him a little more.

His phone buzzed on the nearby table, the screen lighting up with a name that managed to break through the storm of thoughts in his mind.

Marcus.

With a sigh, Luca picked it up and answered. "You have the worst timing."

"Ciao to you too, amico mio," came Marcus's unmistakable voice—teasing, warm, a little smug. "Tell me you're not brooding again on that oversized luxury bathtub you call a yacht."

Luca pinched the bridge of his nose. "What do you want?"

"I'm getting married," Marcus said, just like that. No preamble. No buildup. "Tomorrow. In Tuscany."

Luca blinked. "Married? Tomorrow?"

"Married," Marcus repeated, his voice filled with an infectious joy Luca hadn't heard in a long time. "Elena said yes. I don't know why or how, but she did. So, I'm locking it in before she changes her mind."

Luca leaned back against the couch, a slow grin pulling at his lips despite the knot still sitting low in his chest. "You're serious."

"Dead serious. And you, my friend, are standing next to me when I say 'lo voglio.' So, cancel your meetings, dock that floating palace, and get your brooding ass to Tuscany."

Luca let out a breath, the tension easing slightly from his shoulders. "You really think she's the one?"

"I know she is," Marcus said without hesitation. "You'll get it when it happens to you."

Luca's gaze drifted toward the stairwell, where Willow had disappeared just moments ago. His chest tightened.

"Maybe," he murmured. "I'll be there."

"Bene. Bring a suit."

A faint smile tugged at Luca's mouth. "Can I bring a plus one?"

Marcus's laughter was immediate. "Dio mio, who is she? And don't say another supermodel again."

Luca chuckled. "No supermodel this time. Her name's Willow."

Marcus let out a low whistle. "Willow? Sounds poetic. Is she real or did you dream her up during one of your moody walks along the deck?"

"She's real," Luca said, quieter now. "Too real, maybe."

The teasing faded from Marcus's voice. "That serious, huh?"

"I don't know," Luca admitted. "We only just met… but she's different. She makes me forget who I'm supposed to be."

There was a pause, then Marcus spoke gently. "Maybe that's the point, amico. The right one doesn't make you forget who you are. She makes you remember."

Luca swallowed hard, his gaze still fixed on the stairwell. "Yeah… she's doing that, too."

Willow stepped back onto the deck, freshly showered, her skin glowing and her damp hair curling softly around her shoulders. She wore a simple sundress—sun-washed and delicate—that clung in ways Luca wished it wouldn't. The scent of soap and sea salt lingered as she passed him, stirring something he wasn't ready to name.

Luca glanced over the rim of his glass, letting his eyes linger a moment too long before he forced them away.

"You look… refreshed," he said, his smirk a weak shield.

She raised an eyebrow. "That almost sounded like a compliment."

"Don't get used to it." He turned his gaze back to the water, needing the space—even if it was only a breath of air between them.

Willow joined him at the railing, arms loosely crossed, her presence as natural and effortless as the ocean breeze. "So… what's next? Another private island? More rich people swimming spots?"

He let out a quiet breath. "Change of plans. We're heading to Porto Santo Stefano."

She blinked. "Where's that?"

"A port town on the Tuscan coast. Quiet. Old. Beautiful."

Her brows lifted. "And we're going there because…?"

He paused, watching a distant sailboat drift along the horizon. "A friend of mine is getting married. Marcus Bernardi."

Willow's expression shifted—curious, amused. "You're going to a wedding?"

"I wasn't planning on it," he said, taking a slow sip of his drink. "But he called. Asked me to come."

She tilted her head, studying him. "Must be someone important."

"He is," Luca said, quieter now. "The closest thing I have to a brother."

A breeze picked up, lifting the hem of her dress slightly, and she tucked it down with a small smile. "Are you sure I should come?"

"I told him I'd be bringing someone." His voice stayed light, detached. Too detached.

Willow's lips parted slightly. "Oh."

He glanced at her—just a flick of his eyes—and saw it. The shift. The flicker of surprise. The unspoken question. He looked away before he could start answering it.

"You'll like it," he added quickly, injecting false cheer into his voice. "Free food. Dancing. A bunch of overly emotional Italians making toasts that go on forever. What's not to love?"

She smiled faintly. "Sounds like a fairy tale."

He looked at her again—and this time, the urge to reach out, to touch her, to anchor her somehow—it hit harder than before. Wanting her body was easy. Too easy. But wanting anything more? That was where danger lived.

He took another drink. "We should get there by mid-afternoon. If you want, we can explore the village this afternoon."

Her smile widened, warmer this time. "That sounds like fun."

Luca said nothing, only nodded—and silently braced himself. For Tuscany. For Marcus. For her.

For whatever was coming next.

The yacht docked just before mid-afternoon, the sun high and golden over the terracotta rooftops of Porto Santo Stefano. The small harbour bustled with quiet charm—fishing boats bobbed gently in the water, gulls circled lazily overhead, and pastel buildings hugged the hillside like a well-kept secret.

Luca stepped onto the dock first, offering Willow a hand as she descended. She took it without hesitation, her fingers warm in his. Her sundress fluttered in the breeze, and she looked around with wide-eyed wonder.

"This place is like a postcard," she whispered.

"It has its moments," Luca said, releasing her hand too slowly.

They wandered through narrow cobblestone streets lined with flower boxes and sun-bleached shutters. Children played soccer in an alley. An old man sold gelato from a pushcart and nodded at them with a toothy grin. The smell of espresso and the sea drifted through the air.

Willow tilted her face toward the sun. "You grew up near here?"

He nodded. "About an hour inland. My family used to vacation here in the summer. My mother loved it."

"And you?" she asked, watching him carefully.

"I liked the quiet. Back then, anyway."

They strolled past a small church with open doors and soft music echoing inside. Willow paused near a fountain in a quiet square, trailing her fingers through the cool water.

"Have you ever thought about getting married?" she asked suddenly.

Luca stopped walking. The question hung there, delicate and dangerous.

"I mean, just… in general. You're going to a wedding, it made me wonder."

He studied her for a long moment, then sat on the edge of the fountain, elbows resting on his knees. "I did. Once."

Willow sat beside him, legs crossed at the ankle, her gaze steady. "What happened?"

Luca looked toward the sea, his voice even but distant. "Her name was Jessica. We were together for two years. I thought I was in love. Thought she was the one."

"And?"

"She slept with my best friend." His tone didn't waver, but something flickered in his eyes. "Caught them together. In my apartment. On my birthday, no less."

Willow winced. "God, Luca…"

He gave a half-shrug. "It was a long time ago. I was younger. Stupid. Thought love meant giving someone everything and hoping they wouldn't burn it down."

She was quiet for a beat, then said softly, "That kind of betrayal doesn't just disappear."

"No. But you learn to bury it deep enough not to feel it every day." He glanced at her. "And you stop believing in fairy tales."

Willow looked down at her hands, then back at him. "I think love's still worth the risk."

"Maybe it is," he said. "For someone who hasn't been taught otherwise."

They sat in silence for a moment, the breeze rustling through olive trees nearby.

Then Luca stood, offering his hand again. "Come on. There's a café up the hill with the best view in town."

Willow slipped her fingers into his. "And the best wine?"

He smirked. "Only the best."

As they walked up the winding street, sunlight slanting between the buildings, they passed a flower vendor with buckets of fresh blooms spilling colour onto the cobblestones. Without a word, Luca paused, handed a few euros to the old woman behind the stand, and plucked a single soft-pink bloom from the bucket.

Willow blinked in surprise as he turned to her.

"What are you doing?" she asked, half-laughing.

Luca didn't answer. Instead, he reached out and tucked the flower gently behind her ear, his fingers grazing her cheek.

"There," he said, stepping back to admire his work. "Now you look like you belong here."

She flushed but didn't look away. "You're full of surprises, Luca Lombardi."

His smirk was softer this time. "Don't let it go to your head."

They kept walking, but the air between them felt different—lighter, warmer. Like the flower wasn't the only thing beginning to bloom.

By the time they reached the café at the top of the hill, the sun was beginning its golden descent, bathing Porto Santo Stefano in warm, amber light. The little terrace café was alive with laughter and music—an older man played a lively tune on an accordion while couples danced between tables, their movements full of joy and wine-fuelled abandon.

Luca and Willow found a small table near the edge, where they could look out over the sparkling water below. A breeze carried the scent of lemon trees and the sea.

Willow smiled as she took her seat, cheeks flushed from the climb. "This is incredible."

Luca poured them each a glass of local red wine. "It's not bad," he admitted, sipping. "The view helps."

They sat in companionable silence for a while, taking it all in. The music, the voices, the sensation of being far from reality. Luca watched Willow as she closed her eyes, letting the sunlight kiss her face. He felt that pull again—irresistible, unwelcome.

Then a young man appeared beside their table. Tall, lean, maybe twenty-one at most, with tousled dark hair and bold, eager eyes. He addressed Willow with a smile and a slight bow.

"Perdonami, signorina… would you dance with me?"

Willow blinked, surprised, then glanced at Luca.

Luca raised an eyebrow but said nothing. He swirled the wine in his glass; his mouth set in a line that could have been amusement—or warning.

Willow turned back to the young man and laughed softly. "I'm flattered, really, but—"

"She'll dance," Luca said suddenly, his voice smooth but distant.

Willow looked at him again, startled.

"You don't mind?" she asked.

"Why would I?" he said coolly, not meeting her gaze. "You're free to enjoy yourself."

She hesitated, reading something deeper beneath his words. Then she stood, slowly, letting the young man lead her toward the circle of dancers.

Luca watched them go, the wine suddenly bitter on his tongue.

She laughed as the boy spun her gently, clumsy but charming. Her dress flowed with every step, and her hair caught the light like something out of a dream. Luca leaned back in his chair and forced a smile.

It shouldn't matter. She wasn't his.

But as the music swelled and Willow laughed again—this time, not at his side—he felt something unexpected flicker beneath his ribs.

Jealousy.

And it wasn't just about the dance.

Willow returned to the table breathless and smiling, a faint blush on her cheeks. She reached for her wine, but before she could take a sip, another hand extended toward her—a gentleman this time, older than the last, perhaps in his late thirties. Dapper in a white linen shirt and tailored trousers, with a confident smile and knowing eyes.

"May I have the next dance, bella signorina?" he asked in accented English.

Willow looked surprised, caught mid-sip. She glanced at Luca again, unsure.

Luca set his glass down slowly.

This man wasn't a boy playing at charm—he was practiced, polished. And the way his gaze lingered on Willow's figure didn't escape Luca's notice.

"She's just resting," Luca said, his tone calm, clipped. "Long day."

Willow raised an eyebrow at him. "I didn't say that."

The gentleman smiled patiently. "Only one dance. Then I'll let her rest all she likes."

Luca's jaw flexed. He stood, deliberately slow, placing a hand lightly on Willow's chair—possessive without being overt.

"I'm afraid I'll have to ask you to pick someone else, amico," Luca said, meeting the man's gaze without blinking. "She's spoken for."

The man chuckled, raising his hands in mock surrender. "Ah, capisco. Fortunato, eh?" He gave Willow a charming wink. "Enjoy your evening."

As he disappeared into the crowd, Willow turned in her chair to face Luca fully.

"Spoken for?" she asked, voice light but curious.

He sat again, eyes on the wine, then on her.

"You didn't seem to mind the first dance," she added.

"I didn't," he said. "He was a boy. That one wasn't."

Willow tilted her head. "And that matters?"

"It does to me," Luca replied, his voice lower, quieter now. "Boys flirt. Men take."

She studied him for a moment. "And what do you do, Luca?"

He met her eyes then, and for once, he didn't hide behind charm or detachment.

"I try not to want things I shouldn't."

Silence settled between them, thick with the weight of unsaid things. The music from the café faded into the distance, replaced by the pounding of Willow's heart—and, though he'd never admit it, Luca's.

Then his phone buzzed on the table, the vibration cutting clean through the moment. He glanced down.

Marcus.

Luca exhaled, dragging a hand through his hair before standing and turning slightly away. "Scusa," he murmured.

He answered the call. "Marcus."

"Is that your floating palace I see in the harbour?" Marcus's voice was bright with mischief.

Luca's lips twitched. "Possibly."

"I should've known. Only you would arrive in Tuscany looking like a Bond villain."

"I'm not wearing a tux," Luca said dryly.

"Yet," Marcus replied, chuckling. "You made good time. Want to grab a drink?"

"We are at the café up on the hill."

A pause.

"We?"

Luca's gaze drifted back to Willow. She sat quietly, chin resting on her hand, eyes fixed on him. Calm on the surface, but he knew better. She was listening. Wondering.

"Yes," he said simply. "Willow is with me."

"Ah," Marcus said slowly, a grin laced in his tone. "So, she is real."

"She is."

Another pause. This one deeper.

"Well, now I have to meet her."

Luca glanced at Willow again—sunlight catching in her hair, her fingers tracing the rim of her wineglass.

"Come to dinner," he said. "Bring Elena."

"Tonight?"

"Eight."

"Done," Marcus said. "And Luca?"

"Hm?"

There was a smile in Marcus's voice. "Try not to fall in love before dessert."

Luca ended the call without answering.

He turned back to the table. Willow raised an eyebrow, the corner of her mouth lifting in a question.

"Dinner on the yacht," Luca said, slipping his phone into his pocket. "Marcus and Elena are joining us."

She smiled. "Sounds like a night to remember."

He looked at her longer than he should have.

"Yeah," he said quietly. "It might be."

Chapter Thirteen

The harbour glowed with golden light as the sun dipped behind the hills, casting soft shadows over the water. The Serenissima, moored alongside a private dock, shimmered with quiet opulence—deck lights twinkling like stars, the gentle sound of waves lapping against the hull. Lanterns hung along the railings, casting a warm, amber glow over the polished teak deck and elegantly set dining table.

Luca stood near the gangway, hands in his pockets, watching the pier. Dressed in a tailored navy shirt and slate-grey trousers, he looked every bit the part of the powerful tycoon. But his eyes searched with quiet anticipation.

"They're late," he muttered, though not with annoyance.

"They're fashionably late," Willow said from behind him, her voice like a soft breeze.

He turned—and forgot everything.

She wore a simple white dress that moved with the harbour wind, delicate spaghetti straps framing her shoulders, her hair in a loose up-do with a few strands curling free. There was no jewellery, no pretence. Just Willow. And she was breathtaking.

"I—" He cleared his throat. "You look…"

"Like someone trying not to trip on a yacht?" she teased, stepping carefully in flat sandals.

"Like someone who belongs here," he said quietly.

Before she could respond, a car door slammed on the dock. Marcus and Elena strolled down the pier, arms linked. Marcus waved a bottle of wine above his head.

"Hope this boat's big enough for my ego," he called.

"Barely," Luca muttered, smirking.

Introductions flowed with warm smiles and easy laughter. Elena, tall and effortlessly elegant in a sea-green dress that shimmered in the deck lights, stepped forward and kissed both of Willow's cheeks in the European style.

Then she paused, her hands gently resting on Willow's arms as she took a closer look.

"Oh—look at your eyes," she breathed, a smile blooming across her face. "I don't think I've ever seen blue quite like that. Like the sky after a storm."

Willow flushed, caught off guard by the genuine compliment. "Thank you. That's… very kind of you."

Elena laughed softly. "Kind? It's the truth. If Luca doesn't spend the whole dinner staring into them, I'll be thoroughly disappointed."

Luca gave a quiet cough behind them, clearly amused. He turned to her with a subtle smile. "Willow, this is my closest friend—Marcus Bernardi."

Marcus stepped forward, effortlessly charismatic in an open-collared shirt and linen blazer. He took Willow's hands in his, his grin wide and immediate.

"Well, aren't you a beautiful thing," he said, his voice warm and teasing.

Willow arched a brow, lips curving into a smile. "And aren't you a charmer."

Marcus chuckled. "Guilty as charged. But only when the occasion calls for it."

Luca shook his head with a smirk. "Ignore him. He thinks he's irresistible."

"I don't think," Marcus replied, releasing Willow's hands with a wink. "I know."

As the sun dipped low over the horizon, casting a golden shimmer across the harbour, the group made their way to the candlelit dining table set on the upper deck. Soft music played in the background, mingling with the gentle lapping of water against the yacht's hull.

Plates of antipasti—paper-thin slices of prosciutto, aged cheeses, marinated olives, and golden bruschetta topped with ripe tomatoes—awaited them like edible artwork. A steward moved quietly among them, filling delicate crystal flutes with chilled sparkling wine. Bubbles fizzed and caught the glow of the setting sun.

Elena raised her glass with a radiant smile. "To unexpected meetings," she said, her voice light and lyrical.

Glasses clinked gently, the sound crisp against the backdrop of lapping waves and soft music.

Conversation flowed like the wine—effortless and warm. Elena regaled them with stories of her latest gallery opening in Milan, complete with flamboyant art collectors and the minor scandal of a forged Monet that had nearly caused a bidding war.

Marcus jumped in with his usual flair, offering dry quips and exaggerated tales from Monaco, including the time he accidentally bet against a prince in a poker game and had to escape through a kitchen window.

Laughter echoed across the deck. Willow found herself relaxing, drawn in by the easy camaraderie, the sparkle of lights above, and the magic of an Italian evening that felt entirely out of time.

"So, Willow," Elena said, tilting her head thoughtfully. "What is it that you do when you're not charming Italians into falling at your feet?"

Willow blushed, chuckling. "I work in publishing. Small house, mostly fiction."

"Oh, how romantic!" Elena sighed. "Books and stories. I always thought I'd write one someday, but I can barely finish a grocery list."

Marcus leaned forward. "Let me guess—romance novels?"

"Guilty," Willow said. "Though I read a little of everything. Lately it's been a lot of submissions that need… serious work."

"She's being modest," Luca said, his voice low and proud. "She has an eye for words. And a spine when it counts."

Willow glanced at Luca, surprised by the warmth in his voice. His gaze lingered on hers a moment longer than it should have—intense, searching, almost soft.

Marcus, never one to miss a beat, smirked into his wine glass. "Well, well. Isn't this interesting."

Elena grinned. "I have to agree. I haven't seen Luca look at someone like that in… ever."

Willow laughed nervously, brushing a strand of hair behind her ear as she looked away.

By the time dessert was served—an impossibly delicate tiramisu drizzled with espresso syrup—Willow's cheeks ached from so much smiling and laughter. The mood had shifted into something delightfully light, full of banter and teasing, and for the first time in days, she felt like herself again.

Eventually, Marcus excused himself to take a call, and Luca stepped away to speak with the captain, leaving Elena and Willow alone beneath the soft string lights that glittered above the deck.

Elena leaned in, her tone curious but kind. "So, how did you two meet?"

Willow hesitated for a beat. "Through my sister. She used to work for Luca's company in Rome."

Elena tilted her head, clearly intrigued but too polite to press further. Willow didn't add that she was only on the yacht because of a desperate bargain to save her sister from prison. Some truths didn't belong at a table filled with laughter and tiramisu.

Inside the yacht's lounge, Marcus sipped the last of his wine and watched through the window as Luca lingered by the railing, his gaze occasionally drifting back toward the table.

"She's lovely," Marcus said casually.

Luca didn't look at him. "Who?"

Marcus chuckled. "Who? You can't fool me, Luca. You like her more than you're letting on."

Luca finally turned, a flicker of something unreadable in his eyes. "It's complicated."

Marcus raised a brow. "It always is. But don't wait too long to figure it out. Women like that don't come around twice."

By the time Marcus and Elena left, it was very late. The sky above the harbour was a deep velvet, scattered with stars, and the gentle lapping of the water against the yacht created a soothing rhythm. Willow stood beside Luca as their guests prepared to depart, her heart light from the evening's laughter and unexpected connection.

Elena pulled Willow into a warm, lingering hug. "Keep in touch," she said sincerely, her sea-green eyes shining. "You're someone I'd like to keep as a friend."

Willow smiled, touched by the genuine affection. "I'd really like that."

Marcus stepped forward next, his usual smirk softened with real warmth. He took Willow's hands, then leaned in to kiss her cheek. "Goodnight, bella. It has been a pleasure."

As he stepped back, Marcus added with a teasing glint in his eye, "I'll see you tomorrow at our wedding."

"I will," Willow replied with a laugh, playing along.

As they descended the gangway, Willow watched them go, a gentle breeze lifting strands of her hair. The night was warm, the harbour lights flickering on the water like tiny stars.

Luca turned to her. "Are you tired?"

"Not really," she said, meeting his gaze.

He nodded toward the lounge. "Nightcap?"

"Yes, please."

They walked in comfortable silence across the deck, the sound of their footsteps soft against the polished wood. The air between them buzzed with something unspoken—familiar now, but still electric. Inside, the glow of the yacht's low lighting cast a golden warmth over everything, making the space feel intimate, almost like a cocoon separate from the rest of the world.

They sat close on the leather couch, glasses in hand, the low lighting casting golden shadows across the room. The soft clink of ice in their drinks punctuated the silence, a gentle echo in the stillness.

Willow glanced at Luca—and found his gaze already on her, steady and unreadable.

Neither of them spoke.

Without a word, he reached for her glass, his fingers brushing hers as he took it. Then with his own, he set them both on the coffee table with a quiet finality, as if removing any last barrier between them.

When he turned back to her, it was different.

He didn't just look—he saw her.

Every detail. Every flicker of emotion behind her eyes. And for the first time, she felt completely exposed and entirely safe all at once.

Then he leaned in.

The kiss started soft. A question. A breath. His lips brushed hers like a secret, tender and unhurried. But when her hand slid up his chest and curled into the fabric of his shirt, Luca deepened the kiss, his mouth claiming hers with a hunger that had waited far too long.

She answered him with equal fire. Her fingers tangled in his hair as he tilted his head, their mouths moving together in perfect, aching sync. His arm wrapped around her, pulling her close until there was no space left between them.

Everything else—the yacht, their bargain, the risk—melted into nothingness.

Luca shifted, gently easing her back onto the couch beneath him, never breaking the kiss. His weight braced on one arm, the other trailing down her side, exploring. He kissed her like a man starved. Like she was air. Like he was desperate to memorise every sound she made.

Willow arched beneath him, her hands roaming his back, his shoulders. He groaned into her mouth when her fingers slipped beneath his shirt, skimming the heat of his skin.

"Tell me to stop," he rasped against her lips, his forehead resting against hers, breathless.

She didn't.

Instead, she pulled him back down to her, kissing him deeper, harder—her body trembling with need. That was all he needed. His control, already frayed, began to unravel.

His mouth moved to her neck, trailing fire, then lower, while his hands traced the soft lines of her waist, her thighs, the curve of her hip. Willow gasped, her back arching as he whispered her name like a vow, a confession.

She was his undoing. The crack in his control. And he... he was quickly becoming hers.

They moved together on the narrow couch, tangled in heat and breathless laughter and desperate, whispered truths. It wasn't polished or planned. It wasn't the perfect moment.

But it was real.

And raw.

And burning.

"I want you, Willow," he confessed, his voice low and fierce. "I can't deny it any longer."

She met his gaze, her breath trembling, fragile yet fierce.

"I want you too," she whispered, her voice barely more than a breath, but filled with everything she felt.

Without a word, he rose from the couch, his gaze locked on hers—intense, unwavering. Then, with quiet purpose, he scooped Willow into his arms as if she weighed nothing, his strength effortless, his touch achingly tender. She curled into him, her arms slipping around his neck like it was the only place she belonged. When he kissed her again, it was slow and reverent, a kiss that lingered—not of urgency, but of quiet devotion. As if he was memorising the shape of her lips, the way she tasted, the way she felt—just in case the moment slipped away.

She didn't need to ask where they were going—she already knew. It was in the heat between them, in the way his hands held her like a vow, in the unspoken promises woven into every breath. And she wanted it—all of it. She was ready to surrender to this moment, to him, to the magnetic pull that had been building from the very beginning.

Because she knew now—without hesitation or doubt—she loved him. And she would never take this leap if she didn't.

Chapter Fourteen

Willow wasn't under any illusion that he loved her. His heart was too guarded. She knew that. But in this quiet, raw moment, it didn't matter. Not when every inch of her was burning with the truth she'd been hiding—when all that mattered was that they were here, together, finally unguarded and real.

Luca didn't break their kiss as he cradled her against his chest. Her arms wrapped instinctively around his neck, her heart hammering against her ribs. She had never been touched like this before—never been wanted like this. And yet, in his arms, she didn't feel fear. Only heat. Only longing.

He carried her through the quiet yacht, down the polished hallway to his private cabin. The space was dimly lit, shadows flickering across the elegant wood-panelled walls. Still holding her close, he nudged the door open with his shoulder, then kicked it shut behind them. The soft click of the door felt final—intimate.

He set her gently on her feet beside the bed, his hands lingering at her waist. His forehead rested against hers for a breathless moment. "Willow," he whispered, his voice husky, reverent. "If you want me to stop, just say the word."

She met his eyes—those stormy, beautiful eyes—and shook her head, barely able to speak past the knot of nerves and desire in her throat. "I don't want you to stop."

Her voice trembled, but her gaze didn't. She meant it. She had never done this before— never even come close—but with him, it felt right. Maybe it didn't make sense. Maybe it was reckless. But her heart knew. Her body knew.

Luca didn't ask again. He didn't have to.

He kissed her—slower this time. Tenderly. His mouth moved over hers with aching reverence, like he was memorising her taste, the shape of her lips, the way she sighed into his kiss. Her knees weakened, but she didn't pull away. She stepped closer. Into him.

His hands slid up the length of her arms, over bare shoulders, and came to rest at the delicate straps of her sundress. He hesitated for only a breath, giving her one final out. But she met his eyes and nodded.

He eased the straps down, inch by inch, the backs of his fingers grazing her skin as the dress fell in a whisper to the floor.

Willow stood before him in nothing but lace panties and the soft glow of the cabin light. Her skin was kissed gold by the low lamps, every inch of her lit in warm, honeyed tones. Her breath hitched—she had never been this exposed, never shown herself fully to anyone. But Luca's gaze wasn't ravenous. It was reverent.

"My God," he breathed, voice thick with awe. His fingers ghosted along her waist, barely there. "You're even more beautiful than I imagined."

Instead of shrinking, Willow lifted her chin. The way he looked at her—like she was sacred, irreplaceable—gave her a strength she didn't know she possessed.

He stepped closer, sliding his fingers into her hair, tilting her head just enough for his lips to find the soft hollow beneath her ear. He kissed there—slow, deliberate kisses— and her breath caught, her hands finding the front of his shirt.

His other hand rose to cup one breast, warm and sure, his thumb brushing across her nipple in gentle, deliberate circles. Pleasure darted through her like lightning, and she gasped, clinging to him as heat pooled deep in her belly.

He lowered his mouth, pressing open-mouthed kisses across her collarbone, then down, his breath hot on her skin. When his lips closed around her nipple, Willow cried out— sharp, breathless. Her fingers tangled in his hair, holding on as his tongue moved over her with exquisite control.

The sensation was too much. Not enough. Perfect.

Luca scooped her into his arms as though she weighed nothing, carried her to the bed, and laid her down like she was breakable. Precious. He stood for a moment, unbuttoning his shirt with slow precision, his eyes locked to hers. Then his pants followed, leaving him gloriously bare and devastatingly beautiful in the warm lamplight.

He joined her again, stretching out beside her, and placed one hand flat against her stomach.

"You're shaking," he whispered.

"I know."

"I'll go slow."

She nodded, breathless.

His fingers trailed along her stomach, dipping lower, to the waistband of her panties. He looked at her, asking without words.

Willow gave him her answer in a whisper: "Yes."

He slid the lace down, kissing each inch of newly exposed skin—hips, thighs, the inside of her knee. When she was bare, he didn't rush. He took his time. He kissed her like he was worshiping her. His mouth moved between her thighs, slowly, reverently, tasting her with a groan of sheer wonder.

Willow arched off the bed, her hands fisting in the sheets, as pleasure rippled through her like fire. He didn't stop. He learned her responses, coaxing sounds from her she hadn't known she could make. She was unravelling—completely undone beneath him.

When her climax hit, she cried out, his name the only word she could find.

He rose then, kissing his way back up her trembling body. Her thighs still trembled beneath his hands.

He reached for a condom, rolled it on with care, and kissed her mouth—softly, sweetly—before positioning himself at her entrance. She felt the thick press of him, her body stretching to accommodate something entirely new.

But then he paused.

His eyes flew to hers, stricken. "Willow—are you a virgin?"

She nodded slowly, lips parted, her eyes glassy with feeling. "Yes. But please, don't stop."

Emotion flared across his face—tenderness, protectiveness, reverence. "You should have told me."

"I didn't want you to treat me like I'd break."

He swallowed hard, brushing her hair back from her face. "I won't. I promise."

He entered her slowly, inch by inch, careful and focused, his brows furrowed with control. She tensed, and he kissed her until the sting eased, until her body accepted him.

Then—fullness. Wholeness.

He moved carefully at first, watching her face, adjusting when she winced, pausing when she needed. And then—when she lifted her hips and met him—he let go.

They moved together in a rhythm that felt like fate. His name fell from her lips again and again, like a prayer.

Her climax came like a wave, fierce and unstoppable, her body clenching around him, pulling him deeper. And when he followed, it was with a groan of pure surrender, his release crashing through him in powerful waves.

They collapsed together, bodies tangled, breath ragged.

Luca held her close, pressing kisses to her hair, her temple, her bare shoulder. Willow curled into him, her body spent, her heart wide open.

And as she drifted into sleep, she felt safe. Loved.

Changed.

Luca watched her for a long moment, brushing a strand of hair from her cheek, his heart a tangle of emotion. Then, careful not to wake her, he slipped from the bed and padded into the bathroom.

He disposed of the condom, but what he saw confirmed what his body had already told him—what he had felt in the tight resistance of her body, in the way she trembled beneath him, in the startled cry that had broken from her lips.

She had been a virgin.

He stood frozen for a moment, the weight of it settling over him like a leaden blanket.

She hadn't told him. Hadn't asked for anything. Had given herself to him freely—not out of obligation, not out of seduction, but from something deeper. Trust. Vulnerability. Feeling.

She had given him something sacred. And he hadn't known. He hadn't been ready.

Luca stared at his reflection in the mirror, jaw tight, emotions warring behind his eyes. He felt awe… and guilt. A tenderness he didn't know he was capable of, and a sudden, irrational fear.

What did she want in return?

His heart clenched at the thought. Was she expecting a declaration? A promise? Something more than he could give.

Was this a price he wasn't ready—or willing—to pay?

He braced his hands on the counter, breath slow and unsteady. The truth pressed against him, quiet but undeniable—this wasn't casual anymore. At least not for Willow.

They woke in the quiet hours before dawn, the sky outside still painted in deep shades of indigo. Willow stirred first, her body still humming with the warmth of the night before.

This world—his world—was new to her. The silk sheets, the gentle rocking of the yacht, the way Luca's arm was still wrapped protectively around her waist. Every part of it felt dreamlike.

But dreams didn't last. And neither would this.

Luca didn't do forever. She knew that.

Maybe that was why she wanted to imprint every second of this night into her memory. To feel everything—every breath, every moan, every moment of being truly his, even if it would never last.

The cabin was still cloaked in the hush of early dawn, golden light beginning to filter in through the gauzy curtains. Beside her, Luca slept deeply, one arm thrown across his chest, the sheet tangled low on his hips. He was all golden skin and sinewed muscle, his face relaxed in sleep, utterly unguarded.

Willow shifted slowly, rising onto her knees and sliding a leg over his hips. She straddled him carefully, the cool air brushing against her bare skin as her fingertips traced the contours of his chest—every dip, every ridge, every hard line that had held her, moved within her, worshipped her.

Then she leaned down and pressed a kiss just above his heart.

He stirred beneath her with a quiet groan, his breath catching as she kissed him again. Lower. Slower. Her mouth explored the hard plane of his torso, her lips dragging over the line of his sternum, her tongue circling a nipple, drawing a sharp inhale from him. She smiled softly, wickedly, against his skin, emboldened by the way his body responded.

When she reached the sculpted ridges of his abdomen, she kissed each one like a secret, her breath warm, her tongue teasing. She felt him harden against her, the thick length of him stirring beneath the sheet. And then, when she finally slid down and exposed him fully, he whispered her name—hoarse and reverent.

"Willow…"

She didn't answer. She just met his gaze for one breathless second—his eyes now heavy-lidded and dark with arousal—before lowering her head.

Her tongue flicked out, slow and experimental, tracing the velvety crown of him. He shuddered. Her lips wrapped around him, gradually, taking more with each pass until he was deep in her mouth, her cheeks hollowing with gentle suction. She moved with unhurried precision, learning the rhythm that made him lose control.

His hand slid into her hair—not forcing, just anchoring—his hips twitching involuntarily as a groan broke from his throat.

"Cristo, Willow…"

The power of his unravelling was intoxicating. Her own arousal surged at the guttural sounds he made, the sharp tension in his abs, the way he gritted her name like a prayer through his teeth. She felt the weight of her control—how easily she could undo him. And she wanted to give it all.

But before she could take him over the edge, his hand tightened in her hair.

"Stop," he rasped, his voice strained and rough. "I need to be inside you. Now."

She rose slowly, licking her swollen lips, breath shallow with want. His eyes tracked every movement like a man starved.

He reached for a condom, but she beat him to it. Her fingers tore the foil, and with surprising steadiness, she rolled it onto him, her touch both reverent and bold.

Then she climbed back over him, her knees straddling his thighs, her body humming with anticipation. She guided him to her, not breaking eye contact as she slowly—achingly—lowered herself onto him, inch by inch, until he was fully seated inside her.

Her head fell back, a moan escaping her lips. He filled her so completely it was almost too much—but it was perfect. She rolled her hips once, experimentally, and his hands gripped her thighs like he was holding on for dear life.

"Gesù… Willow…"

He sat up, wrapping an arm around her waist, the other hand gripping the nape of her neck as he kissed her—deep, dirty, and all-consuming. Their bodies found a rhythm, slow at first, but building—each thrust a little harder, each roll of her hips a little wilder.

Her hands splayed on his shoulders for balance as she rode him, the wet slap of skin against skin filling the room, the scent of sweat and sex and need thick in the air. She cried out as he angled his hips upward, hitting a spot inside her that sent stars bursting behind her eyes.

Her movements grew erratic, desperate, driven by pure instinct. The pressure coiled tight in her belly, that exquisite edge approaching fast and fierce.

"Luca—oh God—I'm going to—"

She shattered with a scream, her body locking around him, pulsing, trembling. Her nails dug into his skin. Her head dropped to his shoulder as pleasure wracked her, wave after blinding wave.

He grunted, hoisting her up and flipping her onto her back in one fluid motion, never slipping free. His thrusts grew more urgent, deeper, more primal. She welcomed him eagerly, legs wrapping around his hips, pulling him deeper still.

"Look at me," he growled, his voice guttural and wild. "I want to see you when I come."

She obeyed, eyes wide and dazed, and he came with a feral groan, hips driving hard one last time before he collapsed over her, trembling from the force of it.

For a long, breathless moment, they lay tangled together—his weight warm and solid on top of her, her body still fluttering in aftershocks. His face buried in her neck, her fingers stroking through the damp hair at his nape.

No promises were made. No futures spoken of.

But in that moment, their bodies said everything.

She had given him all of her. And for one unforgettable night, he gave everything back.

The next time Luca woke; the sky outside had shifted from night to the pale blush of dawn. He reached for her instinctively—but his hand met only cool sheets.

She was gone.

He sat up slowly, his brows drawing together as he ran a hand through his hair. The space beside him was empty, her scent lingering faintly on the pillow. Her clothes were no longer on the floor.

Odd.

Luca rose, took a quick shower, and dressed. A sense of unease threaded through him—not panic, but something quieter. Something unsettled.

He knocked gently on her cabin door. No answer.

Then he climbed the steps to the deck.

There she was.

Willow sat at the edge of the yacht, facing the rising sun. Her knees were drawn up, arms loosely wrapped around them, the light breeze lifting strands of her hair. Her eyes were closed; face tilted toward the warmth of the morning light.

She wasn't posing. She wasn't trying.

She was just… being.

And God, she was beautiful.

Something tightened in his chest.

She didn't even have to try.

He watched her for a moment longer, silently, unwilling to disturb the stillness that clung to the morning like mist.

Then he moved—quietly, barefoot across the deck, the soft thud of his steps muffled by teak and breeze.

He stopped a few feet behind her.

"You always wake this early," he said gently, his voice low and warm.

Willow didn't open her eyes, but a faint smile touched her lips. "Only when the world feels different."

Luca lowered himself beside her, resting his arms on his knees, mimicking her posture. "And does it?"

She finally turned her head, opening her eyes. They were clear and quiet, reflecting the soft gold of sunrise.

"Yes," she said simply. "It does."

They sat in silence, the waves lapping softly against the hull, a gull crying in the distance.

"I woke up and reached for you," he murmured. "And you were gone."

"I needed a moment," she said, her voice not apologetic, just honest. "To think. To feel it all before it faded."

He nodded, watching her face. "And?"

Willow looked back toward the horizon, the sun rising slowly, steadily. "I'm glad I came here. Even if it's not forever."

Luca's jaw flexed slightly. "Why do you say that? That it's not forever."

"Because I know you don't do forever," she said, not accusing, just truthful.

He looked away, something unreadable in his expression.

"I didn't expect you," he said quietly. "I didn't expect any of this."

Willow reached out, her fingers brushing his. Her touch was light, almost fleeting.

"It's okay," she said softly. "I'm a big girl. I just want to enjoy the last two days."

Her words settled like a stone in his chest.

The seven days. Their bargain. Almost over.

He turned to look at her, but she'd closed her eyes again, face tilted toward the sun, serene and unreadable.

She wasn't asking for more. Not a promise. Not a declaration.

And somehow, that unsettled him more than if she had.

She didn't expect anything.

He didn't know if he should be relieved... or offended.

Because for the first time in his life, he wasn't sure he wanted it to end either.

Chapter Fifteen

While they were having breakfast on the deck, Luca's phone rang. He glanced at the screen and smiled.

"It's Marcus," he said, then answered. "Happy wedding day."

"Thanks," came Marcus's voice, slightly rushed. "Is Willow there?"

Luca's brow furrowed. "Yes, why?"

"I need to speak to her."

"Why?" Luca asked again, more firmly.

"Just put her on, Luca."

Still looking puzzled, Luca handed her the phone. "It's Marcus. He says he needs to speak to you."

Willow took it, eyebrows raised. "Hello?"

"Oh, thank God," Marcus said in a relieved rush. "I need a massive favour."

"Okay… anything, Marcus. What's going on?"

"Elena's really upset—her bridesmaid broke her leg this morning and can't make it to the wedding."

"Oh no, that's awful," Willow said, her face falling. "Is she okay?"

"She'll be fine, but Elena's gutted. She was really close to her. Listen… would you consider stepping in? Just for today. Elena loves you—she said so last night—and I know it would mean the world to her."

Willow blinked. "Wait… me? Are you sure?"

"I wouldn't ask if I wasn't," Marcus said sincerely. "And neither would she."

Willow glanced at Luca, then back at the phone, a slow smile forming. "Well… if you really think she wants me to, I'd be honoured."

Marcus thanked her profusely, his voice full of genuine relief.

"You're a lifesaver, Willow. Honestly."

She smiled and handed the phone back to Luca.

"What was that all about?" he asked, already dialling back into reality.

Marcus explained quickly on the other end, and Luca nodded.

"Understood," he said. "Can you give us an hour?"

A pause, then a quick, "Perfect. See you soon."

Luca ended the call and looked over at Willow.

"They need us there in an hour."

Willow gave a quick, determined nod. "Then let's not keep the bride waiting."

They both returned to their cabins to dress. The energy between them was different now—warmer, charged, but also edged with something unspoken. Maybe it was the ticking clock of the two days they had left, or maybe it was the way he'd looked at her after their morning on the deck. Like she was something fragile and precious, even if he didn't know how to say it aloud.

Willow slipped into her red dress—the same one she'd worn on the last night with Dennis. But now, it felt like armour. A declaration. She wasn't the same woman who had boarded this yacht days ago.

When she stepped out, Luca's eyes darkened with appreciation. He reached for her hand and pulled her in gently, brushing a kiss against her lips.

"You look beautiful," he murmured, as they stepped off the yacht and onto the dock.

But before she could respond, a voice sliced through the moment like a blade.

"So, you're sleeping with him now."

Willow froze.

That voice.

She turned, heart sinking, to see Dennis standing just a few feet away. His arms crossed, jaw clenched, eyes radiating betrayal and fury.

"Dennis?" she said, stunned. "What are you doing here?"

"I came to take you home," he growled. Then, before either she or Luca could react, he lunged forward and grabbed her by the upper arm, yanking her toward him.

"Let go of her," Luca snapped, stepping forward instantly, his entire posture coiled with barely contained rage.

Dennis sneered, not releasing his grip. "She's not yours. Just because you've got money doesn't mean you can buy everyone you meet."

Willow winced, his hand digging painfully into her arm. "Dennis, you're hurting me!"

"I gave you everything," he hissed at her. "Security. Plans. A future."

Luca's voice turned deadly. "I won't ask again. Let. Her. Go."

But Dennis tightened his grip, even as Willow tried to pull away.

And then—swift as a storm—Luca moved. He yanked Dennis's hand from her arm and shoved him back a step, placing himself protectively between them. His voice was low and controlled, but his eyes burned.

"You touch her again, and I'll forget I'm a gentleman."

Willow clutched her arm, stunned by the sheer force of tension crackling between the two men. A small crowd was beginning to form at the edge of the dock, murmuring.

"Dennis, stop," Willow said, her voice finally breaking through the chaos. "You told me we were done. I believed you."

His eyes returned to hers. "I was wrong, Willow. You and I were supposed to get married."

"No, Dennis," she said, eyes steady. "We weren't. I would have never said yes."

His expression twisted, caught between heartbreak and resentment. "He's changed you."

Willow shook her head, her voice soft but unwavering. "No. I changed myself. And you need to leave."

Dennis's mouth opened like he had more to say, but no words came. His gaze flicked to Luca, who stood like a storm waiting to strike, then back to Willow. Finally, he stepped back, his face hard, his pride crumbling at his feet.

Without another word, he turned and walked away, shoulders stiff, jaw clenched.

Silence felt heavy in his absence.

Luca stepped closer, his jaw tight with anger he hadn't unleashed. He gently lifted her arm, his thumb brushing the red mark Dennis had left—already darkening with bruising. His touch was tender, but his voice was low and sharp with protectiveness. "Are you okay?"

She nodded slowly. "I think so."

He didn't press, just took her hand—this time firmer, possessive, but careful.

"Come on," he said, his tone softening. "We've got a wedding to save."

Willow stepped into the bridal suite, taking a moment to let her eyes adjust to the soft glow of the morning light spilling in through the tall windows. The space smelled faintly of roses and perfume, bustling with stylists and whispered excitement.

Elena stood near the vanity in a flowing white robe, her dark hair pinned in soft waves, her makeup barely begun. When she saw Willow, her eyes lit up.

"Oh, thank God," she said, rushing over and enveloping her in a hug. "I can't believe you said yes. Marcus told me, and I just—thank you. I didn't know what I was going to do."

Willow smiled, returning the embrace. "Of course. I'm honoured. You look... breathtaking, Elena."

Elena pulled back slightly, her eyes shining. "You're a lifesaver. Seriously. I was about five minutes away from having a meltdown."

As she stepped back, her gaze caught on Willow's arm. Her smile faltered.

"Wait—what happened?" Elena asked, her eyes narrowing as she gently reached for Willow's arm. Her fingers brushed the darkening bruise just below her sleeve. "Who did this to you? Luca didn't... did he?"

"No," Willow said quickly, pulling her arm back instinctively. "Not Luca. Never."

Elena's expression shifted immediately—from suspicion to alarm, then to concern. She waited silently, giving Willow the space to continue.

"It was someone from home," Willow said after a moment, her voice quieter now. "He showed up this morning, tried to take me back. He didn't want to accept that things were over."

Elena's brows drew together, her voice steely. "Did Luca see it happen?"

Willow nodded. "He stopped it. Stepped in before it got worse."

Elena exhaled, clearly still angry on her behalf. "Are you okay?"

"I will be," Willow said softly, offering a small smile that didn't quite reach her eyes. "I just... I feel bad that I hurt him. But I had to be honest."

Elena reached out and took her hands gently. "You didn't hurt him. He hurt you. And no one who loves you would ever put their hands on you like that. You did the right thing, Willow. I'm just glad you're safe—and that you're here today."

Willow squeezed her hands in return. "I'm glad I'm here too."

Just then, a stylist appeared with a tray of makeup brushes. Elena stood and gestured to the chair beside hers. "Now come on. Let's get you glammed up. We've got a wedding to go to."

Willow smiled as she sat down, letting the energy of the room envelop her. For the first time in days, she felt like she could breathe again.

Meanwhile, downstairs, Luca stood off to the side of the ceremony space, his jaw tight and his hands shoved into the pockets of his suit pants. Marcus spotted him and walked over, raising an eyebrow.

"What's with the murder face?" Marcus asked. "Did you and Willow have a fight?"

"No," Luca said flatly.

"Then what's wrong? You look like you're about to strangle someone."

"I am," Luca muttered. "His name's Dennis."

"Who the hell is Dennis?"

"Her ex. He showed up this morning, grabbed her—left bruises on her arm."

Marcus stared at him, stunned. "He what?"

Luca's eyes darkened. "I wanted to kill him. Still do."

Marcus let out a low whistle, shaking his head. "You're lucky you didn't. You'd never make it to the wedding."

"I don't give a damn about the wedding," Luca said, his voice low and tight. "I care about her."

Marcus looked at him for a long beat, then gave a slow, knowing nod. "Yeah. That's what I figured."

Luca stared off toward the water, jaw clenched. What startled him wasn't just how much he meant it—it was how violent the feeling was. Fierce. Raw. Unshakable.

He would've torn Dennis apart without a second thought. And that scared him a little.

Because this wasn't just about protecting someone.

This was about *her.*

And he was in deeper than he'd ever planned to go.

The music started, soft and elegant, drifting through the garden as guests rose from their seats. Luca stood at the front beside Marcus, hands clasped tightly in front of him, outwardly composed—except for the way his heart thudded in his chest.

He hadn't seen Willow since she disappeared into the bridal suite. Not since she gave him that small, brave smile after Dennis. He didn't know what dress she'd wear, how her hair would be styled, if she'd be smiling when she walked toward him… but he was unprepared for what he did see.

She stepped into view.

And time simply stopped.

Willow moved down the aisle slowly, sunlight catching on the soft blush of her bridesmaid dress. Her hair flowed in polished waves over her shoulders, a few pieces pinned delicately back. The makeup was light but transformative—emphasising her eyes, her lips, her grace. She didn't look like someone playing dress-up.

She looked like someone he could spend forever looking at.

His breath caught.

Willow.

She was radiant. Not just in beauty, but in poise, in quiet strength. And in that moment, Luca felt everything shift inside him. All the walls he'd spent years building—around his heart, around his past—crumbled at the sight of her.

She glanced up and met his gaze.

And she smiled.

A small, private smile meant only for him. The kind of smile that undid a man completely.

Luca's fingers curled at his sides, resisting the instinct to move toward her, to claim her right there in front of everyone. His chest ached with something raw and real.

Marcus leaned in quietly. "You okay?"

"No," Luca whispered. "I think I'm in deep."

Marcus grinned. "No kidding."

Willow reached the front, took her place beside the bride, and didn't look at him again. But Luca couldn't stop looking at her.

He wasn't sure he ever would again.

The celebration faded into a golden haze behind them. Music, laughter, clinking glasses—it all blurred in Luca's ears as he followed the path down toward the water. He wasn't even sure what he planned to say. All he knew was that Willow was out here, alone, and he couldn't stay away.

She stood at the edge of the stone terrace, moonlight silvering her hair, the breeze teasing soft tendrils around her face. She was so still. So heartbreakingly beautiful it made something inside him ache.

She turned when she heard him. "Hey."

"Hey," he said, voice quieter than intended.

For a moment, neither of them moved.

"You were incredible up there," he managed. "Beautiful. Graceful. Like you belonged in that dress."

Willow smiled, but it didn't quite reach her eyes. "Thanks. Elena was happy. That's all that matters."

He nodded, stuffing his hands into his pockets like they might keep him grounded. "You keep surprising me."

"How?"

"I don't know," he said honestly. "Just… every time I think I've figured you out, you show me something else."

Willow glanced out at the ocean. "People are complicated. Even the ones who seem simple."

Luca exhaled. "That's not it. You're not complicated. You're… real. And I think that scares the hell out of me."

She turned back to him, brows drawing together. "Why?"

He hesitated, the truth clawing up his throat.

"I don't do forever," Luca said, the words gravel in his throat. "This was supposed to be a bargain. A temporary detour."

Willow's expression didn't flicker with surprise—only something sadder, quieter. Acceptance. "Stop overthinking it, Luca. We have two more nights. Then you go back to your world, and I go back to mine."

He looked at her like she'd just slapped him and kissed him in the same breath. "I don't want to hurt you," he said. "But I will. I wasn't made for this. For you."

Her voice was calm, but her eyes shimmered. "I'm not asking for forever," she said softly. "Just for now. Two nights. That will have to be enough."

Luca looked at her like she'd handed him a moment he didn't deserve—but couldn't let go of.

Willow reached out and took his hand, her fingers cool against his warmth. She didn't beg. She didn't plead. She simply said, "I think you need to dance with me."

Wordlessly, he followed her back to the reception, back to the music and laughter and everything that suddenly felt distant except her. He pulled her into his arms like it was the only place he still understood.

Willow rested her head on his chest, trying not to hear the echo of his words—I don't do forever.

It hurt. God, it hurt more than she wanted to admit.

But she'd made her choice.

She could walk away now and let this end with distance and dignity.

Or she could stay, just two more nights, and hold on to whatever this was—fleeting, fragile, beautiful.

She chose to stay.

Because when the memories were all she had left, she wanted them full of light, laughter, and Luca's arms around her.

Even if she couldn't keep the man—

She could keep the moment.

Chapter Sixteen

The next day passed in a golden haze—blurring the lines between day and night, between laughter and longing, between where their bodies ended, and their hearts began.

They couldn't keep their hands off each other.

In the morning, Willow woke to Luca's lips trailing over her bare shoulder, his voice rough with sleep murmuring, "Stay with me just a little longer." And she did. Wrapped in sunlit sheets, her body warm and aching with the memory of him, she clung to those stolen hours like they were air.

They made love with a kind of reverence—as if they were writing their names in each other's skin. In bed, with the sea breeze drifting in through the open balcony doors, he worshipped her like a man starving. She lost herself in the sound of his voice, the way he whispered her name like a prayer.

In the afternoon, they laughed like children. He chased her down the private stretch of sand, catching her waist and spinning her in circles until she was breathless, dizzy with joy. She collapsed into him, and he held her like the most precious thing he'd ever touched.

In the water, they swam together, splashing, teasing, stealing kisses just below the surface. When he lifted her in his arms and carried her back to the beach, dripping wet and laughing, she clung to him like a woman drowning. Maybe she was—drowning in a love she couldn't keep.

Later, on the beach beneath the stars, with the surf crashing in rhythm with their hearts, they moved together in a world that belonged only to them. The sand was cool beneath the blanket, the sky endless above, and Luca's touch was everywhere—gentle, insistent, desperate. He kissed her like it might be the last time. Maybe it was.

At night, they curled up on the deck wrapped in a single blanket, watching the stars, sharing soft words and long silences. Willow ran her fingers over his chest, memorising the curve of his smile, the timbre of his laugh, the shape of the life they'd never have.

She didn't ask what would happen next. He didn't offer.

But in the quiet moments, when he thought she was asleep, Luca would kiss her temple and hold her just a little tighter.

And when she lay awake beside him, blinking back tears she couldn't explain, Willow would whisper into the darkness, "Thank you."

For the days.

For the nights.

For the impossible, beautiful love she'd never forget.

The moon cast silver light across the waves, the soft rush of the sea a lullaby as Willow lay tangled in the sheets beside Luca. Her head rested on his chest, his fingers drawing lazy circles along her spine, the scent of salt and him thick in the air.

She wanted to freeze time.

Wanted to hold onto this moment where the world felt small and safe and full of possibility.

But even in his arms, reality hovered just beyond the horizon.

Luca shifted, propping himself on one elbow. His other hand reached over to the nightstand.

"I have a present for you," he said, his voice low and careful.

Willow lifted her head, her smile soft. "I don't need presents, Luca."

"I know." He gave a small, almost boyish shrug. "But I wanted to get you something. Something to remember me by.

She sat up, the sheet slipping to her waist, and watched as he handed her a small velvet box. Deep blue. Elegant. Like everything else about him.

Her heart skipped, but her hands were steady as she opened it.

Inside, nestled against black satin, lay the most stunning necklace she had ever seen. A single sapphire teardrop, the colour of the sea just before sunset, encircled by tiny white diamonds. It sparkled even in the low light of the cabin.

"Oh, Luca…" she breathed. "It's beautiful."

And it was.

But it was also something else.

It was goodbye.

A billionaire's version of closure. A gift for her time. For her company. For her body. For playing her part in their week-long fantasy.

She swallowed the ache rising in her throat and reached out to gently touch the gem, tracing its cool surface like it was glass. Fragile. Breakable.

"I'm glad you like it," he said softly, searching her face.

Willow nodded, keeping her smile in place, blinking slowly so he wouldn't see the sudden gloss in her eyes.

"It's perfect."

She didn't trust herself to say more. Not when the room felt smaller now, tighter. Not when her chest ached with the truth she'd been trying so hard not to name.

This was his way of drawing the line.

Of saying thank you, without having to say the rest.

Without having to say goodbye.

She looked down again, pretending to admire the necklace so he wouldn't see the hurt blooming quietly behind her eyes.

Luca reached for her hand, bringing it to his lips.

She let him.

Because she loved him.

And tomorrow, she would leave.

But tonight… tonight she would wear the necklace, press her body to his one last time, and pretend that the gift was something more than what it was.

Pretend it meant stay—when they both knew it meant go.

The yacht had docked in Rome at midnight.

Willow hadn't seen it, but she felt it—the subtle stillness in the water beneath them, the distant hum of the port, the faint clink of ropes being secured to the dock. Their magical time was over, no matter how much she tried to pretend otherwise.

And when Luca made love to her in the early hours of the morning, slow and possessive and heartbreakingly tender, it felt like a final goodbye disguised as a kiss.

She held on to every moment—his hands, his breath against her skin, the way he whispered her name like it meant something more than it did. Like she meant something more than a beautiful detour in his extraordinary life.

But even in his arms, she knew.

He would never say stay.

So, when he fell asleep, arms around her like he didn't want to let go, Willow slipped away.

She moved carefully, brushing a kiss across his shoulder as if to say thank you… and I love you… and goodbye, all at once.

Her bare feet padded silently across the cabin floor and into the cool hallway. Her own cabin waited just a few steps away, neat, dark, and far too quiet.

The suitcase sat beside the bed, packed the afternoon before when she knew this moment would come. She didn't trust herself to wait until morning. She had to leave now, before she broke.

The soft pink bridesmaid dress she'd worn the night they danced onshore lay folded across the bed. On top of it, she placed the small velvet box.

The necklace sparkled faintly in the moonlight streaming through the porthole.

She hesitated for just a second before slipping the folded note beneath the ribbon of the box.

Be happy, Luca.

Below the words, she drew a small heart. Inside it, a simple W.

Tears burned her eyes, but she blinked them away. There was no use crying now.

She couldn't do it.

She couldn't wait for him to say goodbye. Couldn't bear to hear him thank her for the memories or offer some polite, distant farewell while her heart shattered in her chest.

So, she did the only thing she could.

She picked up her suitcase, took one last look at the room, and quietly stepped out onto the deck.

Rome glittered in the distance, the skyline still cloaked in early-morning darkness, the city not quite awake. The gangplank had already been lowered. No crew in sight. The silence made everything feel more final.

Willow paused at the edge of the yacht.

She turned back—not to go, but to memorise it. The place where she'd fallen in love. The place that had shown her passion and heartbreak in equal measure.

She touched the railing one last time and whispered a silent goodbye.

Then, with the soft roll of her suitcase behind her, she walked down the gangplank and into the night—leaving behind the necklace, the note, and the man who had unknowingly broken her heart.

The sun was rising—low and golden, spilling across the silk sheets in a quiet cascade of light.

Luca stirred, stretching his arm across the bed with a lazy smile, expecting to find her warm body curled beside him.

But there was only cool linen and empty space.

His eyes opened slowly. His hand searched again. The sheets were smooth. Untouched.

He sat up, confused at first, his sleep-heavy mind catching up with the silence that wrapped around him like a warning.

"Willow?" he called, his voice rough.

Nothing.

He stood quickly, pulling on the first pair of pants he found and moved through the cabin, checking the ensuite, the small lounge area. Empty.

He didn't panic—not at first. Maybe she'd gone for coffee. Maybe she needed space. Maybe—

His chest tightened.

She hadn't brought anything back to this room. Her suitcase had stayed in her own cabin.

Heart hammering harder than he liked to admit, Luca crossed the hallway to the guest room. The door creaked as he pushed it open.

She was gone.

The bed was neatly made, the air still carrying the faint scent of her shampoo—peach and vanilla and something purely her. Her suitcase was gone. Her presence, erased.

Except for one thing.

Lying across the bed was the soft pink dress she'd worn the night of the wedding, gently folded. And resting on top of it—his gift. The sapphire and diamond necklace, still tucked in its velvet box.

Left behind.

He stared at it like it didn't make sense. Like it didn't belong there.

Slowly, he stepped forward and lifted the lid. The necklace gleamed back at him, untouched and unwanted.

That alone made something ache.

But then he saw it. The note.

Just a small square of paper, folded once and tucked beneath the ribbon.

He opened it with hesitant fingers.

Be happy, Luca.

♡ *W*

That was all.

Three words and a hand-drawn heart.

Three words that cracked something in his chest—something he'd locked away a long time ago.

He sat down heavily on the edge of the bed, the necklace still in his hand, her note pressed between his fingers. The silence around him rang louder now.

She left.

Without drama. Without tears. Without one last plea or question.

She'd loved him. He knew that. He'd seen it in her eyes every time he touched her, in the way she listened, in the way she stayed even when it hurt.

And he let her walk away because he didn't do forever.

That had always been the line. The boundary. The rule.

So why the hell did it feel like his chest was being split open?

Why did this feel like loss?

He stared down at the necklace and thought about how she'd smiled when he gave it to her—beautiful but resigned. He thought he was giving her something to remember him by. A generous goodbye.

But she hadn't needed a necklace.

She had wanted him.

And now she was gone.

He let out a harsh breath and dragged a hand through his hair, still refusing to name the feeling gnawing at him.

Because feelings were dangerous.

Forever was dangerous.

But the empty space she left behind?

It was worse.

Chapter Seventeen

It had been a week.

Seven long days since Willow had stepped off Luca's yacht under the cloak of darkness, her heart shattered and her dignity barely intact. Rome had disappeared behind her, but the man she left behind had not.

She had cried—not in public. But there were quiet moments, curled up in bed with the necklace she hadn't kept, where her chest ached with a hollow kind of sorrow. She knew, in some part of her, that she would always carry a piece of Luca with her. That kind of connection didn't just disappear.

But she had to be brave. She had to move forward.

Luca had honoured his word. All charges against Lily had been dropped, and a quiet wire transfer had been made to cover the full cost of the surgery her mother had needed. No demands. No explanation. Just done.

Willow hadn't told Lily the real price she paid.

Some things were better left unsaid.

"Thank you for everything," Lily had whispered the night she was released. Her voice was choked with emotion, her eyes bright. "I don't know how you convinced him, but I owe you everything."

Willow had just hugged her and smiled.

"You don't owe me anything. Just be happy, Lily. That's all I want."

Lily had promised to keep in touch—bright-eyed and earnest—but Willow knew better. Distance was a funny thing. It could stretch a family thin, especially when secrets were stitched between the cracks. But Willow would try. She always did. Because family mattered to her, no matter how imperfect.

Now, a week later, Willow stepped out of her small publishing office, her coat hugged tight around her. The fall breeze nipped at her cheeks, and the sun was starting to dip behind the buildings, painting the sky in shades of copper and rose.

She was halfway to the subway when she heard the voice.

"Willow?"

She turned.

Dennis stood near the curb, his hands in the pockets of his expensive coat, his hair perfectly styled, as always. But his face looked… softer. Less rigid. Almost human.

She smiled, though her heart didn't flutter the way it used to.

"Dennis."

He stepped closer. "I've been meaning to reach out."

"It's okay," she said gently. "You don't owe me anything."

"I wanted to apologise. For what happened in Tuscany." His voice dropped, low and sincere. "I was angry. I acted like a jerk. That wasn't fair to you."

Willow looked at him for a long moment, then nodded.

"I know," she said softly. "And I'm sorry it didn't work out with us."

Dennis exhaled. "We were never really right, were we?"

She gave a sad smile. "No. But I wanted it to be. I tried."

"I know you did," he said. "And you deserved better than a man who treated you like part of a five-year plan."

Willow laughed quietly. "You said seven years, actually."

He grinned. "Still too long."

There was a pause. Not awkward—just final.

"I hope you find what you're looking for," she said. "Truly."

Dennis nodded. "You too, Willow. Whoever he is… I hope he knows what he lost because I do."

Willow's smile faded a little, but she nodded politely. "Take care, Dennis."

And then she walked away.

Her heart still bruised, still aching.

But her steps were steady.

Because loving Luca had changed her.

And losing him—that had taught her how to survive.

Luca looked like hell.

The Roman sun streamed through the tall floor-to-ceiling windows of his penthouse office, catching on the glass and marble with blinding brilliance. But he didn't see it. Didn't feel it. Outside, the city pulsed with life—motorbikes whining, tourists chattering, fountains spilling into sun-dappled stone courtyards. But inside, Luca Lombardi sat in silence, drowning in stillness.

His suit jacket, usually tailored to perfection and worn like armour, hung carelessly over the back of his chair. The sleeves of his once-crisp white shirt were rumpled and rolled haphazardly to the elbows, exposing forearms corded with tension. His collar hung open, his dark tie discarded on the desk hours ago—or was it days? The stubble on his jaw had grown into a full beard, sharp and shadowed. There were hollows beneath his eyes, smudges of sleeplessness no amount of wealth, grooming, or pride could disguise.

It had been ten days since the yacht docked in Rome.

Just over a week since he'd woken to cold sheets and a colder realisation—she was gone. Willow. Her scent had lingered for a few hours: soft jasmine and sunlight. Now it was gone, just like her. No note of anger. No explanation. Just the necklace she'd left behind. And her words.

Words that had gutted him.

He hadn't eaten a full meal since. Coffee had become his crutch, black and bitter. Work had become his distraction—but not even billion-dollar acquisitions or volatile markets could compete with the echo of her absence.

Because nothing replaced her.

The velvet box sat in his drawer, untouched. He didn't need to open it. He could see it clearly in his mind—the delicate chain, the glint of diamonds, and the folded piece of paper in her soft, looping script.

Be happy, Luca.

How the hell was he supposed to do that?

The office door swung open without warning. Marcus strolled in, sunglasses still on, a walking contrast to Luca's dishevelled wreckage. Tanned from a honeymoon on the Amalfi Coast, wearing a charcoal blazer over a white tee, he looked annoyingly content. The smirk on his face dimmed the second he took in Luca's condition.

He let out a low whistle. "You look like a man who lost everything and deserves it."

Luca didn't answer. Didn't even glance up.

Marcus pulled off his sunglasses, leaned forward, and dropped into the chair across from him. "How's Willow?"

Luca looked up slowly, as if the movement cost him. His voice was gravel. "I don't know."

Marcus blinked. "You don't know."

"She's gone."

"Yeah, I gathered that much. I meant how is she? Have you called her? Tracked her down? Done… anything?"

Luca's jaw tensed, grinding with restrained emotion. "No."

Marcus sat back with a sigh that was equal parts frustration and disbelief. "You let the one real thing in your life walk away because you were scared."

The words hit hard. Like a slap across the face. Luca didn't argue.

Didn't need to.

The silence said it all.

Marcus ran a hand through his hair, then leaned forward again. "Please, for the love of God, tell me you didn't give her some parting gift like she was just another disposable lover."

Luca's hand drifted to the drawer with haunted precision. He opened it slowly and pulled out the velvet box and the folded note. He placed them on the desk like they were relics.

Marcus picked up the box, popped it open, and gave a low whistle. "Jesus. This thing probably costs more than my apartment."

He unfolded the note. His brow furrowed. By the time he reached the bottom, the cocky humour in his face drained, replaced by something quieter. Warmer. Sadder.

He looked up, voice hushed. "If this doesn't tell you what you threw away, you're dumber than you look."

Luca didn't move. Couldn't. His eyes were fixed on the tiny heart she'd drawn beneath her name. That small gesture wrecked him more than diamonds ever could.

Marcus leaned forward, holding the note like a lifeline between them. "She didn't take the necklace, Luca. She left it with a note. That isn't closure—that's heartbreak."

Luca's throat worked hard. "I thought she understood what it was. A gift. A goodbye."

Marcus shook his head. "No, man. It wasn't a goodbye to her. It was a thank you for your time but now we're done."

He jabbed a finger at Luca's chest. "You're in love with her, you idiot."

Luca's eyes fell shut. He held still, but a muscle jumped in his jaw. The truth scraped its way to the surface, heavy and raw.

"I know."

The confession broke out in a whisper, thick and ragged. But it was real.

The dam cracked—just like it had that morning. When he rolled over and saw the indent in the pillow, still warm. When he found her suitcase gone, her note folded under the necklace like the final chapter of something beautiful and brief.

"I love her, Marcus," Luca said, voice wrecked. "And I let her go."

The air in the room changed. It quieted, like the moment before a storm or a prayer. The weight of it settled between them—final and irreversible.

Marcus leaned back, arms folded across his chest. He studied Luca for a long moment. Then he spoke, deadly calm.

"Then the only question that matters is—what the hell are you going to do about it?"

Luca looked up, pain etched in every angle of his face. "She might not forgive me."

"She might not," Marcus agreed. "But if you don't try, you'll never know."

Luca winced, but the hit landed. His pride—what was left of it—burned at the edges.

Marcus wasn't done. "You gave her your body, your time, a glimpse of the man underneath the fortress… but not your heart. Not the truth. Not a future." His voice dropped, sharp as a blade. "She walked away because you made her believe there was nothing here for her but a memory."

Luca dropped his head into his hands. His voice was low, broken. "I didn't know how to ask her to stay. I didn't know if I could… be that man."

"Well, congratulations," Marcus said, standing. "Now you're just the man sitting alone with a necklace you should've never bought and a note that reads like a goodbye letter from the love of your life."

Luca looked up, ruined and raw. His world had been big once—yachts, skyscrapers, power—but now it narrowed to a single decision.

Marcus paused at the door, one hand on the frame. "If you love her, Luca… fix it. Show her. Chase her like she matters. Because if you don't?" He shook his head. "She'll move on. And you'll spend the rest of your life wondering what it would've felt like to be brave."

Then he left.

The door clicked softly shut, but the silence that followed roared louder than a cannon.

Luca sat motionless.

The necklace and the note still on the desk.

The only things she'd left behind.

And yet, somehow… it felt like everything.

Luca remained frozen in his chair, elbows on his knees, fingers tangled in his hair. The necklace still sat on the desk. Her note lay beside it, creased from where he'd read it too many times.

Be happy, Luca.

♡ W

He stared at the words again, his chest aching like something had caved in behind his ribs. Be happy, Luca.

They were simple. Gentle. But they gutted him.

Because happiness had a name now. A laugh like sunlight. A heart bigger than anything he deserved. And he'd let her go.

He pressed his fingers to the folded note like touch alone could change what was written—or what he'd done. For the first time in years, maybe in his entire life, he felt completely, utterly powerless. No amount of influence, wealth, or ruthlessness could fix this. He could buy islands, win court cases with a phone call, dismantle empires with a look—but he couldn't undo this one thing.

Because he'd had everything.

And he'd let it slip through his fingers like sand.

Not because he didn't want it.

Because he was afraid.

She didn't want the yacht, the necklace, or the life he could offer on a silver platter. She wanted him. The man behind the power, behind the name. The man he buried beneath a thousand layers of cynicism. And he'd been too terrified to give her that. Too proud. Too guarded.

Too late.

With a sudden burst of restless energy, he pushed to his feet. His chair skidded back, forgotten. He crossed the room to the massive floor-to-ceiling windows that framed the Roman skyline like a painting. The ancient city stretched out beneath him, beautiful and eternal—glittering, golden, and utterly indifferent to the man unravelling above it.

A week ago, he'd returned to Rome believing he could forget her. That time, distance, and distraction could undo what had happened on that yacht. That he could force himself back into the man he was before her.

But he couldn't.

Because he wasn't that man anymore.

Not after Willow.

He turned from the window abruptly and began to pace, his strides fast and uneven. The silence in the room pressed in around him, thick with memory. He could still hear her laughter echoing in his ears, still feel the warmth of her hand in his, the way she leaned into him when she let herself trust him, just a little.

He thought of her that first night—startled and stubborn in his limousine, setting boundaries with fire in her eyes. And every night after that when those walls began to fall. He remembered her smile at the beach, the way her fingers had threaded through his when she wasn't looking. The way she kissed him like he was more than he'd ever dared believe.

He thought of the last time he touched her. Her breath catching beneath his hands. Her eyes looking up at him like he was safe. Like he was hers.

And he'd crushed it. With silence. With fear. With the cowardice of a man who'd spent his whole life running from anything real.

"Coward," he muttered under his breath.

But no more.

He stopped pacing and turned slowly, facing the desk like it was a battlefield. The necklace gleamed in the morning light. The note sat beside it like a verdict.

And then—without hesitation—he reached for his phone.

"Giovanni," he said as soon as his driver answered, voice sharp and clear. "I need the car in five minutes. And call the airport—I want the jet ready within the hour."

There was a pause on the other end, startled but professional. "Where to, sir?"

Luca stared down at the note again. Her handwriting. That little heart.

And this time, something different stirred in him. A quiet fire. Determination like steel sliding into place beneath his ribs.

"New York," he said.

He ended the call and moved with purpose. Every motion was crisp, decisive. He shrugged into his jacket, grabbed his keys, and after a final glance at the desk—one last look at everything he'd nearly lost—he folded the note and tucked it into the inside pocket of his coat. Like armour. Like a promise. Like a compass guiding him home.

When he stepped into the outer office, his assistant looked up from her desk, startled. "Mr. Lombardi—"

He held up a hand as he passed. "Cancel everything. I'll be out of the country for a few days." He paused at the elevator, the faintest trace of something different in his voice. Something hopeful. "Maybe longer."

She blinked. "Should I ask what for?"

He turned his head slightly, offered a rare, subtle smile. It wasn't the sharp smirk the world knew. This one was quieter. More honest. The kind of smile a man wears when something finally matters.

"No," he said. "But if all goes well, you'll be hearing wedding bells soon."

And with that, Luca Lombardi—the man who never believed in forever—walked out the door, no longer running from love but toward it.

Chasing the only woman who had ever made him want more than power, more than pride.

The only woman who had ever made him believe he could be worthy of something real.

Chapter Eighteen

Willow tucked a strand of hair behind her ear as she glanced over the marked-up manuscript spread across her desk. Across from her, Julian Hart leaned back in the chair with a boyish grin that had probably gotten him out of a lot of trouble in life—and into just as much.

"Be honest," he said, tapping the edge of the paper, "was chapter nine as clunky as I think it was?"

Willow smiled, her professional mask slipping just a little. "Clunky is a strong word. Let's just say it wandered in the woods a bit."

Julian laughed—a low, warm sound that made a few heads turn from nearby cubicles. He had a kind of energy that filled a room effortlessly. Tall, tan, with dark blond hair that fell just shy of unruly and a five o'clock shadow that looked annoyingly deliberate. If she were the kind of woman who got swept up in charm, she'd already be halfway there.

"Fair enough," he said. "I'll rein it in. But in my defence, I was trying to write while flying from L.A. to Prague with a very loud cello player seated beside me."

Willow chuckled. "Well, that explains the chaos and sudden references to violins."

"Guilty." He leaned forward now, eyes warm. "You always give the best notes, Willow. I don't know how you manage to be honest and kind at the same time."

She shrugged, a little caught off guard by the compliment. "It's my job."

"Still," he said, and then paused. Something shifted in his expression—less playful, more sincere. "Look, I was wondering… would you maybe want to grab dinner sometime? Just dinner. No pitch meetings. No edits. Just… us."

The words hit her like a soft wave—unexpected, not unpleasant, but enough to stir something dormant. Her lips parted on instinct.

"I—" She hesitated.

She could feel the familiar wall rising. The one that had protected her heart since she'd stepped off that yacht. Since she'd left a man, she couldn't stopped loving.

She should say no.

She wanted to say no.

But her voice didn't follow the script this time.

"Yes," she heard herself say.

Julian blinked, surprised. "Yeah?"

She nodded slowly. "Yes. Dinner sounds… nice."

A slow smile spread across his face. "Great. I know a place not far from here. Tomorrow night?"

Willow smiled back, still unsure where the yes had come from, but not regretting it. Not yet.

"Tomorrow night."

Julian stood, offering a mock salute. "Then it's a date."

And as he walked away, Willow sat back in her chair, heart oddly quiet. Not fluttering. Not aching. Just still.

Maybe that was okay.

Maybe it was a start.

Even if she wasn't entirely sure where it would lead.

The restaurant Julian had chosen was cozy, all warm wood and soft jazz, tucked between two art galleries on a quiet block in Manhattan. It was the kind of place that whispered intimacy rather than demanded it. The lighting was low, the wine poured freely, and the food was the kind that made conversation slow down.

Willow wore a soft navy dress, nothing dramatic, but she felt beautiful in it. Confident, even. She hadn't expected to enjoy the evening so much. Julian was charming, yes, but also genuinely kind. He didn't try too hard. He listened. He asked questions about her favourite books and actually seemed to care about the answers.

He made her laugh.

It startled her, that warm burst of joy—like sunlight breaking through a cloud she hadn't realised was still hovering. It hadn't been long, just over a week, but somehow it felt like lifetimes had passed since she'd laughed like that. Since she'd felt light.

"I can't believe you've never read The Secret History," she said, wide-eyed as she sipped her wine.

Julian chuckled. "Don't judge me. I grew up on comic books and spy thrillers. But I'll make you a deal—if I read it, you have to read one of mine. And not just because it's in your job description."

Willow smiled. "Deal."

Later, when they stepped out into the cool night, the city was quieter. The breeze lifted her hair, and Julian offered her his arm as they walked. She took it—not because she had to, but because it felt… easy.

When they reached her building, they lingered at the steps.

"I had a really great time tonight," he said, tucking his hands into his coat pockets.

"Me too," Willow said honestly.

He hesitated for a moment, then leaned in. It wasn't a hungry or possessive kiss—just warm. Gentle. A slow press of lips to hers that spoke of hope, not expectation.

When he pulled back, he smiled. "Good night, Willow."

"Good night, Julian."

She watched him walk away before turning toward her building, her smile thoughtful and a little uncertain.

Across the street, hidden beneath the shadows of a tree-lined sidewalk, Luca stood frozen beside his parked car, cloaked in the quiet hush of early evening. The world around him moved gently—cars passing, leaves rustling in the soft breeze, lights flickering on in warm windows—but he felt utterly still. Like the earth had tilted beneath his feet.

He had arrived only moments earlier, heart pounding, adrenaline humming through his veins, every step driven by the words he'd been rehearsing since the plane touched down. Words he should have said weeks ago. Words that might still matter—if he could just get them out.

But now…

Now he couldn't move.

Because he'd seen the kiss.

It wasn't theatrical. There was no sweeping embrace, no desperate clutching like the movies loved to show. No. This was quieter than that—infinitely more devastating. A soft brush of lips. A gentle goodbye. Tender. Familiar. Real.

And it hit him harder than he'd expected.

His breath caught. His chest tightened with a sharp, visceral ache, as if something vital had just splintered inside him. She was there, only a few steps away, standing on the stoop with a man he didn't recognise—one whose hand lingered just a second too long at her waist. And she was smiling. That soft, radiant smile he used to think belonged only to him. A smile that once lit up his yacht like dawn breaking over the sea.

Now it was lighting up someone else.

He stood rooted to the spot, shoulders tense, his jaw clenched so tightly it ached. He had come here to fight. To lay down every shield he'd ever hidden behind. To tell her the truth—about how he felt, about how scared he was, about what had changed in him the moment she'd stepped into his world. The moment she became his world.

But now… now she was kissing someone else goodnight.

Maybe he was too late.

Maybe she'd already started to move on.

And maybe—just maybe—she deserved to.

He dragged in a breath that didn't quite reach his lungs and stepped off the curb, each movement weighted, as if gravity itself had turned against him. The city didn't slow down for heartbreak. The cars kept driving, the wind kept blowing, and the man she'd kissed turned to walk away, completely unaware that he'd just shattered the last fragile hope Luca had been carrying.

Still, he crossed the street.

Still, he moved forward.

Because whatever pain he felt—whatever hope had just flickered out—there was one truth louder than the rest: he couldn't turn back. Not this time. Not without trying. Not without saying everything he'd buried beneath pride and fear.

Even if she slammed the door in his face.

Even if she looked at him like he was a mistake.

Even if it broke him.

He had to try.

Because she wasn't just someone he'd loved.

She was it.

The only one who ever truly mattered.

And Luca Lombardi—who had spent a lifetime building empires, outwitting rivals, and walking away before anyone could hurt him—was finally ready to stay. To fight.

Not for power.

Not for control.

But for the one thing he had never believed he could have.

Her.

He reached the foot of her stairs and paused, staring up at her door like it was the gateway to everything he had ever been too afraid to want.

Tonight, he wasn't a billionaire. He wasn't a CEO. He wasn't a man with power and influence at his fingertips.

He was just a man, standing in the dark, praying that love hadn't left without him.

Hopefully.

Forever started now.

Willow kicked off her heels the moment she stepped inside, the soft thud of leather against hardwood echoing through the stillness of her apartment. The door clicked shut behind her, sealing her off from the world, from the night, from the part of herself that had smiled out of politeness even when her heart wasn't in it.

Her coat followed, shrugged from her shoulders and draped carelessly over the arm of the couch. She let out a long, shaky breath, the kind that deflated her entire frame.

She had told Julian the truth—she had enjoyed herself. He'd been charming in a quiet, British kind of way, thoughtful and self-deprecatingly funny. The dinner had been nice. The wine warm and smooth. The conversation easy.

But no matter how many times she laughed, no matter how many compliments Julian offered or how long she stared out the car window pretending to listen to music she didn't recognise—

The ache stayed.

It clung to her like a second skin.

Because her heart still belonged to the one man who didn't want it.

Luca.

She felt foolish just thinking it. Eleven days. That was all. It wasn't supposed to be enough time to change a person, to dismantle the walls she'd built around herself, to make her believe in forever.

And yet, it had.

Since stepping off the yacht, it felt like she'd lived a hundred different lives. None of them whole. None of them hers. And every night since, she'd curled beneath her blankets with the lights off, one hand pressed to the hollow at the base of her throat—where the necklace used to rest—and cried herself quietly, painfully, to sleep.

Tonight, she already knew, would be no different.

She moved through the apartment with slow, automatic motions, tugging pins from her hair and dropping them one by one onto the kitchen counter. Loose waves spilled over her shoulders. Her bare feet made soft, shuffling sounds on the hardwood, and she barely noticed the sting of faint red marks left by her heels. The ache in her chest dwarfed everything else.

All she wanted now was the comfort of her bed. Her pillow. The kind of sleep that didn't come until sorrow had wrung her dry.

She was halfway down the hallway when it happened.

A knock.

Not loud. Not urgent.

But firm.

She froze mid-step. Her breath caught in her throat, suspended between fear and confusion.

Her eyes flicked to the clock on the wall. Nearly midnight.

Her heart began to pound.

Who…?

Dread tightened her stomach. Please not Julian. He'd been nothing but respectful—considerate even—but she wasn't ready for more. She wasn't ready for anything.

Not when her soul still whispered his name like a prayer.

Not when Luca's memory lived in every shadow of this place.

With arms wrapped tightly around herself, she moved cautiously to the door. Her fingers hovered over the handle, then slowly curled around it. She opened the door—

And the world stopped.

Her lungs forgot how to function.

Luca.

He stood there in the dim light of the hallway like a dream pulled into reality, his dark suit slightly wrinkled, as if he'd been wearing it for hours. His hair was windswept, his face drawn with exhaustion, but his eyes…

God, his eyes.

They burned.

Not with anger. Not with arrogance. But with something far more dangerous. Something that made her knees weaken.

Hope.

"Luca…?" she breathed, barely audible.

He didn't answer right away. Just looked at her—really looked at her—with an intensity that stripped her bare. In that single look, she saw everything he hadn't said, everything he'd kept behind the carefully constructed mask of the man he used to be.

Then finally, softly, his voice cracked the silence.

"I had to see you."

Her fingers gripped the edge of the door, knuckles bloodless and white.

He took a step forward, the space between them shrinking. His voice was rough, like gravel. "I don't expect you to forgive me. But I had to tell you what I should've said before you left."

Her lips parted. She wanted to speak. To tell him to stop. Or to stay. She wasn't sure which. But no words came.

"I love you, Willow," he whispered. "And I'm done running from it."

It shattered her.

She stepped back slowly, her gaze never leaving his, her body moving on instinct until the backs of her knees hit the armchair behind her. She sank down like her bones had melted, like her whole frame had given out under the weight of what she'd been holding in.

And then she broke.

The tears came hard. Uncontrollable, soul-wracking sobs that tore from her chest as though they'd been buried too long. She buried her face in her hands, crumbling into herself, a woman split wide open by love and grief and the unbearable ache of almost.

Luca stepped inside. Quietly. Deliberately. The door clicked shut behind him with a soft finality, like the closing of a chapter—or maybe, mercifully, the beginning of a new one.

He didn't speak.

Didn't explain.

Didn't beg.

He just crossed the room and came to her.

He sank down to the floor in front of her—this powerful, proud man kneeling in a stranger's apartment like a sinner at the altar—and reached for her hands. Gently, patiently, like she was something fragile. Something precious.

She didn't pull away.

She couldn't.

And then, without a word, he gathered her into his arms.

Held her like she was the centre of gravity. Like anchoring her was the only way to keep from falling apart himself.

Willow sobbed harder, her face pressed into his shoulder, her fists curling into the fabric of his jacket. She didn't care how broken she looked. How undone she sounded. Because for the first time since she left that yacht, she wasn't crying into emptiness.

Luca was there.

And he wasn't letting go.

His hand moved in slow, soothing strokes over her back. His lips brushed her temple with the softest whisper of a kiss. His voice, low and hoarse, murmured against her hair.

"I'm here… I'm here…"

And for now, that was enough.

She didn't say anything.

She didn't have to.

Because he had come.

Because he was there.

Because she wasn't alone anymore.

And he wasn't letting go.

Not this time.

Chapter Nineteen

Willow's sobs slowly began to fade, tapering into soft, broken hiccups. Her breathing was ragged, her face damp, but the storm inside her had started to still. She could feel it—like the moment after thunder when the world is silent but still trembling.

Luca didn't move.

His arms remained wrapped around her, strong and steady, his cheek pressed against her temple. She could hear his heartbeat, fast but sure, anchoring her in the silence.

Her fingers, still curled in the fabric of his jacket, finally loosened.

She drew in a shaky breath.

"I didn't think I'd ever see you again," she whispered, her voice hoarse and raw.

Luca pulled back just enough to look at her, his eyes searching hers with quiet desperation.

"I almost didn't come," he said softly. "I was afraid you'd already moved on. That I didn't deserve a second chance."

Her lips parted, but she didn't speak. She just looked at him—really looked. He looked exhausted. Unshaven. Messy. Real.

Different.

And yet, somehow, more himself than he had ever been.

Willow sat back slightly, her hands falling into her lap, still trembling. "You broke my heart, Luca."

His jaw clenched. "I know."

She glanced away, blinking fast. "You let me go like I was nothing."

"No," he said quickly, his voice rough. "You were everything. That's why I let you go. Because I was a coward. Because I thought loving you meant ruining you."

Willow's eyes filled again, but this time, the tears didn't fall. She held them there—fragile and waiting.

"I don't know if I can do this again," she whispered. "I'm still hurting."

Luca reached for her hand and held it gently between both of his, his thumb brushing over her knuckles.

"I'm not asking for all of you right now," he said. "I'm just asking for a chance. One chance… to prove I've changed. That I want forever. With you."

She didn't answer right away. The silence stretched, filled with the weight of everything unsaid.

Then Willow looked down at their hands—at the way his fingers were wrapped around hers—and slowly, carefully, she pulled him toward her.

He let her, his eyes never leaving hers. The space between them shrank, breath mingling, the air thick with the weight of everything they hadn't said and everything they still wanted to.

Her forehead touched his, soft and trembling. Her heart thudded so hard it ached, but she didn't pull back. Didn't shy away.

"Tell me again," she whispered, her voice barely more than air.

Luca cupped her cheek, his thumb brushing a lingering tear. "I love you," he said, voice breaking. "More than I thought possible. I've never loved anyone as much as I love you."

A breath hitched in her throat. The words sank deep, blooming in places that had long felt hollow.

She closed her eyes and leaned in, their lips just a whisper apart.

"I love you too," she breathed, her voice a fragile promise in the quiet.

And when their mouths met—soft, slow, and aching—it wasn't about lust or regret or even making up for lost time.

It was about coming home.

Luca kissed her like she was the only thing tethering him to the earth. His hands framed her face with a tenderness that made her ache. He kissed her with reverence, like he still couldn't believe she was real, like he was afraid she might disappear if he opened his eyes.

Willow melted into him, arms wrapping around his neck, fingers threading through the dark waves of his hair. The kiss deepened—slow turned to searching, careful turned to desperate. Their hearts beat in time, frantic and unspoken.

She broke away just enough to whisper against his lips, "Luca, I need you."

His breath caught in his throat, his eyes dark with emotion. He didn't ask what she meant. He knew.

"I need you too, bella," he said, his voice rough with restraint, with longing, with love. "Always."

He kissed her again, standing now, lifting her with ease. She wrapped her legs around his waist as he carried her through the apartment, their mouths never parting for long. He didn't need directions. He knew where her bedroom was—he'd imagined this moment too many times not to.

He undressed her slowly, kissing every inch of exposed skin as though memorising it— like she was something sacred.

When he laid her gently on the bed, he paused.

Just for a second.

His fingers traced the curve of her cheek, his eyes searching hers for any flicker of doubt.

There was none.

Only her.

Only him.

Only the truth—raw and undeniable.

They had lost and found each other in the space of a single heartbeat.

Luca undressed, his gaze never leaving hers.

Willow reached for him, her touch tender, unshaken. The final walls between them crumbled with a single breath.

She smiled—soft, wistful—and cupped his face in her hands.

"What took you so long?" she whispered.

He didn't answer. He couldn't.

Instead, he kissed her—fiercely, reverently—pouring everything he'd ever felt into that one perfect collision. His mouth claimed hers with aching need, desperation bleeding through every touch, every breath.

She pushed him back with quiet strength, her thighs straddling his hips as her palms glided over the hard planes of his chest—warm, solid, and undeniably hers. Every muscle tensed beneath her touch, a low groan vibrating from deep in his throat, thick with longing and restraint fraying at the edges.

Willow leaned down, her hair falling like a silken curtain around their faces, veiling them in a world of heat and shadow. Her lips brushed the stubble-rough line of his throat. She kissed him there—slow, deliberate—feeling the sharp jump of his pulse under her mouth.

Her kisses moved lower, tasting his skin, the salt of the sea clinging to his collarbone, the heat radiating from the strong ridge of his chest. She lingered, her tongue teasing one nipple, then the other—circling, flicking, drawing him into her mouth with soft, wet pulls that made his breath stutter, and his fingers twist the sheets beneath them.

He was utterly at her mercy, and the knowledge of it thrilled her.

Her mouth continued its slow, sensual descent—every kiss a temptation, every flick of her tongue a silent promise. When she reached his navel, she paused, lifting her gaze to meet his. The hunger in his eyes was molten, his chest rising in shallow, uneven breaths.

Sliding lower still, she settled between his thighs, the heat of him making her ache. His arousal stood proud and pulsing, thick and heavy with need. She let her fingertips trail down his shaft, featherlight, watching the way his body arched at the contact. Then she leaned in and ran her tongue along the underside—from base to tip—so slowly, so deliberately, she felt his hips jerk in raw response.

"Willow," he groaned, her name a broken prayer on his lips.

She wrapped her hand around him, teasing the flushed head with her tongue—soft, slow licks—tasting the salt, the heat, the need. Then she took him into her mouth, inch by torturous inch, her lips stretching around him in a slick, exquisite glide.

Luca gasped, head falling back, hands tangling in her hair—not to guide, just to hold. As if she were unravelling him with every stroke, every swirling flick of her tongue. He let her set the pace, let her claim him with purpose and grace.

She hollowed her cheeks, drawing him deeper, then eased back with a slow drag of her tongue that left him panting her name. Her rhythm built with practiced control, sensual and devastating. Every movement was a worship, a declaration. His hips flexed helplessly beneath her, his groans dark and ragged, the sound of a man losing the last threads of restraint.

"Enough," he choked out, voice shredded. "I'm going to lose it…"

Before she could react, his hands gripped her waist and lifted her to him, kissing her fiercely, tasting himself on her lips. The kiss turned wild, hot, desperate as he flipped her gently onto her back and settled between her thighs.

His body was fire and steel above hers; all heat and weight and masculine need. One hand slid down her stomach—slow, reverent—until his fingers found the slick heat between her legs.

Willow gasped, her hips lifting to meet him as two fingers slid inside her—deep and sure. His thumb circled her clit with devastating precision, coaxing soft cries from her throat as his lips found her neck, her collarbone, the swell of her breast.

He took her nipple into his mouth, suckling gently, then harder, while his fingers moved inside her in perfect rhythm. Tender. Demanding. Irresistible.

"Luca... please," she whimpered, writhing beneath him, every nerve ending lit with fire. "I need you. Now."

He kissed her jaw, then her mouth, groaning low. "I want you too, amore mio. I need to feel you."

She opened to him, legs falling apart, welcoming him home. He positioned himself at her entrance, his arousal slick with her heat, then slowly pressed inside.

Thick. Deep. Devastating.

Willow cried out, nails digging into his shoulders as he filled her completely. Inch by aching inch until there was no space left between them—only heat, only him.

He held still, breathless, trembling. "Ti senti come il paradiso," he whispered hoarsely. You feel like heaven.

Then he began to move.

Long, slow thrusts at first, dragging groans from both of them. His body rocked into hers with deep precision, every stroke sending pleasure spiralling through her. Gradually, his pace built—deeper, rougher, more urgent—until they were moving together in a wild, consuming rhythm.

His hands gripped her hips, lifting her to take him deeper, angling just right—until he found that perfect spot that made her cry out, clutching at him like he was the only solid thing in the world.

Their bodies slapped together, slick and frantic, the bed trembling beneath them. Willow arched into him, legs wrapping around his waist, fingers tangled in his hair as their mouths met again and again in frantic, open-mouthed kisses.

"Luca... oh God... don't stop..."

"Never," he growled, voice rough, eyes wild. "I want to feel you come for me. Let go, bella mia."

The pleasure built to an unbearable peak, sharp and beautiful, and then she shattered— her climax tearing through her like lightning, her body clenching around him in tight, pulsing waves.

Luca followed a heartbeat later, thrusting deep with a broken moan as he came inside her, filling her, his body shuddering with the force of it.

He collapsed against her, trembling, breathing her in.

They stayed that way—locked together, bodies tangled, limbs trembling, sweat-slick and sated.

Eventually, he shifted, rolling to his back and pulling her with him so she sprawled over his chest, still joined, still connected. His hand stroked her back in slow, endless circles, like he never wanted to stop touching her.

They lay in the silence, heartbeats slowly steadying, breath mingling.

He kissed her shoulder, then her temple, and whispered into her hair, "Ti amo, Willow. I'll spend the rest of my life proving it."

Her eyes fluttered open, warm and sleepy. She tilted her face toward his, a soft smile curving her lips.

"Don't leave me again," she whispered.

"I'm never leaving," he murmured, pressing a kiss to her forehead. "Not for anything."

And this time, when Willow fell asleep in Luca's arms, there were no doubts.

No fears.

Only peace.

Only love.

Only them.

Golden morning light filtered through the curtains, painting the room in soft hues of amber and rose. Willow stirred as the warmth of the sun kissed her bare skin, but it wasn't sunlight that truly woke her—it was the sensation of Luca's lips brushing along the curve of her shoulder.

She turned, still wrapped in the haze of sleep, and found him watching her. His eyes, dark and full of something deeper than desire, searched hers as though trying to memorise her all over again.

"Buongiorno," he murmured, his voice still thick from sleep.

She smiled. "Good morning."

His hand slid over her waist, then lower, fingers skimming the curve of her hip. "Do you know how beautiful you are in the morning?"

She laughed softly, burying her face in his neck. "You're just saying that because I didn't run away."

He kissed her—slow and sensual, tasting, teasing—and then suddenly they were tangled again, breathless and hungry, the night's intensity giving way to a morning made of softer edges and lingering heat.

Willow moaned against his mouth as Luca rolled her onto her back, his hands and lips rediscovering every inch of her. She welcomed him without hesitation, legs parting to cradle him as he slipped inside her again—this time slower, deeper.

They moved in a rhythm of quiet devotion, of whispered names and long-held promises, of skin brushing skin and hearts beating in perfect time.

When they came together again, it wasn't fire—it was light. Warm, golden, consuming.

Afterward, he lay on his side, propped up on one elbow, watching her trace lazy patterns across his chest. Then, with a soft sigh, he leaned down and kissed her forehead before slipping out of bed.

Willow blinked up at him, dazed and content, as he crossed the room and grabbed his pants from the floor. He dug into one of the pockets and pulled out something small.

She sat up, the sheets falling to her waist as he returned to the bed and slid in beside her.

"I want to give you something," he said quietly, gathering her in his arms.

Willow froze.

Her heart tripped.

Her mind immediately flashed to the necklace—the one he'd given her as a farewell. The one that had broken her heart.

Luca felt her stiffen. His arms tightened slightly, anchoring her.

He looked down into her wary eyes, and his voice came low, firm, and full of regret. "Willow... I'm not going to make that mistake again."

She blinked, caught off guard by the rawness in his voice.

He opened his hand between them.

Nestled in his palm was a delicate ring—gold, simple, elegant. A single, flawless sapphire sat at the centre, deep blue like the Mediterranean Sea.

Not cold.

Not distant.

But true.

Her lips parted, words lost to the rush of emotion that clogged her throat.

"This isn't a goodbye," Luca said, his voice rough. "It's a beginning. If you'll let it be."

She stared at the ring, her vision blurring.

"I know I failed you before," he whispered, brushing her hair back gently. "But I've never been more certain of anything. I love you. And I want every morning of my life to begin like this—with you."

Willow reached for his face, her hand trembling. "I was so afraid," she breathed. "Afraid you'd break me again."

"I was afraid too," he admitted. "But not anymore. Not when I have you."

She let out a shaky laugh, tears slipping free. "Well, that's not fair. You're proposing and making me cry before breakfast."

His smile curved slowly. "Say yes and I'll make you breakfast. In nothing but an apron."

She laughed through her tears, then nodded, her voice a breath of hope. "Yes."

Luca exhaled softly, as if he'd been holding that moment in his chest for a lifetime. He took her hand with reverence and slipped the ring onto her finger. It was cool against her skin—delicate, perfect, real.

Then he kissed her—slow and certain—like a vow sealed in silence.

And for the first time, Willow didn't just feel loved.

She felt home.

Epilogue

Five Years Later – Tuscany

The sun dipped low over the rolling hills of Tuscany, casting the vineyard in a rich, golden glow that made everything it touched seem suspended in magic. Long shadows stretched across the manicured gardens, where laughter mingled with the faint notes of classical guitar. The villa, with its terracotta roof and ivy-covered walls, looked almost exactly as it had five years ago—on the day Marcus and Elena had vowed forever beneath an arch of olive branches and white roses.

But today, it wore celebration once again.

Their fifth anniversary.

Lanterns hung from the trees like stars, flickering gently in the breeze. Tables draped in white linen were scattered across the lawn, each adorned with arrangements of white hydrangeas and pale blue delphiniums. Wine glasses clinked, heels crunched softly on gravel, and the scent of lemon blossoms drifted on the warm summer air.

Willow stood near one of the flower-laden tables, her fingers absently brushing the stem of her untouched wine glass. She wore a soft blue chiffon dress that caught the wind like a whispered secret, the fabric fluttering lightly around her legs. Her hair had been pinned up in a loose twist, stray tendrils curling against her cheeks. Nestled among the soft waves were delicate pearl pins—gifts from Luca that morning, slipped wordlessly into her palm while their son babbled cheerfully in the next room.

Behind her, footsteps crunched on the grass.

"Hello, gorgeous," Marcus said, approaching with his trademark swagger and a glass of prosecco in each hand. His grin was boyish, eternal, the same one he'd worn since university.

Willow turned, lifting a brow in amusement.

Elena appeared beside him, effortlessly elegant in a flowing champagne-coloured dress, her hand sliding around Marcus's waist as she gave her husband a mock glare. "If I were a jealous woman, I'd be worried."

Before Willow could respond, the warmth of a familiar hand settled against her lower back. Luca.

"I'm not thrilled about the way he flirts with my wife," he murmured, his voice rich with dry amusement.

Willow leaned subtly into his touch, her smile soft and teasing. "I only have eyes for you."

Marcus staggered back, clutching his chest in mock betrayal. "Oh, you wound me."

"You'll survive," Luca replied with a smirk, though the smile tugging at his lips gave him away.

Laughter rippled between them like the breeze through the olive trees.

Out on the grass, their three-year-old son, Riccardo, let out a gleeful shout as he chased bubbles floating through the air. His curly dark hair bounced with each step, his tiny feet bare and grass stained. Nico, Marcus and Elena's equally wild toddler, followed close behind, the two boys shrieking in delight, a blur of innocence and sunshine.

Willow's gaze followed them, and something in her heart stretched wide—so full it ached in the best way. This life, these people, the moments she never dared dream for— every piece had become her home.

As dusk deepened and the sky turned lavender, guests began gathering near the stone patio for speeches, dancing, and more wine. Candles flickered to life in tall glass vases lining the steps, casting soft shadows that danced along the walls of the villa.

Willow found herself walking beside Elena through the quiet candlelit halls, the murmur of the party fading behind them.

They moved past familiar rooms—the library where Luca had once kissed her in stunned silence, the hallway where Marcus had drunkenly attempted to play matchmaker. The walls held memories, and tonight they felt like they were whispering.

"I don't know if I should say anything yet," Willow whispered, voice barely audible over the rustling of their skirts. Her hand brushed over her stomach in an absent, almost reverent gesture.

Elena stopped short and turned to her, eyes narrowing with playful suspicion. "Willow. Spit it out."

Willow bit her lip, eyes shining. "I think I might be pregnant."

Elena gasped and immediately grabbed her by the wrist. "Oh my God. You're coming with me." She yanked her down the corridor with comical determination. "We are taking a test right now. No arguments."

Moments later, they were holed up in the nearest guest bathroom, Elena standing guard like a general while Willow paced barefoot on cool marble tiles, her heart rattling in her chest.

When the test finally blinked to life, everything else fell away.

Positive.

Willow stared down at the tiny window, her breath catching. Emotion surged—disbelief, wonder, joy so sudden it felt like flying. Her knees gave a little.

Elena squealed. "Oh my God! You're having another baby!" She flung her arms around Willow, both of them laughing, crying, holding on tight.

When they returned to the garden, laughter still hanging in the air like twilight mist, Elena wasted no time. She intercepted Marcus and dragged him away, whispering furiously in his ear while he raised his eyebrows and grinned like a man who'd just heard the best secret in the world.

Luca stood beneath the golden string lights, one hand in his pocket, a wine glass in the other. He watched his wife approach, his brow furrowing at Elena's sudden theatrics.

"What's going on?" he asked, eyes narrowing slightly as Willow stepped up to him.

Wordlessly, she reached for his hand and placed the pregnancy test gently into his palm.

He looked down at it. Blinked once. Then again.

His head snapped up.

"You're…?"

She nodded slowly, her voice a breath. "Yes."

A beat of silence. Then—

He let out a sound that was half laugh, half gasp. Disbelief gave way to joy, unfiltered and overwhelming. With a cry of pure happiness, he grabbed her and spun her around in his arms, laughing into her hair, kissing her cheeks, her forehead, every inch of skin he could reach as guests turned to watch and broke into cheers.

Elena and Marcus returned a moment later, Marcus grinning from ear to ear. He slapped Luca's shoulder with a hearty clap. "Well done, Papà," he said, winking.

Luca laughed again, unable to contain it. He pulled Willow close, his other arm reaching just in time to catch Riccardo as the little boy came barrelling toward them, grass-stained and cookie-covered, a whirlwind of mischief and sunshine.

Luca held his son in one arm, his wife in the other.

He looked around—at Marcus whispering something that made Elena throw back her head in laughter, at the villa bathed in candlelight, at the tiny miracle already taking shape inside the woman he loved.

He had once believed love was a myth. That it wasn't meant for men like him—men with walls built too high, with scars too deep.

But he'd been wrong.

Because he had found it.

Real. Fierce. Eternal.

And it was even better than he could have ever imagined.

The End

The Billionaire's Unexpected Heir

Alison Reid

A complete standalone romance

Previously published individually

Chapter One

The scent of antiseptic and fading lilies clung to the air like a sorrow that refused to lift—thick, inescapable, and suffocating in its familiarity.

Calista Georgiou sat perched on the edge of the hospital bed, her slender fingers laced gently through her half-sister's frail hand. Danica's once-luminous skin—so often lit by the flashbulbs of Paris runways and Tokyo billboards—now seemed translucent under the harsh white lights. Her cheekbones, once envied by designers and photographers alike, were too sharp now, her features fragile and hollow. Her golden hair, dulled and brittle from the months of chemo, was tucked beneath a silk scarf in muted lilac—less an accessory now, more a final piece of dignity.

A soft whimper drew Calista's gaze to the corner of the room.

Little Chloe, curled up in a faded pink armchair much too big for her tiny frame, clutched a threadbare white bunny to her chest. Her fair hair formed a halo around her sleeping face, and her thumb rested in her mouth, the habit recently returned—an old comfort in the strange, sterile rhythm of hospital life. She had adjusted far too quickly, as if her toddler heart already sensed the tides of loss.

"She should be outside," Danica murmured, her voice thin and cracked like old porcelain. "Running barefoot in the grass… not waiting for me to die in here."

Calista's throat closed. She gave her sister's hand a soft squeeze. "Don't say that," she whispered, even though part of her knew they had moved past denial weeks ago.

Danica's lips twitched into a faint, tired smile. "We both know what's coming," she said, her breath hitching. "I've stopped pretending. There's no runway left to walk. No miracle hiding behind another scan."

She shifted slightly, her back arching with a subtle wince she tried to mask—but Calista saw it. She saw everything now.

"I need to know something," Danica said. Her eyes fluttered open, bloodshot but still eerily striking beneath dark lashes. "When I'm gone… you'll take care of her?"

Calista blinked through a rush of tears, her lashes wet. "You don't even have to ask. She's already mine."

"I know," Danica whispered, emotion catching in her throat. "You've raised her more than I have. I was never meant to be someone's mother—not really. Modelling always came first. The shoots, the brands, the travel. And I told myself I'd make it up to her later. But cancer doesn't wait for later, does it?"

The silence that followed was thick and reverent. The only sound was the rhythmic beep of the heart monitor, steady and indifferent.

A single tear slid down Danica's temple. Her voice broke as she whispered, "Promise me…you'll do what's best for Chloe."

Calista nodded, the ache in her chest almost too much to bear. "I swear. On everything I have. I'll protect her. Always."

Danica's body sagged slightly into the mattress, as if a weight had lifted. "You were always the better sister," she said. "Even when I pretended not to see it."

Calista leaned forward and kissed her forehead, brushing a damp lock of hair from her temple. "You gave me Chloe," she said softly. "That's more than enough."

But a part of her—deep inside—ached for the truth she never voiced aloud. Danica had never been kind to her. Not truly. Growing up, their relationship was built on fragile strings: competition, criticism, dismissal. Calista, the quiet, bookish shadow to Danica's golden light, had learned long ago to love her sister from a distance. Even after Danica had unexpectedly shown up pregnant and scared, Calista had taken her in without question. Raised Chloe as if she were her own.

Danica hadn't thanked her. Not for years. Not until the diagnosis came crashing down six months ago, erasing vanity and grudges and sharpening what truly mattered. She'd softened since then. Apologised, in quiet moments. Tried to make amends. And Calista—because her heart always forgave too easily—had held her sister's hand through it all, never once tallying the past.

Her gaze drifted to Chloe. The little girl's chest rose and fell in steady rhythm, her lashes fluttering with dreams. She was beautiful. Fair-haired like Danica, with her wide blue eyes and porcelain skin. A child too young to understand that her world was about to change forever.

Calista didn't know who Chloe's father was. Danica had always claimed she didn't know, brushing off questions with a wave of her manicured hand. But Calista had always suspected that was a lie. The protectiveness in her sister's eyes whenever the subject came up had been too fierce, too sharp.

Now, the truth would die with her.

As night crept through the high hospital windows, casting long shadows on the walls, Calista pulled Chloe into her arms and curled beside Danica's bed. One hand cradled her niece, the other remained wrapped tightly around her sister's.

She listened to the steady rhythm of Danica's breathing. To the machines. To the hush that filled the room with quiet finality.

And then—

The rhythm stopped.

It didn't gasp or scream. It simply… ceased.

Calista sat still, frozen in the silence, unable to look away from Danica's face. Her sister lay peaceful now. Eyes closed, features relaxed in a way they hadn't been for weeks.

Chloe stirred slightly in her arms, murmuring in her sleep, oblivious to the fact that her mother had just slipped away.

Tears spilled down Calista's cheeks—warm, silent, unstoppable. They traced delicate lines along her pale skin as she leaned forward, pressing her forehead gently against the back of Danica's cooling hand.

"I'll keep my promise," she whispered, her voice barely a breath. "No matter what. She'll never feel alone."

She stayed there for hours, through the long hush of night into the pale grey light of morning. The machines had long gone quiet, but Calista couldn't bring herself to leave. She sat in the heavy silence of loss, holding Chloe close, her niece's small, steady breath a grounding anchor in a world that felt like it was unravelling.

Calista knew Danica would be taken soon—by orderlies in quiet uniforms, escorted down sterile corridors into another kind of silence. But she couldn't let them come just yet. Chloe had to wake first. Chloe needed to see her mother one last time, even if her two-and-a-half-year-old mind wouldn't fully understand.

She had a right to say goodbye.

Curled against Calista's chest, Chloe stirred with a soft whimper and blinked into the morning light. Her fair lashes fluttered like fragile wings, and she looked up sleepily, her thumb still tucked into her mouth.

"Mommy?" she mumbled, reaching instinctively for Calista.

Calista's heart twisted. Chloe had always called her "Mommy"—a title she never corrected. Danica had been her biological mother, yes, but rarely present. Photoshoots, fashion weeks, exotic islands—Danica's life had always existed in motion, never pausing long enough to nurture. Calista had been the one who rocked Chloe to sleep through colic, who sang lullabies at midnight and cleaned up spilled milk with a tired smile.

She wiped her eyes quickly, trying to steady her voice. "Good morning, sweetheart."

She brought Chloe closer, letting the toddler settle into her lap as she gently guided her tiny hand to Danica's still fingers.

"Say good morning to Mommy," Calista said softly. "She's sleeping now. A special kind of sleep."

Chloe looked up, confused. Her little brows furrowed, and her lips trembled as if she sensed something was wrong, even if she couldn't name it. She leaned forward and kissed her mother's hand with a tenderness that shattered Calista's heart.

"Bye-bye, Mommy," she whispered.

A sob caught in Calista's throat, and she held the little girl tighter.

The door creaked open behind them, and soft footsteps entered the room. Calista didn't have to look to know who it was.

"Calista," came the gentle voice, laced with sorrow.

Henry Collins.

He stepped closer, the scent of his familiar aftershave drifting into the room—woodsy, clean, grounding. He had once lived next door when their world had still been intact. When their parents were alive, and Danica's laughter had rung through the yard like bells in summer. He had gone to school with Danica, but it was Calista he had gravitated to as adults. Quiet, steady Calista, who never asked for anything.

He knelt beside her, his hand resting gently on her shoulder. "It's time to get you and Chloe home."

She didn't move. Didn't speak. Just stared at the motionless figure on the bed, trying to imprint every detail of her sister's face before they came to take her away.

Henry's hand lingered, warm, and patient. "You've done everything you could. She knew you were here. She knew Chloe was safe."

Calista closed her eyes for a moment, breathing in slowly.

Henry had asked her to marry him once—just after Danica's diagnosis, when everything felt uncertain and fragile. He said he loved her. And Calista did love him, in a way. He was kind. Loyal. Dependable.

But it wasn't the kind of love that made your heart ache at the sight of someone's smile. It wasn't the kind of love that kept you up at night, wondering what their laugh sounded like in the dark. It wasn't the love she dreamed about—the kind she secretly believed wasn't meant for people like her.

She had told him the truth. That she loved him, but not the way a wife should love a husband. And to his credit, he hadn't walked away. He stayed. As a friend. As someone who showed up when it mattered.

Now was one of those times.

She looked up at him finally, her eyes red-rimmed and raw. "Just a few more minutes."

Henry nodded. "Take all the time you need."

He rose and stepped back, giving her space.

Calista turned her gaze back to Danica, brushing her fingers one last time over her sister's knuckles.

"You were never easy," she whispered with a soft, broken smile. "But I loved you anyway. And she will always know how much you meant."

She pressed a final kiss to Danica's forehead, then stood slowly, lifting Chloe into her arms. The little girl wrapped her arms around her neck, her head resting against Calista's shoulder.

And together, with Henry waiting quietly by the door, they stepped out of the hospital room, leaving behind the silence of goodbye and stepping into the fragile beginning of everything that came next.

Henry drove them home through the quiet streets, the early spring sunlight too bright, too cheerful for a day wrapped in grief. Calista sat in the backseat with Chloe nestled against her chest, the child already drifting into sleep, her small fingers clutching the edge of Calista's blouse.

The hush of the hospital still clung to Calista, a phantom weight she couldn't shake. Outside, the world moved on—cars passed, neon signs glowed—while she sat in silence, numb beneath the rhythm of her own breath.

By the time they reached her little house—modest, but warm and filled with memories—Chloe was fast asleep. Calista carried her gently to her bedroom, laid her down in the soft pink sheets, and tucked her bunny beside her. Chloe didn't stir. She was exhausted, her small body heavy with the kind of bone-deep fatigue that only sorrow and confusion could bring.

Calista brushed back a strand of golden hair from her niece's forehead, then leaned down to kiss her cheek. "I've got you," she whispered. "Always."

When she came out into the kitchen, she found Henry standing by the counter, two mismatched mugs sitting between them, steam curling from the coffee he'd made. He moved comfortably in her space, as he always had—fitting into her world without demanding more than it could give.

"Is she okay?" he asked softly as she entered.

"She will be," Calista replied, pulling her cardigan tighter around herself. "I don't think she really understands yet."

Henry nodded and slid a mug toward her. "Kids feel more than we give them credit for. But she has you. That's something solid to hold on to."

Calista curled her hands around the mug. The warmth seeped into her fingers but did nothing to ease the chill in her chest. She gave him a tired smile. "Thank you. For everything today."

Henry reached across the table and placed his hand gently over hers. His touch was familiar, steady—comfort, not sparks. "You know I'm here for you. Always."

She looked down at their hands, his larger one covering hers with quiet strength. "I know, Henry. And I appreciate it more than I can say. You've been a godsend these past few months. I don't know how I would've managed without you."

He watched her for a moment, then said softly, "You know I love you, Calista."

The words hung between them—not a declaration, but a quiet truth he had offered before. She met his gaze, and her heart ached—not because she didn't care, but because she couldn't give him what he wanted.

"I love you too," she said gently, "but not the way you deserve."

"I know," he said, not flinching. His smile was small, a little sad. "I just needed to say it. I know you have a lot on your mind. But that doesn't change how I feel."

She swallowed hard, touched by his honesty, by the unshakable loyalty he carried for her. "You deserve someone who sees you as the centre of their world, Henry. Someone who can give you back everything you offer. I don't want to keep you waiting for something that's not going to change."

Henry leaned back in his chair, nodding slowly. "You've just lost your sister. You're raising a child now. Your life is upside down. I'm not asking for anything from you right now. Just… let me be here."

Her eyes shimmered. "That's more than enough."

They sat in silence for a while, sipping coffee as the weight of the day settled around them. Outside the window, the wind rustled through the trees, and the house was quiet except for the soft hum of the fridge and the occasional creak of settling wood. A home in mourning, but still a home

"Do you need help with the funeral arrangements?" Henry asked gently, his voice breaking the stillness between them.

Calista shook her head, her fingers tightening slightly around her coffee mug. "No. I've already taken care of most of it. I just have to let the funeral home know what day I want the service. I'm thinking Thursday. That gives me time to let people know."

Henry nodded, his expression unreadable for a moment. "Alright. I'll bring her will with me when I come to the funeral."

Calista looked up, her eyes heavy with fatigue but steady. "I'm not expecting any surprises. Everything will be left to Chloe—as it should be."

A flicker passed over Henry's face—too brief to name but not missed entirely. Concern? Regret? She couldn't tell. He looked away before she could study him further.

"You'll find out soon enough," he said carefully. "Danica was adamant about making sure everything was in order."

Calista sighed and leaned back in her chair, her limbs aching with more than just exhaustion. "I'm not worried about that. I'll need to go through her things. Sort everything out. There's a lot… I don't even know where to start."

"If you need help, just say the word. I mean it."

She offered a faint smile. "I will."

Henry lingered for a moment, then stepped closer and pressed a gentle kiss to her cheek. His palm rested briefly on her shoulder. "I'm here for you, Cal. Always."

She nodded, her throat tight. "I know. And I'm grateful."

As the door closed behind him, the silence returned, wrapping around her like a too-heavy coat. In the quiet, the weight of everything settled in her chest—grief, responsibility, and the looming unknowns.

She had kept her promise.

But she had a feeling that the hardest part was still ahead.

Chapter Two

The day of the funeral arrived cloaked in a slate-grey sky, as if the world itself had taken on the hush of mourning.

Chloe had accepted Danica's passing better than Calista expected. There were no tantrums, no tears in the night—just quiet questions, asked with the kind of clarity only children possess. Why did mommy have to go? Is she coming back? And then, the one that shattered Calista's composure: Will you go, too?

She had knelt beside her daughter, her voice steady despite the crack threading through her chest. "Not for a very, very long time. I promise."

Now, as they stood outside the church, Calista's promise echoed like a vow made in a different life. The building loomed, tall, and still, its stained-glass windows catching the weak light and throwing fractured colours across the pavement. Henry's hand rested gently at the small of her back, a silent tether. She hadn't said much all morning.

Inside, the scent of lilies was thick in the air, cloying. Calista hated lilies now.

Danica's photo stood on an easel at the front of the sanctuary—smiling, radiant, a version of her that seemed impossibly alive. Calista sat in the front pew, Chloe beside her clutching a small stuffed bear, Henry on the other side, their shoulders nearly touching but not quite. The space between them felt vast.

As the eulogy began, Calista didn't hear the words. She only saw moments: Danica laughing in the kitchen, holding Chloe as a baby, arguing over something silly and storming off, then returning with wine and apologies. The messy, brilliant, complicated years of their friendship, their entanglement, all of it both too much and not enough.

Tears slid silently down her cheeks. Chloe leaned her head against her arm.

After the service, mourners gathered in hushed clusters, sharing stories, casseroles, and condolences. Calista moved through them like a ghost—gracious, grateful, numb. Everyone wanted to say something, to offer a memory or an "if you need anything." But what could they give her that would bring Danica back?

Outside, the cold had sharpened. The cemetery was small, ringed with bare trees that clawed at the grey sky. As they lowered the casket, Chloe tucked the bear into her coat and whispered something Calista couldn't hear. Henry held her hand now. She let him.

She felt the finality in her bones.

Afterward, when the crowd thinned and the wind picked up, Calista lingered. Chloe had gone with Henry to the car. Alone, she placed a hand on the dark earth, newly turned. "I loved you," she said. "Even when I hated you, I loved you."

It wasn't forgiveness. But it was truth.

And for now, that would have to be enough.

Henry drove them home through the quiet streets, the sky now streaked with pale amber light that filtered weakly through the clouds. The city seemed indifferent to their grief—cars still moved, shop signs still blinked to life, and pedestrians bundled in coats passed by, unaware of the weight pressing on the people inside the black car.

Calista sat in the front passenger seat; her hands folded tightly in her lap. Chloe was in the back, half-asleep, her small head resting against the window. The silence between them was not uncomfortable, just fragile. Held together by the thin threads of exhaustion and emotion.

When they reached the apartment, Chloe perked up only slightly. Calista helped her out of her black coat, smoothing her hair as they stepped inside. The warmth of home rushed over them like a blanket, but it brought no comfort. Just the ache of familiarity in a world suddenly altered.

"I'll set her up in the living room," Calista murmured to Henry.

He nodded, removing his own coat and gloves, waiting in the kitchen.

Chloe, ever resilient, clutched the stuffed bear she'd brought to the funeral and let Calista settle her on the couch with a soft throw, her tablet, and a tray of crackers and apple slices. The quiet click of the tablet powering on gave Calista a moment of strange gratitude—for simple distractions, for small routines that made the pain tolerable.

Then she turned, her breath catching slightly, and walked into the kitchen.

Henry stood by the island, a manila envelope in his hand. His expression was gentle but unreadable, that lawyer's calm returning now that grief had done most of its tearing. The soft hum of the refrigerator was the only sound between them.

"She asked me to do this with you," he said quietly. "Not in an office. Here. Where you'd feel safe."

Calista gave a small nod. "Just… get it over with."

Henry opened the envelope, sliding out a few sheets of paper. "Danica updated her will six months ago."

Calista's eyes narrowed faintly. "Six months…?"

"She didn't tell anyone, not even me, until she sent me a sealed copy." He paused. "She left everything to you, Calista."

The words hit her like a gust of cold air.

She blinked. "What?"

Henry looked down at the paper, confirming what he already knew. "Her entire estate—real and liquid assets, investments, the trust fund, her properties in New York and Paris—all of it. It's yours."

Calista took a step back, as if physical distance could blunt the impact. "No. That… she didn't mean that. She couldn't have."

"She did. She left a letter with it too. I can show you—"

"No," Calista said, voice sharp, then softened. "I don't want it, Henry. I don't want any of it. Chloe should have it all. She was Danica's daughter, not me."

Henry set the paper down gently. "Calista, she made you Chloe's guardian. She left all her fortune to you. It wasn't a mistake."

Calista turned away, bracing her hands on the counter. Her eyes burned, not from tears—but from disbelief, confusion, guilt. "She spent her whole life resenting me. Punishing me. Why would she leave me everything?"

Henry hesitated. "Maybe she knew she'd never get the chance to say it, so she did the only thing she could."

Calista pressed her lips together, breathing through the lump in her throat. "I don't want her money. I want her to be here. I want Chloe to grow up knowing who her mother really was—before everything fell apart."

"She trusted you to give her that," Henry said softly. "And to decide what to do with the rest."

Calista closed her eyes.

"I'm not ready," she whispered.

"You don't have to be. Not tonight."

He gently folded the will and slipped it back into the envelope, leaving it on the counter. Then he stepped back, giving her space, watching her with something like tenderness in his eyes.

"She left you her fortune," he said, almost to himself. "But maybe the real gift was her trust."

Calista didn't answer.

The house had settled into a soft hush. Chloe had fallen asleep on the couch; the tablet dimmed to black beside her. Calista tucked a blanket around her and kissed her forehead, then returned to the kitchen.

The envelope still sat on the counter like a quiet challenge.

She stared at it for a long time, unsure what frightened her more—the weight of what Danica had left behind, or the words she might have saved for last. Words Danica never gave her when she was alive. Not fully. Not without venom or silence trailing behind.

Her fingers trembled slightly as she opened the flap.

Inside, beneath the will and legal documents, was a smaller envelope. Handwritten. Her name in Danica's slanted cursive: Calista.

She sank into a chair before she dared open it.

Calista,

If you're reading this, I'm gone—and you're probably furious. That's all right. I deserve it. There's so much I should have said while I was alive, but I never found the right time. Or maybe I was too proud to try.

You were never a mistake.

I know I made you feel that way more times than I can count. I carried a lot of bitterness, some of it earned, most of it not. I blamed you for things that were never yours to carry— because you were always mum and dad's favourite. But I realised too late that that was not your fault, it was theirs. But I always blamed you.

But even though I was not worthy, you stayed through it all. You took care of Chloe like she was your own, even when you had every reason to walk away.

I watched you.

Every bedtime story. Every doctor's appointment. Every tantrum you soothed with more grace than I ever had.

You became the kind of mother I wish I had been from the start.

That's why I left everything to you—not as a burden, but as a correction. A way of saying: I see you. I trust you. I love you.

Yes, I said it. Don't roll your eyes.

Give Chloe the life I couldn't give her. Make better choices. Love boldly. And please, forgive me—not for leaving, but for the years I wasted before I understood how much you meant to me.

Yours,

Danica

The morning was brisk; the kind of cold that made the city feel sharper around the edges. Calista pulled her coat tighter and kept her hands tucked into her sleeves as she walked through the glass doors of Henry's law office. The space was quiet, sterile, filled with the soft hum of printers and the click of shoes on tile.

Henry met her in the reception area, his expression gentling when he saw her. "You didn't have to come in. I could've—"

"I needed to," Calista interrupted. "I needed to do this in person."

He nodded and led her to a modest but well-appointed conference room. A manila folder sat on the table, neatly labelled, waiting.

Once the door closed behind them, Henry gestured to a seat. "I finalised the paperwork last night. The estate is substantial. Danica's investments, assets, and life insurance—"

"I want it all transferred," Calista said before he could finish. "Into a trust for Chloe."

Henry paused, his brow furrowed. "Calista, I understand your instinct, but Danica named you as the sole beneficiary. It's legal and clear."

"I know," she said, her voice steady. "And I appreciate what she was trying to do. But this money—it's not for me. It was never meant to be. Danica wanted Chloe to be cared for. That's what I'm going to do."

Henry leaned back in his chair, considering. "You'd be entitled to manage it, even in trust. But you wouldn't technically own it."

"That's the point. I don't want ownership. Just access—for her needs. School. Medical expenses. Anything she requires. But it should be hers, not mine. When she turns twenty-five, she can make her own decisions."

Henry gave a slow nod. "All right. We can set up a revocable trust, name you as trustee. You'll have the ability to authorise distributions for Chloe's benefit, and at twenty-five, full control passes to her. I'll write in a clause for earlier partial disbursement if needed—college, emergencies, things like that."

Calista let out a breath she hadn't realised she'd been holding. "That sounds right. That sounds… fair."

He opened the folder and began drawing up notes with practiced ease. "It'll take a day or two to finalise. In the meantime, if there's anything Chloe needs—"

"She's okay," Calista said softly. "Better than I thought she'd be. She's been… resilient."

Henry smiled faintly. "Like someone else I know."

Calista looked away, but a small smile tugged at her lips. She gave a small shrug, her eyes drifting to the window. The city outside moved on, indifferent and alive.

"I don't want to be tethered to this money," she said. "I just want to raise Chloe with as much honesty as I can. No guilt. No games. Just… a life she can trust."

Henry looked at her for a long moment before speaking. "Danica made the right choice. Even if she never told you."

Calista blinked, eyes stinging again. "I hope so."

She stood as Henry rose too. The folder lay between them now—still heavy with memory, but lighter with purpose.

"I'll be in touch when the documents are ready," he said gently.

"Thank you," she murmured, then added, "for seeing me through all of this."

As she stepped out into the cold again, Calista felt something she hadn't in days—clarity. The grief was still there, wound tightly inside her. But now, so was direction. Chloe's future was no longer a question tangled in regret or resentment.

It was a promise.

Chapter Three

Chloe's life didn't change much.

She still went to her preschool every morning, clutching her little backpack with the pink unicorn charm that jingled when she ran. She still insisted on jelly sandwiches cut into stars. She still sang the same off-key lullabies in the bath and told elaborate stories to her stuffed animals at bedtime.

She still laughed.

She still cried.

To a casual observer, it would be hard to tell that anything monumental had shifted in her young life.

Calista noticed it most in the quiet moments—the ones that used to hold a heaviness she couldn't name. The stillness before dinner. The sound of one fewer voice in the house. The absence of clipped heels across the tile or the sharp rustle of expensive handbags being dropped on the table.

Danica was gone, and Chloe… Chloe didn't seem to feel it. Probably because Danica was hardly ever there.

Calista sat on the couch one afternoon, watching Chloe build towers from her coloured blocks on the living room rug. She had her tongue between her teeth in concentration, a little furrow in her brow.

There had been no questions. No weeping tantrums. No whispered "where's Mommy?"

It unnerved Calista at first. But then she reminded herself of something simpler. Danica had always been more presence than person to Chloe—an elegant silhouette coming and going, a perfume trail, a late kiss on the forehead if Chloe was still awake. A mother in name, but not in rhythm. Not in the texture of Chloe's days.

And now, with Danica gone forever, Chloe's world had barely rippled.

Calista leaned back and closed her eyes for a moment. The guilt had come in waves the first few days after the funeral. Not for herself—but for what Chloe didn't feel. For what she'd never gotten the chance to have.

But grief, Calista was starting to learn, wasn't always loud or dramatic. Sometimes it was just the soft hush of absence. Sometimes it was quiet acceptance.

She opened her eyes again as Chloe looked up and grinned. "Look, mommy! I made a zoo!"

"You did," Calista said, smiling back. "It's perfect."

Chloe beamed, then crawled over to add a plastic tiger to the mix, completely immersed again in her game.

The world hadn't stopped. Not for Chloe. And maybe that was all right. Maybe Danica's absence didn't have to be a defining wound.

Maybe, Calista thought, as she curled her feet under her and watched Chloe giggle, maybe this was what healing looked like—when a child didn't have to unlearn pain, because she'd never been taught it in the first place.

The rhythm of normalcy had begun to thread itself back into Calista's days—quietly, gently, like the cautious return of spring after a long, bitter winter.

She'd gone back to work at the elementary school, slipping into her old routines with the grace of someone relearning muscle memory. The children were small, noisy anchors, their laughter like medicine. She helped with spelling and shoelaces and playground disputes. No one there asked too many questions. They just welcomed her back with soft smiles and fresh stacks of worksheets.

In the quiet afternoons, after Chloe's bath was finished and dinner simmered gently on the stove, Calista would slip into the bedroom and open the closet door—the one where Danica's clothes now hung like whispers of another life.

Silk blouses, tailored coats, bold prints, and vintage treasures filled the space. Each piece carried the echo of Danica's impossible style: effortless, fearless, unforgettable. The scent of her perfume still clung faintly to the fabric—sharp and expensive, a fragrance that lingered like memory.

Calista had kept every garment.

She had promised. They're a part of me, Danica had said in a rare moment of quiet seriousness. Wear them. You'd look beautiful.

But weeks had passed, and Calista hadn't worn a single thing. Not because she didn't want to—but because they felt too extravagant for her quiet life. She couldn't imagine wearing silk to pick up groceries or heels for a schoolyard pickup. Still, a promise was a promise. So, she kept them, hung lovingly on padded hangers, waiting.

They had been identical in shape and height—Danica and Calista—but their colouring had always set them apart. Danica was pale, with cool blonde hair and icy blue eyes, a porcelain elegance Chloe had inherited. Calista, by contrast, had olive-toned skin and wild dark hair, her wide green eyes earthy and intense. Fire and frost, their mother had once said.

After sorting the clothes, she moved on to the boxes.

Jewellery came first—glittering traces of Danica's glamorous world. Calista handled each piece with reverence, sifting through delicate chains, cocktail rings, art-deco cuffs. She selected the most valuable ones and placed them carefully in a velvet-lined box labelled For Chloe.

One day, when she was older, they'd be hers. A piece of her mother's story. A shimmer of love passed down through memory and time.

Next came the notebooks—some filled with poetry, others with sketches and fragments of thoughts. Then documents: receipts, contracts, folded letters, old birthday cards with lipstick-stained signatures. The fragments of a vibrant, complicated life, preserved in manila folders and leather portfolios.

It was during one of those quiet Saturday afternoons—Chloe napping, the light soft and grey through the curtains—that Calista found it.

A letter.

Thick envelope. Heavy paper. Danica's distinctive handwriting—sharp, slanted, and elegant—curved across the front. There was no return address. Just a name, and beneath it, an address in Athens, Greece.

Nicholas Drakos

Vasilissis Sofias Avenue, Athens 106 74

Greece

Calista's breath caught.

The envelope was sealed, the flap perfectly pressed. It hadn't been mailed. It looked pristine, as though Danica had written it, meant to send it—and then couldn't. Or chose not to.

She stared at the name. Her hands, so steady moments ago, trembled now with something that felt like dread… or anticipation.

Danica had never spoken of a Nicholas Drakos. Not once.

But this wasn't just a name. This was deliberate. A sealed letter, addressed, ready—and left behind.

Carefully, Calista turned the envelope in her hands. No date. No clue as to when it had been written. But the paper was heavy and expensive. And Danica's pen had pressed hard against the page, the ink slightly embossed. There had been emotion behind it.

She didn't open it. Not yet.

Instead, she set it gently on the desk and leaned back, her mind whirling with possibilities. Who was he? An old lover? A regret? A secret never told.

She reached for her phone and typed the name: Nicholas Drakos, Athens.

A dozen results appeared. A corporate bio for a shipping magnate. A gallery owner in Plaka. A professor at the University of Athens. A few LinkedIn profiles.

Then, a photograph.

She froze.

One of the results included an image—tall, striking, dark hair brushing the collar of a suit jacket. Strong jaw. Bronze skin. A presence that seemed to leap from the screen.

A Greek god, she thought. And he looked real. Grounded. Intense.

But was he the Nicholas?

There were four with the same name in Athens. None of the addresses listed matched the one on the envelope.

Calista looked back at the letter, heart pounding. She didn't know what Danica had written. She didn't know if she had the right to open it. But Danica had left it for a reason. A letter like this didn't survive years of travel and reinvention by accident.

It had been kept. Protected. Intended.

Gently, Calista picked it up again, letting her thumb trace the edge of the envelope. Then she placed it inside a folder and set it aside, away from the others.

She'd think on it. Not act yet.

But the weight of it lingered, long after the sun dipped below the horizon. Long after Chloe was tucked into bed, her small breaths rising and falling in the dark. Long after the house fell still and silent.

Some stories didn't end when a life did. Some just waited—quietly, patiently—for someone else to turn the page.

Calista sat at the desk, the letter in her hands, her fingers trembling as she broke the seal. The sound was soft, but it echoed in her chest like a drumbeat.

She unfolded the thick paper and read.

Nicholas,

I'm writing to let you know that you're going to be a father.

I know you never wanted children. You made that quite clear. Still, I'm pregnant, and I know this baby is yours.

What you choose to do with this information is entirely up to you. I'm not asking for anything. But if you ever want to know your son or daughter, you know how to find me.

Danica Georgiou

Calista stared at the words, the air thinning around her. Her heartbeat pulsed in her ears.

She whispered Danica's name, but it was only silence that answered back.

Calista sat frozen in the chair, the letter open in her lap, her breath shallow. Her mind raced, stumbling over the same sentence again and again.

You're going to be a father.

She pressed a hand to her mouth, tears prickling behind her eyes—not from sadness, not entirely, but from the sheer weight of it. Of what it meant. Of what Danica had never said.

Nicholas Drakos wasn't just a mystery. He was Chloe's biological father.

Danica had never told her. Never even hinted. All those late-night talks when Danica had been sick, when Calista had asked about Chloe's father—she'd always brushed it off with a wry smile and a deflection. It's complicated. It's better this way.

But this—this wasn't complication. This was a choice. A deliberate silence. And now, months after Danica's death, Calista was holding the truth in her hands.

She stared at the name again. Nicholas Drakos. Athens, Greece.

Her gaze drifted toward Chloe's room, where soft breathing floated through the baby monitor. Chloe was still so small. So perfect. And yet... half of her came from someone Calista had never met.

She didn't sleep that night. Instead, she sat by the window with the letter folded in her hands, watching the Boston skyline blur into the soft grey of morning.

By late morning the next day, she was walking across the Boston Common, her phone clutched tightly in her hand. She pressed the call button.

Henry answered on the third ring.

"Cal?" His voice was warm, familiar. "Everything okay?"

"No," she said, her voice catching. "I need to talk to you. Are you free?"

"Always. You want to meet at the café?"

"No. Your office. Please. I—" She swallowed. "I found something."

Henry's office was tucked above a quiet bookstore downtown, filled with old wood, legal briefs, and the faint scent of bergamot tea. He waved her in without question, concern creasing his forehead.

"What is it?"

Calista didn't sit. She handed him the letter, still sealed in the envelope she'd carefully reinserted it into.

He read silently, his brow furrowing. Then he looked up slowly.

"Do you know who he is?"

"No. Not at all. I searched the name. There are a few men in Athens. No idea which one, or if any of them are him."

"And you're sure it's… Chloe's father?"

Calista nodded. "Danica never told me anything. But the letter—she was pregnant when she wrote it. She never sent it. And she kept it. That has to mean something, right?"

Henry leaned back in his chair, thoughtful. "Legally, Chloe's yours now. Danica made that clear in her will. But this…" He tapped the envelope. "This complicates things emotionally. Maybe legally, depending on what you want to do."

"I don't know what I want," Calista confessed, her voice barely above a whisper. "Part of me wants to burn it. Pretend I never found it. But then I look at Chloe, and I think… one day she might ask. About where she came from. Who her father was. And I won't lie to her. I can't."

Henry gave a slow nod, his expression softening. "You don't have to decide anything today. You have time. But if you do choose to reach out, we'll do it thoughtfully. Quietly. I'll help you."

She let out a breath she hadn't realised she was holding, the words offering a sliver of steadiness in the swirl of doubt.

"I think he deserves to know Chloe exists," she said after a long pause. "Whatever his past with Danica was… this is different. He has a daughter. It's not something I can keep from him. It wouldn't be right."

Henry studied her, then asked gently, "Are you certain?"

Calista's eyes flicked to the window, where early spring light slanted across the floor. "I feel like I have a moral obligation to tell him. Not for me. For Chloe. For the truth."

Henry nodded again, this time with a quiet gravity. "Then we'll find him, Cal. And we'll do it the right way."

Chapter Four

The villa's terrace glowed under the golden haze of the late Athenian afternoon, light spilling across the marble tiles like liquid honey. Bougainvillea framed the archways, vibrant and defiant, and in the distance, the sea shimmered with careless brilliance.

Nicholas Drakos stood with his back to the view.

He looked like he belonged in another era—an untouchable god carved from bronze and shadow. Tall, broad-shouldered, and exuding the kind of cold authority that made people drop their gazes when he entered a room. His suit was navy linen, tailored within an inch of perfection, the open collar of his crisp white shirt revealing just the edge of sun-brushed skin at his throat. Dark hair curled slightly over his ears and collar, unruly in a way that dared anyone to tame it. His jawline was sharp, his cheekbones cruel, and his eyes—those eyes—were a piercing storm-grey, unreadable, and cold.

He wasn't looking at the view.

He was looking at the woman in front of him.

"I don't understand," she said, her voice cracking with the effort to remain composed. "You told me—"

"I told you nothing," Nicholas interrupted smoothly, his tone silk-wrapped steel. "You told yourself stories. That isn't my responsibility."

The woman—tall, elegant, the kind of blonde that turned heads in every room she walked into—clutched the front of her designer dress as if the fabric could hold her dignity together. Her name was Amalia. She was the daughter of a shipping rival, the kind of woman who had grown up with yachts and champagne and tailored illusions.

"I cared about you," she said, stepping forward, tears threatening to undo her mascara. "This wasn't just… casual for me."

"But it was for me," Nicholas replied, not unkindly—just honestly. Brutally so. "Amalia, you're beautiful. Charming. And entirely delusional if you thought this was ever going to be more than what it was."

Her breath hitched. "You're not even trying to be gentle."

"I don't lie," he said coolly. "You asked for time. Distraction. A taste of freedom from your father's expectations. And I gave it to you. Generously, if I may say so."

"You slept with me!" she cried.

He didn't flinch. "And now I've stopped. That's what arrangements do. They end."

She stared at him, the tears beginning to fall. "You're a bastard."

He shrugged one shoulder, expression unreadable. "So I've been told."

Amalia stepped back, shaking her head in disbelief, humiliation burning in her cheeks. "I thought you were different. That beneath all that arrogance, there was something—someone—real."

Nicholas's eyes narrowed, but his voice remained calm. "What you see is what there is, Amalia. I never pretended otherwise."

There was a long silence. Then, with a shuddering breath, she turned on her heels and walked quickly across the terrace, her heels clicking like gunshots against the marble.

Nicholas remained still.

When the sound of the gates opening below signalled her departure, he turned slowly back toward the view. The sea was unchanged. Eternal. Just like him.

No ties.

No regrets.

No weaknesses.

At least, that was what he told himself.

And he'd believed it.

Nickolas Drakos had built a life most men envied and few survived. Billionaire. Tycoon. Kingmaker. His empire stretched across continents—real estate, shipping, global tech investments—anything that promised dominance and control. And he never missed. He didn't believe in luck, only leverage. And he had plenty of it.

His homes were coldly beautiful—glass and marble fortresses perched over oceans or skylines. Always high, always apart. Women came and went with the same elegance as his cars: sleek, expensive, and never around too long to leave a mark.

He had a reputation for ruthless business acumen and equally ruthless relationships. Lovers were handpicked, discreet, stunning, and temporary. Champagne in Monaco, skiing in Verbier, private islands in the Maldives—it was all curated perfection. No feelings. No mess. No chance of entanglement.

Children had never been part of the equation. He didn't do family. He barely tolerated his own. A child meant unpredictability. Dependence. Emotion. The very things he had spent his life avoiding. Even the idea of a legacy bored him—his name was carved into buildings, corporations, and balance sheets. What more did he need?

He was Nickolas Drakos.

Untouchable. Unshakeable. Unattached.

Nicholas Drakos stood at the floor-to-ceiling window of his office, the glass cool beneath his fingertips as he stared out over the city of Athens. The skyline shimmered under the midday sun, but his thoughts were elsewhere—grudgingly circling back to the brief, cryptic call from Demetri earlier that morning.

"There's a situation," his friend and long-time legal counsel had said. "You need to hear it from me. In person."

Nicholas didn't like surprises. Especially ones that came with no detail, only tension laced beneath a familiar voice.

A knock echoed through the room.

He didn't turn. "Come in."

The heavy door opened, and Demetri Papadakis entered, a man in his early fifties with silver at his temples and a briefcase that had survived more scandals than most marriages. He walked with purpose, but not panic—still, there was something in the tight line of his mouth that Nicholas didn't like.

"Whatever it is," Nicholas said, finally turning, "get it over with."

Demetri exhaled slowly, placing a manila envelope on the sleek, dark wood desk between them. "This arrived by courier this morning. From a law firm in Boston."

Nicholas arched a brow but didn't move to touch it. "And?"

With deliberate calm, Demetri opened the folder, extracting a single-page letter and a notarised document. His expression remained neutral, but his eyes were watchful.

"There's a woman claiming you're the father of a thirty-two-month-old girl. Her name is Chloe Georgiou."

Silence fell like a blade between them.

Nicholas didn't flinch. Not visibly. But something flickered in his eyes—disbelief, annoyance, and something colder beneath.

"That's absurd," he said evenly. "I don't know anyone named Georgiou."

Demetri gave a small nod. "According to the letter, the child's mother, Danica Georgiou, passed away recently. The girl is now in the care of her aunt. Apparently, the aunt found this letter among Danica's belongings." He handed the paper to Nicholas.

Nicholas read it silently.

Nicholas,

I'm writing to let you know that you're going to be a father.

I know you never wanted children. You made that quite clear. Still, I'm pregnant, and I know this baby is yours.

What you choose to do with this information is entirely up to you. I'm not asking for anything. But if you ever want to know your son or daughter, you know how to find me.

Danica Georgiou

Nicholas let out a low, humourless laugh. "A gold digger with a long game. Creative. But no."

"The lawyer says the child is with the mother's sister now, a Calista Georgiou," Demetri added.

Nicholas leaned back against the edge of the desk, folding his arms—cool, composed, completely unshaken. "Demetri, I always use protection. Every time. I don't revisit past affairs. I have no interest in being a father. I'm meticulous."

"I know," Demetri replied, though his voice held a note of caution. "But this doesn't feel like a typical play for money. They're not asking for anything. No financial support. No legal action. Just… awareness."

Nicholas's jaw tightened. "They all start that way. First, it's just information. Then it's the house, the trust fund, the nondisclosure agreements."

Demetri paused, then slid a photo across the desk.

Nicholas picked it up without thinking—then froze.

Something tugged at the edge of his mind.

A small girl stared back at him. She couldn't have been more than three. Golden-blonde curls framed her delicate face, and her wide blue eyes were impossibly vivid. She was beautiful. Innocent. But unfamiliar.

"She looks nothing like me," he muttered, though his gaze lingered longer than it should have.

"No request for a paternity test," Demetri said. "That's what makes this unusual. They're not demanding anything. Just said you have a right to know."

Nicholas stared at the photo, brows low, lips pressed into a hard line. A thousand thoughts moved behind his stormy gaze—calculations, memories, consequences.

Finally, his voice came—quiet, sharp, and unmistakably firm.

"Arrange the paternity test," Nickolas said coldly. "Quietly. I want it handled off the record. No names. No loose ends. We'll put this to rest quickly—it's going to come back negative."

Demetri gave a single nod. "Understood. I'll go personally, make sure nothing leaks."

"Good," Nickolas said, his tone final. "Handle it fast. I don't have time for distractions."

He didn't speak again. Didn't have to. Dismissal was a language Nickolas spoke fluently.

Demetri stepped out of Nickolas' office, the door clicking shut behind him, and exhaled a breath he hadn't realised he was holding. His footsteps echoed down the marble hallway, but his thoughts were louder.

This wasn't the first time someone had come forward with a claim like this. Nickolas Drakos—wealthy, powerful, reckless with his charm—was no stranger to opportunists and long-shot schemes. But this one… this one felt different.

Demetri frowned, the envelope still tucked under his arm. There had been no demand, no legal threat, no subtle play for attention. Just a name. A photo. A letter written by a woman who, by all accounts, was now dead.

It wasn't Nickolas' sharp denial that unsettled him—it was how fast he'd dismissed it. How completely. As if the possibility of fatherhood was so absurd it didn't even warrant a second thought.

But Demetri had a feeling. A quiet, persistent tug in his gut that whispered: This time might not be like the others.

And that little girl in the photograph? She didn't need anything from Nickolas Drakos.

Just because she didn't look like him. Didn't mean he wasn't her father.

Chapter Five

Calista walked into Henry's office just after ten, her curls still damp from the morning mist, her hands clutching the leather strap of her worn satchel like a lifeline. She was dressed simply—a pale blue blouse and dark jeans—but the tightness around her eyes betrayed the nerves she was trying to hide.

Henry rose from his desk and met her halfway, brushing a light kiss against her cheek.

"How are you holding up?" he asked, his voice warm, familiar.

She offered him a faint smile. "I'm okay, Henry. Just… worried for Chloe. I don't want to do the wrong thing for her."

"I know," he said gently. "You're not."

He motioned toward the small round conference table tucked near the window, where the sun slanted across the polished wood in long, golden streaks. A pitcher of water and three glasses waited, untouched.

"His lawyer should be here soon."

Calista lowered herself into the chair, smoothing her blouse out of habit. "So… he's not coming."

Henry gave a soft, bitter scoff as he sat across from her. "I didn't expect him to. Now that I know who he is… it's best he doesn't."

She looked up, brows lifted. "That bad?"

Henry hesitated for half a breath. "Let's just say he's not the family type."

Before Calista could respond, a soft knock came at the office door. Her breath caught. She straightened instinctively, her spine stiffening as her fingers tightened on her knee, grounding herself for whatever came next.

"Come in," Henry called, his tone calm but watchful.

His secretary stepped inside with her usual quiet efficiency, holding the door open with a slight nod. A tall man in his early fifties stepped through, his presence commanding without being overbearing. His hair—dark with dignified streaks of silver at the temples—was neatly swept back, and he wore a tailored navy linen suit that looked effortless but precise. His olive-toned skin and sharp, intelligent gaze gave him an air of quiet authority. He didn't need to announce who he was; the room simply adjusted to him.

Henry rose to his feet and offered his hand. "Mr. Papadakis. Nice to meet you. Thank you for coming."

Demetri returned the handshake with a firm nod. "Mr. Collins. The pleasure is mine."

Henry turned to Calista, who stood as well, her expression composed, though her heart fluttered in her chest like a trapped bird. "This is Calista Georgiou. She's Chloe's legal guardian."

Demetri shifted his attention to her, and something in his expression softened as he extended his hand. "Pleasure to meet you, Miss Georgiou."

Calista offered her hand, steady and warm despite the tension curled around her ribs. "Likewise, Mr. Papadakis."

There was a pause—brief but heavy with unspoken questions—before Henry gestured toward the conference table. "Please, sit."

Demetri nodded, taking the seat directly across from Calista. Henry poured water into three glasses, then sat between them like a quiet mediator.

"I appreciate you making time on short notice," Calista began, her voice quiet but steady. "This... is an unusual situation."

Demetri inclined his head, signalling for her to continue.

"It's been three months since Danica passed," she said gently.

"I'm sorry for your loss," he said, his voice low, formal but sincere.

She offered a small smile in thanks. "After her funeral, I found the letter among her things. It was addressed to Nickolas Drakos, in a sealed envelope, she obviously didn't post it."

Demetri's brow twitched slightly, the only outward sign of reaction. Still, he said nothing—just listened, watchful and measured.

"I sat with that information for a couple of days," Calista continued. "Trying to figure out what was right—for Chloe. She's almost three now. Bright, curious, gentle. Since Danica passed, she's settled into a quieter rhythm. My sister's modelling career kept her traveling, so in many ways, I've been Chloe's mother since she was born."

She glanced down briefly, then met his gaze again. "I've loved her as my own. But she deserves to know the truth about where she came from. And he—Mr. Drakos—has a right to know she exists."

A long pause followed. Demetri remained silent, his expression unreadable, but his attention never wavered. Then finally, he spoke, his voice even and sincere.

"I'm glad you came to us."

Calista lifted a brow, slightly sceptical. "Are you?"

His lips curved faintly, almost a smile. "I didn't say he was glad. But I am."

Calista gave a small nod, acknowledging the distinction. "Mr. Collins explained a bit about how public Mr. Drakos's life is. I understand what kind of chaos this could create. That's why I came here first—quietly, through the proper channels. I don't want Chloe's life becoming fodder for the tabloids. She's already lost her mother. She doesn't need to be dragged through courts or public scandal."

Henry spoke up gently. "Calista's made it very clear she isn't seeking money, recognition, or legal action. Just the truth. On Chloe's behalf."

Demetri leaned back slightly in his chair, folding his hands over his stomach. "You realise that even handled discreetly, this could impact his name. And hers."

"I do," Calista said without hesitation. "That's why I'm trusting you with this first step. I'm not here to stir trouble. I just want Chloe to have the choice—someday—to understand where she came from. And for Nickolas to have the choice to be part of her life... or not."

Demetri studied her for a long, quiet moment. There was something in her—an unflinching calm, a quiet conviction—that struck him. Then, without warning, his expression softened.

"You're a rare woman, Miss Georgiou."

Calista blinked, caught off guard by the compliment. "I'm just trying to do right by Chloe."

"And you are," he said, with no hint of flattery in his tone. Then he turned to Henry. "I believe a paternity test is the appropriate first step."

Henry nodded in agreement. "We can use a discreet private clinic outside the city. I'll arrange it so there's no paper trail and no link to the Drakos name."

"I'll speak to Nickolas personally," Demetri said. "He'll have questions, but I'll handle it—and ensure it remains private."

Calista exhaled slowly, as if releasing breath, she hadn't realised she was holding. Some of the weight on her chest eased.

"Thank you," she said. "I appreciate it more than you know."

They agreed on a time the next day for the test—early morning, quiet, and far from cameras or curious eyes. No headlines. No drama. Just the first step toward truth.

As the meeting wrapped and they stood, Demetri offered his hand again. "For what it's worth, Miss Georgiou… Chloe's lucky to have you. You've already given her the most important thing—a life built on love."

Calista's eyes shimmered with emotion, though she blinked it away quickly. "I hope so."

Nickolas Drakos sat behind his sleek glass desk, the skyline behind him smeared with the golden hues of a late afternoon. His eyes flicked over spreadsheets on his laptop, though he wasn't really reading them. He was restless—his fingers tapping against the desk, jaw tight.

When his phone buzzed, he didn't even glance at the screen before answering.

"Yes."

"Nickolas." His lawyer voice came through, calm but weighted. "I just met with Calista Georgiou and her legal advisor, Henry Collins."

Nickolas leaned back in his chair with a sigh. "Of course. What does she want?"

There was a pause—brief, but intentional.

"Nothing."

That made him sit up. "What?"

"She says she doesn't want anything from you. No money. No public acknowledgment," Demetri said calmly. "She only wants you to have the choice to know your daughter."

Nickolas let out a dry, humourless scoff, the sound edged with disbelief. "She's not my daughter."

"We'll find out soon enough," Demetri replied evenly, unshaken. "Your sample's already been submitted. The child is scheduled for her test in the morning. We'll have the results by tomorrow afternoon."

Nickolas pushed back from his desk and stood abruptly, his jaw tightening as he walked toward the window. The skyline sprawled before him, sharp and glinting, but it brought him no calm. "She's just another gold digger," he said, voice clipped. "They all are. This is just a new angle—she plays the noble guardian while waiting for her payday."

"I don't think she's playing anything," Demetri said, and there was steel in his tone now. "She was composed. Thoughtful. She's a woman who's been raising a little girl with love and stability since the day she was born. She didn't come into that office to manipulate you, Nickolas. She came to protect that child."

Nickolas turned sharply, his expression unreadable but cold. "So, I'm supposed to believe she found a letter—three months after her sister's death—and suddenly decided I deserve to know this kid exists?"

"Yes," Demetri said without hesitation. "Because I believe that's exactly what happened. She took her time. Thought it through. She's not impulsive—she's careful. That's why I trust her motives."

Nickolas's hands curled into fists at his sides. "We'll see."

There was a pause on the line, then Demetri's voice dropped, calm but heavy with meaning. "You're angry. I understand. But don't let your past cloud your judgment. This isn't about you—it's about a little girl who may be your daughter."

Nickolas didn't answer. A beat later, the call ended.

He stood frozen in the silence of his office, the phone still in his hand, the words 'your daughter' echoing louder than he wanted them to.

She's not mine, he told himself again, though the certainty behind the thought felt thinner than before.

A child was the last thing he wanted. A family? Even less. His life was calculated, controlled. And this—this was chaos in the shape of a three-year-old girl with someone else's eyes.

And yet… he couldn't stop himself from wondering what she was like.

Chapter Six

"Positive?" Nickolas barked, the word cracking through the room like a whip. His voice echoed off the glass and marble of his penthouse, sharp with disbelief. He stared at Demetri, eyes blazing, shoulders coiled with tension. "That's impossible!"

Demetri sat quietly across from him, composed in the way only a man seasoned by decades of boardrooms and family crises could be. He had flown back to Athens for this very moment—because he knew Nickolas would never accept the truth unless it was delivered face-to-face.

He placed the envelope on the low table between them with deliberate care. The seal was broken. The truth had already been read.

"It's not impossible," Demetri said calmly. "It's reality. You are the father of Danica Georgiou's daughter."

Nickolas let out a harsh breath, stepping back as if the words had struck him physically. "No. No, there has to be a mistake. These things aren't always accurate—maybe the lab screwed up. We'll redo it. Use a different sample. A different lab."

Demetri didn't flinch. "We used three. Independently. The results all matched."

Nickolas stared at the envelope as though it might burst into flames. His chest rose and fell in shallow breaths. He looked younger in that moment—not the polished, ruthless heir of the Drakos empire, but a man blindsided by something deeply human.

A child.

His child.

Nickolas turned away, pacing toward the windows with jerky, disbelieving steps. He raked a hand through his hair, the tension in his shoulders like a drawn bow. "For the love of God…" he muttered under his breath, barely containing the surge of emotion rising in his chest. "What happens now? What does she want?"

"Nothing," Demetri replied quietly. "Not a single thing. She made it very clear that the next move is entirely up to you."

Nickolas swung around. "She doesn't want money? My name on a birth certificate? Custody?"

"She already has custody. You would find it very difficult to win custody of the child, even if you wanted to." Demetri met his gaze steadily. "She wants nothing. She said if you want to meet the child, you can. But if you choose not to, she won't force the issue. She'll respect your decision. She just wanted you to know."

Nickolas stared at him, chest rising and falling with shallow breaths. "She said that."

"She did," Demetri confirmed. "Word for word. She's not looking for publicity or leverage. She's not trying to shame you or trap you. She came forward because she believes the child has a right to the truth—and that you deserve the choice."

Nickolas sank into an armchair, silent, stunned. The room felt too still, too quiet.

A child. His child.

And he had no idea what to do with that.

Nickolas stood, turned away, pacing toward the tall window that overlooked the Athens skyline. His voice was low now, almost disbelieving. "So, I can ignore this? Walk away? She doesn't care if I don't claim her?"

Demetri leaned forward slightly in the chair, folding his hands. "No, she doesn't care in the way you mean. She's not chasing you down, Nickolas. She said the decision is yours—entirely."

Nickolas turned his head just enough to glance back. "Then why even tell me?"

"Because she believes Chloe deserves to know the truth. And because she's given this child her heart. She loves her like her own." Demetri paused. "But she also said that if you choose not to be involved, she won't lie to the girl. When Chloe is old enough and starts to ask questions—about her mother, about her father—Calista will tell her. Gently. Honestly."

Nickolas's jaw tightened.

"She's not asking you for anything, Nickolas. Not money. Not help. Just the choice. And she's already prepared to carry the weight of your silence if that's what you decide."

Nickolas didn't speak. He stared out at the glittering city, his reflection ghosting faintly in the glass—tall, powerful, successful… and suddenly unsure of everything.

Demetri watched him in silence for a moment, then spoke gently, but clearly. "Do you want to ignore the child?"

Nickolas didn't turn around. His voice was rough, like gravel under pressure. "I don't know."

He exhaled slowly, running a hand through his hair. "I never planned to have children. Ever. That part of life… it was never meant for me."

Demetri nodded, his tone even. "Life rarely asks for our permission when it hands us the unexpected."

Nickolas gave a bitter huff of laughter, but it lacked any humour. "A daughter? I don't even know what that means—what that looks like. What the hell would I even do with her?"

Demetri didn't answer right away. He simply said, "That's not something I can tell you. Only you know what kind of man you want to be when she learns your name."

After Demetri left, the silence in Nickolas's penthouse felt heavier than usual. The city lights outside his floor-to-ceiling windows flickered like distant stars, cold and untouchable. He poured himself a scotch, the amber liquid catching the light as he sank into the leather armchair Demetri had vacated.

Danica.

He leaned his head back, eyes drifting to the ceiling as he summoned the memory. Blonde. Tall. Legs that seemed to go on forever. A model—yes, he remembered that. They'd met at a charity gala; some event with flashing cameras and shallow conversation. He remembered her laugh, smoky and flirty, the way her hand had lingered on his chest.

A one-night stand.

That's all she had been.

He hadn't even remembered her last name.

He reached for the envelope on the table and pulled out the photo Demetri had left with the test results. Chloe. She was sitting on a swing, midair, a blur of golden curls and pink sneakers. Her smile was wide; eyes crinkled with joy.

Happy.

Nickolas stared at the photo for a long moment, his scotch forgotten in his hand. She didn't look like him, not really—except maybe the shape of her mouth, the arch of her brow. It was hard to say. He didn't know how to look for himself in a child's face.

He set the glass down and rubbed a hand over his face. "A daughter," he muttered under his breath, the word foreign on his tongue.

He could walk away. Calista had made that clear—no demands, no strings. She must be a rare woman. He could file this away as a mistake, pretend the photo and the truth inside the envelope had never touched his world.

But as he looked down at the picture again, that smile burrowed under his skin like a quiet ache.

Should he meet her?

He didn't know the answer.

But for the first time in years, he wasn't sure walking away would feel like winning.

Calista sat on her couch, the soft glow of the lamp casting a golden halo around her as she stared at the silent hallway where Chloe had just gone to sleep. Her hands twisted together anxiously in her lap. "Can he take her from me?"

Henry, seated beside her, looked over with quiet steadiness. He placed a reassuring hand over hers. "It's very unlikely, Calista. You're her legal guardian. You've raised her since she was born. That holds weight—legally and morally."

"But he's her father," she whispered, her voice trembling. "What if he decides he wants her after all? He has money. Influence. I'm just…" She shook her head. "I feel like I could lose her, and that would—" Her voice broke. "That would kill me."

Henry gave her hand a gentle squeeze. "You are more than just anything. You are Chloe's whole world. Her comfort, her safety, her mommy in every way that matters. No court is going to rip her away from that. And if he tries—he'll have to go through me, and through you."

Calista nodded, swallowing hard. "I just want to protect her. That's all I've ever wanted."

"And you've done it beautifully," Henry said softly. "Don't doubt that now."

Calista looked up at him then, her eyes shimmering. "Thank you, Henry. You've been my rock through all of this. I don't know how I'd have gotten through the last three months without you."

Henry gave her hand a firm squeeze. "You would have found a way. But I'm honoured to stand with you—for Chloe, and for you. Whatever happens next, you're not alone."

A soft breath left her, and for the first time that night, her shoulders eased just a little.

Later that night, the house had gone quiet—too quiet.

Calista sat curled into the corner of the couch, an untouched cup of tea cooling on the table. She had tried reading, even flipping on the TV for background noise, but nothing could quiet the storm in her chest.

A soft shuffle broke the silence.

She looked up just in time to see Chloe, pyjama-clad and sleepy-eyed, padding into the room clutching her worn bunny. Her curls were mussed from sleep; her little face creased from the pillow.

"Chloe, baby," Calista said gently, sitting up. "What are you doing awake?"

Chloe rubbed one eye. "I had a dream." She walked closer and climbed into Calista's lap, resting her head against her chest. "You were gone."

Calista's throat tightened. "Oh, sweetheart. I'm right here. I'm not going anywhere."

Chloe looked up at her, eyes wide and solemn in the dim light. "Are you my mommy forever?"

The question was simple—pure—but it struck like a lightning bolt through Calista's chest.

She held the little girl tighter. "Yes. Yes, I am. Forever and ever, no matter what."

Chloe sighed against her, nodding with the sleepy trust only a child could give. "Okay. I love you."

"I love you too," Calista whispered, kissing the top of her head. "So much."

And as Chloe fell back asleep in her arms, Calista closed her eyes, holding her as if to anchor them both—because no matter what came next, she would fight for this little girl with everything she had.

Chapter Seven

The late afternoon sun bathed the quiet suburban street in a golden glow as Nickolas stood motionless in front of the modest white house. His jaw was clenched, his pulse hammering in a way that felt foreign. This wasn't a boardroom where he held all the power, nor a courtroom where precision ruled. This was something entirely different. Something unpredictable. Personal.

It had taken him a week to tie up loose ends in Athens—meetings postponed, decisions delegated—just to get here. To Boston. To the doorstep of a child he hadn't known existed.

Of course he hadn't called. Hadn't warned them. He wasn't sure he could face it if Calista told him not to come.

So now, he was here. Standing under a maple tree, sunlight dappled on his shirt, holding his breath like a man bracing for impact.

He lifted his hand and knocked.

For a moment, there was only silence.

Then, faintly from inside—laughter.

Light, lilting giggles. A woman's soft laugh and a little girl's delighted squeal, floating through the door like music from another world.

His world now, whether he liked it or not.

His hand dropped slowly to his side. He wasn't prepared for this. Not really. No DNA test or photograph could have prepared him for the reality waiting behind that door.

The moment it opened, his breath left him.

She was… stunning.

Not in the way he was used to—in designer gowns or cocktail dresses—but in a raw, natural way that hit him like a gut punch.

Long black hair spilled over her shoulders, tousled and wild from play. Her cheeks were pink, flushed from laughter, and those eyes—dear God—those eyes were the most brilliant green he had ever seen. She was tall, leggy, barefoot, wearing nothing more than short denim cutoffs and a soft tank top. Her legs seemed to go on forever, smooth and toned, and her lips—full, pink, kissable—parted slightly in surprise.

She blinked up at him. And for a moment, neither of them spoke.

Because Calista felt it too.

The man standing on her porch wasn't just striking. He was breathtaking. Towering, broad-shouldered, with curling black hair and eyes so deep and dark they looked like melted chocolate. His features were sharply cut—aristocratic cheekbones, a strong jaw, and a mouth that seemed like it was carved from marble. He wore a tailored black shirt rolled up at the sleeves, and he looked like sin wrapped in silk.

A Greek god. On her porch.

Her throat went dry.

They stared at each other—two strangers connected by something that neither of them could see but both could feel humming like electricity in the air.

Then—

"Mommy?"

A tiny voice.

Both of them looked down at once.

Chloe had padded up behind Calista and was clinging to her leg, wrapping her arms around the toned length of it and peeking shyly out from behind her thigh. Her curls were a mess, her cheeks sticky with remnants of fruit snacks, and her eyes—so wide, so curious—blinked up at Nickolas.

"Mommy," she asked, her voice small and inquisitive, "who is this man?"

The question broke the spell. Calista's hand instinctively dropped to Chloe's soft curls.

Nickolas stared at her—his daughter. The same girl from the photograph, now real and living and inches away from him. She looked even smaller than he'd imagined, and so much more real. His throat tightened.

Calista straightened, her voice calm but cautious. "This is… this is Mr. Drakos. He came to visit."

Nickolas looked up sharply at the title—Mr. Drakos—but said nothing. Not yet. His eyes returning to the little girl.

Chloe tilted her head, studying him with a seriousness that belied her age. "Do you know my mommy?"

Nickolas looked at Calista, his voice low, uncertain. "We've just met."

Calista nodded once, brushing her hair behind her ear, steadying herself even as her heart beat like a drum. "Chloe, why don't you go finish building your tower? I'll be there in a minute."

Chloe looked from her mother to Nickolas and back again. Then she gave a small nod and scampered away, her little feet pattering across the hardwood floor, her bunny trailing behind her.

Calista stepped out onto the porch, gently closing the door behind her, the screen between them and the rest of the world. "You're here. I wasn't expecting you."

Nickolas nodded, so she knew who he was, but his voice was hoarse when he spoke. "I didn't think I would be here either. I hope you don't mind. But I had to meet her."

He looked toward the closed door, something raw and unguarded flickering in his eyes. "I didn't know a laugh could feel like that," he said quietly, as if the revelation surprised even him.

Calista's throat tightened. "She has that effect on people."

She meant Chloe, of course. She assumed it was the child's laughter that had moved him.

But then he looked back at her—and their eyes met.

And in the quiet that followed, she realised the laugh he meant wasn't Chloe's. It was hers.

The silence between them shimmered with the weight of everything unspoken.

"I wasn't sure how you wanted to be introduced," Calista said quietly, her voice barely above the whisper of the breeze around them. She shifted, her arms crossing lightly over her stomach, a subtle gesture of protection—and vulnerability.

Nickolas didn't hesitate. "I think we should tell her the truth."

Calista's gaze didn't waver, but her lips curved into a small, guarded smile. There was something brave in it. Something aching, maternal, and strong. "Okay," she said softly. "I'll talk to her."

She stepped aside, holding the door open for him, and nodded once. "Please… come in."

Nickolas crossed the threshold into the house, the scent of lavender and something sweet—apple juice and graham crackers, maybe—wrapping around him. He felt like he was stepping into another world entirely.

Nickolas stood just inside the cozy living room, every nerve stretched taut. Toys were neatly tucked into baskets, a blanket draped over the couch, and the faint sound of a cartoon echoed from down the hall. It smelled like home—warm, lived-in, safe. A far cry from the sleek, cold perfection of his penthouse.

Calista crouched in front of Chloe, who was sitting cross-legged on the rug, hugging her bunny.

"Sweetheart," she began gently, brushing a curl behind the child's ear. "Do you remember how we talked about families? How sometimes people have mommies and daddies, and sometimes just one, and every family looks a little different?"

Chloe nodded, wide-eyed. "Like my friend Emma has two mommies."

"That's right," Calista said with a smile. "Well… today you get to meet someone very special."

Chloe glanced past her to Nickolas, curiosity dancing in her eyes. "The man?"

Calista nodded, her voice soft but steady. "Yes, love. His name is Nickolas. And he's your father."

For a moment, the room felt completely still.

Chloe blinked, glancing between them. "My daddy?"

Nickolas stepped closer, slowly kneeling down so he was at her eye level. His throat tightened as he looked at her—really looked—and saw himself in the tilt of her chin, the set of her mouth. "Yes," he said, voice low and sincere. "I'm your daddy, Chloe."

The little girl studied him, as if deciding whether that word fit him. Her brow furrowed.

"Do you like ice cream?" she asked.

He blinked. Then, slowly, a smile tugged at his mouth. "I do. Especially chocolate."

Chloe nodded solemnly. "That's my favourite too."

Calista let out a shaky laugh, tears glittering in her eyes. Nickolas looked up at her then, and something passed between them again—unspoken but powerful.

Hope. Hesitation. Maybe even the beginning of forgiveness.

And Chloe, as children do, felt it all but understood only what mattered.

"Can he stay for dinner?" she asked.

Calista met Nickolas's eyes. "Would you like to?"

He nodded. "I'd like that very much."

It was a simple meal—grilled chicken, roasted vegetables, and buttered rice—but it was warm, fragrant, and comforting in a way Nickolas hadn't expected. They ate at a small round table in the kitchen, where Chloe sat between them, swinging her feet and chattering away.

Nickolas barely touched his food at first, too busy watching the two of them.

Calista moved around the kitchen with an easy grace, her long black hair pulled into a loose ponytail, her face still free of makeup. She laughed softly when Chloe dropped a piece of carrot, wiped little fingers, poured more water. There was no pretence. No show. Just instinctive care.

She loves her, he thought, not with obligation or guilt—but with her whole heart.

He couldn't stop watching her. The way she listened. The way she leaned down to kiss the top of Chloe's head. The way her green eyes sparkled when Chloe told a story about a purple dragon and a lost sock.

This woman had raised his daughter.

And Chloe had questions. So many questions.

"Do you live in a castle?"

"No," Nickolas answered, smiling faintly. "But my apartment is very high up. You can see the whole city from the windows."

"Do you like dogs?"

"I've never had one. Do you?"

Chloe nodded. "I want one. A tiny one. Named Pancake."

He bit back a laugh. "That's a very good name."

"Are you coming back tomorrow?"

That one caught him off guard. He glanced at Calista, but she didn't answer for him.

"I'd like to," he said gently. "If it's okay with you."

Chloe considered him carefully, chewing her rice. Then she nodded. "Okay. You can come back. But bring pancakes."

"Deal," he murmured.

And something in his chest—something long frozen—gave the smallest, reluctant crack.

After Calista had tucked Chloe into bed, the house settled into a softer quiet. She returned to the kitchen where Nickolas was waiting, leaning against the counter. She poured two mugs of coffee, handing him one before sitting opposite him at the small table.

For a moment, neither of them spoke. The low hum of the refrigerator filled the silence, warm and strangely intimate in the stillness.

Nickolas looked over the rim of his cup. "You and Danica are sisters."

Calista nodded, wrapping both hands around her mug. "Half-sisters. Danica's father died when she was a baby. My father married my mother when she fell pregnant with me. He adopted Danica. She was three years older."

"That explains the colouring," he said slowly, studying her face again in the low light. "Danica was blonde."

Calista gave a small smile. "Yes. Blue eyes, high cheekbones, a little more flash. People always noticed her first."

"And you?"

"I was the quiet one," she said with a shrug. "I liked books, art, quiet things. Danica… liked to be seen. Applause. Being the centre of attention."

Nickolas studied her for a moment longer. "I was told you raised Chloe from birth."

Calista's gaze dropped to the coffee between her hands. "That's right. Danica wasn't very maternal, and her career got in the way. So, she left her with me. She didn't see Chloe much."

"Lucky, she had you."

"I didn't have much of a choice. I wasn't going to let her go into the system. I loved her before she was even born."

Nickolas nodded slowly, his voice softer now. "I can see that."

Their eyes met again. The silence stretched, not uncomfortable this time—just full of things not yet said.

Nickolas shifted in his seat, then cleared his throat. "I better go."

"Okay," Calista said softly.

They both stood at the same time, the small kitchen space closing in around them. In the motion, she turned too quickly and bumped into him—her shoulder brushing his chest, her hand catching his arm for balance.

The contact was brief, but electric.

Calista met his eyes, startled—and froze. He was closer than she realised, his body warm, solid. The rich scent of his cologne—something woodsy and expensive—wrapped around her. Her breath caught.

Nickolas didn't move. His hand instinctively steadied her at the waist; his gaze locked on hers. Her hair fell forward in a silken wave, and in the soft light of the kitchen, her eyes looked almost unreal—deep green, wide, surprised.

Neither of them spoke.

The moment hovered.

Then Calista stepped back slightly, breaking the spell, her voice just above a whisper. "Sorry. Small kitchen."

Nickolas let out a breath, low and rough. "No need to apologise."

But he didn't take his eyes off her.

Something was shifting between them—something neither of them had planned for.

Chapter Eight

As they walked toward the front door, the silence between them felt charged, as though neither quite knew what to do with the tension lingering in the air.

Just as Calista reached for the handle, there was a knock on the other side.

Nickolas paused. "Are you expecting someone?" he asked casually, though his voice was a touch tighter than before.

Calista glanced at the door, then offered a small smile. "It's probably Henry."

Henry.

Something in Nickolas tensed, his jaw tightening involuntarily. Who the hell was Henry?

She opened the door—and there he was.

Tall. Fit. Confident. A few years younger than Nickolas, dressed in jeans and a grey sweater, with easy charm radiating from his smile. He had a bouquet of wildflowers in one hand and a takeout bag in the other.

"Thought I'd bring you dessert," Henry said, grinning. "And the flowers are from Mrs. Lantos's Garden—she insists they're magic."

Nickolas's brows rose slightly.

Calista's smile warmed. "That's sweet of you. Chloe's asleep, but she'll love the flowers in the morning."

Henry leaned forward to kiss her cheek in a way that was almost too familiar for Nickolas's liking. "You look tired. Everything okay?"

"Fine," she said gently. "We had a visitor."

Henry glanced past her then—and his eyes met Nickolas's.

There was a flicker of something: curiosity, maybe surprise. But it passed quickly, replaced by polite interest.

Nickolas straightened, a subtle shift in posture that made him appear even more formidable. He didn't like the way Henry looked at her—or how effortlessly he moved in her space, like he belonged there.

Henry extended a hand, confident and easy. "Mr. Drakos, I'm Henry Collins."

Nickolas took it, his grip firm, his expression unreadable. "Nickolas Drakos."

In that brief handshake, something passed between them—cool evaluation, silent sizing up. Neither man blinked.

Calista, sensing the change in atmosphere, stepped lightly between them, her voice smooth but not entirely relaxed. "Henry's a close friend. We've known each other since school."

Nickolas gave a curt nod. "That's nice," he said, though it tasted bitter on his tongue.

Henry's smile stayed, but his gaze sharpened, just slightly. "So… you met Chloe?"

Nickolas flicked a glance at Calista before replying. "I did."

Henry studied him again, slower this time, more cautiously. "That's good," he said, voice lower, almost thoughtful.

Nickolas didn't answer. He only looked at Calista—his gaze lingering on her face, unreadable, but far from indifferent.

With a final flicker of a smile, Henry turned away and stepped further inside the house, as though he'd done it a hundred times before. "I'll be in the kitchen, Cal."

Nickolas's neck tensed. Something primal and possessive stirred in him—and he wasn't sure he liked it.

As Henry disappeared into the kitchen, the air between them shifted again—thicker now, charged with something unsaid.

Nickolas turned to her slowly. "So," he said, his voice low, rougher than before, "Henry seems… very at home here."

Calista met his gaze—steady, calm, but unreadable. "He is. Henry's been a good friend. To me… and to Chloe."

Nickolas gave a short nod. "That's nice."

It wasn't. Not even close. He didn't like it at all.

She moved to the door and opened it, a polite signal that their evening was over.

"What time can I come by tomorrow?" he asked, lingering.

"Anytime. It's Saturday—we usually just spend it at home. You're welcome to join us."

His chest eased, just slightly. "Okay. I'll see you tomorrow."

"Goodnight, Nickolas."

He paused, her voice wrapping around his name like silk.

He liked how it sounded coming from her lips—soft, certain. And what lips they were.

A surge of desire curled low in his gut, unexpected and hot.

He gave her one last look—long, quiet, and filled with the kind of awareness he hadn't felt in a long time.

Then he turned and walked into the night, already counting the hours until morning.

The night air hit him like a splash of cold water, but it did nothing to quiet the storm inside.

Nickolas walked down the steps slowly, each one measured, controlled—but his thoughts were anything but.

He had come here expecting to feel nothing. What he hadn't expected was her.

Calista.

No makeup. Long legs. Wild black hair and green eyes that looked like they could see right through him. And the way she'd looked holding his daughter—his daughter—like she was the safest place in the world.

He'd been so prepared to feel nothing.

Instead, all he could feel was… pulled.

To her.

To them.

He got in his car but didn't start it. His fingers flexed once on the steering wheel.

Then there was Henry. Of course there was a Henry. Young, charming, entirely too familiar with Calista for his liking. Nickolas hadn't missed the way the man smiled at her—or how easily he had walked into her kitchen, like it was his second home.

That had lit a fire in his chest he hadn't felt in years. Not since he was a younger man.

Nickolas let out a breath and leaned back in the seat, eyes closed for a moment.

This was dangerous ground.

He'd come here to do right by his daughter. To understand the past. Not to feel this.

He had no right to want her—not a woman he barely knew, and certainly not a child he'd only just met. But the ache was there. Low and persistent. A longing that curled deep in his chest and refused to let go.

It didn't belong in a man like him.

And yet… it was there.

Undeniable.

Clear as day.

And he wasn't sure he could walk away. Not now. Not anymore.

He pulled out his phone and called Demetri.

"Do you know who this Henry Collins is?" Nickolas asked, voice low and tight.

Demetri didn't hesitate. "Calista's legal advisor. Why?"

"They seem… very close."

There was a pause on the other end. Then Demetri's voice dropped with a note of sly amusement. "Yes, I noticed that. To be honest, I think he's in love with her."

He said it lightly—but he knew exactly what he was doing.

There was a long silence. Then a clipped, "I see."

Demetri smirked to himself. Nickolas sounding interested in someone—truly interested—was a rare thing.

And maybe, just maybe, this wouldn't be such a bad thing after all.

"So, Nickolas Drakos finally presented himself," Henry said, placing the dessert on the table and taking the seat across from her.

Calista let out a soft breath of laughter, half a smile tugging at her lips. "To be honest, I didn't expect him at all."

Henry arched a brow as he leaned back in his chair. "He's… intense."

She gave a small nod, swirling her spoon through the untouched dessert. "That's one word for it."

"And how did it feel," he asked carefully, "seeing him at your door?"

Calista looked at him then, her expression unreadable. "I was shocked at first. But… he seemed genuine. Like he really wants to get to know Chloe."

She hesitated, her voice softening. "He's nothing like I imagined."

Henry's brow lifted slightly. "How do you mean?"

She traced the rim of her spoon against the edge of her bowl. "He just seemed… normal. Not like some untouchable billionaire. He was present. He listened. Chloe liked him."

Henry's gaze sharpened, but his voice stayed even. "She likes anyone who smiles at her."

Calista offered a faint smile. "Maybe. But still, she was drawn to him. And she's all that matters."

Henry leaned forward slightly, his voice low. "Just be careful, Calista. You don't really know him. Not yet."

She nodded, the moment pressing heavier than before. "I know. I'll be careful."

She stood and leaned in to kiss his cheek, her touch light. "You've always looked out for us."

His eyes softened, but something in his jaw still tensed. "Always."

Chloe was practically bouncing on the couch, her eyes flicking between the cartoons on the screen and the front door. She'd been talking about her daddy all morning— what she wanted to show him, ask him, tell him. Her excitement was a bright, beautiful thing. Too bright, Calista thought.

Her fingers tightened slightly around the edge of the kitchen bench.

She was happy for Chloe—of course she was. But behind that happiness was a thread of worry winding tighter by the minute. What if Nickolas couldn't be consistent? What if he realised the responsibility was more than he'd bargained for and disappeared? It wasn't fair to Chloe. She was too young to understand the politics of betrayal and too innocent to guard her heart.

But it wasn't Nickolas's fault. Calista reminded herself of that, again and again. He hadn't known. Danica had made sure of it. And now… he was here.

The knock came, sharp and clear.

Chloe's head whipped around, curls bouncing. "Daddy's here!" she squealed, leaping off the couch.

Calista's heart tugged as she smiled at her daughter's unfiltered joy. "Okay, slow down, sweetheart," she said gently, heading to the door.

She opened it—and froze for half a beat.

Nickolas stood there, not in the tailored armour of wealth and power, but in worn denim jeans and a soft charcoal sweater. His hair was slightly tousled, and there was a casual ease in the way he held himself that was completely different from the man who'd arrived last night.

He looked… approachable. Even boyish. And devastatingly handsome.

"Good morning," he said, a smile curving his mouth—slower, warmer than she expected.

"Morning," Calista replied, suddenly aware that she wasn't wearing makeup and had flour on her shirt, possibly on her face too. Still, his eyes held hers like she was the only thing he saw.

Then Chloe burst through the gap between them, launching into his legs. "Daddy!"

Nickolas knelt without hesitation, sweeping her into his arms. "There's my girl," he murmured, voice thick with wonder.

And just like that, Calista's heart softened again. Because whatever fears she had—whatever reservations lingered—Nickolas wasn't pretending. Not with Chloe.

Chapter Nine

Nickolas scooped his daughter up like it was second nature, his arms instinctively strong and sure around her tiny frame. Chloe fit against him perfectly, her arms wrapping around his neck without hesitation, as if she'd known him forever.

It startled him—how natural it felt. How right.

This little person had weaved her way into his heart so quickly, it shocked him. He had only met her the night before, yet something fundamental in him had shifted. The world looked different now. Smaller, clearer. Centred around this bright-eyed, curly-haired girl who smiled at him like he was her entire universe.

He glanced over at Calista, catching the soft, uncertain smile on her face as she watched them.

He was drawn to Chloe, yes—but he was also drawn to the woman who had raised her with so much love. It was unexpected. Unplanned. And overwhelming.

But as Chloe giggled and buried her face in his neck, something shifted deep in Nickolas—something permanent.

He didn't want to walk away from this.

Not from the little girl who had claimed his heart with one smile… and not from the woman who had quietly captivated him with her strength, her beauty, and the way she loved his daughter.

In that moment, Nickolas knew with absolute certainty—

He wanted them both.

But that was madness.

Nickolas didn't do commitment. He didn't do roots or promises or forever. His world was built on control, on clean exits and no strings. Fleeting arrangements were all he'd ever allowed himself—and they'd always been enough.

But Calista?

She wasn't the kind of woman you touched lightly and left behind. She was all-in or nothing. Fire wrapped in calm. Strength beneath grace. And Chloe…

Chloe made "forever" suddenly feel terrifying.

And, for the first time in his life—

Worth wanting.

Chloe's eyes lit up as she bounced on the balls of her feet. "Did you bring pancakes?" she asked, full of excitement.

Nickolas chuckled, the sound warm and genuine. "Not this time. But I was hoping you and your mommy might come with me to a place that makes the best pancakes in all of Boston."

Chloe turned to Calista, her face hopeful and bright. "Can we, Mommy? Please?"

Calista smiled softly, brushing a strand of hair from Chloe's forehead. "Of course, sweetheart. But you'll have to go get changed into a pretty dress first, so you're ready— your daddy wants to show you off."

Chloe lit up, spinning on her heel toward the hallway. "Okay, Mommy! Can I wear the pink one? That's my favourite," she added, looking up at Nickolas with hopeful eyes, as if his approval suddenly meant everything.

Nickolas crouched down so he was at her level, his gaze tender. "The pink one sounds perfect. You'll look like a princess."

Chloe beamed, practically glowing with delight. "I'll be right back!" she squealed, then suddenly grabbed Calista's hand with both of her tiny ones. "Come on, Mommy, you need to put on a pretty dress too!"

Calista laughed, startled by the demand. "Oh, do I now?"

"Yes!" Chloe nodded with complete seriousness. "You have to look like a princess too. Daddy's taking us out."

Calista's eyes flicked to Nickolas at the sound of Chloe calling him Daddy so naturally. Something about it tugged deep in her chest—unexpected and fierce.

Nickolas watched them, a quiet warmth in his eyes. "She's not wrong," he said, his voice low and smooth. "I think it's only fair you match your daughter."

Calista raised an eyebrow, but there was a teasing smile on her lips. "We'll be right back."

"Take your time," Nickolas replied, his smile slow and lingering, his gaze holding hers for a heartbeat longer than necessary.

She turned away, but not before something fluttered low in her stomach—unsettling, unfamiliar. Like the start of something she hadn't planned on but couldn't ignore.

As they made their way to the bedroom, Chloe chattered excitedly about syrup and whipped cream and whether pancakes could come with sparkles, but Calista's thoughts were far quieter.

She didn't want to read too much into a smile. Or the look in his eyes. Or the way it felt having him here, barefoot, warm, and real, like this could be a Saturday morning that belonged to them.

But that flutter in her stomach? It hadn't gone away.

And part of her, the part she didn't trust yet, didn't want it to.

Calista knelt beside Chloe as she helped her wriggle into her favourite pink dress—the one with the frilly skirt and the little heart-shaped buttons. Chloe beamed, her curls bouncing as she twirled once in front of the mirror.

"All done," Calista said with a smile, smoothing the hem.

Chloe reached for her hand immediately. "Now it's your turn, Mommy. Come on!" She tugged eagerly, leading Calista down the hall to her room.

"Oh?" Calista laughed softly, following her daughter. "Are you picking out my outfit today?"

"Yes," Chloe said with serious determination. "You have to look really pretty. Daddy's here."

Calista arched a brow, amused but a little caught off guard by the way Chloe said daddy. It still felt surreal hearing the word used so casually. So naturally.

Chloe marched straight into the closet and began rifling through the hanging dresses with far more confidence than an almost three-year-old should have. Her tiny hands paused on a dress tucked toward the back—a green A-line dress with delicate cap sleeves and a soft, silky sheen.

It was one of Danica's. Calista had never worn it.

"This one," Chloe said, pulling it out with both hands. "It goes with your eyes."

Calista's breath caught for just a second. She hadn't even known Chloe had noticed that.

"Sweetheart," she said gently, "Mommy's never worn this one before…"

"But it's so pretty," Chloe insisted, pushing it toward her. "And Daddy's waiting."

With that, she spun on her heel and darted out of the room, little feet padding down the hallway.

Calista stared at the dress for a moment, fingertips brushing over the fabric. She hadn't worn it because she hadn't felt like she had a reason to. But now, with Chloe's sweet encouragement still echoing in her ears—and the thought of Nickolas in the next room—something inside her shifted.

She caved.

Sliding the dress on, she was surprised by how well it fit. Simple, but elegant. Soft against her skin, and somehow… right. She dabbed on a little mascara, a sweep of lip gloss—just enough to feel polished without looking like she was trying too hard.

When she stepped out into the hallway, Chloe was waiting, bouncing on the balls of her feet.

"There she is!" her daughter squealed. "See? I told you she looks beautiful!"

Calista's eyes followed Chloe's excited gesture to where Nickolas stood in the living room.

He had been talking with Chloe's stuffed bunny in hand, a crooked smile on his lips—but the moment his eyes landed on Calista, the rest of the world seemed to still.

His expression changed.

Gone was the casual ease. In its place was something else—stillness. Heat. A kind of reverence that made her heart give a stuttering beat.

"You were right," he murmured, eyes never leaving her. "She does."

His gaze lingered—on her hair, her mouth, the way the green of the dress made her eyes look deeper, richer. She hadn't expected him to look at her like that. Not with such open, undisguised admiration.

Calista cleared her throat, her cheeks warming. "It was Chloe's idea."

"Smart girl," he said softly, a smile curving at the edges of his mouth.

Chloe twirled again in her pink dress, completely unaware of the charged silence settling between the two adults.

"Are you staying all day, Daddy?" she asked, wide-eyed.

"If your mommy lets me," Nickolas said, his voice lower now, laced with something almost tender as he glanced at Calista again.

For a second, she forgot how to speak. The air between them pulsed with something fragile and real—and far more dangerous than she wanted to admit.

She gave a quiet nod, her voice soft. "You're welcome to."

Chloe beamed and immediately grabbed his hand, her little fingers wrapping trustingly around his. "Come on, Daddy! Pancakes and puzzles!" she declared, tugging him toward the front door with all the determination of someone who'd made up her mind.

Calista followed, a half-smile playing on her lips as she watched them. The sight of Chloe swinging their joined hands made something warm unfurl in her chest—something she hadn't let herself feel in a very long time.

They ended up at a small, cozy restaurant just off the square. Nickolas claimed it had the best pancakes in town, and to Calista's surprise, he was right. Light, fluffy, and golden, they were the kind of pancakes that didn't need syrup to be good—but Chloe, of course, insisted on both syrup and a scoop of vanilla ice cream on top.

"She's going to bounce off the walls," Calista said under her breath, watching her daughter devour the sugar-laden stack with glee.

Nickolas just smiled. "She's happy."

Calista glanced at him across the table. He wasn't watching Chloe this time—he was watching her. Steady, quiet, like he was memorising the way the light fell on her cheek or the way she tucked a stray strand of hair behind her ear. His gaze held something unfamiliar but gentle. Something that made her breath catch.

For a moment, she couldn't remember the last time someone other than Henry had looked at her like that. Not with pity, or polite interest, or distracted affection—but with the quiet wonder of someone who was simply glad she existed.

She looked away, her fingers tightening slightly around her coffee cup. Flustered. But even as she lowered her gaze, the warmth in her chest bloomed, stubborn and unexpected, like the first hint of spring after too long a winter.

Chloe licked syrup off her fingers and grinned, cheeks sticky with sugar. "Best day ever," she declared with a happy sigh, clearly not caring that ice cream was melting down the sides of her plate.

Calista laughed under her breath, then smiled—soft and involuntary. "You always say that when there's ice cream involved."

Calista excused herself with a gentle smile. "I'll be right back," she said, standing from the table and heading toward the restroom.

As soon as she was out of earshot, Nickolas leaned in a little, resting his elbows on the table. He gave Chloe a conspiratorial smile. "So... I met your friend Henry last night."

Chloe's eyes lit up, and she practically bounced in her seat, syrup still on her fingers. "Henry loves my mommy!" she announced proudly, her voice rising with excitement. "He wants to marry her!"

Several heads at nearby tables turned at the little girl's declaration. Nickolas blinked, caught off guard for a second—but then he smiled, tight-lipped, his eyes drifting in the direction Calista had gone.

"Oh really?" he said, trying to sound amused, though his tone held an edge Chloe didn't notice. "And what does your mommy think about that?"

Chloe shrugged, her expression matter of fact. "She likes him. But I don't think she loves him yet."

Then she leaned forward, lowering her voice as if revealing something sacred. "She still gets shy when he looks at her."

Nickolas raised an eyebrow, but before he could respond, Chloe added brightly, "I like Henry too. I love him."

"You do?" he asked, a flicker of amusement crossing his face. "Do you want him to be your stepdad?"

Chloe giggled. "I told him I would marry him myself! But he just laughed and said I'm too little." She frowned, then sighed dramatically. "Grown-ups are always saying that."

Nickolas chuckled, though the laughter didn't quite reach his eyes. "Yeah… they do." He glanced toward the hallway where Calista had gone, his smile fading slightly. "They say a lot of things."

Nickolas didn't like the idea of Henry becoming Chloe's stepdad. He told himself it was only because he cared—because he didn't want anyone stepping into the place he'd only just begun to claim.

But deep down, in the quiet corners of his mind he rarely dared to explore, he knew that wasn't the whole truth.

The thought of Henry standing beside Calista, of another man tucking Chloe in at night and being called Dad—it stirred something fierce and unwelcome inside him.

A mix of regret, jealousy, and a longing he hadn't expected to feel.

Chapter Ten

By the time they got back home, Chloe was nodding off in her car seat, her head lolling to one side.

"She always has an afternoon nap," Calista said softly as she unbuckled her. "But with all the excitement today, it's a bit earlier than usual."

Nickolas watched as she carried Chloe inside, the little girl already half-asleep against her mother's shoulder. He heard the quiet creak of the bedroom door, the murmur of Calista's voice as she soothed her, the hush of a lullaby she probably didn't realise she was humming.

When she returned to the living room, Nickolas was standing by the window, hands in his pockets and a scowl etched across his face.

Calista paused, instantly alert. "Is everything okay?"

He turned to face her. "There's something I'd like to talk to you about, actually." He hadn't planned to bring it up—not like this—but the thought had been growing louder in his mind all day, and he couldn't push it down any longer. "I'd like to take you and Chloe to Greece. To see where I live."

Calista blinked, stunned. For a moment, she wasn't sure she'd heard him right.

"You... want us to come to Greece with you?" she asked slowly.

Nickolas gave a small nod, his expression unreadable. "Yes. I want you to see my home. My life there."

She stared at him, words momentarily lost. It was so far beyond what she'd expected.

"I—Nickolas, that's... that's a big ask."

"I know," he said, his voice quiet but steady. "And I'm not asking for an answer right now. I just... wanted you to know I'm serious. About being part of your life. About being part of hers."

Calista exhaled slowly, heart thudding in her chest. "It's just that... neither of us has a passport."

He gave a half-smile then, the tension easing slightly from his features. "That's something we can fix."

She wasn't sure what surprised her more—that he wanted them to go, or that a part of her wanted to say yes.

"I'd like her to meet my family while you're there," Nickolas added, watching her closely.

Calista blinked. "Oh. What family?"

"My mother and sister," he said. "They live in Athens; they will come to my island in Greece to meet you two."

She stared at him. "Sorry—what?"

"My island," he repeated calmly.

There was a long pause as her brain tried to compute that sentence. Then she blinked again, slower this time. "You… own an island."

"Yes."

"Oh my god." She sat down on the edge of the couch like her legs had given out. "I knew you were wealthy but that's next level."

Nickolas gave a faint smile, his eyes never leaving hers. "It's just home to me. But I'd like you to see it. I want you to understand where I come from."

Calista let out a breath, somewhere between a laugh and a gasp. "Nickolas, you're full of surprises."

"And you're taking this better than I expected."

She looked up at him, dazed but amused. "Give me a minute. I might still faint."

He laughed—a deep, unguarded sound that surprised even him. It had been years since anything made him laugh like that.

Later that afternoon, after Chloe woke from her nap, Nickolas stayed a little longer, gently coaxing her to laugh with him as they played with her favourite toys. Calista gave them space to bond, watching from the doorway as her daughter's giggles filled the room. There was something heartwarming about seeing the two of them together, and for a moment, she allowed herself to believe that maybe this could be more than just a fleeting connection.

Nickolas, on the other hand, was realising something profound. Calista was nothing like any woman he had ever met. The women he was used to were self-absorbed, only showing interest when they could gain something from a relationship. They were often calculating, with one eye always on what they could get. But Calista? She was different. She was genuine, warm, and real. Her care for Chloe wasn't for show, and her quiet strength made him admire her more with every passing minute.

Not that he was interested in Calista, beyond the fact that she was the mother of his child. He didn't do commitment. It wasn't part of his world, nor did he want it to be. He liked his life uncomplicated, no strings attached, no promises.

But then there was Calista. The attraction to her was undeniable, stronger than anything he'd felt in years, if ever. It was a pull, an unexplainable magnetism that stirred something deep inside him. The way she moved, the way she cared for Chloe—there was a quiet strength in her that was both captivating and disarming.

He knew he had to resist it. Getting involved with Calista would only complicate things. He couldn't afford to lose his freedom, to let his emotions get tangled up in something as messy as a real connection. Eventually, he'd get bored, like he always did, and it would all fall apart. The last thing he needed was to put himself in a position where walking away would be more difficult than usual, especially when Chloe was involved.

After Nickolas left for the day, Calista sat in silence for a few minutes, her thoughts tangled in a whirlwind of uncertainty. Finally, she picked up her phone and called Henry.

"Hi, Cal," he answered warmly. "Everything okay?"

"Yes… I think so," she said, hesitating.

"What's wrong?" Henry asked, instantly picking up on the tension in her voice. He knew her too well not to notice when something was bothering her.

She exhaled slowly. "He wants me and Chloe to go to Greece. To his private island."

There was a beat of silence on the other end. Then Henry said, "You can't be serious."

"He is," she replied quietly.

Henry let out a low whistle. "That's… a lot to process."

"Tell me about it."

"How do you feel about it?" he asked, his voice gentle, cautious.

Calista hesitated. "I get why he wants us to go—so Chloe can meet his mother and sister. It makes sense, in a way. But it's such a long way, and I'm not sure. It feels… overwhelming."

"Don't do it if you feel uncomfortable," Henry advised gently.

"Yeah, I know," Calista murmured. "I just need to think on it."

There was a pause, then Henry sighed, the sound heavy with something more, there was a pause. "I… I've been thinking a lot about us."

The moment she heard him say that Calista knew something was different. Henry's voice was too careful, too measured—like he was balancing on a ledge.

"Why won't you marry me, Calista?"

She closed her eyes, the guilt hitting her like a wave. "Henry…you know why."

"The feelings you have will grow," he said quietly. "With time. They always do."

"Henry, please," she whispered, her voice thick with emotion. "I don't want to hurt you. You mean too much to me."

"But not enough to marry me," he said, not bitterly, just sadly. "I would make you happy, Cal."

She swallowed hard, her voice barely above a breath. "But would I make you happy?"

"Of course you would," Henry said without hesitation. "You know I love Chloe like she's my own. You'd never want for anything."

"I wish I could say yes, Henry… but I just can't." Tears welled in her eyes. "Please, Henry… understand."

"I love you so much, Calista. You're all I think about. You and Chloe—you're my whole world."

"I'm sorry, Henry," she whispered, her heart breaking even as she said the words.

They said their goodbyes, soft and final. When the call ended, Calista sat in silence, her phone still in her hand, tears slipping down her cheeks. She didn't regret being honest—but God, she wished she could've said yes. That life with Henry would've been safe, kind, easy. But her heart didn't move in that direction, no matter how hard she tried.

A knock at the door startled her. She wasn't expecting anyone.

Wiping her eyes quickly, she opened it—and froze. Nickolas stood there, a faint furrow in his brow. "Sorry… I think I must have dropped my wallet. What's wrong?" he asked, his tone softening as he took in her tear-streaked face.

Without waiting for permission, he stepped forward and wrapped his arms around her.

She leaned into him instinctively, her head against his chest. "It's nothing," she murmured. "It's silly."

He held her tighter, his hand instinctively cradling the back of her head as she leaned into him. What the hell is wrong with me? he wondered, startled by the intensity of his reaction. He hated tears—always had. They made him uncomfortable, brought back memories of messy endings and emotional manipulation. But this… this was different. Calista's tears weren't manipulative or dramatic. They were soft, quiet, and real—and seeing them carved something open in him he didn't know existed. It twisted deep in his chest, an ache he didn't understand. All he knew was that he wanted—needed—to make it stop.

"Please tell me," he said gently, his voice rough with restraint. "What's going on?"

She hesitated, then whispered, "Henry asked me to marry him."

He froze. Slowly, he pulled back, just enough to lift her chin and look into her eyes. "And that made you cry?"

Her eyes shimmered, lashes damp. "I don't want to hurt him. He means a lot to me."

Nickolas stared at her, and for a moment, the world around them fell silent. The way her voice caught, the way her eyes held such raw honesty—it undid him. He was mesmerised. Her beauty wasn't just on the surface. It was in the way she cared, the way she carried her pain quietly, with grace.

Without thinking, without allowing himself the space to second-guess, he lowered his head. His lips brushed hers once—soft and tentative. Testing. A question, not a demand.

But when she didn't pull away, when she let out the smallest sigh against his mouth, something in him gave way. The kiss deepened, slow and searching at first—tender, as though he was trying to memorise her. Then, suddenly, it shifted. Passion surged between them like a wave breaking loose. His hand slid into her hair as his mouth claimed hers, deeper, more urgently. She responded with equal need, her fingers gripping his shirt, pulling him closer.

It wasn't just a kiss—it was everything unspoken between them. Frustration, desire, fear, longing. All of it poured out in that moment, wrapped in heat and vulnerability.

When they finally pulled apart, breathless and dazed, Nickolas rested his forehead against hers, eyes still closed as he tried to steady his heartbeat. Silence stretched between them, but his mind was anything but quiet.

What the hell was that? The kiss had lit something inside him—hot, consuming, and completely unexpected. He'd kissed plenty of women before. Too many if he were being honest. But nothing—nothing—had ever felt like that. There was a weight to it, a depth that rattled him to his core. Her lips had been soft, familiar yet new, and the way she'd responded… it wasn't just chemistry. It was connection—raw and real.

He tried to dismiss it, to rationalise the rush flooding his chest. It's just been a while, he told himself. Too long without someone. That's all this is.

But the lie didn't land.

Before he could make sense of anything else—before he could even find the words to ask her what she was feeling—Calista stepped back. The loss of her warmth hit him like a gust of cold air. Her eyes dropped to the floor, her lashes shielding whatever storm was brewing beneath them.

"That was a mistake," she said quietly, her voice raw and fragile.

The words sliced clean through him. Not because she was wrong—maybe it was a mistake—but because of how much he didn't want it to be.

And just like that, the fragile warmth between them fractured. The moment that had felt so powerful, so impossible to ignore, turned into something delicate and breakable—something they weren't ready to face.

"We can't complicate things," she added, hugging her arms around herself. "Chloe needs to come first."

He nodded stiffly. "Yes. You're right." The words burned like acid on his tongue. A lie, every syllable of it. He wasn't sorry, not even a little. But admitting that would only push her further away. So, he did what he always did—he buried it. Buried the feeling. The ache. The truth.

"Sorry," he added, even though it made him feel like a coward.

She gave a small, quick nod, still not meeting his gaze.

Nickolas stood there for a moment, caught in the echo of what had just happened— what had almost happened again. He wrestled with everything he hadn't said, every word that rose to the back of his throat but never made it past his lips.

Calista bent down and picked something up from the floor—his wallet. She walked over and placed it gently in his hand, her fingers brushing his. The touch was brief, but it lingered like a spark in the air.

"Is this what you were looking for?" she asked, her voice composed, too composed.

He forced a tight smile. "Yeah. Thanks."

He hesitated—just for a second—then turned to go. Each step felt heavier than the one before, like gravity was pulling harder with every footfall. The weight wasn't in his body, though—it was in his chest.

And as he walked away, the door closing softly behind him, a quiet voice whispered the truth he didn't want to face:

He wasn't sure if he was capable of walking away from her again.

Because after that kiss… pretending he didn't want her felt impossible.

Chapter Eleven

The next morning, Calista stood at the kitchen sink, hands motionless under the stream of water, lost in the memory of the kiss. It had been nothing like she expected—not rushed or careless, but deep, certain, electric. It sent a shiver through her even now, hours later, as if her body hadn't quite caught up with her better judgment.

She had never been kissed like that before—deep, certain, electric. And it terrified her.

Nickolas was the last man she should be getting tangled up with. Not just because of Chloe—though that should've been enough—but because he didn't stay. He never had. His relationships were short bursts of charm and intensity, followed by a silence that never explained itself.

What if she was just another novelty?

What if this was only about the thrill of chasing something that felt real—until it required staying?

She glanced at the clock, her stomach knotting. He said he was here for Chloe. He said he wanted to be in her life. But she couldn't help the doubt that crept in, stubborn and sharp-edged. Words were easy. Staying was something else.

And if he left… again… it wouldn't just be her heart he'd break.

It would be Chloe's.

Calista's chest tightened. She pressed her palm flat to the counter, steadying herself against the weight of that thought. Her fingers were damp; the dishcloth still bunched in her other hand. She shook her head and muttered under her breath, Stop it. Stop thinking about something that never should have happened.

But the memory of his kiss lingered, warm and unwelcome, like a flame licking at the edges of her resolve.

From the living room came the sound of Chloe's laughter—pure, high-pitched, and bubbling with joy. It cut through her thoughts like sunlight through fog. Calista blinked, then turned off the tap and wiped her hands on the cloth, forcing herself to leave the ache behind as she joined her daughter.

Chloe sat cross-legged on the rug, building towers from her wooden blocks, her face glowing with the kind of happiness only small children seemed to possess so freely.

Calista sank onto the couch, watching her. She needed to make a decision—and soon. Nickolas had asked only last night. He wanted Chloe to visit Greece. To meet his mother. To see the place where he grew up.

A part of her knew he was right—Chloe did have a right to meet her grandmother, her aunt. To know her roots. But another part of her, the wounded part, clung to caution. What if this trip only made it harder when he drifted away again?

She cleared her throat gently. "Sweetheart?"

Chloe looked up from her tower, eyes bright. "Yes, Mommy?"

Calista forced a smile and tucked a curl behind Chloe's ear. "Your daddy asked me if you might like to visit the country where he lives. It's called Greece. He wants you to meet your grandma—and your aunt, too."

Chloe gasped. "Oh! Can I, Mommy? Please?"

"If you wanted to," Calista said slowly, choosing her words with care, "we'd need to get something called passports first."

"What's a passport?" Chloe asked, tilting her head with innocent curiosity.

"It's a special document that lets you travel to different countries," Calista explained. "Like a little book with your picture in it. You need one to get on an airplane."

"I want a passport!" Chloe said, bouncing to her feet and twirling in a little circle. "I want to go on an airplane! And meet Grandma! And see Daddy's house!"

Calista's heart ached as she watched her. She wanted all those things for Chloe, too. But she also wanted to be sure—really sure—that Nickolas wouldn't vanish just when Chloe began to believe in him.

Because for Calista, a broken heart was survivable.

For Chloe… it might be something else entirely.

Something lasting.

"We'll see," she said softly, brushing a kiss to her daughter's forehead.

But suddenly, the air felt too thick to breathe—cluttered with memories she didn't want to unpack. She needed to get out—move, breathe. "How about we go to the park?"

"Yes please!" Chloe squealed, already racing to find her shoes.

The afternoon was warm, the breeze light, and the neighbourhood park was alive with the usual weekend chorus—children squealing, dogs barking, parents calling out names across the playground. Chloe ran ahead, her pink shirt fluttering as she dashed toward the slide, immediately finding a group of kids to chase and giggle with.

Calista found a spot on a bench under the shade of an old tree and sat down with a contented sigh, letting the sun kiss her face through the leaves.

Not long after, a tall man with dark hair and kind eyes wandered over, glancing between her and the playground. He had a relaxed, open manner, and when he smiled, it was warm but unassuming.

"Your daughter… she the one in the pink shirt?" he asked.

Calista nodded. "Yes, that's Chloe. And your son?" She pointed to a boy clambering up the jungle gym.

"Yep, that's Tyler. Five going on fifteen." He laughed and rubbed the back of his neck. "You ever wonder where they get all that energy?"

"All the time," Calista said, chuckling. "If someone could bottle it, they'd make a fortune."

They shared a laugh, easy and companionable, and the conversation drifted from work to parenting challenges to favourite cartoons. It was light, pleasant—normal. Something she hadn't felt in a long time.

The man—Daniel, she learned—had a gentle way about him, the kind that didn't push but simply existed. Chloe waved at her from the top of the slide, and Calista waved back, smiling.

"So, is Chloe an only child?" he asked casually.

Calista hesitated, her answer quiet. "Yes… she is."

"Well, she's lovely. You're doing a great job."

Calista flushed slightly at the compliment, a rare warmth creeping into her chest. "Thank you."

Daniel smiled again and was just about to say something else when a low, cool voice interrupted them from behind.

"She is. She is a wonderful mother."

Calista froze. She didn't have to turn around to know who it was. The shift in the air was unmistakable.

Nickolas.

She looked up slowly. He stood just behind the bench, sunglasses in hand, dark eyes trained not on Chloe—but on Daniel.

Tension crackled in the space between them. Calista saw the way his jaw flexed, the stiffness in his shoulders. He looked every bit the man who'd just walked in on something he didn't like—even if it wasn't his place to dislike it.

Daniel cleared his throat and stood, extending a hand with practiced politeness. "Hey, I'm Daniel. Tyler's dad."

Nickolas didn't take the hand.

"Nickolas," he said, cool and clipped. "Chloe's father."

Daniel let his hand fall, the mood tilting from light-hearted to uncomfortable in a heartbeat. "Right. Well… good to meet you. I'll go check on Tyler. Thanks for the chat, Calista."

He offered her a brief, polite smile—more strained than warm now—and walked away, his shoulders a little stiffer than before.

Calista turned to Nickolas, her expression cooling fast. "What are you doing here?" she asked, voice low but laced with warning.

"I came to see Chloe," he said evenly, though his eyes lingered on Daniel's back as he disappeared into the crowd. "Didn't realise I'd be crashing… something."

"You weren't," she snapped, standing to face him properly. "We were just talking."

Nickolas stepped in closer—too close—his presence suddenly far too imposing. "You looked like you were enjoying yourself."

"I was. He was nice." Her eyes flashed, a spark of irritation igniting. "And why shouldn't I be? That was completely uncalled for, Nickolas. You could've at least shaken his hand."

His jaw tightened, the muscle in his cheek ticking like a silent metronome. "Do men usually try to pick you up at the park?"

She let out a sharp, incredulous laugh. "He wasn't trying to pick me up. That's what normal parents do—they talk. About their kids. About life. It's not a crime."

There was a flicker in his eyes—something darker, something possessive—but before he could reply, Chloe came dashing toward them, breathless and radiant with laughter.

"Daddy!"

Nickolas's expression shifted instantly, melting into a smile as he crouched to scoop her into his arms.

"Hey, mou. Did you have fun?"

They walked home beneath the soft gold of the afternoon sun, Chloe perched on Nickolas's hip, chatting animatedly about the swings, the slide, the little boy with the funny laugh who'd raced her to the monkey bars.

Nickolas nodded along, offering the occasional "Really?" or "That sounds fun," but Calista noticed the way his jaw was still set, his smile not quite reaching his eyes.

She walked a few steps behind them, arms folded loosely, lost in her thoughts.

Daniel.

His easy laugh. His kindness. The normalcy of their conversation. The lack of emotional weight, of complicated history. It had felt… simple.

And then Nickolas had appeared—tense, silent, and bristling with something that looked an awful lot like jealousy.

But why?

They barely knew each other. A few days, a handful of conversations, one reckless kiss.

A kiss she hadn't stopped thinking about.

She glanced up at him now, his tall frame blocking the sun as he bent his head to listen to Chloe's rambling. He looked like he belonged there, with her. Like a father.

But the tightness in his shoulders hadn't eased, and neither had the questions swirling in her mind.

Was it jealousy?

Did he think he had a right to be?

And more importantly—why did a part of her wish he did?

They turned onto her street, the little white house coming into view. Chloe pointed to it with glee, declaring, "That's our home, Daddy!"

Nickolas smiled then, wide, and real. "It's lovely. Just like you."

Calista's heart gave a traitorous tug.

Lovely. Just like you.

Damn it.

Inside, the house was quiet, save for the soft clatter of wooden blocks and Chloe's occasional hums as she played contentedly on the living room rug. Afternoon sunlight spilled through the gauzy curtains, casting golden streaks across the worn hardwood floor and lending a cozy warmth to the slightly cluttered space.

Nickolas sat in silence, his elbows on his knees, watching Calista move through the kitchen with quiet efficiency. She filled the kettle, set out two mugs, her motions calm, practiced—like she'd done it a thousand times before, like this was her rhythm, her sanctuary. He should have felt at ease here. Instead, his mind was buzzing.

What the hell was wrong with him?

He wasn't the jealous type. Never had been. In his world, relationships were temporary, uncomplicated. But watching that man—Daniel—laughing with Calista, sitting close enough to touch her, looking at her like she was something rare and worth keeping… something had snapped inside him. Something raw. Possessive.

He didn't like it. Not one damn bit.

He'd told himself this was about Chloe. But the heat in his gut when Daniel made her laugh—that wasn't fatherly.

Calista poured the hot water and returned to the table, placing a steaming mug in front of him before settling into the chair across from his. She curled her fingers around her cup, letting the warmth soak into her palms. Her gaze lingered on the swirl of rising steam as if it held the answers she hadn't quite found yet. Nickolas watched her in silence, sensing the shift in her mood—measured, cautious.

She blew gently on the surface of her coffee, her eyes still avoiding his, the silence between them stretching long enough to carry weight. Something fragile hung there—hope or hesitation, he couldn't tell.

"I've been thinking about your request last night," she said finally, her voice quiet, steady. "About going to Greece."

He straightened slightly, something flickering in his eyes. "Yes?"

"I think… Chloe should meet her family. Your mother. Your sister." She paused, as if testing the words in the air. "She deserves that. To know where she comes from."

Nickolas nodded slowly, trying to read her tone. "But?"

"But it's not as simple as just packing a bag," she said, meeting his eyes now. "We'll need passports—Chloe and me. And I'll need to talk to my boss, figure out if I can get the time off work. It's not a no, Nickolas. But I need to plan."

His shoulders relaxed slightly, though his expression remained unreadable. "Of course. I didn't expect it overnight."

Calista studied him for a beat. "This isn't a vacation for me. It's a huge decision, and it affects Chloe's whole world. I'm not going to uproot her life on a whim."

"I wouldn't ask you to," he said softly.

She nodded, then looked down at her coffee again. "Good. Because if we're doing this, we do it with care." Her voice was even, but her fingers tightened on the mug like it anchored her resolve.

Nickolas leaned back slightly, watching her with something that looked like admiration—or maybe guilt.

"I know," he said. "And I want to do this right. For her. And for you."

Chapter Twelve

The limousine cruised toward the airport, early morning sun spilling golden light through tinted windows. Chloe sat between them, practically vibrating with excitement, her little legs swinging off the edge of the leather seat as she chattered non-stop to Nickolas.

"And then I painted a butterfly!" Chloe bounced. "Mommy helped, but I did the wings all by myself."

She barely paused for breath. "And at school, we had pyjama day, and I wore the unicorn ones! And guess what, Daddy? I made a new friend—her name is Ava—and she likes dinosaurs too!"

Nickolas smiled, nodding with sincere interest, though Calista could see the exhaustion edging into his expression. He had flown back to Greece the Monday after their conversation—the day after she'd agreed, with cautious hope, that Chloe should meet her family. In just two weeks, he had orchestrated passports, paperwork, and travel plans with the relentless precision she was coming to expect.

All of it—passports, paperwork, travel plans—handled.

Calista, for her part, had somehow managed to wrangle four weeks off work—a feat she'd thought impossible. Yet her boss had surprised her with unexpected kindness and support when she explained the importance of the trip. She'd packed their bags with a careful blend of nerves and excitement, trying to convince herself this was right.

Because it was.

Wasn't it?

Henry had his reservations. As a close friend—more like family, really—he'd been by Calista's side through every twist and turn since Chloe was born. He wasn't trying to interfere, but he couldn't help feeling protective.

"This just feels fast," he'd said quietly a few nights before the trip, sipping coffee at Calista's kitchen table while she folded laundry. "You've just started finding your rhythm again. Chloe too. What if this stirs up more questions than answers?"

He didn't doubt Nickolas's sincerity—but Henry had seen what hope could do when it crashed. He'd been there for the late-night tears, the hesitant mornings, the long process of helping Chloe understand the absence in her life without turning it into pain.

"It's a lot for a little girl," he continued. "A different country. A new family. A father she barely knows. What if it's overwhelming?"

Calista had paused, her hands stilling on a little pink sundress. "I know," she said softly. "But she deserves to see where she came from."

Henry had offered a quiet nod. He didn't argue. He trusted her instincts. Still, as she zipped the final suitcase, he couldn't shake the weight in his chest.

When the limousine pulled to a stop outside a sleek, private terminal, Chloe gasped, pressing her palms to the window. "Is that it? Is that the airplane we're taking?"

Nickolas leaned forward with a smile. "Yes, mou. That's our jet."

"Our jet?" Chloe squealed, looking up at him like he'd just promised her a ride on a unicorn.

He chuckled. "It's a little different than the big airplanes. Smaller, faster, comfier."

Calista stepped out of the car behind them, her heels clicking on the tarmac as a soft breeze lifted the hem of her dress. She adjusted the strap of her bag and took Chloe's hand, letting Nickolas guide them toward the hangar.

Everything had happened so fast—too fast, maybe. But as they moved through security and customs with astonishing ease, she couldn't help but marvel at the surrealness of it all.

Then they stepped onto the tarmac, and she saw it.

The jet gleamed in the sunlight, white and sleek, the Drakos family crest subtly painted near the door. Two flight attendants waited at the bottom of the stairs, smiling in welcome.

Calista stopped.

Her feet froze, rooted to the spot.

Nickolas stood at the top of the stairs, holding Chloe's hand like it was the most natural thing in the world—like he'd always been part of her life.

And suddenly, it hit her.

This was real.

Too real.

Her heart thudded hard. The weight of it all—the past, the future, the fragile now—pressed down on her.

Nickolas turned, his brow knitting. "Calista?"

She didn't move. Just stared—at the plane, at the staff, at the sky stretching wide above them.

Without hesitation, he came down the steps and reached her, voice low and steady. "What's wrong?"

"I don't know," she whispered. "It just feels like… too much."

He took her hand, warm and anchoring. "It is a lot. But you don't have to carry it all at once."

She swallowed hard, eyes searching his. "What if we get there and it's a disaster? What if your mother hates me? What if Chloe doesn't fit in? What if—"

"Then we deal with it," he said softly. "Together."

She looked for doubt in his face. Instead, she found calm conviction—like he'd already considered every worst-case scenario and still believed this was worth it.

"My mother's been waiting years for this," he added gently. "And my sister? She's going to fall in love with both of you in five minutes. I promise."

Still, Calista hesitated.

Then Chloe's voice rang out from halfway up the stairs.

"Mommy, come on! We're going to Greece!"

Calista looked up. Her daughter's face glowed with joy, her little backpack bouncing with each step.

Nickolas extended his hand again. Not demanding. Just offering.

This time, she took it.

They climbed the stairs together, Chloe skipping ahead like the plane might leave without her. Inside, the jet was serene—cool leather seats, polished wood trim, orchids in elegant vases. The flight attendant greeted them with warm professionalism.

They buckled in. Calista's grip on the armrest was white knuckled as the engines came to life.

Nickolas leaned close. "You okay?"

She gave a breath of a smile. "Ask me again when we land."

As the jet soared into the sky, the city shrank beneath them—familiar streets, her little house, the comfortable life she was leaving behind for something far less certain.

Nine hours later, they stepped onto the sunlit tarmac of a private airfield outside Athens. The air was warm, fragrant with sea breeze and olive trees. A sleek helicopter waited nearby, its blades whirring lazily in the golden light.

Calista climbed in beside Chloe and Nickolas. As they lifted off, the vibration of the rotors hummed through her chest—and then the world opened up.

The Greek coastline unfurled beneath them like a painting brought to life: terracotta rooftops, olive groves in neat silver rows, and wildflowers spilling across green meadows. The Aegean Sea stretched endlessly below, shifting from turquoise to deep sapphire as the light danced over it.

They passed jagged cliffs and hidden coves where fishing boats bobbed in gentle waves. Tiny islands dotted the water like forgotten myths, each one kissed by sun and time.

"Look, Mommy!" Chloe pressed to the window, wide-eyed. "Is that where we're going?"

Ahead, Nickolas's island rose from the sea—lush, green, ringed with white sand and crowned with elegant villas peeking through the trees. A road snaked upward toward a grand estate nestled among cypress and bougainvillea.

Nickolas leaned close, his voice warm in her ear.

"That's home."

Home.

The word lingered, soft and strange. Not quite hers—yet.

The helicopter banked toward the island, and Calista felt it again—that quiet, undeniable shift deep inside her.

This wasn't just a vacation.

It was the start of something new. For Chloe. And maybe, for herself too.

The helicopter touched down on a marble helipad tucked into the hillside, the downdraft stirring petals from a flowering bougainvillea vine that spilled over a stone wall. Calista shielded her eyes against the wind, Chloe clinging to her side with wide, unblinking eyes.

And then the blades slowed, the engine powering down into silence that was somehow more dizzying than the roar that came before it.

Nickolas stepped out first and turned to help them both down. Calista's heels clicked softly on the pale stone as she took in the scene—lush gardens cascading in terraced steps, olive trees dancing in the breeze, and beyond them, an estate that looked like it had been plucked from the pages of a Mediterranean fairy tale.

The villa rose in soft, sun-warmed stone, its arched windows trimmed in pale blue shutters, its balconies laced with curling vines. Jasmine perfumed the air, and the scent of the sea drifted in on the wind.

A car waited at the edge of the helipad, sleek and silver, and within minutes they were winding up a cobbled drive, the gardens growing more manicured with every turn. Calista gripped Chloe's hand as they rounded the last bend, and the estate came fully into view—grand without being ostentatious, elegant without feeling cold.

Waiting at the top of the steps were two women—one older, elegant, and still, the other younger, closer to Calista's age, with an open, curious expression.

The older woman stood tall and regal, her silver-blonde hair swept into a flawless twist at the nape of her neck. She wore a linen dress the colour of cream and seafoam, perfectly pressed, effortlessly elegant. Even from a distance, her presence radiated quiet authority—but it was her eyes that held Calista captive. Piercing. Intelligent. Unnervingly familiar.

The same eyes that looked back at her from Chloe's face.

Nickolas stepped out first, and something in him changed. His easy charm shifted into something more contained, more proper. A quiet formality settled over him.

Calista climbed out with Chloe, who had grown suddenly still, her little hand tightening around her mother's fingers.

The younger woman descended the steps with a sunny, practiced smile. She was beautiful—olive-skinned, with dark, glossy hair and a dimple that deepened as she spoke. "You must be Calista," she said warmly, as if they'd known each other for years. "I'm Cassia. I've been dying to meet you."

Calista blinked at the enthusiasm, then took the offered hand. "It's lovely to meet you, Cassia."

"Nickolas has told us all about you," Cassia added with a mischievous glance in his direction. Then she bent down to Chloe's level, her smile softening. "Would you like to see your room, sweetie?"

Chloe hesitated, glanced up at her mother. "Yes, please."

Cassia extended her hand, and after a moment's pause, Chloe took it. Calista watched as the two of them disappeared into the house, laughter already echoing faintly from the entryway.

And then she was alone—with Nickolas, and the woman who had yet to speak.

The older woman descended the steps slowly, with a dancer's grace and a diplomat's precision. Her gaze moved—first to Nickolas, then to Calista, and finally to the doorway where the girls had vanished.

Nickolas stepped forward. "Màna," he said quietly. "This is Calista."

The woman's eyes fixed on her. Cool. Discerning. Not unkind—but not warm, either.

"I am Eleni Drakos," she said, extending a hand with practiced elegance.

Calista took it. Her pulse skittered in her throat. "It's very nice to meet you."

A silence followed—just long enough for it to feel deliberate.

Then Eleni gave a single nod. "Welcome to our home."

She turned without another word and moved inside, her heels clicking softly against the stone.

Calista stood there for a moment.

The silence she left behind felt colder than any words she could have spoken. She looked up at Nickolas. "She doesn't like me."

"She doesn't know you yet," he said gently, brushing a hand against the small of her back. "Come, I'll show you to your room. You must be exhausted."

"I am," she admitted softly.

But it wasn't the journey that had tired her.

It was the feeling of walking into a house that wasn't quite sure it wanted her inside.

After showing Calista to her room and pointing out where Chloe would be sleeping, Nickolas left her to rest. But as he closed the door behind him, the worry on her face lingered in his mind like a bruise. It unsettled him.

He found his mother in the sunroom, seated in a high-backed chair near the open terrace. A book rested in one hand, a delicate glass of white wine in the other. She looked every inch the Drakos matriarch—composed, elegant, and entirely unbothered.

"Mána," he said from the doorway.

Eleni looked up. "Nickolas."

"May I speak with you?"

She closed her book with a soft snap and set it aside. "You already are."

He stepped into the room, hands in his pockets, tension in every line of his body. "It's about Calista."

Her expression didn't flicker. "Of course it is."

He drew a breath. "She's here as my guest. As Chloe's guardian. I'd appreciate it if you could be a little more… welcoming."

"She is not Chloe's guardian," Eleni replied coolly. "She is Chloe's caretaker. At best. More likely a gold digger."

His jaw clenched. "She hasn't asked for a single thing. Not once. She's the only mother Chloe has ever known."

"And whose fault is that?" Eleni's voice was silk wrapped around steel. "Don't confuse convenience with legitimacy. That child is a Drakos. She should be here, with you. Not tucked away in some little house in Boston with a woman who—"

"Stop." His voice was low but hard. Final. "Calista raised Chloe with love. With patience. She's protected her, taught her, loved her. She's earned more than your scorn."

Eleni took a measured sip of wine, then lowered the glass with a soft clink. "Love is not the same as blood."

"No," he said quietly. "Sometimes it's better."

A silence settled between them, taut and bitter. Beyond the terrace, the olive trees swayed in the wind. Somewhere deeper in the house, Chloe's laughter rang out—a small, bright sound that made Eleni's mouth tighten.

She set down her glass. "Do you know what people will say when they find out you brought her here? That you're playing house with a woman who has no claim to your daughter?"

"I don't care what anyone says." His voice was calm, but there was iron beneath it. "Calista is her legal guardian. She was there when Chloe took her first step. When she got sick. She knows what books she loves, what food she hates. She knows Chloe's fears, her dreams—her soul. And Chloe loves her."

Eleni's eyes narrowed, but Nickolas didn't look away.

"And if you can't see that," he said, his voice quiet but firm, "then you're the one who's out of place. I won't allow the woman who raised my daughter to be disrespected in my own home."

Eleni's expression remained composed, but something cold and cutting flashed in her eyes. "She is not her mother."

"She is in every way that matters," he said, steady as stone. "And as far as the law is concerned, that makes her exactly that."

Chapter Thirteen

After Chloe drifted off—her small hand curled around the ear of her stuffed bunny—Calista lingered beside her, watching the soft rise and fall of her daughter's chest. Peaceful. Safe.

She leaned down and pressed a gentle kiss to Chloe's forehead, breathing in the familiar scent of baby shampoo, then quietly slipped from the room.

Back in her temporary quarters, Calista opened the suitcase she hadn't planned to touch just yet. Most of what she'd packed was practical—soft blouses, worn jeans, the cardigan she always reached for when she needed to feel grounded. But folded carefully at the bottom were a few of Danica's dresses.

Her sister would've belonged in a place like this. Calista wasn't sure she ever would.

She pulled out the royal blue gown—the one with the off-the-shoulder neckline and the faint shimmer that danced in the light like moonlight on water. She'd never worn anything like it before. Never had reason to. Slipping it on felt like stepping into someone else's life—part disguise, part declaration.

She added a touch of makeup. Just enough to look composed, like someone who wouldn't flinch at polished silver and linen napkins.

A soft knock startled her.

Cassia stood on the other side of the door, radiant in a deep green dress, her smile immediate and warm.

"You look beautiful," she said, eyes sparkling. "That colour is stunning on you."

Calista flushed. "Thank you. You look lovely too."

Cassia offered her arm with a theatrical little bow. "Shall I escort you to the dining room? It's easy to get lost in my brother's... excessively grand house."

Calista smiled and slipped her arm into Cassia's. "Thank you. I appreciate the rescue."

As they walked, their heels clicking softly against the marble floor, Cassia's voice dropped slightly.

"I hope my mother didn't offend you earlier."

Calista glanced over. "Why would you think she did?"

Cassia shrugged delicately. "She's… not known for her warmth. Nickolas barely tolerates her, and I'm related by blood."

Calista gave a small, uncertain smile. "She seems very… polished."

Cassia let out a quiet laugh. "That's one word for it."

They reached the top of the staircase. Voices murmured below—elegant, low, and vaguely intimidating. Calista paused, steadying her breath.

Cassia gave her arm a reassuring squeeze. "You look incredible, and you belong here. Don't let her make you doubt that."

Calista didn't reply, but as they descended the stairs together, she lifted her chin just a little higher.

The dining room opened before her like a stage set—tall windows veiled in sheer fabric, candlelight glinting off crystal and polished silver.

Only two people were present: Eleni, statuesque at the far end of the table with a wine glass held like a sceptre, and Nickolas, seated at the head. His gaze found her the instant she entered.

He rose slowly, as if something had stolen the breath from his lungs.

His eyes swept over her—not with the lazy detachment of a man used to beauty, but with focused reverence. The royal blue gown hugged her in elegant lines, the neckline skimming her collarbones, the fabric catching the candlelight like starlight. Her hair was swept back, her features subtly highlighted.

Nickolas didn't speak right away. Something in him was visibly recalibrating.

Then—softly, genuinely—he said, "You look… beautiful."

Calista met his gaze, unsure what to do with the way he said it—like it mattered.

Eleni's voice cut the air. "Well. I see someone's trying to make an impression."

Calista didn't let her smile falter. "Good evening."

Nickolas moved around the table, pulling out the chair beside him. "Sit here."

She did, her pulse a little louder than before. His hand brushed her back as he guided the chair in—light, warm, lingering for a second longer than necessary.

When he sat again, he didn't look away.

A hush fell as the first course was served—white asparagus soup with a delicate swirl of cream and a hint of lemon zest. The silverware gleamed beneath the soft chandelier light, and the servers moved in seamless precision.

Calista kept her hands steady, though she felt anything but. Nickolas sat to her right, quiet but present. She could feel his attention on her even when he wasn't looking directly at her. Across from her, Eleni sipped her wine slowly, her expression unreadable behind carefully painted features.

The silence stretched, brittle and polite.

Then Eleni set her glass down with a soft clink. "I suppose we should talk about the child."

Calista's spine straightened. "Of course."

"Why didn't your sister tell Nickolas about Chloe?" Eleni asked, voice like velvet laced with steel. "She must have known who the father was."

Calista's spoon paused halfway to her mouth. She lowered it gently into the bowl. "I can't answer that. I asked Danica about the father when she was pregnant. She told me she didn't know who he was."

Eleni's eyes narrowed slightly, though her expression remained polite. "How convenient."

Nickolas shifted beside Calista, his jaw tight, but he said nothing.

Eleni went on. "Your last name—Georgiou—is Greek, isn't it?"

"Yes," Calista replied evenly. "My father was Greek."

Eleni's smile was brittle. "How traditional. I imagine your family has strong feelings about legacy."

Calista met her gaze without flinching. "My family valued loyalty and love more than bloodlines and titles."

A flicker of something—annoyance? amusement? —passed through Eleni's eyes. "Still, don't you think it's time you stepped aside and let Nickolas take charge of his own daughter?"

Calista blinked slowly. Her voice, when it came, was calm but resolute. "I'm her mother. I'm sorry if that disappoints you, but that will never change. I will always be Chloe's mother."

The room stilled.

Eleni tilted her head, studying her. "I see."

Nickolas cleared his throat. "That's enough."

Eleni raised a brow but said nothing more, returning to her soup with measured grace.

Dinner continued, the quiet tension weaving between crystal and silver, between the spaces where things were said and where they were very deliberately left unsaid.

But Calista didn't shrink.

Not once.

The dining room doors closed behind them with a soft, final thud, sealing off the clinking of silverware and the fading echo of Eleni's imperious voice.

Calista walked ahead, the long gown swaying around her legs, her spine stiff with the effort of keeping her composure. She needed air. Space. Anything that didn't smell like wine, wealth, and judgment.

Her hands curled unconsciously at her sides. The silk rustled with every step—elegant, composed, a contradiction to the storm still crashing in her chest.

Nickolas caught up with her just beyond the terrace doors.

"Calista."

She paused but didn't turn. The marble was cool beneath her heels, the breeze carrying the faint scent of night jasmine and the distant sea. Her voice was quiet when it came.

"She wanted to provoke me."

"Yes," he said, equally soft. "She did."

Calista turned then, her gaze direct. "Is this what it's going to be like? Every time I sit at a table with her, I have to defend my place in Chloe's life?"

"No," he said firmly. "Not from me."

There was a weight to his words that made her chest tighten. But she couldn't let it in—not yet.

"She was cruel," he added, jaw tight. "And wrong."

Calista looked at him for a long moment, searching for something. Maybe sincerity. Maybe courage. Whatever it was, she didn't find enough of it to stay.

"I think it's time I went to bed," she said quietly, starting to turn away.

But he reached out—not forcefully, just a gentle touch to her arm.

"Please—Calista."

She turned slowly, eyes meeting his. There was something unguarded in his expression—something she hadn't expected to see.

"I'm here for Chloe," she said quietly. "I want her to know her family—your mother, your sister. And I want her to spend time with you. I just hope I don't come to regret it."

Nickolas flinched almost imperceptibly, the line hitting harder than she'd meant it to.

"I'm sorry," he said, his voice gentler now. "For tonight. For her."

Calista gave a small nod, her gaze skimming past his shoulder.

"Good night, Nickolas," she murmured.

And then she turned, walking away with quiet grace, the deep blue of her gown catching the low light—trailing behind her like a thread of midnight silk unravelling into the shadows.

Nickolas remained rooted where she'd left him, the faint whisper of her gown still echoing in his mind long after the sound had faded. The night air had turned sharp, crisp with the scent of salt and jasmine drifting in from the gardens. Somewhere beyond the terrace, cicadas sang in rhythmic pulses, a quiet counterpoint to the silence she'd left behind.

He ran a hand through his hair, exhaling slowly.

Calista.

There had been a strength in her tonight that surprised him—an unshakable grace beneath the vulnerability. She never raised her voice. Never flinched beneath his mother's barbs. But he'd seen her fingers curl beneath the table. The way she blinked too long when Eleni questioned her place in Chloe's life.

She had every right to be furious, yet she walked away with her dignity intact—leaving him the one in tatters.

Nickolas crossed to the low wall at the edge of the terrace, resting his hands against the stone. The moon hung low above the horizon, casting silver streaks across the marble floor.

He thought of Chloe. Of her small hand in his. The bright, curious eyes that mirrored his own.

And then of Calista—so fiercely protective, so composed even when her world was being dissected over dinner like it was a matter of polite conversation.

He couldn't stop thinking about the way she'd looked when she entered the room. Regal. Unapologetically herself. And utterly unforgettable.

He hadn't protected her tonight. Not the way he should have. And he felt ashamed.

Chapter Fourteen

Morning sunlight spilled across the breakfast table, soft and golden, warming the crisp linen and bouncing off the delicate china. The room, a sunlit corner of the sprawling villa, felt more like a retreat than a palace—airy, quiet, a pocket of peace tucked away from last night's sharp edges.

Calista sat beside Chloe, helping her spread strawberry jam onto a warm croissant. Her daughter's cheeks were flushed with sleep, her curls still tousled. She wore a cotton sundress dotted with tiny lemons and had insisted on picking her own shoes—mismatched sandals that Calista hadn't had the heart to correct.

"You're getting really good at that," Calista said with a smile, as Chloe carefully lifted the croissant to her mouth.

"It's sticky," Chloe said, licking a smudge of jam from her finger.

Calista chuckled softly. "That's half the fun."

The scent of coffee and citrus lingered in the air, blending with the faint perfume of blooming gardenias just beyond the open terrace doors. For a while, it was just the two of them—easy, familiar, unspoken comfort weaving between bites and quiet smiles.

Then footsteps echoed lightly in the corridor.

Cassia entered first, her hair pulled back in a sleek braid, wearing soft cream trousers and a loose silk blouse. Her face lit up when she saw them.

"Good morning," she said brightly. "You two look cozy."

"We are," Calista said, offering a genuine smile. "There's coffee, if you haven't had any."

"Already three cups deep," Cassia said with a wink.

Behind her, Nickolas appeared, more casual than usual in an open-collared shirt and dark jeans. His gaze went first to Chloe and softened.

"Morning," he said, quieter.

"Hi," Chloe said around a mouthful of croissant, then grinned. "I had jam."

Nickolas smiled, stepping closer. "Lucky you. I missed breakfast."

"We can share," Chloe offered, holding up a crumb-covered half of her croissant.

Calista bit her lip, watching the exchange. There was something about the way he crouched beside Chloe's chair, accepting the soggy offering with unfeigned gratitude, which tugged unexpectedly at her chest.

"I was thinking," she said gently, waiting until his eyes met hers. "Maybe you and Chloe could spend the day together."

Nickolas blinked, surprised. "Just us?"

She nodded. "If she's comfortable with it."

He glanced at Chloe, who had resumed chewing with casual interest.

"Chloe?" Calista said softly. "Would you like to go with daddy today? Just the two of you?"

Chloe considered this, brows drawn. "Will you be there?"

"I'll be here," Calista said, brushing a curl from her daughter's forehead. "But I thought you might want some special time with daddy. You can tell me all about it later."

Chloe's eyes drifted to Nickolas. "Will we get ice cream?"

He gave a quiet laugh. "Absolutely."

"Okay then," Chloe declared, nodding firmly. "But I get to pick the flavour."

"Deal," he said, his expression somewhere between amused and awestruck.

Calista smiled, but there was a hint of something bittersweet in it. Chloe trusted easily— but only when she felt safe. And right now, she did.

Cassia, leaning casually against the sideboard, watched it all with a soft glint in her eye.

"If Nickolas is on Chloe duty," she said, "I was actually thinking I might steal Calista for a bit."

Calista turned, intrigued. "Oh?"

"There's a small village not far from here," Cassia said. "Stone houses, olive groves, a little market where the old men argue about olives and politics. I thought we could take a walk. Give you a breather from all the…high-society intensity."

Calista's smile grew. "That sounds perfect."

"Then it's settled." Cassia straightened, looking pleased. "You and I will disappear after breakfast, and these two,"—she gestured between Nickolas and Chloe— "can go off on their own grand adventure."

Calista glanced at Nickolas again. "You're sure?"

His expression was steady. "I'd like that."

And for the first time since arriving, something between them loosened. No expectations. No battle lines. Just the quiet promise of trying.

Chloe finished her croissant and looked at Nickolas expectantly. "I need my shoes. The matching ones."

He stood and offered his hand. "Lead the way."

She grabbed it without hesitation, hopping off the chair.

As they walked off toward the hallway—his large hand wrapped gently around her small one—Calista let out a slow, quiet breath.

Cassia handed her a second cup of coffee. "You okay?"

Calista nodded. "I think so."

Cassia smiled. "Good. Because trust me, the village may be small, but the pastry shop? Life-changing."

Calista laughed softly. "You're speaking my language."

And as they stepped out into the sunlight, the breeze warm and filled with birdsong, it felt—if only for a little while—like things were beginning to shift.

The village was tucked into the hillside like a forgotten gem—stone walls softened by ivy, terra cotta rooftops glowing under the late morning sun. A narrow path led through the centre, flanked by weathered storefronts and cafés with rickety chairs and colourful umbrellas. The scent of roasting chestnuts, fresh bread, and wild lavender hung in the air.

Cassia guided Calista through the winding cobbled streets like someone born to them, waving to familiar faces and slipping easily into the village's gentle rhythm. Calista stayed close, her eyes wide, taking in the quaint charm of sun-bleached walls, terracotta roofs, and lazy shutters.

"It's beautiful," she murmured.

Cassia smiled. "It's my escape. Especially when mother's around."

They paused at a shaded bench beside a bubbling fountain. Calista tilted her face to the sun, sighing softly.

"I can see why," she said. "It feels like time forgot this place."

Cassia chuckled. "It has its own rhythm. The old men gossip more than the women, and if you linger too long, someone will insist on feeding you."

Calista's gaze wandered to the stone chapel nestled at the top of the hill, then down to the sleepy shops clustered in the square. "I thought Nickolas owned the island?"

"He does," Cassia replied, nodding to a woman sweeping her stoop. "But he rents part of it to the villagers. It's far too big for one family."

Calista arched a brow. "Do you live here?"

"No," Cassia said with a light laugh. "I live in Athens. I came to meet you and Chloe."

"And your mother?"

"She's in Athens too."

Calista frowned slightly. "Then whose home is this?"

Cassia's lips curved with something between mischief and affection. "Nickolas'. He could never live with our mother. She doesn't exactly approve of his... lifestyle."

"Lifestyle?" Calista echoed.

Cassia gave her a mock-serious look. "You know. Male gigolo."

Calista let out a short, surprised laugh. "You're not serious."

"Oh, painfully," Cassia deadpanned. "The brooding stares. The mysterious silences. The habit of never staying with one woman for more than two weeks—textbook."

Calista shook her head, amused. "At least he's consistent."

Cassia grinned. "Don't tell him I said that. He likes to think he's misunderstood. In reality, he's just not interested in commitment."

Calista's smile softened. "Some people don't suit it, I suppose."

Cassia's gaze flicked to her. "Is there someone? Someone special?"

Calista hesitated. "No... not really."

Cassia raised a brow. "Not really?"

"Well... there's someone. Henry. He's proposed a couple of times. I said no."

Cassia blinked. "Oh? I thought you and Nickolas..."

Calista's laugh came too quickly. "No. No, no, no. I'm a commitment girl. He and I would never work."

Cassia leaned back, folding her arms loosely. "Interesting."

"What?"

Cassia's voice gentled. "I've seen the way he looks at you."

Calista blinked. "How does he look at me?"

"Like he's trying to figure out how someone like you exists," Cassia said simply. "Like you surprised him."

Something in Calista's breath hitched. She tried to brush it off with a laugh, but there was a flicker in her eyes she couldn't quite hide. "He barely knows me."

Cassia reached out, letting her fingers trail along a flowering vine curling over a nearby wall. "You know, he never wanted children."

"I know," Calista said quietly. "When I contacted him about Chloe, I honestly thought he'd want nothing to do with her."

"I was shocked when he told us," Cassia said. "He didn't just accept her—he's trying."

Calista nodded slowly, her gaze distant. "That's the part I didn't expect."

They strolled a bit farther before stopping at a sun-dappled café on the square. Cassia chose a table shaded by trailing bougainvillea, and they each ordered a coffee. The air was warm and laced with the scent of fresh bread and citrus blossoms.

They were quietly sipping their drinks when, as if on cue, a group of young men spilled out of the bakery across the square. Casual and sun-kissed, they laughed amongst themselves—one wore a loose linen shirt, another still had flour in his hair, clearly the baker's son. Their voices fell as they caught sight of the two women at the café.

The tallest of the group, golden-skinned and grinning with mischievous eyes, nudged the flour-covered boy and said something that made them all laugh—too loudly—before they scrambled to compose themselves.

Cassia leaned toward Calista, voice low and amused. "Brace yourself."

"For what?"

She didn't get an answer—because the tall one was already striding over, his charm turned all the way up.

"Cassia," he said in lilting, accented English, "you didn't tell us you were bringing Aphrodite herself to the village."

Cassia rolled her eyes, setting her cup down with deliberate calm. "Luca, behave."

Luca pressed a hand to his chest, mock wounded. "I'm only being hospitable. It's not every day the gods send us a beauty like this."

Calista laughed, caught off guard. "That might be the most dramatic compliment I've ever received."

"Ah, and she has a laugh like music," Luca said, clearly pleased with himself. "A rare gem, indeed."

Cassia took a slow sip of her espresso, watching him over the rim of her cup. "She's not remotely interested in charming village boys with flour on their shoes."

Luca glanced down at his flour-dusted sandals, sighing theatrically. "But these are my finest shoes."

The other young men passed by, offering respectful nods and murmured greetings—but more than one sent a lingering glance Calista's way.

When they were gone, Cassia turned to her with a grin. "You're famous now."

Calista smirked. "I wasn't expecting that kind of welcome."

"Oh, that was nothing," Cassia said, waving a hand. "Wait until Luca tries to write you a sonnet in the bakery window. He once serenaded a Swedish tourist with a mandolin and a basket of croissants. She nearly missed her flight."

Calista laughed, shaking her head. "He's certainly bold."

"He's also harmless. All charm, no bite," Cassia said with a smirk. Then, more softly, "But it's good to see you smile."

They resumed their walk through the village, the cobbled streets warm beneath their feet, winding between whitewashed houses with cobalt shutters and riotous bursts of bougainvillea. Flower boxes spilled geraniums over wrought-iron balconies, and the air carried the comforting scents of rosemary, yeast, and sun-dried linen.

Children darted between doorways, their laughter ringing like wind chimes, while an old man waved from his stoop, a cat curled at his feet. Calista walked in easy step beside Cassia, her sandals brushing softly against the stone.

The sea glinted at the far edge of the village, a thin ribbon of blue that shimmered like glass. The silence between them felt companionable but laced with the threads of things left unspoken.

Then a familiar voice called out from behind.

"Cassia!"

They turned to see Luca jogging toward them, grinning like he'd just won a prize. In his hands was a wild bouquet—sun-bleached daisies, sprigs of thyme, and something purple Calista didn't recognize but looked freshly plucked.

Cassia groaned under her breath. "Oh dear. I think Luca's in love."

Calista raised a brow. "You're joking."

"He's never given a girl flowers before," Cassia whispered, eyeing the bouquet like it might explode. "I think you've broken the village flirt."

Luca skidded to a halt in front of them, just slightly out of breath. "For you," he said, holding the flowers out to Calista with all the solemnity of a knight presenting a sword.

Calista blinked. "Oh. Thank you. They're... lovely."

Luca beamed, clearly pleased with himself.

Cassia folded her arms, her voice dry. "Careful, Calista. Accepting wildflowers might be a marriage proposal around here."

Luca only winked, his grin widening. "Then I'll start preparing the dowry."

Calista laughed again, the sound light and easy, like the weight of the world had briefly lifted. For the first time in a long while, it felt good to be somewhere she didn't have to pretend.

Cassia rolled her eyes but smiled nonetheless, watching the exchange with a knowing look.

Luca took a half-step closer, still holding the bouquet out toward Calista. "Your name, Calista," he said, his voice suddenly more serious, as though the playful banter had turned a corner. "Do you know what it means?"

Calista glanced down at the flowers, still not quite sure how to handle the attention. "Uh... no, I don't. What does it mean?"

Luca's gaze softened, the playful glint in his eyes replaced by something almost reverent. "It means 'the most beautiful.'"

Calista blinked, startled by the intensity of his words. She laughed awkwardly, unsure if he was joking or serious. "I'm not sure that's true," she said, a little too quickly, deflecting.

Luca only smiled, a hint of warmth in his eyes. "The name says it all," he replied, his voice low. "You're Calista. Of course, you're beautiful."

Cassia chuckled beside her, nudging her with an elbow. "See? Even the village heartthrob agrees."

Calista's cheeks flushed with warmth, but despite her best efforts to remain composed, a small, genuine smile tugged at her lips. "I think I'll hold off on the dowry for now. But thank you for the flowers," she said, her voice light but laced with appreciation.

Luca, grinning broadly, handed her the bouquet with a flourish, as though it were a grand gesture rather than a casual offering. "Of course. But the offer stands, whenever you're ready."

He gave a playful bow, his eyes sparkling with mischief. With a wink, he straightened up and turned, whistling as he strolled back toward the bakery, leaving a trail of laughter in his wake.

Chapter Fifteen

The sun dipped low on the horizon, casting molten gold across the terrace where Nickolas and Chloe sat. Their quiet conversation was interrupted by the soft, rhythmic sound of footsteps and the rustle of silk. Calista appeared, laughter still lingering in her voice as she stepped into view, sunlight catching in her hair.

"Hello, sweetheart," she said warmly, bending down to press a gentle kiss to Chloe's head.

Chloe tilted her face upward, curious eyes scanning the bouquet in her mother's hand. "Mommy, where did you get the flowers from?"

Calista opened her mouth to reply, but Cassia swept in with a glint in her eye, crouching beside Chloe before the answer could come.

"One of the villagers fell in love with your mommy," she said sweetly, though her voice carried that pointed edge only the adults could hear.

Nickolas' jaw tightened, his teeth clicking softly as he forced himself to stay composed. His gaze flicked between Calista and Cassia, then landed on Chloe again—but something in him had shifted. The moment was simple on the surface, but it unravelled something deeper, more personal.

Cassia noticed. She always noticed. And the subtle flicker of triumph in her eyes made it clear: she was stirring the pot on purpose.

"Really, Mommy?" Chloe asked, her voice a mixture of awe and concern. Then, more seriously, "I don't think Henry will like that."

Nickolas' hands clenched slightly at his sides. "I'm sure Henry can handle it," he muttered, his tone dry and barely audible.

Cassia feigned innocence. "Chloe is Henry your mommy's boyfriend?" she asked lightly, as if the question didn't carry weight like iron.

Chloe nodded eagerly. "He wants to marry Mommy."

Cassia's smile curved into something darker. Her gaze flicked toward Calista as she leaned closer to Chloe, her voice coated in exaggerated sweetness. "Well, Luca wants to marry your mommy now too. Looks like you get to pick your stepdaddy."

Chloe's brow furrowed, her little hands clutching the edge of her seat. "Two?"

Calista let out a tight laugh, clearly uneasy. "Your Aunt Cassia is teasing, sweetheart."

But Cassia wasn't paying attention to Chloe anymore—her eyes were on Nickolas, watching the tension rise in his shoulders, in the hard line of his jaw. She was playing a game, and she was winning.

Nickolas could feel the sting of her words, every syllable sharpening a truth he wasn't ready to name. He said nothing at first, but the silence only made it worse.

Finally, his voice cut through the tension, low and controlled. "Enough, Cassia. This isn't a conversation for children."

But the damage was done. The seed had been planted, and it nestled easily in the space between them. Cassia's smirk lingered, sly and knowing, as if to say this is only the beginning.

Cassia's voice broke through the charged silence, light and coaxing, but laced with that ever-present undercurrent of mischief.

"Come on, Calista," she said, smiling like she hadn't just upended the moment. "We'll leave Nickolas and Chloe to enjoy their afternoon together. You need to get your bikini on."

Nickolas said nothing, his eyes fixed on Calista. She hesitated just a second, then bent to press another kiss to Chloe's head.

"Have fun, sweetheart."

"I will, Mommy," Chloe chirped, innocent and unaware of the emotional tangle unravelling around her.

Nickolas watched them walk away—Calista's figure graceful, calm, untouched by the storm Cassia had quietly summoned, and Cassia... well, Cassia walked like a woman who'd gotten exactly what she wanted. She didn't look back, but her smirk was obvious even in profile. It was deliberate. A parting shot.

His jaw ticked again, involuntarily this time. He didn't know whether he was angrier at Cassia for toying with him—or at himself for letting her words get under his skin. The idea of Calista having suitors, admirers, men lining up to propose... He shouldn't care. He had no right to. But the ache in his chest said otherwise.

He turned back to Chloe, who was humming softly to herself and rearranging the little petals that had fallen from Calista's bouquet.

Nickolas forced a smile. "Just us now, kiddo."

But as the sunlight warmed the terrace around them, he couldn't shake the image of Calista walking away—her laughter, her softness, the way Chloe lit up when she looked at her.

And he definitely couldn't shake the way Cassia had said bikini.

He ran a hand through his hair and exhaled slowly.

This was going to be a long afternoon.

The afternoon sun shimmered on the surface of the pool, casting golden ripples across the pale stone deck. Cassia lay sprawled on a lounger, sunglasses perched on her nose, a half-finished cocktail in hand. She looked every bit the queen of mischief, basking in the sun like a cat that had already caught the canary.

Calista stood at the pool's edge, adjusting the strap of her deep blue bikini, the colour striking against her sun-kissed skin. Her posture was effortless, poised, the subtle tension in her limbs promising grace. Her dark hair was twisted up, a few damp tendrils clinging to her neck in the heat. She seemed unaware she was being watched.

But from the terrace above, Nickolas leaned silently against the railing, arms crossed, gaze fixed.

He'd just settled Chloe down for her nap—two stories, one read twice, her sleepy voice murmuring again, please—and now, instead of returning inside, he found himself rooted there. Watching.

He told himself it wasn't intentional.

Yet the moment he stepped out, his eyes had gone straight to her. Calista. Laughing at something Cassia had said, her face lit with unguarded warmth. That laugh—it struck him like a chord from a forgotten melody. So easy, so real. And it echoed somewhere inside him where he hadn't let anyone reach in a long time.

He had never seen her quite like this. Relaxed. Playful. Happy.

Cassia's voice floated up, sweet and singsong, laced with wicked amusement. "We have an audience."

Calista glanced up reflexively, following his sister's gaze. Her eyes found Nickolas's, and a slow smile spread across her lips as she lifted her hand in a carefree wave.

Nickolas hesitated a beat, then returned the gesture. The moment felt simple—harmless, even—but he knew better. Calista didn't yet understand the games Cassia liked to play. Normally, he ignored his sister's antics. But when they involved Calista, he couldn't seem to look the other way.

Their eyes lingered.

Then, without warning, Calista dove into the water in one fluid, elegant motion. She slipped beneath the surface like silk, leaving barely a ripple in her wake.

Nickolas's jaw tightened, his fingers curling around the railing, the faint scent of sun-warmed chlorine and mischief drifting up from below.

Cassia chuckled lazily, tilting her face back to the sun, entirely pleased with herself. "Well," she murmured, mostly to the sky, "let the games begin."

Calista swam smooth, measured lengths of the pool, her strokes precise, rhythm steady. The water was cool against her skin, a welcome contrast to the heat simmering beneath the surface of her thoughts. She told herself it was just the sun—the afternoon warmth, the exercise—but it wasn't. Not really.

It was him.

That look Nickolas had given her from the terrace still lingered behind her eyes, sharp and unsettling in a way that made her chest flutter. There had been something possessive in it. Something unspoken, tightly wound.

She reached the edge of the pool and paused, fingers curling over the warm stone lip, catching her breath. Her limbs ached in the satisfying way that came with exertion. She rested her cheek against her arm, turning slightly to glance at the lounger where Cassia had been moments ago. Empty.

Gone for another drink, she figured. Nothing unusual.

Then, behind her, the water shifted.

A sudden splash broke the calm, and before she could fully turn, a shadow surged up in her periphery. Nickolas emerged from the water like a myth—smooth, silent, closer than she expected. Droplets traced down his jaw, his dark hair slicked back, eyes locked on hers with quiet intensity.

Calista's breath caught in her throat.

"Oh," she said, startled but not retreating. Her voice was softer than she intended, coloured by the rush of her pulse. She offered a breathless smile. "Hello."

Nickolas didn't smile back.

He was too close. Too quiet. And for one suspended moment, the water between them shimmered with something charged—unspoken, electric.

Calista's brows knit slightly, nervous now. "Is… is something wrong?"

"Yes," he said, his voice low and clipped.

She straightened, alarm flashing in her eyes. "Is Chloe, okay?"

"She's fine," he replied quickly. "Fast asleep."

Relief washed through her, and she exhaled. "Oh. Good." She gave a shaky little laugh. "You scared me. So… what is it?"

He didn't answer right away. Just moved closer. A single, steady stroke through the water brought him nearly chest to chest with her, the space between them evaporating.

Calista's back met the pool's edge, cool stone pressing into her spine as her hands gripped the lip behind her. Her heart pounded.

"Nickolas?" she said, barely above a whisper.

His gaze was locked on hers, unreadable but intense. Too intense.

Then he said, just as quiet, "You're driving me mad, you know that?"

Calista blinked, her breath catching. "What… what do you mean?"

Nickolas's hands moved to the edge of the pool, caging her in without touching her. The water dripped down his shoulders, glistening in the sun, but his eyes—those eyes— held hers fast, unwavering.

"I mean," he said, voice husky and low, "I can't stop thinking about you. About the way you laugh when you think no one's listening. The way you look at me like you're not sure whether to trust me… or run."

She swallowed hard, her throat inexplicably dry despite the water surrounding them.

"I don't mean to do any of that," she whispered.

"I know," he murmured, closer now—so close. He knew Calista wasn't playing games. She wasn't trying to lure or provoke. She was just her—unfiltered, unknowingly captivating.

For a moment, neither of them moved. The world faded to a hush: the gentle hum of summer, the wind rustling through leaves, the faint lapping of water against the stone.

Then his voice dropped, low and rough. "But here we are."

Calista's fingers tightened on the edge of the pool. Her heart beat loud and fast, thudding in her ears like a warning—or a dare.

"Nickolas…" she breathed, her voice shaking with something that sounded like fear and hope all at once.

"I know," he said again, softer this time, his eyes lingering on her lips, "But if I don't kiss you right now, I'll regret it."

Chapter Sixteen

He leaned in slowly, giving her every chance to pull away. She didn't.

Their lips met—warm, hesitant, a slow burn igniting between them. The tension that had wrapped itself around them for days unravelled in a single, searing touch.

Nickolas moved one hand from the edge of the pool to her jaw, brushing his fingers along her cheek, then her neck, like she was something delicate and rare. His other hand slid around her waist, pulling her body tight against his.

Calista's hands found his shoulders, fingers digging in, then climbed to the nape of his neck as she kissed him back, bolder now. She let out a soft moan as her lips parted beneath his. He didn't hesitate—his tongue slid against hers, deepening the kiss with hungry precision.

"Wrap your legs around me," he murmured against her mouth, voice thick with restraint.

She obeyed, her legs locking around him as the water buoyed their bodies, weightless in everything but want.

The press of her body against his sent a shudder through him, and she moved instinctively, seeking friction, chasing the delicious pressure building low in her belly.

"I've dreamt about your legs around me," he groaned, lips trailing along her jaw, his breath hot against her ear.

She made a sound—half whimper, half plea—as her head dropped back and her fingers tightened around his neck.

Everything else fell away.

The water was all around them now, lapping against their skin as their bodies pressed closer, clinging to one another with an urgency neither could fight. Nickolas' hands roamed over her, exploring, memorising, as if he needed to anchor himself to her.

Calista's breath hitched as she ground herself against him, feeling the tautness of his body, the heat that burned through the cool water. Every movement sparked a deeper need, a pull she couldn't ignore.

Her legs wrapped tighter around his waist, locking him in place, and she felt the growing pressure between them, a tangible friction that made her pulse quicken. She didn't have to speak. Her body said everything—each subtle shift, every desperate, breathless motion.

"You drive me crazy, Calista," he rasped, his lips brushing her ear as a tremor ran down his spine.

His hands moved to her back, pressing her closer, as if he couldn't get close enough. His lips found her neck, trailing wet, heated kisses down to her collarbone, each one searing into her skin, marking her in a way that felt permanent.

She gasped as she tilted her head back, her fingers gripping his hair, urging him to take more, give more, and she met him with equal fervour, her body pressing against his as the water swirled around them. The soft splash of their movements only heightened the intimacy, the sound of it mingling with the rushing of her heartbeat.

"Nickolas…" She barely whispered his name, but it was enough to unravel the last thread of restraint between them.

His hands slid down her sides, fingers dipping into the curves of her waist as he pulled her in even closer, until she could feel every inch of him—his breath, his heartbeat, the undeniable ache of desire that pulsed between them.

"I can't hold back anymore," he said, his voice strained, broken.

And with that, he kissed her again—slower, deeper, as if savouring each taste, each touch. The water enveloped them, a quiet sanctuary around the fire that burned between their bodies. The world outside the pool was forgotten. Time ceased to exist. It was just the two of them, suspended in this moment, drowning in everything they hadn't said, in everything they were feeling.

Calista's fingers slid over his chest, tracing the hard line of his muscles, feeling the tension in his body. Her breath came in shallow gasps, each one hitching as she lost herself more completely in him.

Nickolas' lips moved to her jaw, down her neck, tracing a path of fire over her skin. "Calista…" His voice was ragged now, the weight of his desire impossible to hide. "Tell me you want this…"

Her body responded before her mind could catch up. She nodded, the truth too big for words, her eyes saying what her lips couldn't. Her hands gripping his shoulders, pulling him back to her, crashing their lips together in a kiss that promised everything and nothing all at once.

In the water, nothing mattered but the feeling of his touch, the heat that radiated from him, the electric charge between them that could no longer be denied.

And Calista—she gave herself to it. To him. To the wild, consuming passion that was as inevitable as the current beneath them.

Nickolas kissed her again—slower this time, but no less intense. It was a claiming, a confession, a surrender wrapped in the heat of a summer afternoon. Calista clung to him, her hands buried in his hair, her legs still wrapped tight around his waist. The water moved around them in soft ripples, warm and lazy, a stark contrast to the fire building between their bodies.

His mouth trailed down her throat, each kiss sending tremors through her. When he reached her shoulder, he whispered against her damp skin, "You don't know what you're doing to me.

She shivered, though the sun still warmed her back. "I think I do," she whispered back, her voice breathless and trembling with anticipation. She could feel his heartbeat, fast and erratic, against her chest. Every inch of her body was alive, aware of every place he touched and every place he hadn't touched yet.

Nickolas's hands slid beneath the surface, warm and sure, finding her thighs before gliding up to her waist. His fingers splayed wide, anchoring her to him, reverent in their touch. "You feel incredible," he murmured, his voice rough with awe—as if this, she, was something sacred.

Calista inhaled sharply as she shifted against him, the friction subtle but devastating. The sound he made in response—low, guttural, barely restrained—reverberated between them like a pulled string about to snap.

Then—

"Am I interrupting?" came Cassia's voice, light and casual, like she hadn't just shattered something electric.

Calista froze.

Heat rushed to her face faster than she could blink. She ducked her head instinctively, burying it against Nickolas's shoulder as if she could vanish into the water—or into the sunlit silence that followed.

"Oh my God," she whispered, mortified. "Kill me."

Nickolas let out a slow, controlled breath, lifting one hand from her waist to pinch the bridge of his nose. He didn't bother looking at Cassia. "Do you ever knock?"

Cassia's laughter floated across the pool, syrupy-sweet and utterly unapologetic, like she owned the space and every moment in it. "It's a pool, Niko. There's no door to knock on."

Calista made a strangled noise in the back of her throat and tried to pull away, but Nickolas held her steady, his grip gentle but firm. "Don't," he muttered under his breath, not ready to let the moment go, even if it had been ambushed.

Cassia, perched now at the edge of the deck with a fresh drink in hand and sunglasses still in place, watched them with feline satisfaction.

"You two are so dramatic," she teased. "I was just coming to tell you the lemonade's running low. But this is much more entertaining."

Nickolas turned his head slowly, fixing his sister with a look that could curdle wine. "Leave."

Cassia raised her hands in mock surrender, clearly delighted. "Fine, fine. Don't get your swim trunks in a twist." She winked at Calista. "Carry on, lovebirds."

And with that, she sauntered off—her laughter trailing behind her like a ribbon of smoke.

For a long moment, silence returned.

Nickolas turned back to Calista, brushing a strand of wet hair from her cheek. His gaze dropped to her lips, still parted from their last kiss.

"Where were we?" he murmured, fingers grazing the small of her back.

But Calista stilled beneath his touch.

"Nickolas…" she said quietly, drawing back just enough to place a hand gently on his chest. Her pulse thudded against her wrist, her breath uneven—not from desire now, but from nerves.

"We need to stop."

His brows pulled together, not in anger, but confusion. "Why?"

She looked down, struggling to meet his eyes. "Because I'm not like you."

His body went very still. "What does that mean?"

"I don't take lovers," she said softly. "Every fortnight or otherwise." Her fingers curled slightly against his chest. "I've never taken one. Ever."

It landed with a hush. A shift in the air, as if the weight of her words pulled the steam from the water itself.

Nickolas blinked, something unreadable flickering in his expression—like a shadow briefly crossing the sun. "Calista…"

"I'm not ashamed," she said quickly, voice tight, trembling, but still firm. "It's just… I don't do this. I don't know how to do this."

The heat in his gaze cooled, not with indifference, but with something deeper—something quieter. Reverent. As if he'd stumbled upon a truth he hadn't expected.

"You've never had a lover?" he asked, his voice low, almost disbelieving.

She shook her head, the motion small, but final. "No."

Then, softer still: "I'm sorry."

Nickolas didn't move for a heartbeat. Just let out a breath that raked through his chest, all sharp edges and restraint.

She pushed out of his arms, and though his hands lingered a moment longer—thumbs brushing her skin like a silent plea—he let her go. Reluctantly. Like releasing something rare and breakable.

Calista turned, water cascading off her like silver ribbons, and moved toward the steps.

"Calista…" His voice cracked behind her, hoarse with emotion. "Wait."

But she didn't stop.

She climbed out, her movements swift, the moment unravelling with each step. She seized a towel and wrapped it around herself like armour—barrier and boundary in one. Her back to him, but her posture said it all: don't follow.

"I have to go. Sorry, Nickolas."

And then she fled, bare feet slapping against stone, vanishing into the house before he could speak again.

She was gone.

Nickolas dragged a hand through his wet hair, the sting of chlorine doing nothing to cut through the haze she'd left behind. Her words still echoed—sharp and soft all at once—like a bell tolling just beneath his ribs.

I don't do this… I've never had a lover… I'm sorry.

Sorry?

He stared at the water, at the ripples where she'd been, the heat of her still lingering on his skin. Something shifted inside him—something he couldn't quite name. Not lust. Not anymore.

Calista—so fearless, so damn alive—had never been touched like that before. Never given herself to anyone. And she'd trusted him enough to get that close.

He swore, quiet and low. Not from frustration—but something closer to reverence. And guilt.

He hadn't known. Couldn't have. The way she kissed, the way she met his gaze without flinching—it hadn't occurred to him she was carrying something so rare. So unspoken. So sacred.

And now?

Now she probably thought he was just another man waiting to collect a conquest and move on.

The worst part? She might be right.

Because he didn't do forever. He didn't do promises or fairy tale endings. That wasn't who he was. He liked his life clean, uncomplicated. Temporary.

But Chloe had changed that. She was a commitment—one he hadn't chosen, but one he'd embraced without question. His daughter. His responsibility. His softest point.

And he loved her.

So maybe that meant he was capable of more than he thought.

But Calista… Calista wasn't a responsibility. She wasn't a mistake he had to fix or a loose end he needed to manage.

She was a choice.

And if she ever gave herself to someone, it should be someone who could cherish her. Steady her. Stay.

Someone like Henry.

Nickolas exhaled harshly, his jaw tight.

She deserved poetry. Loyalty. Certainty.

And him?

He was chaos with a pretty smile.

God, he wanted her. More than he'd wanted anything in his life.

But he might not be the man she needed.

He was only the one she almost chose.

Chapter Seventeen

Calista got back to her room shaking.

Her hand fumbled with the doorknob, and once the door shut behind her, she leaned against it like it might be the only thing keeping her upright. Her breath came in shallow gasps, her pulse thundering in her ears.

What just happened?

No, seriously—what nearly happened?

She stared at her reflection in the mirror above the dresser. Her cheeks were flushed, eyes wide, lips still swollen from his kiss. Water clung to her skin like a ghost, reminding her—taunting her.

You nearly made love to a man for the first time… in a pool.

A strangled sound escaped her throat. Not a laugh, not a sob—something in between.

"What is wrong with you?" she whispered, dragging both hands through her wet hair.

Not just a man. Nickolas.

Nickolas, who changed women like he changed his clothes. Who smiled with that lazy charm and made it look real—even when it never was. Who walked away from her sister years ago without looking back, leaving her with a child and a long list of reasons not to trust him.

In the pool, she'd all but melted in his hands.

She paced the room, robe clinging to her damp skin, her legs still trembling. Her body ached in places she hadn't even known could ache. Every nerve ending still sang with the memory of his touch.

But it wasn't just physical.

That's what scared her the most.

Because there'd been a moment—just a flicker—where she looked into his eyes and saw something that felt true. Like maybe he wanted her not just for the night, but for something… more.

And that was the most dangerous lie of all.

She stopped pacing, stared down at the floor, and swallowed hard.

She couldn't be another notch on his bedpost. Another pretty distraction. Another story he'd forget by next week.

She wouldn't survive it.

Calista woke the next morning with the weight of too many unsaid things pressing heavily on her chest. The kiss in the pool—the almost—still burned beneath her skin like a fever that refused to break. She needed to put it behind her. Chloe was the reason she was here. Chloe, who had just found her father. That was where her focus needed to be.

And that, she told herself as she pulled her hair into a loose ponytail and avoided her reflection in the mirror, was for the best.

Nickolas didn't mention it either. Not a glance. Not a single accidental brush of his hand. Their conversations were polite, even warm at times, but a quiet, careful civility had replaced the tenderness that had once hummed between them.

Cassia noticed.

She tilted her head one morning as they sat in the garden, sipping iced coffee under the shade of a lemon tree. "So… something weird is going on between you and my brother."

Calista's heart skipped. She forced a faint smile. "Define weird."

"You were all over each other three days ago," Cassia said, lifting her brows. "Now you're barely making eye contact. He's acting like he's tiptoeing through a minefield, and you treat him like he's just another houseguest—not the guy you were making goo-goo eyes at not so long ago."

Calista let out a soft laugh. "That's ridiculous."

Cassia stared at her. "You're not denying it very hard."

Calista took a long sip of her drink, then set it down. "Whatever was happening… it's better this way. Nickolas needs to focus on Chloe."

And he was. Because she made sure of it.

Every morning, Calista stepped back, gently nudging Chloe toward her father with subtle encouragements and soft reassurances. Art lessons in the sunroom. Walks through the vineyards. Quiet afternoons curled up with books in the library. At first, Chloe had clung to Calista's hand, glancing at her as if for permission. But slowly—beautifully— she began to let go.

Soon, she was spending long stretches of time alone with Nickolas, her laughter echoing down corridors Calista hadn't dared to walk before. Each afternoon, Chloe would rush back to her, eyes bright, voice tumbling with excitement as she recounted every detail—how her daddy let her braid his hair—badly, how he'd read her favourite story in silly voices, how he'd pretended to be a clumsy pirate just to make her laugh.

Calista knew then, without a shadow of doubt—Chloe already loved her father with the full, open heart only a child could give.

And Nickolas—he surprised her. He was good with her. Not just present but engaged. Intentional. There was no awkwardness to him, no fumbling attempts at connection. He listened—really listened—when Chloe spoke. He met her energy with humour, her emotions with patience. He laughed at her impressions, even the ones that skewered him with comical accuracy. When she missed the canvas, he let her paint directly on his shirt and wore the abstract smudges like medals of honour.

And from a distance, Calista watched. Smiling. Proud. But aching.

Because every laugh that echoed between them, every small triumph and growing bond, came with a bittersweet twist in her chest. She had wanted this for Chloe— fought for it, even—but she hadn't anticipated how much it would hurt.

Not because she felt excluded. But because it was everything she'd ever wanted, and none of it was hers.

Not really.

And as she stood on the outside of something so beautiful, Calista knew she would never forget these days. Or the quiet, aching truth they revealed.

She had fallen for him.

And that was the one thing she knew would only lead to heartache.

She kept mostly to herself, or spent time with Cassia, whose sharp wit and probing eyes made her both laugh and squirm. But at night, when the house was quiet, and no one was watching, she let herself remember.

The pool. His hands on her waist, her thighs, the way he'd cradled her cheek with such unexpected tenderness. The way he'd whispered her name like it meant something.

And then she'd remember the next morning. His expression—cool, controlled, distant. As though he'd packed away the memory into some quiet corner of his mind and turned the key for good.

It was for the best.

It had to be.

She couldn't fall for a man who lived on the other side of the world. She couldn't let herself become another brief chapter in the long story of Nickolas Drakos's charm. Another woman dazzled, then discarded, once the fantasy gave way to reality.

But none of that stopped the ache in her chest when she heard his laughter echo down the corridor.

None of it stopped the flutter in her stomach when he looked her way during dinner.

And none of it silenced the truth she whispered to herself in the dark when the world was still.

She was already in love with him.

And that was the most dangerous truth of all.

Nickolas's mother was another element in the equation—a thorn wrapped in silk.

Eleni Drakos was never openly hostile, not in a way anyone could accuse. But her words came laced with barbed sweetness, her smiles edged in disdain. Snide remarks delivered with perfect poise. Compliments so carefully constructed they unravelled into insults by dessert.

Dinner became a daily exercise in composure. Calista sat through courses of veiled judgment, hands steady, smile pleasant. She didn't flinch when Eleni praised the staff for their discretion— "So important, especially with unfamiliar guests around." She didn't react when Eleni marvelled at how quickly "some women" became comfortable in someone else's home. She kept her head high when Eleni mentioned family lineage and European etiquette as if Calista had grown up in a barn.

But she didn't allow Eleni to walk all over her, either.

Her responses were always gracious, always calm—but never submissive. When Eleni made a thinly veiled jab about "those who chase security where they can find it," Calista simply lifted her glass and replied, "True security comes from within. Some people spend their whole lives chasing it through money and titles, and still never feel safe."

Cassia nearly choked on her wine.

Nickolas, seated at the head of the table, went still. He didn't look at her, but Calista could feel the smirk tug at the corner of his mouth. Sense the glint of amusement—and admiration—in his peripheral gaze.

Eleni didn't flinch. Her expression remained pristine, untouched, as she lifted her champagne flute with a deliberate grace. "How poetic," she murmured coolly.

Calista met her gaze and smiled sweetly. "Thank you. I read it in a fortune cookie."

After that, dinner passed in a tense sort of peace. Eleni quieted, at least for the moment, and Nickolas seemed…conflicted. His silence wasn't cold, but contemplative. He caught Calista's eye once when Chloe made a joke about octopus tentacles and she laughed, full and unguarded. His gaze lingered, unreadable.

But Calista knew better than to hope.

Because no matter how many stolen glances or tense silences hung between them, there was a war playing out beneath the surface. Not just between them—but around them. Between her past and his future. Between the life she knew, and the world she was now orbiting on borrowed time.

And Eleni Drakos, polished and polite as she was, had made it very clear—

Calista didn't belong.

Nickolas missed Calista. She avoided him now, always careful to keep Chloe between them like a buffer.

It frustrated him more than he cared to admit.

He knew he shouldn't want her. He told himself that often. But he did—more than he'd ever wanted anything. And that, in itself, was disarming.

Nickolas Drakos didn't chase. He didn't have to. Women came easily—too easily. But with Calista, it was different. She didn't fall for the charm, didn't lean into the pull between them. Instead, she resisted it. Resisted him.

And still, he wanted her.

It wasn't just her beauty, though that alone was enough to unsteady him. It was her quiet strength, the grace with which she navigated every challenge—especially his mother's veiled barbs. Calista met them all with composed politeness, never rising to the bait. It stunned him. Moved him. He was in awe of her.

He cherished every moment with Chloe—those hours were fast becoming the best of his life—but it was the times the three of them were together that undid him completely.

In those moments, it felt like something real was within reach. A future he'd never let himself imagine.

And Calista—

She was at the heart of it.

It had been a week since the kiss in the pool, and the memory still haunted him. It lingered in his mind like the echo of a song—her soft gasp against his lips, the silk of her skin beneath his hands. He could still feel her in his arms. And he wanted to feel it again—desperately.

But Calista had drawn a line. And Nickolas, for once, didn't know how to cross it without pushing her further away.

At dinner that evening, the conversation drifted around the table—wine, weather, vineyard yields—until Cassia casually asked, "You're going to that charity gala on Saturday, aren't you, Nickolas?"

He looked up from his plate, his instinctive answer forming on his lips. "I—"

"You should take Calista," Cassia said, too casually to be innocent. A sly smile tugged at the corner of her mouth.

Across the table, Eleni's fork froze mid-air. Her eyes narrowed just slightly, but her voice remained smooth. "I don't think that would be… appropriate."

"Why not?" Cassia asked, feigning surprise. "She's beautiful, intelligent, and—let's be honest—a vast improvement over the usual socialites you drag to those things."

Nickolas's gaze shifted to Calista. She didn't react. Her eyes stayed fixed on her plate, cutting her food with careful precision. Poised. Controlled. But he noticed the slight tension in her shoulders.

Before he could think better of it, the words slipped out. "I actually think that's a good idea."

Eleni's lips pressed into a fine line. "Oh, I don't," she said, ice in her tone.

Cassia leaned back in her chair; one brow arched with theatrical innocence. "Why not? It's just a gala, not a marriage proposal. It might even be… fun."

"Cassia," Eleni snapped, her voice low but laced with steel. "That's enough."

Nickolas's jaw tightened. He turned to his mother, calm but firm. "With all due respect, Mother, the invitation is mine to offer."

The air at the table stilled. Even the clink of cutlery stopped. Calista finally lifted her gaze, her expression composed but inscrutable, her eyes flicking between Eleni and Nickolas.

Nickolas looked at her directly now, his voice softer. "Will you come with me, Calista?"

She hesitated. "Oh… I don't know. I'm not sure I have anything suitable to wear."

Cassia jumped in with a grin. "That's not a problem. I have at least three gowns that would look better on you than they ever did on me."

Calista gave her a startled look, touched but unsure.

Eleni set down her glass with a delicate clink. "You don't have to push her, Cassia. She wouldn't exactly fit in."

Silence.

Calista's spine straightened slightly, her face remaining neutral. "Then it's a good thing I'm not trying to."

Nickolas turned his head sharply toward his mother, his eyes hardening. But before he could speak, Cassia cut in breezily, "Excellent. It's settled then. We'll pick a dress tomorrow."

And just like that, battle lines were drawn—with Calista, poised and quiet, sitting in the eye of the storm.

Chapter Eighteen

The bedroom was awash in soft afternoon light, filtered through gauzy curtains that fluttered in the breeze. A sea of cosmetic brushes, jewellery boxes, and hairpins covered the vanity, while a rich emerald gown lay draped over the edge of the bed like spilled jewels.

Calista stood in the centre of it all, arms folded over her camisole-clad chest, her bare feet curling into the plush rug. "I still think this is excessive," she murmured, watching as Cassia uncapped a lip gloss with clinical precision.

Cassia arched a brow. "It's a charity gala, not a PTA meeting. And you're going to look like a goddess."

Calista snorted. "I'm not looking to impress anyone."

"Sure," Cassia said with a knowing smile. "You're just going to wear a floor-length emerald gown with a thigh-high slit and stilettos for yourself."

"I am." Calista held her chin high. "Nickolas isn't even going to notice. He is used to much more beautiful women than me."

"Mommy, you're sparkly," Chloe said from her nest of pillows on the bed. Her curls bounced as she clutched her new elephant that Nickolas had given her, eyes bright. "You gonna be a princess."

Calista softened instantly. She walked over and kissed her daughter's forehead. "Only if you say so, sweetheart."

Cassia grinned from behind the vanity. "Come sit. Time for the magic touch."

Reluctantly, Calista obeyed, perching on the stool as Cassia tied a silk robe over her shoulders and assessed her face like an artist before a canvas.

"You don't have to do all this," Calista said quietly, eyes drifting to the mirror.

"I want to," Cassia replied, dabbing foundation onto the back of her hand. "Besides, it's been a while since I got to glam someone up who isn't a bridesmaid or an influencer."

As Cassia worked—sweeping soft gold across Calista's eyelids, coaxing colour into her cheeks, defining her eyes with smoky liner—Calista stared at her reflection. It felt like watching someone else appear, someone more confident, more composed. Someone who might not break at the sight of Nickolas Drakos in a tux.

Not that she cared if he looked.

Not that she wanted him to.

Cassia's voice broke through her thoughts. "You should wear this colour more often. It brings out your eyes."

"It's your dress," Calista said.

"And now it's your dress," Cassia corrected. "At least for tonight."

The gown had a cinched waist adorned with a scattering of diamond-like gems that caught the light when she moved, and the slit—well, the slit was dramatic. Scandalous, even. Calista still wasn't sure she could walk without tripping or blushing.

Cassia stepped back to admire her work. "Okay, hair next."

While Chloe hummed softly from the bed, Cassia gathered Calista's thick black waves, twisting them into an elegant chignon with soft strands left loose to frame her face. Her fingers were quick but gentle, and every so often she'd glance at Calista in the mirror.

"You're thinking about him," Cassia said, quiet and without judgment.

Calista stiffened. "I'm not."

"You are."

"I don't care if he notices."

"Of course not."

Calista met her gaze. "I'm serious. I'm not dressing up for him. I just—I want to feel good tonight. For myself. I've never been to something like this before."

Cassia gave a small nod, her voice softening. "I know and I believe you. But if he happens to look at you and forgets how to breathe, well… that's just a bonus."

Calista looked down, brushing a fingertip over the gemmed waistline of the gown. "He won't even notice."

Cassia smiled faintly. "Oh, he'll notice."

When they were finally finished, Cassia handed her the silver stilettos. Calista stepped into them gingerly, balancing on unfamiliar height.

Chloe gasped in delight. "Mommy, you look like magic."

Calista turned toward the mirror—and for a second, she didn't recognise the woman staring back.

Not tired. Not afraid. Not trying to stay invisible.

She looked… radiant. Powerful. Like a woman who might be able to walk into a room and hold her own—even with Nickolas Drakos there.

She swallowed hard.

"I don't care if he likes this," she whispered to no one in particular. "I'm doing it for me."

Cassia walked over and slipped a pair of diamond stud earrings into her hands. "Then wear these. Just in case you don't care a little too loudly."

Calista laughed, the sound nervous and fragile—but real.

She clipped the earrings on.

And let herself hope—just a little—that he would look.

Nickolas stood at the base of the grand staircase, his phone idle in his hand, forgotten. He was dressed in a tailored black tuxedo, the crisp white of his shirt stark against the deep tan of his skin, the slight scruff along his jaw giving him an edge no designer could refine away.

He'd been checking the time, waiting to see Calista. His yacht was at the dock waiting. Then he heard a noise.

He looked up.

And forgot how to breathe.

Calista descended slowly, one hand light on the banister, the emerald-green gown clinging to her curves like it had been made for her. The slit revealed one toned leg with every graceful step, and the way the gem-studded waist shimmered under the chandelier lighting made her look like a woman pulled from a dream. Her dark hair had been swept up, elegant and understated, and her makeup only enhanced the striking natural beauty he could never quite forget.

She paused halfway down, adjusting slightly as her heel caught on the carpet. His hand was at the rail instantly—instinct—but she steadied herself without him.

"Careful," he said, his voice deeper than usual. Gravelly. Unsteady.

She glanced down at him, that soft smile playing on her lips. "I'm not made of glass, Nickolas."

No. She wasn't. She was fire and steel under all that grace. And it was that strength— more than the gown, the heels, the polished elegance—that made it hard to look away.

"I didn't realise Cassia was loaning out gowns fit for royalty," Nickolas said, his voice low, his mouth suddenly dry as she reached the final step.

Calista gave a soft laugh, adjusting the delicate silver clutch in her hand. "It's just a dress."

He looked at her—really looked. "Not on you."

Her gaze faltered, something unreadable flickering behind her eyes. She turned slightly, fingers brushing the side of her neck in a nervous gesture. "I told her it was too much."

"It's not," he said quietly, like a confession. "It's perfect."

She hesitated, her eyes dropping for a second before meeting his again. "I just… I hope I don't embarrass you. This world of yours—this is all new to me."

His jaw tightened slightly. "How could you embarrass me looking like that?" His gaze swept over her slowly, reverently. "Calista, you'll stop the room."

She laughed again, but it was quieter this time. Almost shy.

He offered his arm, steady and sure. "Then let's make an entrance."

She took it. Lightly. Carefully. As if it didn't mean anything. But it did.

To him, it meant everything.

As they slid into the waiting car, silence settled between them—not awkward, just charged. Her perfume—faint jasmine, with something warmer beneath—wrapped around him, tightening the invisible thread that had been pulling him toward her since the day they met.

By the time they stepped onto the private dock, where his yacht shimmered under the harbour lights like something out of a dream, Nickolas knew he was already in too deep.

And the most dangerous part?

She wasn't even trying.

Calista paused at the edge of the dock, her breath catching as her eyes swept over the sleek, stunning lines of the yacht. It gleamed under the harbour lights, all white curves and polished steel, like something out of a dream.

She turned to him, awed. "That's yours?"

Nickolas gave a faint smile. "She's mine. Althea."

Calista blinked, laughing softly. "It's… incredible. I've never even seen a yacht this beautiful."

He looked at her, not the boat. "You're easily the more breathtaking of the two tonight."

Her cheeks flushed, but she turned her attention back to the vessel. "You keep saying things like that and I might start to believe you."

He didn't answer. Not with words, anyway.

They boarded the yacht for the short cruise to the mainland, where a waiting limousine swept them toward the gala. Calista sat quietly beside him, watching the glittering coastline slide by. His presence filled the space—tall, still, entirely composed—but she could feel the energy between them crackling like static.

When they arrived at the gala, the car barely slowed before she heard them.

Voices. Cameras clicking. A sudden eruption of flashing lights like fireworks as the limousine door opened.

She stiffened, caught off guard by the chaos. "Are they—are they waiting for you?"

"Just stay close," he murmured, sliding out and turning to offer his hand.

She took it, stepping down. The moment she did, the shouting intensified.

"Nickolas!"

"Mr. Drakos—this way!"

"Who is she?"

"Smile for us!"

Calista froze for half a second, stunned by the frenzy. The bulbs strobed in her eyes, disorienting, and her fingers tightened slightly around his.

He leaned down, his mouth brushing her ear. "Just ignore them," he whispered, low and smooth.

It looked intimate. Too intimate. Like a secret meant for her alone.

The photographers caught it instantly.

Her breath caught. She felt it—the whisper, the nearness, the heat of him—and she wondered.

Had he done that on purpose?

Nickolas straightened, face calm, hand still wrapped around hers as they moved up the carpeted steps. She tried to focus, to block it all out, but her mind wouldn't stop turning.

He told her to ignore them.

But how was she supposed to ignore him?

The heavy glass doors parted ahead of them, and they stepped into a world that felt like another realm entirely.

Chapter Nineteen

Golden light spilled from towering crystal chandeliers, casting a warm, shimmering glow across the grand ballroom. The ceilings soared high above, painted with frescoes, and the marble floors gleamed beneath their feet. Waiters in white jackets glided through the crowd with silver trays, the air alive with the clink of champagne flutes and the quiet hum of string music drifting from a live quartet near the terrace.

Calista stopped just inside the entrance, her breath stolen.

It wasn't just beautiful—it was overwhelming. Like walking into a modern fairy tale.

Nickolas leaned close. "Breathe."

She blinked up at him, almost laughing at herself. "I'm trying."

He guided her forward gently. She felt the weight of attention shift as they moved. Heads turned. Faces watched. And though no one said it aloud, she knew what they were wondering.

Who is she?

It wasn't just the gown or the heels or the way her hair had been swept up with Cassia's practiced hands. It was the man beside her. Nickolas Drakos didn't bring unknown women to events like this—certainly not as his date. His companions were usually models, heiresses, women whose names already echoed through the ballroom long before they entered it.

Yet here he was, with his hand resting at the small of Calista's back like he couldn't quite bring himself to let go.

She swallowed, lifting her chin, even as nerves danced like butterflies beneath her skin.

"Are they all like this?" she murmured as they passed under a floral arch into the reception hall, her voice quieter than she intended.

He glanced down at her. "Some are worse."

A shaky laugh slipped from her lips. "I can't tell if I'm Cinderella or a contestant on The Bachelor."

A faint smile tugged at his mouth, but his eyes remained unreadable. "You're neither," he said. "You're Calista."

She looked up at him, startled by the quiet certainty in those words.

And just like that, the noise around them dimmed. The crush of chandeliers and diamonds, the hush of whispered speculation—it all fell back. Not because the room was any less intimidating, but because he was grounding her. Steady. Silent. Present.

Still, as they were led to a table with his name etched in gold, a small voice stirred inside her—quiet, uncertain.

Did the fairytale ever end well…for the girl who didn't belong?

And what happened, she wondered, when midnight inevitably came?

Their table was near the centre of the ballroom, set under a cascade of suspended orchids and a slow-turning crystal chandelier. Every plate gleamed, every napkin folded with military precision. Place cards bore names Calista recognised from headlines and magazine covers, names that moved money and influence like chess pieces on a global board.

Nickolas pulled out her chair, and she murmured a thank you before smoothing her gown and sitting down.

To her left sat an older gentleman with a distinguished silver beard and eyes that twinkled with mischief, his elegant wife beside him in a sapphire silk gown. On her right—Nickolas, watchful and composed. Across the table, two men in tuxedos appraised her with a little too much interest.

Calista met their glances with polite indifference, then deliberately turned her body toward the elderly couple.

"Calista, may I introduce Lord and Lady Ashcombe," Nickolas said smoothly.

"Please, call me Richard," the gentleman said, extending a warm hand. "And this is Eleanor. We're thrilled to meet you. Nickolas never brings anyone we actually want to talk to."

Eleanor chuckled. "It's true. Last time it was a Russian heiress who thought Oxford was a brand of shoe."

Calista laughed lightly, grateful for their warmth. "Well, I can promise I've never owned Oxford shoes, but I did read Middlemarch in college. Does that count?"

"Oh, a reader," Eleanor said approvingly, her eyes lighting up. "You'll have to join our literary dinner next season. Richard never finishes the books, but he comes for the wine."

"Wine's the best part of War and Peace," Richard quipped.

Nickolas watched the exchange in silence, his mouth curved faintly, but his gaze occasionally slid across the table—sharp, dark, and assessing. One of the men across from them—a hedge fund magnate with a grin that didn't reach his eyes—leaned a little too far forward during dessert.

"You're not in fashion?" he asked, eyeing Calista's dress with deliberate slowness. "Because you wear it like a campaign."

"I work in education," Calista said coolly, not flinching.

"Ah," the second man said, his eyes dragging lower than they should. "Well, beauty and brains. Dangerous combination."

Nickolas's hand tightened slightly around the stem of his wine glass. His voice was soft when he spoke, but lethal.

"She's not on the market, gentlemen."

The men stilled, taken aback.

Calista said nothing, but she felt the subtle shift in his posture—the protective lean of his body, the quiet possessiveness in his tone. It shouldn't have thrilled her. But it did.

Lady Ashcombe leaned in, smiling gently. "Ignore them, dear. Some men think charm is measured in decimal points."

Calista smiled in return. "I think they just assume I didn't come with Nickolas."

"Oh, they know," Eleanor said knowingly, "but some men always test fences that aren't theirs."

Nickolas's gaze flicked to her then, a flare of something darker in his eyes before he looked away again, jaw tight.

The first part of the evening passed with laughter and easy conversation. Calista charmed the Ashcombe's without effort, her warmth and wit a gentle contrast to the curated sharpness of so many in the room. But she never quite relaxed. Not with the weight of Nickolas's presence beside her.

Not with the memory of his voice in her ear, low and protective.

Not with the flicker in his eyes when he looked at her like she was his—and didn't know how to stop.

After dinner, the ballroom had slipped into a more relaxed rhythm, the orchestra shifting from sweeping overtures to a sultry waltz. Glasses clinked. Laughter bloomed in pockets across the floor. Calista had just finished a soft exchange with Eleanor when a tall man in a charcoal tuxedo approached their table.

"Nickolas," the man greeted smoothly, holding out a hand. "It's been too long."

Nickolas stood to greet him, his smile polite but reserved. "Luca. I thought I saw your name on the donor list."

"I never miss the chance to network over caviar," Luca said with a grin. He looked to be in his early thirties, handsome in a sharp, polished way, his smile easy. His eyes drifted to Calista with interest. "And you must be the reason every head turned when you entered."

Calista stood slowly, caught off guard but graceful. "Calista. It's lovely to meet you."

"Luca Moretti," he said, offering her his hand. "Drakos mentioned he was bringing a guest, but he undersold it. You're a vision."

Nickolas's jaw ticked. "Luca works in international real estate. Primarily in Monaco and the south of France."

"Mostly admiring views," Luca said, eyes still on Calista. "Speaking of—may I steal you for a dance?"

Calista blinked, then glanced instinctively at Nickolas.

He didn't say a word. Didn't move. His expression didn't shift—but the air around him did. Tighter. Sharper.

Calista hesitated just a second longer than polite before giving Luca a smile. "I'd like that."

Luca held out his hand, and she took it.

Nickolas sat down without a word, but his gaze never left the floor.

They moved to the centre, where the music had softened into a moody, elegant sway. Calista followed Luca's lead easily, her movements fluid, her emerald gown catching the light with every turn. She laughed at something Luca said, and it made Nickolas's chest constrict.

He barely heard Lady Ashcombe murmuring something about "young men and their wandering eyes." He only watched the way Calista tilted her head back slightly when she smiled. The way her hand rested lightly on Luca's shoulder. The way the world seemed to pay attention to her now—and so did he, like a man unable to help himself.

She wasn't his.

He'd told himself that.

And yet, watching her in another man's arms—no matter how innocent the dance—it lit something dangerous in him.

Something possessive.

And deeply, deeply unwelcome.

Nickolas hadn't touched his wine since she walked onto the dance floor.

The first dance was tolerable. Barely.

But when the orchestra shifted to a more playful rhythm and Luca—ever bold—slid his hand just a touch lower on Calista's back and leaned in, to whisper something that made her laugh again, Nickolas's grip on the stem of his glass tightened.

The second dance began without Luca so much as looking back for permission.

Across the table, Lady Ashcombe leaned in, her pearl earrings swaying gently. "My dear," she said in that refined drawl honed over decades of subtle social combat, "I do believe you've lost your date."

Nickolas didn't smile. "She's not my date."

"Hmm," Lady Ashcombe hummed, sipping her champagne with deliberate grace. "That's certainly not how it looked when you whispered in her ear at the entrance. The photographers were practically salivating."

Nickolas's jaw flexed. He hadn't meant to. But the moment she descended the stairs, he hadn't been thinking clearly.

Richard gave a little laugh beside his wife. "Oh, I saw that, too. Very Mr. Darcy at the ball if I may."

Nickolas didn't take his eyes off the floor. Calista's dress shimmered like a forest under moonlight. Her head tilted toward Luca again, smiling at something he said.

"She's a natural," Lady Ashcombe murmured, softer now. "You may want to reconsider letting someone else notice it before you do."

Nickolas rose from his chair, sharp and silent.

"Excuse me," he said, his voice low. Controlled. But Lady Ashcombe smiled as if she'd won something.

He stepped away from the table, moving along the edge of the dance floor, not rushing but unmistakably heading in one direction.

Chapter Twenty

Calista had just turned toward Luca, laughing again as they pivoted—and then she saw Nickolas standing just beyond the crowd, watching her with that unreadable intensity she was beginning to understand far too well.

Her smile faltered. Her body, instinctively, adjusted—her posture straightened, her touch with Luca lightened.

Nickolas extended a hand toward her.

A silent invitation.

Or maybe a warning.

She hesitated. Then gently stepped back from Luca.

"I think I need a break," she said, her voice light but her pulse fluttering as she walked toward Nickolas, every step as deliberate as his gaze.

As Calista turned to walk away, Luca caught her wrist gently, his smile playfully wicked.

"If Nickolas doesn't live up to your expectations…" he said, lowering his voice just enough to graze her nerves, "give me a call."

Her breath caught. A flush crept over her cheeks—not from attraction, but from the audacity of it. She gave a tight, polite smile and slipped from his grasp without a word.

Nickolas waited at the edge of the dance floor, hand extended. Without a glance back, she stepped into his orbit. His hand found the small of her back. Warm. Possessive. Tense.

They moved together in time with the music, but the air between them crackled with something far less graceful.

"What did Luca say?" Nickolas asked quietly, his lips near her ear, his jaw set like stone.

She looked up at him, defiant. "Does it matter?"

"It does."

Her eyes narrowed, then flicked away. "He said… if Nickolas doesn't live up to your expectations, I should give him a call."

Nickolas didn't speak for a moment. But his hand tightened ever so slightly on her waist, and the muscle in his jaw ticked.

Her brow arched. "I don't know why you look so put out. We're not a couple."

His eyes met hers—dark, searching. "No," he said slowly, voice low. "We're not."

But the way he held her said otherwise. The way his hand refused to drift away. The way his breath slowed when she met his gaze and didn't look away.

The orchestra swelled around them. Glittering chandeliers spilled golden light over her hair. His thumb brushed the curve of her spine, just once.

Calista swallowed.

They weren't a couple.

But the space between them was dangerously thin—and getting thinner by the second.

They stayed on the dance floor for more than one dance.

At first, Calista kept a careful inch between them, maintaining a fragile boundary—one he respected, though barely. But as the music shifted into something slower, warmer, she found herself easing closer. His hand rested at her waist, firm but not forceful, and his other hand held hers in a way that made her feel… wanted. Not claimed. Not caged. Just wanted.

It was disarming.

Nickolas didn't speak again. He simply moved with her, guiding her effortlessly across the polished floor, his gaze fixed on hers in the dim golden light. And every so often, his fingers would shift slightly on her back—as if memorising the shape of her.

Her breath grew shallow. Her guard slipped, bit by bit, like silk unravelling.

She let her palm rest more fully in his. Her body relaxed into his hold.

Her head tilted toward him—almost without thought—and her cheek brushed the crisp lapel of his tailored jacket. The scent of his cologne enveloped her again: cedar, spice, and something unmistakably, maddeningly him.

"Thank you for bringing me," she murmured, her voice softer than the music. "I've had a wonderful time."

He didn't respond right away.

Instead, he leaned in, his breath grazing the shell of her ear, warm and unguarded.

"So have I," he said at last, the words gravel rough.

Her pulse stuttered. Her lashes fluttered, but she didn't step back.

The violins swelled around them, distant and dreamy, as his fingers trailed the seam of her gown at her lower back. Every movement—every shift in his hold—felt like a question neither of them dared ask aloud.

She should have moved away. Redrawn the lines.

But tonight, in the golden hush of chandeliers and champagne laughter, she let the world fall away. Let herself melt into him. Let herself be something she'd forbidden for so long—

His.

Just for this moment.

And even if the spell broke by morning, she wanted to remember the way it felt to belong somewhere.

To Nickolas.

Even if it wasn't forever.

They had just stepped off the dance floor, her hand still resting lightly against his chest as they paused near the shadowed edge of the ballroom. Her cheeks were flushed from dancing, her eyes bright with something unguarded—something that made it hard for him to think.

She looked up at him, smiling softly, and for a moment—just one—everything else fell away: the music, the guests, the rules she had clung to so tightly.

God, he wanted to kiss her.

Wanted to forget every reason he shouldn't and close the space between them. Right there. In full view of this glittering, opulent room. He'd never been the man to kiss women in public—but he wanted to now.

To hell with the consequences.

He leaned in, just slightly, his hand brushing hers—

"So, this is the flavour of the month," a voice cut through the moment, velvet-edged with venom.

Nickolas stilled, his jaw tightening as he turned.

"Amalia," he said, voice low and even.

She stood poised in all her icy elegance—polished, precise, a cobra in couture. Her lips were curved in a mimicry of a smile, but her eyes were fixed on Calista with barely concealed disdain.

She didn't even look at him.

She stepped up to Calista, a venomous smile curving her lips.

"Run now," she said softly, just loud enough to carry. "While you still can."

Calista's smile froze—but only for a breath. Then she straightened, shoulders back, chin high. When she spoke, her voice was cool silk lined with steel.

"Why? Because you regret not having the courage to?"

Amalia's smile faltered.

Calista leaned in just enough, her voice soft but razor-edged. "If you truly believed he was dangerous, you'd be warning him about me. Not the other way around."

There was a beat of stunned silence.

Amalia's eyes narrowed, her jaw tightening as if she were biting back something bitter. Then, with a sharp huff, she turned on her heel—retreating like smoke, furious but smart enough not to make it worse.

Nickolas stood silent beside Calista, but when she glanced up at him, something in his gaze had shifted. The heat was still there—but now it was laced with something steadier.

Respect. Admiration. Maybe even awe.

And for the first time all night, he didn't just want her.

He wanted everyone to know she was his.

Calista gave him a sweet, innocent smile—like she hadn't just verbally undressed a viper in heels.

That did it.

He leaned in, hand gentle at the small of her back, and kissed her. Soft. Certain. Possessive.

And for a breathless second, the world tilted. Not from surprise, but from the weight of how much she wanted it. Wanted him.

He didn't care that they were in a ballroom filled with hundreds of people.

Let them all see.

Let them know.

When he finally pulled back, Calista's breath caught. Her cheeks flushed as the noise of the room came rushing back in. She blinked, suddenly aware of the crowd, of the stares.

But Nickolas didn't move away.

His hand remained at the small of her back like a silent vow, his gaze steady—anchoring her.

"I… I'll be right back," she murmured, breathless.

He let her go, reluctantly, his fingers trailing after her as if unwilling to break the contact.

In the powder room, Calista leaned over the marble sink, dabbing at her lipstick with a trembling hand. The adrenaline was still fizzing through her veins. She hadn't meant to say it like that. But she had. And she'd meant every word.

The door creaked open behind her.

"Calista?"

She turned.

Lady Ashcombe swept in like the hush before a storm—elegant, composed, her expression unreadable but not unkind. There was wisdom in her eyes, the kind carved from years in high society trenches.

"I saw Amalia speak to you," she said quietly, her voice neither accusatory nor consoling—just… aware. "Whatever you said must've hit a nerve. She looked ready to combust."

Calista offered a slow smile, cool and unrepentant. "I don't do well with bullies."

Lady Ashcombe let out a quiet, knowing chuckle as she stepped closer. "No, I rather suspected you didn't," she murmured. Her head tilted slightly. "And I saw Nickolas… stake his claim."

Calista winced, her cheeks flushing. "Oh dear. You saw that."

"I did," Lady Ashcombe replied, her eyes twinkling. "So did half the ballroom. Possibly the orchestra too."

Calista lowered her gaze to the sink, her voice softer, more vulnerable. "I think I've been living a little too… carefully."

Lady Ashcombe's smile deepened, tempered with understanding. "We only get one life, my dear. The trick is to live it fully—and without apology."

The orchestra had just begun a new piece when Calista re-entered the ballroom.

Her smile arrived before she did—warm, poised, luminous. It softened the lines of her face, lit her eyes with something unspoken and sure. Heads turned as she passed, drawn not by spectacle but by the quiet confidence that clung to her like silk. She didn't notice them.

Her spine was straight. Her stride unhurried. There was a gleam in her gaze that hadn't been there before—one born not of defiance, but of clarity.

She had made a decision.

Life was unpredictable. Messy. Often cruel around the edges. But it was also fleeting—and she was done living it in half-measures.

Nickolas stood near the edge of the dance floor, speaking with a senator when he caught sight of her—and stopped midsentence.

She looked…

Not just graceful.

Radiant.

As if the moon had stepped into lamplight and dared it to compare.

Something flickered across his face—something sharp, reverent, almost shaken. For a heartbeat, he didn't move. Then, without a word of excuse or a glance back, Nickolas crossed the room with single-minded focus.

He reached her just as she stopped beside their table.

There was no preamble. No explanation. He simply took her hand and led her to the dance floor.

Their final dance.

He held her closer than decorum allowed, his hand splayed at the small of her back, his breath warm against her temple. She didn't protest. Neither did he pretend to care who watched. The world had shrunk to this—her body pressed against his, the silent rhythm between them more intimate than words.

They left soon after.

Chapter Twenty-One

The moment they stepped onto the yacht, the world fell away.

Behind them, city lights shimmered like fallen stars, the harbour water lapping softly against the hull. But Calista saw none of it. Heard none of it.

All she saw was him.

Nickolas—tall, still, and devastating beneath a canopy of midnight sky. The polished teak deck gleamed beneath their feet, but the air between them sparked with something far more dangerous than elegance.

He turned toward her slowly, his expression unreadable, his eyes storm-lit.

"Calista—"

She didn't let him finish.

She didn't need another word. No caveats. No reasons to pause. Life was short, uncertain—and she was done waiting.

She stepped in and kissed him.

Her hands slid up his chest, fingers curling into the lapels of his jacket, her mouth finding his with a certainty that made his breath stutter. For one stunned second, he didn't move.

And then—he did.

Everything broke loose. His arms wrapped around her, hard and fast, pulling her against him as if he'd been holding back for years. The kiss deepened, threaded with hunger and heat and everything they'd tried to deny. Weeks of tension. Nights of wanting. Every stolen glance and unspoken thought collided in that moment.

He backed her gently against the rail, one hand threading into her hair, tilting her head just enough to kiss her deeper. Her clutch slipped from her fingers, thudding softly onto the deck. Neither of them noticed.

He kissed her like a man starved—and she kissed him back like she didn't care if they both burned.

When he finally drew back, their breath mingled in the space between them. Her lips were parted, her eyes dazed. His thumb traced along her cheekbone, reverent.

"I've wanted to do that all night," he said, voice thick. "Hell… longer than that."

Calista swallowed, her voice barely above a whisper. "Then don't stop now."

And in the hush of the night, with the sea rocking gently beneath their feet, he didn't.

He kissed her again—this time slower. Deeper. Like a man giving in.

Nickolas's hands lingered at her waist, his forehead brushing hers. Her lipstick was smudged, her breath shallow, but her gaze—God, her gaze—held something bold. Decided.

Calista laced her fingers with his.

"Maybe," she said softly, "we should go downstairs."

His breath caught.

For a beat, he didn't move—just searched her face as if memorising it. "Calista…"

"I know what I'm saying," she murmured.

His jaw clenched, a visible war between desire and restraint. Still, he didn't let go.

"I don't know what this is," she said. "Maybe it's nothing. Maybe it's everything. But I've spent too long playing it safe. Tonight, I want to take the risk."

His throat worked. His grip on her hand tightened slightly.

"Even if it's just for now?" he asked.

She tilted her head, brushing her fingers over the edge of his jacket. "So what if it is? I'd rather feel something real for a moment… than wonder forever."

That undid him.

The tension in his body gave way to something softer—warmer. The corners of his mouth curved, but his eyes were still full of fire.

"You have no idea," he murmured, voice husky, "what you do to me."

She smiled—genuine, unguarded, just a little breathless.

"Then show me."

And he planned to.

Not in haste. Not in conquest.

But like a man who finally understood he was holding something rare. And meant to savour it.

The cabin door clicked shut behind them, sealing out the night and the world above. The hush of the sea beyond the windows was the only sound, soft, and endless.

Before Nickolas could say a word, Calista turned to him—no hesitation now, no lingering doubt. She stepped into his arms as if they were the only place she'd ever belonged. Her hands slid up his chest, palms flat against his heart, and when she looked up at him, her eyes were lit with something fierce and unguarded.

"I want this," she said, her voice low and steady. "I want you."

Something in him stilled, unravelled, all at once.

His hands framed her face, thumbs brushing her cheekbones. "Calista…"

But whatever he meant to say was lost the moment she rose onto her toes and kissed him—deep, sure, and hungry. He responded with a groan that came from somewhere deep in his chest, pulling her closer, anchoring her against him.

It wasn't gentle.

It wasn't careful.

It was the unravelling of restraint, the shattering of every boundary they'd tried to honour. Weeks of tension came undone in the space between breath and touch—every stolen glance, every unspoken confession, all of it combusting in the fire that now roared between them.

This wasn't the soft brush of a hesitant beginning.

This was hunger. Raw and unfiltered.

This was what happened when longing was finally given permission.

Calista wasn't fragile in his arms. She was wildfire wrapped in silk, sweetness laced with power, a woman who burned and bloomed at once. And Nickolas—he didn't hold back. Not this time. Not when she'd just looked him in the eye and dared him to fall.

He kissed her like he was learning her by heart. Like reverence could be written in skin.

Slowly, deliberately, he undressed her—his fingers sliding beneath fabric with almost painful precision, his mouth trailing behind every inch he revealed.

"You are…" he whispered against her collarbone, "…magnificent."

His voice was hoarse, reverent.

"So beautiful."

She flushed, the colour rising in her cheeks—but she didn't turn away, didn't try to hide. Her gaze held his as she stood before him, bare and unashamed.

Then she moved closer.

She slid his jacket off his shoulders, letting it fall soundlessly to the floor. Her fingers found the first button of his shirt, then the next, parting the fabric one slow breath at a time. With each inch of skin she revealed, she pressed her lips to him—his chest, the centre of his sternum, the edge of his ribs.

He closed his eyes, jaw taut, his hands still resting at her hips. Letting her take the lead, letting her show him this wasn't about dominance or surrender. This was about mutual, molten need.

When his shirt finally joined her dress on the floor, her hands splayed across his chest, her fingers dragging lightly over the warm, smooth plane of him. His body was tense, restrained. But his eyes—they burned.

He cupped her face, tilted her chin, and kissed her again.

Slower this time.

Deeper.

More certain than before.

And when they sank to the bed, it wasn't just heat between them—it was the quiet, breathless realisation that something had shifted. That this wasn't just about desire.

It was the beginning of something neither of them could name—

Something fragile and fierce, trembling just beneath the surface.

It had lived quietly in the spaces between their glances, in the breathless silences, in every restrained touch.

And now, it bloomed—wild and unrepentant—in the dark.

Nickolas worshipped her with his hands and mouth, as though he were discovering a language spoken only in her sighs and gasps. His touch was reverent, unhurried, a slow unravelling of all her defences.

When his thumb rasped over one of her nipples, she cried out, her back arching into him. He caught the sound with his mouth, greedy for every note of it.

His hand slipped between her thighs, fingers parting her gently, exploring her with a hunger sharpened by patience. He touched her like she was sacred—like pleasure was a form of devotion.

When he lowered his head and tasted her, she nearly sobbed.

"You taste," he murmured, voice like gravel and silk, "incredible."

"Nickolas…" Her voice was breathless, trembling. "Please."

He smiled against her, and then he gave her everything.

His tongue teased and stroked until her legs trembled, until her hands gripped the sheets and her head fell back in abandon.

She shattered with his name on her lips, a broken, beautiful cry that he would never forget—

A sound that etched itself into his soul, unforgettable.

He kissed his way back up her body, slow and tender now, like he was memorising every inch of her. Her skin was flushed and dewy, her breath shallow, her limbs boneless from release.

But her eyes—her eyes were wide open, dark with want and wonder.

He hovered over her, brushing a thumb across her cheek.

"Calista," he said softly, his voice unsteady, "I want you. But only if you're sure."

She reached up, framing his face with both hands, her touch steady despite the tremble in her fingers.

"Yes, Nickolas," she whispered. "Please. I want this. I want you."

He nodded, a muscle ticking in his jaw as he positioned himself between her thighs.

And then—slowly, carefully—he began to enter her.

When he met resistance, he paused. His gaze searched hers, a flicker of awe and something like pain in his expression.

"I'll go slow," he murmured, breath catching.

And then, with a tenderness that nearly undid him, he breached her innocence.

She gasped, her nails biting lightly into his back, her body clenching around him as he stilled—waiting, trembling with restraint.

For a moment, the world stopped.

It was just the sound of their breath, the thrum of her heart against his chest, the quiet miracle of something sacred beginning.

He brushed his lips against her temple.

"Tell me if I hurt you."

"You haven't," she whispered, eyes shining. "You've only made me feel… everything."

And so, he began to move—slow, reverent strokes that built a rhythm of intimacy more powerful than anything either of them had ever known.

It wasn't just about pleasure.

It was about letting go.

About surrendering to the ache, they'd both carried in silence.

And with every thrust, every sigh, every whispered name, the distance that had once stretched between them dissolved.

They were no longer two people from different worlds, bound by caution and circumstance.

They became something else.

Something raw.

Something real.

A tangle of heartbeats and hunger, of trust given in trembling silence.

When she finally shattered, it was with his name on her lips—

A breathless, broken prayer that filled the room like music.

He followed moments later, groaning her name as he buried himself deep, his release crashing through him like a wave too long held back.

Every muscle in his body tensed, then gave way to the exquisite unravelling she alone could bring.

For a long time, neither of them moved.

Only the sound of their breathing, the heat of their skin, the slow return to earth after a fall they hadn't known they were ready for.

And in that hush, tangled in sheets and moonlight, they held onto each other—

Not as a mistake. Not as a secret.

But as something they could no longer deny.

Chapter Twenty-Two

The villa was quiet when they returned, the hush of the early morning casting a soft stillness over the marble floors and dimmed lights. Calista slipped off her heels in the foyer with a sigh of relief, but before she could take another step, Nickolas scooped her into his arms.

She gave a breathless laugh, her hands instinctively curling around his neck. "Nickolas—"

"Shh," he murmured, brushing a kiss against her temple. "Let me."

She didn't protest. Not when he carried her down the hallway with such ease, not when he pushed open the door to his room and walked her over the threshold as though it meant something. Maybe it did.

He set her down gently, but before her feet could fully touch the floor, his mouth found hers again—urgent and aching now, without the watchful eyes of the world, without restraint.

Her fingers slid into his hair, pulling him closer as he backed her toward the bed, their kisses growing hungrier, need deepening between them like a current neither of them could resist. His jacket dropped to the floor. Then her dress. Then the last layers between them until there was nothing but skin and heat and the sound of their breathing.

When they came together again, it was different from before.

Slower at first. Softer. Not because she was inexperienced, but because something unspoken had passed between them—something real. She wasn't shy now. She moved with him, responded to him, touched him as though she was beginning to understand what she did to him. And he let her.

He whispered her name over and over, his hands reverent on her body, his lips trailing along her shoulder, her throat, the curve of her breast.

"Calista…" he breathed, voice rough and low. "You undo me."

They moved together in a rhythm that felt inevitable, like the sea meeting the shore— crashing, retreating, coming back again. And when they finally stilled, tangled in the sheets, their bodies slick with sweat, she pressed her cheek to his chest and listened to the strong, steady beat of his heart.

She belonged there.

Even if it couldn't last. Even if tomorrow changed everything.

Tonight, she had him.

And he had her.

Dawn light filtered through the sheer curtains, casting the bedroom in a wash of silver light. Calista moved carefully, slipping one leg out from beneath the sheets, then the other. Her bare feet met the cool marble floor as she reached for the silk camisole draped over the back of a nearby chair.

But before she could rise fully, a strong arm wrapped around her waist, drawing her back into the warmth of the bed.

"Where are you going?" Nickolas murmured, his voice low and rough with sleep, his lips brushing the curve of her shoulder.

She froze, her breath catching. "Back to my room," she whispered, though the words lacked conviction—even to her own ears.

"Not yet," he said, his palm splaying across her stomach, holding her there.

She turned slightly, just enough to see the dark stubble along his jaw, the sleep-blurred edges of his gaze. There was something unguarded in his face—something that disarmed her completely.

Then he kissed her.

Unhurried. Deep. Certain.

As if the answer to her hesitation lived in that kiss.

And it did.

The camisole slipped from her fingers, forgotten, as he pulled her beneath the sheets once more. Their bodies found each other in silence, every touch threaded with a new kind of knowing. The world outside ceased to matter. Not here. Not in this fleeting, infinite moment.

The sun began to rise, but neither of them noticed. They were wrapped in the hush between heartbeats, in the language of skin and breath, in the way she whispered his name like a secret—and the way he answered as if it were something sacred.

She had tried to leave.

But he made her stay.

Hours later, Calista padded softly down the hallway, her emerald gown a little rumpled, her hair tousled from sleep and something far more intimate. Morning light stretched across the marble like a whisper, glinting off the polished floor as she slipped back toward her room.

She didn't know she was being watched.

Eleni stood just beyond the curve of the grand staircase, still as stone.

She hadn't meant to linger—not exactly. She was leaving early for Athens and had come upstairs to retrieve a book from her bedroom. But the sight that met her eyes stopped her cold.

Calista.

Barefoot. Flushed. Emerging from the private wing of the house—Nickolas's wing.

A low, bitter twist coiled in Eleni's stomach.

"So," she whispered, her voice a silken thread of venom, "the gold digger is sleeping with him now."

Her words hung in the air, soft and lethal.

Her fingers curled into fists at her sides, fury sparking beneath her skin like dry brush ready to burn. Her son had no sense. No judgment. And this woman—this outsider— did not belong here.

Not in his house.

Not in their world.

And certainly not as the mother of her granddaughter.

No. Eleni would not allow it.

Not if she had anything to say about it.

Nickolas stepped into the shower, the hot water cascading over his shoulders, but it did little to wash away the thoughts consuming him. His mind was still with her—Calista.

The sheets still held her scent. His skin still tingled from her touch. The night they'd shared had left a mark on him, deeper than he'd expected, more lasting than he was willing to admit. It hadn't just been passion—it had been something else. Something real.

The way she'd looked at him in the quiet after, her fingers tracing lazy patterns on his chest, like she was memorising him. The way her body fit against his. The way she whispered his name like it meant something.

It hadn't just been a night. It had been *the* night.

And now she was gone—just minutes ago, slipping quietly out of his room, leaving behind nothing but the imprint of her body on his sheets and the ache of her absence in his chest.

Nickolas closed his eyes as the hot water poured over him, but it couldn't wash her away. Not from his skin. Not from his mind. Not from the place she'd carved in his heart.

Somehow, without him noticing, she'd gotten in.

Calista.

She had slipped past every wall he'd built, disarmed every defence. Nickolas Drakos— the man who never wanted permanence, who never believed in forever—now had a daughter he adored and a woman he couldn't stop thinking about.

A woman who mattered more than he was ready to admit.

She'd told him she didn't care if what they had was temporary. That one night was enough.

But maybe it wasn't.

Maybe, for the first time in his life… he didn't want it to end.

Calista stepped into the shower, the warm spray cascading over her skin, but it couldn't ease the ache settling deep in her chest.

Last night had been unforgettable—a night she would carry with her for the rest of her life. She closed her eyes, letting the memory of his touch wash over her like the water sliding down her back.

She was in love with Nickolas. There was no more pretending, no more denying it. She wouldn't have given herself to him if she wasn't. That wasn't who she was.

But she also knew the truth—Nickolas Drakos didn't believe in forever.

And she couldn't fault him for that. He'd never lied to her. He'd been clear from the beginning. No promises. No illusions.

She was the one who had agreed. The one who said she didn't care if it didn't last.

Only… she did.

She cared more than she wanted to admit, more than she ever thought she would. But telling him? That would only make it harder when it ended.

So, she would smile. She would act as if everything was exactly as it should be.

And when the time came to walk away, she would do it with grace.

Even if it shattered her.

Chapter Twenty-Three

The sun rose lazily over the Aegean, casting a warm golden glow across the terrace where Calista sat with a cup of coffee in her hands. The sea sparkled in the distance, calm and endless, but her thoughts were anything but still.

Chloe sat across from her, swinging her legs under the table, her chin smeared with apricot jam as she took a big bite of a croissant. "Mommy, can we go swimming later?"

"If you finish your breakfast and behave like a little lady, absolutely," Calista replied, smiling as she reached to wipe Chloe's mouth with a linen napkin.

The terrace was peaceful—just the clink of cutlery, the soft rustle of the breeze through the olive trees, and the occasional chirp of cicadas beginning to wake. Calista tucked a loose strand of hair behind her ear, still feeling the whisper of last night on her skin, the press of his hand at the small of her back, the heat of his mouth on hers. She flushed at the memory and took a sip of coffee to compose herself.

"Okay," came a bright, familiar voice. "Spill."

Cassia swept onto the terrace like a gust of coastal wind, sunglasses perched on her head, her curls piled high in a loose knot. She dropped into the seat next to Calista and plucked a strawberry from Chloe's plate, who giggled and offered her another without hesitation.

"Good morning to you, too," Calista said wryly.

"Don't 'good morning' me." Cassia leaned forward, eyes sparkling. "How was it? The gala. The dress. The atmosphere. And don't leave anything out."

"It was… amazing," Calista said, smiling as she set her cup down. "I ate—like, really ate. There was this truffle risotto I'm still thinking about. I drank champagne that didn't come in a plastic flute. And I danced."

"With?" Cassia asked, lifting a perfectly shaped brow.

Calista shrugged, attempting—and failing—to keep her tone breezy. "Nickolas, of course."

Cassia blinked. "So, my brother actually danced with you?"

Calista laughed, her cheeks flushing at the memory. "Yes. Of course."

Cassia leaned forward, narrowing her eyes. "What, no one else? Just my brooding, control-freak, billionaire brother?"

Calista tapped a finger to her chin, feigning thought. "Well… Luca Moretti."

Cassia dropped her fork with a clatter. "Shut up. The Luca Moretti? Italian heir. Notorious heartbreaker. That Luca?"

"For two dances," Calista said, nonchalant. "He asked, I was being polite."

Cassia stared at her like she'd sprouted wings. "You've officially gone full Cinderella. What's next? A glass slipper and a royal decree?"

Calista smirked. "No glass slipper. But I might've left a little dignity behind."

Cassia gasped and reached across the table to swat her arm. "No! Don't go vague on me now. What happened?"

Before Calista could answer, Chloe pointed to a slice of watermelon on her plate. "Mommy, this one looks like a heart!"

Calista smiled, gently brushing her daughter's curls. "You're right, sweetheart. It does."

She turned back to Cassia, her voice softer, her expression distant. "It was a beautiful night. One I won't forget."

Cassia studied her for a long moment, the mischief fading from her face. "You're falling for him."

Calista didn't answer right away. She turned her face toward the sea, letting the breeze sweep through her hair and cool the heat rising in her chest.

"I already have," she whispered. "That's the problem."

Cassia's brow furrowed. "Why is that a problem?"

Calista exhaled. "Because he doesn't do forever. You know your brother better than I do." She hesitated, then added quietly, "And please don't say anything to him. I don't want to lose what little pride I have left."

Just then, footsteps approached from behind. Nickolas stepped onto the terrace, dressed in crisp linen, his presence commanding as always.

"Good morning," he said smoothly.

"Daddy!" Chloe beamed. "Did you think Mommy looked like a princess last night?"

Nickolas's eyes met Calista's. She tried not to look at him, but the weight of his gaze made her breath hitch.

"Yes, sweetheart," he said, his voice gentler now. "She looked exactly like a princess."

Cassia didn't miss a beat. "And I hear you weren't the only one who thought so, Nickolas. Apparently, Luca Moretti noticed, too."

His jaw tensed, just slightly.

"Yes," he said, his voice clipped.

Calista finally looked up—too late to pretend she hadn't seen the flicker of possessiveness in his eyes.

Chloe munched on a strawberry, then looked up at her father with shining eyes. "Daddy, Mommy and I are going swimming after breakfast!"

Nickolas arched a brow, his tone playful. "Oh really? And can you swim, little mermaid?"

Chloe lifted her chin with pride, her curls bouncing. "Of course! Henry and Mommy taught me."

"Is that so?" Nickolas said, his mouth curving into a grin. "Well then, you'll have to show me just how good you are."

Chloe giggled. "I will! I can float and everything!"

Calista sipped her coffee, trying to hide her smile as she watched father and daughter. The way Nickolas looked at Chloe—with so much affection, so much wonder—made her chest ache. Moments like this made it dangerously easy to forget the walls she'd so carefully built around her heart.

After breakfast, Calista and Chloe changed into their swimsuits—matching one-piece suits in soft shades of teal. Chloe was practically vibrating with excitement as she grabbed Calista's hand and tugged her down the stone path to the pool.

"Hurry, Mommy! Come on!"

The sun was warm overhead, the pool shimmering like liquid sapphire. Chloe didn't hesitate—she dove in with a splash and surfaced laughing, her little arms paddling.

Calista slipped in after her, smoothing back her wet hair as they played, swam, and splashed in the water. Chloe's giggles echoed off the villa's white stone walls.

A little while later, Nickolas appeared at the edge of the pool, barefoot and in swim trunks, watching them with quiet amusement.

"Daddy! Watch!" Chloe called, her voice bright with excitement. She kicked off from the shallow end and swam a short distance, then turned with wide, expectant eyes. "Did you see, Daddy? Did you see me?"

Nickolas smiled, stepping closer to the water. "I saw, sweetheart," he said, his voice warm and low. "You were perfect."

Chloe beamed, splashing happily, and Calista, floating nearby, tilted her face up to him. The sun glinted off the surface of the water, but it was the tenderness in Nickolas's eyes that made her chest tighten, her heart suddenly too full to contain.

The morning unfolded like a dream. The three of them played in the pool, laughter echoing through the villa's sunlit courtyard. Chloe shrieked with delight as they played water tag, clung to Nickolas's back during a piggyback race, and declared herself the queen of the pool during a pretend tea party on the shallow steps.

She didn't notice the lingering glances exchanged between her mother and Nickolas, the way his hand would settle on Calista's waist during a game, or how her laugh softened whenever he looked at her like that.

But Calista noticed. She felt every brush of his fingers, every look that held just a little too long. And when Chloe darted off to the bathroom, wrapped in her towel and singing to herself, Nickolas didn't hesitate.

He moved toward her, water lapping around them, and before she could speak, his hands were on her waist—firm, possessive—and his mouth found hers in a kiss that stole the breath from her lungs.

It was deep, slow, and full of everything she hadn't let herself hope for. His arms pulled her closer, and for a moment, the world fell away. There was no caution, no guilt, only the quiet ache of two people trying not to fall—and failing.

When they broke apart, her forehead rested against his, their breaths mingling.

"I shouldn't feel like this," she whispered.

"But you do," he said simply.

And she did. She felt like she belonged—in this villa, in this pool, in this moment. Like she wasn't just a guest or a passing phase in his glittering world.

For the first time in a very long time, Calista felt like she was part of a family.

That feeling lasted until dinner.

After a long day in the sun, Chloe had eaten a hearty meal and slipped into a warm bath. Calista helped her into her favourite star-print pyjamas, drying her curls with a soft towel as Chloe chattered nonstop.

"Can we go swimming again tomorrow?" she asked, yawning but too excited to sleep. "It was so much fun! Daddy was so funny when he slipped, remember? And you looked so pretty in the water, Mommy. Like a mermaid."

Calista smiled, brushing her daughter's hair back and kissing her forehead. "We'll see, sweetheart. Now close those eyes."

She waited until Chloe's breathing softened before quietly slipping out of the room. She was still smiling as she headed downstairs—until she heard the raised voices echoing through the marble corridor.

"Don't be ridiculous, Mother! She would never do something like that!"

Nickolas's voice—sharp, disbelieving—rang out first.

Calista slowed her steps, her stomach knotting.

"She's been here a little over a week," Eleni snapped, her tone icy and imperious. "And now my necklace is missing. A diamond necklace, mind you, not a trinket."

Cassia's voice rose, a blend of shock and exasperation. "Do you hear yourself? You can't just accuse someone of stealing because you don't like her!"

"I'm not accusing, I'm stating the facts," Eleni said coolly. "It was there this morning. It's gone now. And the only new person with access to my room is her."

By the time Calista reached the foot of the staircase, she could see them—Nickolas standing rigid, hands clenched at his sides, Cassia pacing with frustration, and Eleni seated regally on one of the damask chairs, her spine ramrod straight, a silk scarf around her neck, and a glass of wine untouched on the table beside her.

The room was thick with tension.

Nickolas raked a hand through his hair. "You have no proof. You're accusing the mother of my daughter—"

"She's not her mother," Eleni hissed. "She's her aunt. Let's not forget that little detail."

Calista's breath caught. The words stung more than she expected.

She stepped into the room, all eyes turning to her.

"If something's missing," she said calmly, though her voice wavered at the edges, "you're welcome to search my room. My bags. My things."

Eleni stood. "No one asked you to eavesdrop."

"And no one asked to be accused," Calista replied, lifting her chin. "I won't stand here and let you imply that I'm some common thief."

Nickolas moved immediately to her side. "You don't have to defend yourself, Calista. This is absurd."

But Calista could feel the heat rising in her chest, the familiar flush of humiliation creeping in. She had worked so hard to protect Chloe from this—this exact kind of judgment, the sideways glances, the whispers that came from people who thought they were better.

"I'll pack our things," she said, her voice barely above a whisper. "We'll leave in the morning."

"No," Nickolas said firmly, turning to her. "You are not leaving."

Eleni scoffed. "So, you'd rather let a woman of questionable background remain in this house and play family with your child than admit the truth?"

Calista blinked, but her eyes stung anyway.

"You're out of line," Cassia said, her voice trembling with anger. "That necklace could've fallen under your dresser for all you know. You could have misplaced it."

Nickolas stepped in front of Calista, shielding her from the blast of Eleni's venomous glare.

"You think money gives you the right to tear people apart," he said quietly. "But it doesn't. Not this time."

Silence fell. Heavy and suffocating.

Calista didn't want his protection—not like this. Not when it meant becoming the crack in a family already stitched together by silence and expectation. Most of all, she didn't want Chloe to wake up tomorrow and feel the ground shift beneath her feet again.

But somewhere deep inside, beneath the wounded pride and rising fear, another memory clawed its way forward—sharp and uninvited. Her sister's voice, cold and accusing.

"What did you take this time, Calista?"

The constant suspicion. The casual cruelty. The way no one ever gave her the benefit of the doubt.

Her throat tightened, but she forced herself to breathe through it.

Because this time, like all the rest, she had nothing to hide.

A small, aching truth whispered to her then:

She hadn't just fallen for Nickolas—she'd handed over her heart, piece by piece, when she wasn't even watching.

Her heart already belonged to him.

And now… it might cost her everything.

She stepped out from behind Nickolas, her voice quiet but clear. "I insist that you search my room."

Nickolas turned sharply. "No."

Cassia echoed, frowning. "Absolutely not."

Calista lifted her chin, forcing herself to meet Eleni's stare. "If you don't, this will hang over me. Over Chloe. Over all of us. It will fester. And I won't have your mother—or anyone—thinking I'm afraid of the truth."

"But you shouldn't have to prove your innocence," Cassia said, her voice tight with emotion.

"I shouldn't," Calista agreed, her tone soft but firm. "But I've lived long enough to know that sometimes you have to stand in the fire just to prove you won't burn."

Nickolas stared at her, something dark and unreadable moving behind his eyes. "This isn't right."

"No," she said quietly. "It's not. But let's end it here. Tonight. So that tomorrow, Chloe doesn't wake up to tension and whispers. Let her wake up in peace."

For a moment, no one moved. Eleni looked smug, certain she'd won. But Calista wasn't doing this for Eleni. She was doing it for Chloe. For herself. For the chance to move forward with her head held high.

"Then let's go," she said, and turned toward the stairs.

Nickolas hesitated, then followed her—not because he believed she was guilty. But because she believed this was the only way to protect what mattered most.

And he couldn't let her walk that path alone.

Chapter Twenty-Four

Eleni's hands moved with sharp, almost gleeful precision as she searched the guest room. She opened drawers, lifted pillows, checked behind picture frames. Calista stood ramrod straight near the door, her face blank, her arms folded tightly across her chest.

Cassia stood at her side, jaw clenched, eyes blazing with fury. Nickolas remained silent on Calista's other side, unreadable, though tension pulsed from him like a storm barely held at bay.

"She's not going to find anything," Cassia muttered.

Calista said nothing. She wouldn't give Eleni the satisfaction of reacting. She kept her eyes fixed on the far wall, not even blinking as Eleni rifled through her closet.

Finally, Eleni stepped back, her hands empty.

Cassia crossed her arms. "Well? Now apologise to Calista."

Eleni didn't move. Her gaze swept the room one more time, then landed on the bed. "Where is your suitcase?" she asked coldly.

"Under the bed," Calista answered, her voice even.

With a sharp tug, Eleni pulled the suitcase out and unzipped it. She rummaged through it for a moment—then suddenly froze.

Her fingers emerged, clutching a gleam of diamonds.

The necklace.

Cassia gasped. "No—no way."

Nickolas stared, the blood draining from his face. "What the hell…"

Eleni held it up like a trophy. "There it is. Exactly where I said it would be."

For a moment, there was only silence.

Then Nickolas stepped forward, eyes locked on the necklace as though trying to make sense of what he was seeing. "That's impossible."

Calista couldn't move. Her heart thudded in her ears, a hollow, sick rhythm.

Cassia turned to her slowly, her brows drawn together in disbelief. "Calista?"

"I didn't put it there," Calista whispered, stunned. "I don't even go in her room. I swear to you—"

But Nickolas cut in, his voice low and bitter. "You stole my mother's necklace," he said, as though confirming it aloud made it real. "Why?"

Her breath caught.

"Nickolas…" Cassia said, shaking her head.

But he wasn't looking at his sister. His eyes were locked on Calista. Cold. Confused. Hurt.

"I let you into my home," he went on, his voice cracking under the weight of something darker. "I trusted you. I believed you were different. Not like the rest."

Calista's throat closed. "I didn't—Nickolas, please. I would never—"

He took a step back, the necklace still glittering in his hand. "Of course not," he said bitterly, almost to himself, his voice dropped to almost a whisper. "Just another gold digger with a good act."

The words slammed into her with staggering force.

Calista flinched, as though he'd slapped her, she swayed slightly.

Cassia's mouth opened in protest, but Calista held up a trembling hand to stop her.

It was too late.

The damage had already been done.

Her voice was barely audible, but it trembled with pain. "You think I'd use my daughter for something like this?"

Nickolas didn't answer.

And that silence was louder than any accusation.

His jaw clenched, eyes flashing with something unreadable, Nickolas turned and stormed out of the room.

"Nickolas!" Cassia called, hurrying after him. "This doesn't make sense—you know it doesn't!"

He didn't stop. Didn't look back. The sound of his footsteps and hers faded down the hall, swallowed by the stillness they left behind.

Eleni lingered, her chin tilted high, a cruel smile curling at her lips.

She stepped closer, her voice low and cold. "Just as I thought. Money-grubbing harlot. You fooled him for a while; I'll give you that."

Calista didn't move. She couldn't. Her spine was stiff with shock; her hands numb at her sides.

Eleni gave a satisfied sniff and turned to leave. "I look forward to seeing him throw you out. Then he can take you to court and get his daughter back. She's not yours."

The words hit harder than any slap.

The door closed behind her with a soft, final click.

Calista didn't move. Couldn't. Her legs felt hollow, her breath shallow and tight in her chest. Betrayal coated her tongue—bitter, thick, impossible to swallow. Her hands curled into fists at her sides, as if bracing against a wave she couldn't hold back.

Just down the hall, Chloe slept peacefully—still dreaming of pools and sunshine and the family she thought she finally had.

She had no idea that, by morning, everything could be gone.

Calista stared at the suitcase under the bed, the one she hadn't touched since arriving. Her vision blurred.

She hadn't just lost Nickolas tonight.

Now, she might lose Chloe too.

And that—that—was the heartbreak she wasn't sure she could survive.

Nickolas stormed into his study, the door slamming against the wall as he paced to the windows. His jaw was tight, hands raking through his hair. Cassia was on his heels, her heels clicking sharply on the marble floor.

"You can't seriously believe Calista took that necklace," she snapped, crossing her arms.

Nickolas turned, his eyes stormy. "It was in her suitcase, Cassia. In her room."

"And that proves what? That she planted it there herself while our mother conveniently 'searched' the room?" Her voice was sharp with disbelief. "You know what mother is capable of when she feels threatened."

Nickolas looked away, jaw working. "What am I supposed to think?"

"That she's not like the others," Cassia said. "Because she's not. You know it."

He ran a hand over his face, frustration lacing every breath. "You saw where it was. It doesn't make sense. But—God, Cassia—I've been here before. Every woman I've dated, every one of them—eventually, it's all about what I can give them. The lifestyle, the money, the name. They smile, they charm, and then they take."

Cassia stepped closer, her voice lower now. "She's not them."

He met her gaze, his own uncertain. "Then why didn't she deny it? Why did she just stand there?"

"Because she was in shock! Because she couldn't believe you were even questioning her." Cassia's voice cracked with emotion. "She loves that little girl like she's her own. She's not a thief, Nickolas. She's not a liar. But she is a woman who's been through hell—and tonight, you didn't stand beside her. You stood in judgment."

Nickolas looked away again, pain flickering across his face.

Cassia's voice softened. "You're so afraid of being used that you can't see when someone's standing in front of you for you—not your name, not your wealth. Just you."

He didn't speak.

And Cassia's heart broke a little for both of them.

Calista sat on the edge of the bed, her hands clenched tightly in her lap. Her eyes were red-rimmed, her cheeks blotchy from crying, but the ache in her chest refused to dull.

How could he think I stole it?

How could Nickolas think I was capable of that?

She had never stolen anything in her life. Not a trinket as a child, not a dollar from her mother's purse, nothing. And now, here she was—branded, judged, betrayed—all because a diamond necklace had somehow appeared in her room.

She didn't know how it got there.

Only that it had.

And that Nickolas had looked at her like he didn't know her at all.

A soft knock broke the silence.

Calista hesitated, then dragged herself to her feet. She opened the door just a crack— and saw Cassia standing there, her expression full of worry.

Without a word, Calista stepped back and let her in.

"Oh, Calista…" Cassia's voice was gentle. "Are you okay?"

Calista gave a humourless laugh. "Not really."

Cassia stepped closer, her arms wrapping around her in a firm hug. "I can't believe my brother actually thinks you tried to steal that necklace."

Calista pulled back, searching her face. "You believe me?"

"Of course I do," Cassia said fiercely. "I know who organised this."

A sick twist of confirmation tightened in Calista's stomach. "Your mother."

Cassia nodded grimly. "She's never liked anyone who could take his attention away from her influence."

Calista swallowed hard, her voice barely above a whisper. "I need to go home. I can't stay here, not after this. Can you... help me?"

Cassia didn't hesitate. "Yes. I'll help you pack; I can get you to the marina in the morning. My brother is an idiot, but he'll figure it out—just too late, as always."

Calista managed a small, grateful smile through the tears still brimming in her eyes.

She didn't know where things would go from here.

But she did know she couldn't stay in a place where love turned to suspicion with a single lie.

It was still early when the sun began to rise over the Aegean, casting a soft golden light over the villa. The house was quiet—too quiet—as Calista quietly packed the last of their things into a worn overnight bag.

She turned and knelt beside the bed where Chloe sat, already dressed in her favourite pink sundress and clutching her stuffed rabbit.

"We're going home, sweetheart," Calista said gently, brushing a curl behind her daughter's ear.

Chloe's face fell. "But what about Daddy? He'll want to come swimming today..."

Calista's throat tightened, but she forced a smile. "I know, baby. I promise you'll see him again soon." Her voice wavered, she knew she would never keep Chloe from Nickolas, she knew he loved her. "I promise."

Chloe looked down at her toy, then back up with wide, searching eyes. "Will he come visit?"

"Yes," Calista said firmly, kissing her forehead. "And Cassia too. She said she'd come see us."

Later, as they made their way down the winding path to the road, Chloe clung to Calista's hand, still half-asleep, her little steps stumbling. The sea breeze tugged at Calista's hair as Luca waited by the car, engine running, his expression unusually sombre. The car door stood open, their ticket to the mainland already tucked in Calista's purse—courtesy of Cassia, who had refused to let them leave without help.

At the dock, Cassia pulled Calista into a fierce hug.

"I'm so sorry," she whispered, voice raw with emotion. "For everything. For what she said. For what he did."

Calista held on a second longer than she meant to. "None of it was your fault."

Cassia leaned back, her eyes damp. "You didn't deserve what happened last night. And I swear—I'll fix this. Somehow."

Calista swallowed. "You don't have to. You've already done more than you know."

Cassia cupped her hands around Calista's. "I'm so glad to have met you."

"So am I," Calista said, her voice quiet.

Luca helped them onto the ferry. As it pulled away from the dock, Calista stood at the railing, Chloe pressed against her hip, watching the island grow smaller behind them.

She didn't cry. Not yet.

But the ache in her chest told her everything had changed—and not just for today.

Chapter Twenty-Five

Nickolas strode onto the terrace, still wearing the same clothes from the night before, his shirt rumpled and the collar open. His jaw was clenched, his eyes red-rimmed and hollow with the weight of a sleepless night. The early morning sun spilled golden light across the tiled floor, but none of it touched him.

The house was too quiet.

Too still.

A flicker of unease twisted in his chest as he paused in the doorway. "Where's Calista?" he asked sharply, scanning the terrace. "And Chloe?"

Cassia, seated at the table with a half-finished cup of coffee, looked up slowly. Her expression was tight, guarded. The circles under her eyes were nearly as dark as his, but the fury simmering just beneath her calm was unmistakable. She set her mug down with a deliberate clink.

"They're gone," she said flatly.

Nickolas frowned. "What do you mean, gone?"

"I mean they left the island. Early this morning."

His body went rigid. "Without telling me?"

Cassia's gaze sharpened. "No. Because why would she? After everything you accused her of?"

He took a step back, disbelief crashing over him. "She took my daughter without—"

"She didn't take anyone," Cassia snapped, rising to her feet, her voice sharp with righteous anger. "Chloe is her daughter. She's the one who raised her. She's the one who brought you into her life—she didn't have to. She gave you the gift of knowing your child. And you threw it in her face the minute things got uncomfortable."

Nickolas's breath caught in his throat. "You helped them?"

Cassia nodded, unflinching. "I asked Luca to drive them to the marina. I booked their tickets myself. And no—I'm not sorry. Not one bit."

Nickolas turned away, running a hand down his face, trying to steady himself against the wave of guilt rising in his chest.

But Cassia wasn't done.

"I stood there and watched her fold up Chloe's pyjamas with shaking hands while you were hiding in your study, punishing her in your head for sins she never committed. You didn't ask her. You didn't give her a chance. You just assumed she was like every other woman who's ever batted her lashes at you."

Nickolas closed his eyes, her words hitting like shrapnel.

"You broke her heart, Nik," Cassia continued, her voice lower now, rough with emotion. "And even then, she still made sure Chloe wouldn't hate you. She told her she'd see you again soon. She said she would never keep you from your daughter. That's love. Real, unconditional love. And you looked her in the eye and shattered it."

He turned, his voice hoarse. "I don't believe she did it. I know now… it wasn't her."

Cassia stepped closer, her eyes narrowed. "Too late, you idiot. Do you really think Calista would have stayed here, let herself be humiliated like that in front of Eleni, in front of you, if she were guilty? You let our mother tear her apart and you just stood there."

He dragged a hand through his hair, the weight of it all settling on his shoulders. "I made a mistake," he murmured. "I didn't trust her."

"No kidding," Cassia said bitterly. "She was the best thing that's ever happened to you. And you treated her like a criminal. Like a—"

"Gold digger," he whispered, the word tasting like ash.

Cassia recoiled, her expression darkening. "God. You actually said it to her?"

"I didn't mean to," he said, but his voice lacked conviction.

Cassia gave a harsh, disbelieving laugh. "Well, you meant it enough. I just hope one day I meet someone who loves me half as fiercely as that woman loved you."

She stepped past him, pausing only at the doorway to say, cold and final:

"You didn't just lose Calista. You lost everything."

And then she was gone.

Nickolas stood in his study, staring at the diamond necklace lying motionless on his desk like a silent accusation.

She was gone.

Calista's room was empty now—void of her voice, her laughter, the soft rhythm of her footsteps. All that remained was the faintest trace of her perfume still lingering in the air. A ghost of what had been. A cruel reminder of what he'd destroyed.

Cassia had been right. About all of it.

She'd helped Calista and Chloe leave the island, and she hadn't looked back. She wasn't sorry.

And he didn't blame her.

The moment he'd seen the necklace tucked into Calista's suitcase, that old, venomous fear had surged up inside him—cold and corrosive. The fear that he was unlovable without his wealth. That no one ever really saw him, only the name, the fortune, the lifestyle.

His mother had called Calista a gold digger. And like the fool he was, he'd believed it.

He hadn't asked questions.

He hadn't trusted her.

He'd let the weight of past betrayals poison something real.

And the look in Calista's eyes when he'd accused her…

It had broken something in him.

He picked up the necklace now, the cold metal sliding like ice through his fingers, then let it drop. It hit the desk with a soft clink, mocking him.

He rubbed the back of his neck, trying to relieve the tension, his voice a rasp in the silence. "Idiot."

He knew now—too late—that Calista hadn't stolen anything.

He slumped into the chair behind his desk, elbows on his knees, head in his hands, his thoughts a chaotic storm of guilt and regret.

The door burst open.

"Go away!" he barked, not even looking up.

"No," came Cassia's voice, firm and clear.

"I already know I'm a bloody idiot, Cass," he muttered. "You don't need to rub it in."

"I'm not here to rub it in."

There was movement. A pause. Then:

"You need to hear this."

He looked up.

Cassia stepped aside—and behind her stood Maria, his mother's maid, wringing her hands, her eyes wide and anxious.

Nickolas straightened, his gaze sharpening. "What is this?"

Maria swallowed hard, glancing nervously between him and Cassia. Then she blurted, "Your mother told me to put the necklace in Miss Georgiou's room."

Silence.

"What?" The word cracked from him like a whip.

Maria flinched. "I didn't want to, sir. I swear it. But she said it was just a test. To see what Miss Georgiou would do. If she'd return it… or keep it. She said it was the only way to know what kind of woman she really was."

Nickolas froze.

The fury came next—slow, rising, volcanic.

His mother had set her up.

And he had walked right into it.

He stood so suddenly the chair behind him hit the wall loudly.

His hands clenched at his sides. His breath came shallow. It took every ounce of control not to scream.

"She planned this?" he said, his voice low and lethal. "She used Calista to feed her paranoia?"

Maria nodded helplessly. "I'm sorry, sir. I liked Miss Georgiou. I didn't know it would go this far. I didn't know she'd leave."

But Calista had left.

And he'd handed her the final reason to walk away.

Nickolas turned to Cassia, his face pale with realisation.

"She thinks I didn't love her," he said quietly.

The truth sat heavy in his chest, heavier than anything he'd ever carried.

Cassia's voice broke the silence, cool and sharp. "No. She knows you didn't trust her. And that's worse."

Nickolas found her in the solarium, seated in her usual spot with a pristine espresso cup in hand, the morning sun gilding the sea behind her. She looked serene, untouched. As if she hadn't just detonated the most precious part of his life.

"Mother," he said, his voice sharp with restrained fury.

Eleni glanced up, her expression calm and composed. "Nickolas. You look exhausted."

He didn't waste a second. "You planted the necklace in Calista's room."

Her brows arched slightly, but there was no trace of guilt. "I did what needed to be done."

"No. You lied. You manipulated a woman who's done nothing but love Chloe—who has done everything to make this family feel like home."

"She doesn't belong in this family," Eleni said coolly, setting her cup down with deliberate precision. "She's a pretender. A woman clinging to a child that isn't hers, hoping it will elevate her."

Nickolas took a step forward, his voice low, vibrating with restrained rage. "You set a trap. And like a fool, I walked right into it. I accused the woman I love because I let you poison my judgment."

"She is what I said she is," Eleni snapped, rising now. "A gold digger. A woman who saw an opportunity and clung to it. If you had any sense, you'd take her to court and fight for your daughter. That child deserves better."

He stared at her, disbelieving. "You think this was about protecting Chloe?"

"She needs stability," Eleni insisted. "Not a woman pretending to be her mother."

"She is her mother," Nickolas said, every word deliberate. "And you—you're going to leave this island."

Her head jerked back. "What?"

"I want you off this island by noon."

Eleni's expression twisted into incredulity. "You can't be serious. Over her?"

"That 'wannabe mother,' as you called her, is the woman I love."

Eleni's mouth parted, stunned into silence.

"And if you can't respect that—if you can't respect her or Chloe—then you are no longer welcome in my life."

"You would cut off your own mother for a woman who—"

"I would cut off anyone who tries to hurt them," he interrupted, deadly calm. "You've meddled in my life for too long. It ends today."

She stared at him, her face tight with fury. "You're making a terrible mistake."

"No," he said, his voice cold and resolute. "I made the biggest mistake of my life believing manipulative woman who's never known a single thing about unconditional love."

He didn't wait for a reply.

He turned and walked away without looking back, leaving Eleni standing alone in the golden silence, her espresso untouched and cooling beside her—just like the hold she once had over him.

The kettle whistled softly, steam curling through the air as the rich aroma of fresh coffee filled the small kitchen. Henry poured the dark liquid into two mismatched mugs, his movements gentle, unhurried.

Calista sat at the table; arms folded tightly across her chest. Her eyes were heavy with exhaustion, but dry now—she'd cried herself empty somewhere over the Atlantic, with Chloe curled beside her in the window seat, sleeping peacefully, unaware.

Henry set a mug down in front of her, then slid into the chair opposite. "I'm so sorry, Calista. You don't deserve any of that."

She wrapped her hands around the warm ceramic, not for the drink, but for the small comfort of something steady. "It's not even about me anymore. I just feel for Chloe. She misses him."

Henry's brow creased, concern softening his features. "It's only been two days. She'll adjust. Kids are tougher than we give them credit for."

Calista nodded, her grip tightening around the mug. "She asked if he was coming to visit. I didn't know what to tell her."

He didn't look away. "Maybe you should get away for a while. You've still got time off work, don't you? Go somewhere quiet. Just you and Chloe. Somewhere you can breathe."

She looked at him, her expression unreadable for a moment. "You think that's what we need?"

"I do," Henry said gently. "You've both been through too much. A change of scenery might give you space to… reset."

Calista exhaled slowly, her gaze drifting toward the hallway where Chloe lay napping. "I don't want to see him. Not yet."

Henry nodded. "I understand."

She stood then, walked to the drawer by the fridge, and pulled out a small, folded envelope. She brought it back to the table and placed it in front of him.

"If he does come looking… give him this."

He looked down at the envelope, then back at her. "What does it say?"

"That Chloe's safe. That I won't keep Chloe from him. And that I just need time."

Henry reached for the note, his fingers brushing hers. "Do you want me to tell him where you've gone?"

She shook her head. "No. Not even if he asks. Promise me."

"I promise," he said, tucking the note into his jacket. "But Cal… if he does come for you—"

"I don't think he will," she said softly, the hurt laced through her voice like a fine crack in glass.

Henry gave her a small, sad smile. "Then he'd better come ready."

She gave him a grateful, broken smile, then quietly turned back to her coffee. The room settled into silence, broken only by the ticking clock and the distant hum of a world that kept turning.

She almost said: I still love him. But she swallowed it. What good would it do now?

Chapter Twenty-Six

Calista wasn't home.

She hadn't been home yesterday either.

Nickolas had called three times already that day. He'd even waited in his car outside her house for hours, watching, hoping—for a glimpse, a chance, anything. But there was no sign of her. Her phone went straight to voicemail.

The silence was maddening. And there was only one man in the world who might know where she'd gone.

The moment Nickolas stepped through his office door; he was met with a glare sharp enough to draw blood.

Henry didn't bother to rise from his chair. "What the hell do you want?"

"I need to know where Calista is."

Henry's jaw tightened. "Why in hell would I tell you that?" His voice was low and flat. "You broke her heart—one you never deserved."

Nickolas swallowed hard. "I didn't mean to hurt her. I know I was wrong."

"You called her a thief," Henry said, rising slowly from behind his desk. "And a gold digger."

"I know what I said." Nickolas's voice cracked. "And I know it was unforgivable."

"You're damn right it was."

Henry came around the desk, eyes blazing as he stood toe to toe with him. "You don't know the first thing about her. You never asked. So let me tell you a few things Calista would never say about herself."

Nickolas stood frozen, jaw clenched.

"Her sister, Danica—the one who gave birth to Chloe—made Calista's life a nightmare. Selfish. Cruel. Left Chloe behind without a second thought when she ran off to chase God knows what. Calista didn't just babysit. She raised that little girl."

Nickolas flinched. "I thought she was helping while Danica was—"

"Gone. She was gone, Nickolas. For two years. And Calista? She gave up everything to be Chloe's mother. She loved her like her own because she was her own. No cameras. No applause. Just diapers, sleepless nights, scraped knees, and bedtime stories. All while trying to survive a sister who despised her."

Nickolas dragged a hand through his hair, breath catching in his throat.

Henry's voice dropped, full of quiet fury. "When Danica got her brain cancer diagnosis. Who do you think she turned to. Calista. And she cared for her until the end, not asking for anything in return. Nothing. And when she died, she left her whole estate to Calista. Millions. Not a dime for Chloe. Not a letter. Not a damn explanation. Nothing. Just one final act of cruelty."

Nickolas blinked, stunned. "She left everything to Calista?"

"Every cent. And do you know what Calista did with it? She put it all in a trust for Chloe. Every last cent. She didn't keep a single dime for herself."

The room spun.

"Does that sound like a gold digger to you?" Henry hissed. "Does that sound like someone who would steal a necklace?"

Nickolas couldn't speak. Couldn't breathe. His mistakes slammed into him like a fist to the chest. He had believed the worst about a woman who had only ever given her best. Out of fear. Out of pride. Out of loyalty to a mother who had never deserved it.

He had shattered the only thing that had ever truly mattered.

"Please…" Nickolas whispered, voice raw. He stepped forward. "Please, Henry. I need to see her. Just tell me where she is. I'm begging you."

Henry stared at him for a long, weighted beat. Then, with a reluctant sigh, he said quietly, "I can't tell you where she is."

Nickolas's heart sank. "She didn't tell you?"

"She did." Henry's expression softened, but only slightly. "And she made me promise I wouldn't tell you."

Nickolas felt like the floor was slipping out from under him.

"But," Henry added, reaching into a drawer, "she did leave this for you."

He handed over a plain envelope.

Nickolas took it like it was made of glass, carefully breaking the seal. The moment his eyes fell on the familiar handwriting, everything else faded.

Nickolas,

I don't regret being with you.

I hope one day, you won't regret being with me—for the short time we had.

I will never stand in the way of you seeing Chloe. She loves you, and she deserves to.

But I need a little time.

Time to heal. To breathe. To stop wondering if I was ever enough.

I'll reach out when I've recovered.

Until then, I wish you peace.

And love.

Even if it's not with me.

—Calista

Tears slipped down Nickolas's cheeks before he even realised, they'd fallen. He read the letter again—and again—clinging to each word like it might undo the damage, like it might somehow bring her back.

He looked up at Henry, his voice barely more than a breath.

"I broke her."

Henry didn't argue. He just nodded, solemn and unflinching.

"Yes. You did."

Nickolas swallowed hard. "Are you going to see her?"

"I am."

A long pause stretched between them.

"Will you give her a note from me?"

Henry considered him for a moment, then gave a curt nod. "Okay."

Nickolas found a scrap of paper and scrawled the only words that mattered.

He folded it with care and handed it to Henry.

"I'll be at the Ritz-Carlton," he said quietly, his voice frayed with emotion.

And then he turned and walked out—each step weighted with regret, with hope, with the silent prayer that it wasn't too late.

The beach cottage smelled of salt and lemons and something sweet baking in the oven. Sunlight spilled across the hardwood floors, and the sound of the ocean murmured in the distance. Chloe was the first to spot him through the window.

"Uncle Henry!" she shrieked, racing to the front door with bare feet and a huge grin.

Henry barely had time to brace himself before she launched into his arms. He caught her easily, laughing as he swung her around in a circle.

"There's my girl," he said, his voice warm.

She giggled, arms wrapped tight around his neck. "I missed you."

"I missed you more."

When he set her down, she tugged him eagerly toward the kitchen. "Come see what I'm making! Mommy let me help with the lemon bars!"

Calista turned from the counter just as they walked in. Her eyes met Henry's, and for a moment, time held its breath.

She looked tired.

Beautiful, as always, but the kind of beautiful that came from endurance, not peace. There were faint shadows beneath her eyes, her smile hesitant as she wiped her hands on a towel.

"Hi," she said softly.

"Hi," Henry replied.

He glanced at Chloe, who was now chattering to a mixing bowl. "Could you give us a minute, kiddo?"

Chloe pouted. "But the lemon bars—"

"I'll eat three," he promised, leaning down. "Four, if you let us talk."

She grinned and skipped out, leaving them in the quiet hum of the kitchen.

Henry reached into his jacket and pulled out the folded note. "He asked me to give you this."

Calista didn't take it right away. Her hands were still, fingers clenched lightly around the edge of the counter. "He came to see you?"

"He did. Looked like hell warmed over."

She exhaled slowly and took the paper. Her name was written in Nickolas's sharp, slanted hand. She unfolded it with trembling fingers.

Calista,

I'm sorry. I love you.

—Nickolas

Tears welled in her eyes before she could stop them. She bit her bottom lip, holding the note close to her chest as if it might disappear.

"I don't know what to do," she whispered.

Henry leaned back against the counter, arms crossed, watching her quietly. "You love him?"

"I don't want to."

"That's not what I asked."

She looked away, blinking hard. "He broke something in me. I trusted him, and he… he didn't even try to understand."

"I know," Henry said gently. "And for what it's worth, I wish you loved me."

Her gaze snapped to his.

He smiled faintly, no bitterness behind it—just a softness, maybe even sadness. "I do. You know I love you. Always have. But I'm not the one you look for when the door opens. Not the one you dream about. It's him."

"I don't know if I can forgive him," she said.

"You don't have to. Not right away. Maybe not ever. But if there's even a piece of you that still believes in him, that still wants to believe in you and him—don't shut that door before you're sure. Regret's a heavy thing to carry."

She looked down at the note again, her thumb brushing over the ink.

"I just don't want Chloe to get hurt."

"Then be honest. With her. With him. With yourself. That's all any of you can do."

The oven beeped, a soft chime that broke the silence. Calista didn't move.

Henry stepped closer and gently placed a hand on her shoulder. "You've always been brave, Calista. Don't stop now."

She closed her eyes, one tear slipping free.

"Will you stay for lemon bars?" she asked, her voice small.

He smiled. "Wouldn't miss it."

And as she tucked the note into her pocket, the wind lifted through the open window, stirring the scent of sugar and citrus—and something new. Not peace. Not yet.

But maybe the beginning of it.

Chapter Twenty-Seven

Nickolas was sitting in the penthouse at the Ritz-Carlton in Boston. He hadn't moved much from the armchair near the window. The view of the city glittered in the distance—glass and steel shimmering like stardust—but he wasn't really seeing it.

His phone sat still on the table beside an untouched glass of whiskey, silent for hours.

The note Henry had handed him was still in his pocket.

He didn't know how many times he'd read it. Each time, her words hit differently. Each time, they hollowed out something deeper.

He hadn't slept. Hadn't eaten. He wasn't sure he'd even breathed properly since she walked away.

The room phone rang from the desk. He blinked, slowly rising, the sound startling in the silence.

He crossed the room and picked up the receiver. "Yes?"

"Mr. Drakos," the receptionist said politely, "there is a Miss Georgiou here to see you."

His breath caught in his throat. For a second, he thought he'd misheard.

Calista.

He gripped the edge of the desk, pulse pounding. "Send her up."

He didn't sit. He couldn't. Every part of him felt like it was bracing for impact.

When the knock came, he crossed the room in four strides. He hesitated just a moment—one hand on the door—before opening it.

There she was.

She wore a white sundress, simple and soft, as unadorned as the truth in her eyes. Her face was bare, untouched by makeup, and all the more striking for it—honest, open. Her hair was pulled back into a loose ponytail, a few wisps escaping to frame her cheeks. She looked tired. Fragile. Radiant in a way that had nothing to do with perfection and everything to do with grace.

"Hi," she said softly.

His breath rushed out like he'd been holding it for days. He couldn't speak—his throat was too tight.

"Sorry, I didn't call," she continued, her voice a little shaky. "I didn't know what to say. But Henry gave me your note. And I just… I needed to see you."

Nickolas stepped aside, gently, silently, and she moved past him into the suite.

The door clicked closed behind her.

He turned, watching as she walked slowly to the window. The same view he'd been ignoring for hours spread wide before them.

She turned toward him, eyes shining with unshed tears. "You hurt me."

Nickolas swallowed hard, his voice low. "I know."

"You judged me without even asking if I did it."

"I know that too," he murmured, shame thick in his throat.

Her gaze didn't waver. "Did you mean what you wrote?"

"Every word," he said without hesitation. "I'm sorry, Calista. And I love you. God, I love you."

Her eyes shimmered, but she blinked the tears back. "You made me feel like I was nothing. Like everything I'd done for Chloe—everything I sacrificed—meant nothing to you."

He stepped closer, his voice raw and aching. "I was wrong. Deeply, unforgivably wrong. I saw what I was afraid to see. And I let someone else's bitterness poison what we had."

Calista's breath hitched. "You believed all I wanted was your money. Your life. Your name."

"I believed I wasn't worthy of what you were giving me," he confessed, the truth cracking open inside him. "You're the most honest, selfless woman I've ever known. And I didn't trust it. I didn't trust myself. I panicked because… I've never had something that pure. Not without strings. Not without cost."

Her expression softened, but the pain lingered in her eyes. "I loved you, Nickolas. I still do. But love… it has to feel safe."

His voice caught as he stepped closer. "Then I'll spend the rest of my life making sure it does—if you'll let me."

She looked away, torn. "I thought you didn't believe in forever."

A faint, wistful smile touched his lips. "I didn't. Not until I met you."

He took a breath, his voice thick with memory. "I think I fell in love with you the very first day. You opened the door in shorts and a tank top; your face flushed from chasing Chloe around the house. You looked at me with those beautiful, green eyes… and I fell. Hard."

Calista's lips parted, but no words came. Her heart thundered in her chest.

"I fought it," Nickolas said, his voice rough with truth. "I wasn't ready for the way you made me feel. I didn't know what to do with it."

He took a tentative step closer, his eyes never leaving hers.

"I never wanted forever," he continued quietly. "Never dreamed of a family. But you… you changed all of that. Now it's the only thing I want. You, me, and Chloe— together. A home. A real life. And maybe someday if you're willing… we could grow that family too."

He stepped in front of her, slowly lifting his hand to gently cup her face. She leaned into his touch, eyes fluttering shut, like she'd been waiting for it.

"I'm scared," she whispered.

"So am I," he said, his voice low, trembling with emotion. "Scared that you'll never forgive me… that I won't get the chance to show you how much I love you. With everything I am. With all my heart."

"I love you," she whispered, barely more than breath.

He leaned down, his gaze searching hers for a heartbeat longer—then brushed his lips against hers in a kiss as soft as a promise, as light as a feather's touch.

He lifted his head, searching her face.

She turned away, her voice barely steady. "How can I do this, Nickolas? Your mother will always be there—judging, interfering, trying to push me out. I can't be the reason your family falls apart."

Nickolas's voice was quiet, but resolute. "My family was fractured long before you entered it. Cassia barely speaks to our mother. And I've spent my entire life trying to earn love from a woman who only knows how to control, not care."

He reached for her hand, holding it gently.

"You and Chloe… you're the only part of my life that feels real. The only thing that's ever felt whole."

Her breath caught, emotion tightening her throat.

"You didn't break anything, Calista," he said softly. "You reminded me what love is supposed to look like."

He paused, then added with quiet conviction, "I won't let her poison this. Not again. And if she ever wants to be part of our lives, it will be on our terms—not hers."

Calista stared at him, her eyes shimmering with unshed tears. Her voice was barely a whisper. "I want to believe you."

Nickolas stepped closer, his hands cradling her face with reverence. "Then let me show you. Not just with words, but every day from now on. I want to build something with you, Calista. Something no one can touch."

She closed her eyes, leaning into his touch as though she'd been holding herself upright for too long.

"Please, Calista" he breathed.

Her eyes opened slowly, locking with his. "I love you," she whispered.

He didn't wait another second.

He bent and brushed his lips over hers—soft as breath, warm as forgiveness. A kiss that asked permission, not possession. Her lips trembled beneath his, but she didn't pull away. She leaned in, pressing closer, her hands finding his chest, curling into the fabric of his shirt like she needed to feel his heartbeat.

The kiss deepened—not rushed, not desperate—but steeped in aching need and quiet promise. It wasn't just a kiss; it was an apology, a vow, a plea for one more chance.

Something in Calista gave way. The walls she'd built to protect herself began to crack, and in their place bloomed the ache of everything she still felt for him.

All she could think about was him—being with him, loving him, touching him. The way his hands framed her face like she was something precious. The way his breath trembled against her skin. The way his heart beat wildly beneath her fingertips, like it had always belonged to her.

She let go of the fear, if only for now, and let herself feel what she'd buried.

What they'd almost lost.

Frantically, Calista tugged his shirt free from his trousers, needing to feel his skin— needing to touch him, to ground herself in the reality of him. Her hands slid beneath the fabric, and the moment her palms met the warmth of his bare skin, he groaned her name like a prayer.

"Calista."

He pulled back just enough to strip the shirt over his head, dropping it carelessly to the floor. Then he was in front of her again, bare, and breathless.

Her hands explored his chest, tentative at first, then bolder—like she was trying to memorise him, rediscover every plane and curve, every scar and hollow. As if her fingers were tracing a truth she'd once known by heart and was desperate to remember again.

Her hands moved over him like a reverent whisper, fingertips grazing the hard lines of his abdomen, mapping the heat of him with aching, unspoken longing. Nickolas inhaled sharply, every muscle beneath her touch taut with restraint. Their mouths stayed connected—kissing, tasting, breathing each other in like something vital.

With a gentleness that trembled with need, he gathered the fabric of her dress in his hands, slipping it over her head in one fluid motion. The white cotton pooled at her feet, leaving her almost bare before him.

He didn't move. Just looked at her.

His eyes darkened, not just with desire—but with awe. With something sacred.

Then he sank to his knees before her, his lips brushing the curve of her bare stomach in a kiss that made her tremble.

"You're so beautiful," he murmured, his voice hoarse with awe, as if the sight of her undid him.

His fingers slipped beneath the elastic of her panties, dragging them slowly down her legs. His mouth followed in their place—hot, sure, devastating.

When she shattered beneath his touch, he rose, his breath uneven.

Calista barely had time to find hers before his lips found the hollow at the base of her throat, lingering in soft, reverent kisses that trailed along her collarbone. His hands circled her waist, drawing her flush against him, fitting their bodies together with aching precision.

She reached for him instinctively, her fingers threading through his hair, holding on like he was the only solid thing left in a world that had tilted on its axis.

Nickolas lifted her with ease, her legs wrapping around his waist like they belonged there. He carried her to the wall, pressing her gently against it—the coolness of the surface a jarring contrast to the fire smouldering between them. His mouth brushed her throat as he groaned her name, the sound low, ragged, hungry.

"I want you," he whispered, voice thick with hunger. "I need you."

Her answer was a breathless murmur, threaded with urgency. "I need you now."

He shifted, adjusting them with a careful reverence that made her shiver. And then—he entered her in one deep, aching thrust.

Her gasp was ragged. "God, Nickolas…"

His forehead rested against hers, his breath mingling with hers, their hearts pounding in shared rhythm.

"I love you," he said, the words falling from his lips like a vow. "With everything I am."

Calista clung to him, arms wrapped around his shoulders, her fingers buried in his hair as he moved within her—slowly at first, like he was memorising every sigh, every shiver. His hands supported her as though she were something precious, something breakable, and in his eyes was that same mix of hunger and reverence that made her chest ache.

Their mouths met in a kiss that was less about passion and more about promise—soft and deep, like a whisper spoken to the soul.

"I missed you," she murmured against his lips, breath catching as he thrust deeper, steadier. "I didn't know how to breathe without you."

"Never leave me again," he whispered, his voice cracking against her skin. "Not ever."

Calista cupped his face, her breath catching. "I won't," she promised, her voice trembling with truth. "You're my whole world."

Their bodies moved in a rhythm that spoke of longing and reclamation, desperate yet reverent—like they were stitching time back together with every breath, every touch. He was everywhere, surrounding her with the strength of his arms, the press of his mouth, the raw, aching love in every motion. She felt it in her bones—in the way he held her like she mattered more than anything he'd ever known.

Calista's head fell back as a cry tore from her throat, unrestrained and pure. He pulled her closer, his own control fraying, unravelling into something beautiful and real.

Their release came like a wave crashing over them—wild, consuming, undeniable. And then the world stilled, leaving only their mingled breaths and the thunder of his heartbeat against hers.

They clung to each other in the quiet aftermath, limbs tangled, hearts bare. It wasn't just passion. It was coming home.

For a long time, there was only the sound of their breathing, the thud of his heartbeat against hers, and the warmth of his body still holding her like a lifeline.

He leaned his forehead to hers again, eyes closed. "You're my home," he whispered.

Tears slipped silently from the corners of her eyes, and she kissed him gently. "And you're mine," she whispered, finally letting the last of her fears slip away.

505

Chapter Twenty-Eight

The morning light crept softly through the blinds, casting a warm, golden glow over the suite. The world outside had begun to stir, but inside, it was still. Quiet. The air felt heavy with the remnants of everything that had happened the night before.

Nickolas lay beside Calista, their bodies still entangled, her head resting against his chest. His fingers gently combed through her hair, marvelling at how right it felt to have her in his arms. They hadn't spoken much after their final, breathless moments, but the silence between them wasn't uncomfortable. It was filled with the unspoken understanding that they were back where they belonged.

Calista shifted slightly, stirring awake. Her eyes fluttered open, and she blinked, slowly adjusting to the morning light. She looked up at him, her gaze soft but filled with something deep and knowing.

"Good morning," she whispered, her voice thick with sleep.

Nickolas smiled, brushing a loose strand of hair away from her face. "Good morning, beautiful."

She stretched, her body still leaning into his, and let out a quiet sigh. "I never thought I'd feel like this again."

He nodded, his chest tightening with emotion. "I never thought I would either. But you're here now. And I'll never let you go again."

Her eyes glistened as she met his gaze. She didn't have to say anything. The sincerity in his words and the way his hands held her told her everything she needed to know.

The late morning sun filtered through the clouds as Nickolas pulled the car to a gentle stop in front of Henry's quaint cottage nestled along a quiet, tree-lined street. Calista's heart beat faster with every step she took toward the front door. Her arms ached to hold Chloe, to smell her hair and feel the little heartbeat that had steadied her through so many storms.

Before she could knock, the door burst open.

"Mommy!" Chloe's delighted squeal rang out like a song, and in the next second, she was flying into Calista's arms.

Calista dropped to her knees and wrapped her daughter in a fierce, tearful embrace. "Oh, baby... I missed you so much."

"I missed you too! Are you okay? Did you see the dolphins? Henry said they make people better," Chloe babbled into her neck.

Calista laughed, brushing her daughter's hair back from her face. "I did. And I'm better now. I promise."

Nickolas knelt beside them, his eyes soft as he watched the reunion. Chloe turned to him with a bright smile. "Daddy!"

His heart lurched as she threw herself into his arms too, no hesitation, no doubt. Just love.

He caught her with practiced ease, lifting her into his arms. "Hey, sweetheart. You ready to come with us? We've got something special to talk to you about."

"Is it ice cream?" Chloe asked hopefully.

"Better," he said, grinning. "But there might be ice cream too."

Behind them, Henry stepped onto the porch, his arms folded across his chest, a knowing smile tugging at his weathered features. "Well, looks like things worked out after all."

Calista stood, cradling Chloe's small backpack, her voice warm. "Thank you, Henry. For everything."

Henry gave her a gentle nod, then turned his gaze to Nickolas. He stepped forward and extended a firm hand. Nickolas took it without hesitation.

"You be good to these girls," Henry said quietly, but with steel behind the words. "They've been through enough."

Nickolas met his gaze and nodded. "You have my word. I'll spend the rest of my life proving it."

Henry studied him a moment longer, then gave a small, satisfied smile. "Then we're square."

As they walked toward the car, Chloe bouncing in Nickolas's arms and Calista beside them, hand brushing his, the sun seemed to shine a little brighter. A chapter had closed, but a new one—one filled with hope, and healing, and the promise of something lasting—was just beginning.

The last bell of the school day echoed through the halls, followed by the usual chorus of giggles, squeaky sneakers, and the rustling of backpacks. Calista stood near the classroom door, waving goodbye to each little face as they filed out with messy art projects and sticky hands.

"Bye, Miss Calista!"

"Have fun in Greece!"

"Don't forget us!"

Calista's smile was bright, but her heart squeezed with emotion. "I could never forget you," she called after them, blinking fast to keep the tears from falling.

The room quieted as the final child disappeared down the hall. She turned back toward the rows of tiny chairs, the scent of crayons and glue lingering in the air like a gentle memory. Slowly, she began clearing her desk—sticky notes, a chipped coffee mug with Best Helper Ever! in glittery print, Chloe's framed drawing of the two of them holding hands under a rainbow.

Her fingers lingered on the drawing. In five more days, she reminded herself. Just five.

Five more days until she and Chloe will board Nickolas's private jet that would take them across the world—to Athens, to Nickolas, to a life that still felt like a dream whenever she allowed herself to believe it was real.

She missed him. Fiercely.

They had parted two weeks ago, their goodbye at the airport tender and quiet, Nickolas holding her a moment longer than necessary, like he didn't trust the world to keep her safe without him. He had to return to his business and responsibilities. She had to pack up her life, quit her job, sort through memories tucked into drawers and boxes. It had all felt overwhelming—except for the way Chloe lit up every morning talking about Greece.

"I'm going to live with my daddy," she'd told her preschool friends proudly. "And my mommy. We're going to be a family. And maybe I'll ride a donkey or meet a dolphin!"

Calista had laughed then, but at night, when Chloe was asleep and the house was quiet, she would sit in bed and scroll through her phone, rereading Nickolas's messages, watching the short videos he sent of Athens—the view from the penthouse terrace, the sparkling sea, a bakery that promised to have Chloe's favourite cheese pies.

He called every day. Morning and night. Sometimes more. But his voice on the phone wasn't the same as feeling his arms around her or watching the way his eyes softened when he looked at her. She missed the way he touched the small of her back absentmindedly, how he knelt to tie Chloe's shoe without a second thought, how he made her feel like no one else in the world mattered.

A soft knock pulled her from her thoughts.

It was Mrs. Townsend, the lead kindergarten teacher. "Just wanted to say goodbye. You've been such a gift here, Calista. They all adored you."

Calista rose and hugged the older woman. "Thank you. This place… it's been home. It's hard to leave."

"You're off to start a beautiful new chapter." Mrs. Townsend smiled knowingly. "And that little girl of yours is over the moon."

Calista laughed gently. "She really is. I just hope we're doing the right thing."

"You love him?"

Calista didn't hesitate. "Yes. Completely."

"Then you're already doing the right thing."

When she was alone again, Calista looked around one final time. She placed the drawing in her tote bag, took a steadying breath, and flicked off the lights.

As she stepped out into the golden afternoon, the sun warming her face, she could almost feel Nickolas's hand in hers again. Five more days. And then the distance between them would disappear.

And this time… she wouldn't have to let go.

The afternoon sun spilled through the glass walls of Nickolas Drakos's high-rise office, casting long lines of golden light across the polished floor. The city stretched out far below him, bustling and vibrant, but his thoughts were elsewhere—halfway across the world, with a woman and a little girl who had become his entire universe.

He was reviewing a contract when the intercom buzzed.

"Mr. Drakos," his secretary's voice came through, crisp and professional. "Miss Drakos is here to see you."

He set the pen down and sat straighter. "Send her in."

The door opened and Cassia stepped inside with her usual graceful poise. Dressed in elegant neutrals with a silk scarf knotted around her throat, she moved like someone who had never known uncertainty. She crossed the room and leaned down to kiss his cheek.

"Hello, Nik."

"Cassia," he greeted warmly. "To what do I owe this visit?"

She smiled as she sat across from him. "I was in the area and thought I'd stop by. We haven't had a proper conversation in weeks. And… I wanted to ask when you're expecting Calista and Chloe."

Nickolas leaned back in his chair, a faint smile tugging at the corner of his mouth. "I'm flying out tomorrow to bring them home. They should be safely here by Saturday afternoon."

His voice softened on that last word—home.

Cassia tilted her head, studying him. "And not a moment too soon, I imagine."

"Exactly," he said, exhaling slowly. "These past two weeks without them… I never realised how quiet life could feel. Empty, even."

She nodded knowingly. "I called Calista last night. Just to check in. She sounded… sad."

Nickolas's brows drew together slightly, the smile fading. "It's a big step for her. Leaving everything she knows behind. Friends. Work. The only home Chloe's ever had. She's doing it for their future—for our future—but I know it's not easy."

Cassia gave a small, wistful smile. "She's brave. And you're lucky."

"I know I am."

"And Chloe?" she asked gently. "How is she handling it all?"

Nickolas's eyes brightened. "She's thrilled. Tells everyone she meets that she and her mommy are going to live with her daddy. She has no fear, no doubts. Just excitement." He paused. "Her joy makes this feel real in a way nothing else could."

Cassia's expression softened. "Children have a way of showing us what really matters."

"She's changed everything," Nickolas said, quietly. "They both have."

There was a brief silence between them, not uncomfortable—just reflective.

"I'm looking forward to seeing them again," Cassia said sincerely. "Really. It'll be good to have them here."

Nickolas gave her a nod of appreciation. "Thank you, Cass. That means a lot."

As she stood to leave, she added with a sly smile, "You better be ready, Nik. Once they're here, everything changes."

He gave a low chuckle, then paused, reaching into the top drawer of his desk. "Before you go… give me your opinion."

Cassia turned back, eyebrows raised with curiosity.

Nickolas pulled out a small velvet box and handed it to her. Her brows lifted higher, a spark of surprise lighting her face as she carefully opened it.

"Oh, Nik…" she breathed, her voice catching. "Is this what I think it is?"

Inside nestled a stunning emerald and diamond ring—elegant, timeless. The emerald was deep green and luminous, framed by a halo of white diamonds that caught the light with every movement.

"It's beautiful," she said softly, her smile growing. "Calista's going to love it."

Nickolas's expression was a mix of anticipation and nerves. "You think so?"

Cassia looked up, her gaze gentle. "I know so. It's bold, rare, and unforgettable—just like her."

He nodded, closing the box carefully. "I wanted it to be something that reminds her of who she is. Strong. Precious. One of a kind."

Cassia placed a hand over his. "She'll say yes, Nik."

"I hope so," he said quietly, more to himself than to her.

Because this time… he wasn't just asking for her heart.

He was asking for forever.

As Cassia turned to leave, she glanced back over her shoulder, a teasing smile tugging at her lips. "I never thought I'd see the day—you, head over heels."

Nickolas leaned back in his chair, the velvet box still in his hand. His expression softened with something close to awe.

"Neither did I," he said quietly. "But I'm so grateful to have met her."

Cassia's smile deepened, this time touched with warmth. "She changed everything, didn't she?"

He nodded. "She made me want more than power and success. She made me want a life… a real one."

Cassia gave him a knowing look. "Then don't waste another second. Make it count, Nik."

As she stepped out and the door clicked shut behind her, Nickolas turned his gaze to the skyline outside.

Four more days.

And then the rest of his life would begin.

Chapter Twenty-Nine

Nickolas carried Chloe in one arm and held Calista's hand in the other as they stepped into his penthouse for the first time. The heavy door clicked shut behind them with a soft finality, sealing them into a space that felt both unfamiliar and oddly comforting.

Calista paused, letting her gaze sweep over the soaring ceilings, the understated elegance, and the soft ambient lighting. The air was cool and faintly scented—clean linen and something subtly masculine, like sandalwood. After ten long hours in the air and another navigating customs and baggage, stepping into this oasis felt like exhaling for the first time in days.

Home.

Chloe's head rested sleepily on Nickolas's shoulder; her tiny arms looped loosely around his neck. Her pink carry-on trailed behind them, caught in Calista's grip. One of Chloe's pigtails had come undone, and her cheeks were flushed—equal parts excitement and exhaustion.

Nickolas walked ahead, then turned near the archway that led deeper into the apartment. His eyes locked on Calista's, warm and unwavering.

"Welcome home," he said, his voice low and full of meaning.

Then he adjusted Chloe in his arms and smiled down at her. "Come on, sweetheart. I have something to show you."

Chloe lit up instantly. "Is it ice cream?"

Nickolas laughed. "Better."

He carried Chloe down the hallway, Calista trailing just behind, her heart tightening at the sight of them together—Nickolas holding their daughter with such care, as if she were something precious and fragile he couldn't bear to drop.

They stopped in front of a pair of white double doors near the end of the corridor. Nickolas turned to Chloe with a conspiratorial smile.

"Ready?"

She nodded, eyes wide with curiosity.

He pushed open the doors.

The room beyond looked like something out of a storybook. The walls were painted the softest blush pink, and a white daybed sat beneath a gauzy canopy, pillows piled high and stuffed animals already waiting. A dollhouse nearly as tall as Chloe stood in one corner, and opposite it, a wall of shelves overflowed with books, puzzles, and art supplies. But it was the mural that stole the breath from the room—a scene of dolphins leaping through painted waves, their silver-blue bodies shimmering under the warm recessed lights.

Chloe gasped. "Mommy!" she whispered, twisting in Nickolas's arms and wriggling free. "There are dolphins!"

Calista pressed a hand to her chest, emotion rising like a tide. "I see, baby," she said softly, blinking back tears. "Aren't they beautiful?"

Nickolas looks at Chloe's flushed face. "Do you like it?"

"I love it!" Chloe declared, throwing herself onto the bed in a flurry of limbs and giggles. "Can I sleep here now?"

Nickolas chuckled. "That's the idea."

They helped her change into pyjamas, tucked her in beneath a lavender quilt, and kissed her goodnight. Chloe barely had time to murmur, "I really like it here," before her eyes fluttered shut. The long day had finally caught up with her.

Calista reached down and gently smoothed the hair back from Chloe's forehead. Nickolas leaned over and switched on the dolphin-shaped nightlight.

Together, they backed out of the room and quietly closed the door behind them.

The hallway was silent, dimly lit by the golden sconces along the wall. Calista turned toward him, her arms wrapped loosely around her waist.

Before she could say a word, Nickolas stepped forward and swept her into his arms with effortless strength.

"Nickolas," she laughed, surprised, her arms instinctively winding around his neck.

He silenced her with a quick, searing kiss to her lips. "I've missed you," he whispered against her mouth.

She melted into him, her cheek pressing to his shoulder as her fingers tangled in his hair. Every part of her relaxed in his hold, as though her body remembered something her mind was just catching up to.

"It feels like an eternity since I've had you in my arms," he murmured, his voice low and thick with longing.

Without another word, he carried her to their bedroom. The door clicked softly shut behind them as he crossed the room and laid her gently on the bed. He came down beside her, half covering her body with his, and kissed her—deep and unhurried, a kiss that said everything words could not.

She kissed him back with equal fervour, arms tight around him, anchoring herself to the one place that felt like home.

"God, I've missed you," he whispered against her lips, his voice trembling with truth.

Her eyes fluttered closed as she murmured, "I love you. I've missed you so much."

Their mouths met again, a long, lingering kiss that spoke of distance closed and time reclaimed. The kind of kiss that silenced the world.

Then, suddenly, Nickolas pulled back. He sat up quickly, breathless, and tugged Calista gently up with him.

She blinked in surprise, her lips still tingling. "What is it?"

"I can't wait any longer," he said, his eyes searching hers. "I have to know."

"Know what?" she asked, brows furrowing in confusion.

Nickolas reached into the nightstand drawer and pulled out a small velvet box.

Calista stared, uncomprehending for a heartbeat. Then she laughed, a breathless sound. "What are you up to?" she asked, a nervous flutter rising in her chest.

But Nickolas wasn't laughing.

His gaze held hers—steady, unwavering—full of something that made her heart stop. Love. Certainty. A quiet promise, waiting to be spoken.

He dropped to one knee in front of her, where she sat on the edge of the bed.

Nickolas took her hand in his, the unopened box resting in his other. He drew in a breath, not from nerves, but from the gravity of the moment—like he needed to centre himself before saying something that would live in both their hearts forever.

"When I met you," he said softly, "you took my breath away. I didn't know I was meeting the woman who would change my life forever. You've rewritten everything I believed about love and family. You and Chloe… you're my whole world now. And you—you're at the centre of it all."

Calista's breath caught. Her eyes shimmered.

Then he opened the box.

Inside, nestled in velvet, was a ring—an emerald, rich and vivid, framed by a halo of white diamonds. Elegant. Understated. Beautiful. Like her. The delicate band sparkled as it caught the soft light of the room.

"I don't want to go one more day without knowing you're mine. Not just in my heart, but in name, in life. Calista," his voice dipped, reverent, "will you marry me?"

For a long moment, she could only stare. Her heart pounded so hard it felt like her whole body beat with it. Her throat thickened, her vision blurred.

Then a laugh broke from her, breathless and full of wonder. She covered her mouth with her trembling hand.

"Yes," she whispered, the word fragile with emotion—then stronger, steadier, tears streaming freely. "Yes. Of course I'll marry you."

Nickolas slid the ring onto her finger with hands that shook ever so slightly. Then he rose and pulled her into his arms, holding her like he never intended to let go again. He buried his face in the curve of her neck, and for the first time in a long time, everything felt right.

Calista pulled back just enough to look into his eyes, her voice husky and low.

"If you don't make love to me soon, I'm going to lose my mind."

His mouth curved in a slow, wicked smile. "Then I guess we'd better not waste another second."

Epilogue

Two Years Later...

The bridal suite was a flurry of soft laughter, perfume, and satin ribbons, but Calista stood still for a moment, her hands gently adjusting Cassia's veil with the kind of tenderness only a sister-by-love could give.

"You look so beautiful, Cassia," she whispered, eyes gleaming as she took in the radiant bride.

Cassia turned, her eyes wide and shimmering with emotion. "I can't believe this day is finally here."

Calista smiled, one hand resting instinctively on the swell of her very pregnant belly. "Believe it. You're about to marry a man who adores you."

It all began at her and Nickolas's wedding—candlelight flickering, champagne flowing, and Henry catching sight of Cassia across the dance floor. One spark, one laugh, one slow dance... and they'd been inseparable ever since. Now, eighteen months and a thousand stolen kisses later, it was their turn to say, 'I do.'

Earlier that afternoon, Calista had seen Henry briefly—nervous in the best way, pacing by the fountain in his suit.

He had taken her hands in his, his voice a little hoarse. "I didn't think I'd ever love anyone more than I loved you."

Calista had smiled at him, full of genuine affection and peace. "I always knew you would. You deserve happiness, Henry. And Cassia... Cassia is a lucky woman."

"No," he'd said softly. "I'm the lucky one."

Now, the ceremony was unfolding like a dream. The vows were tender, the kiss sweet and lingering. No hiccups, no forgotten lines. Just love, bright and boundless, shared beneath a sky of white roses and Grecian sun.

Later, beneath strings of fairy lights and the gentle hum of violins, Nickolas finally found Calista standing at the edge of the dance floor. She was watching Chloe twirl in her flower girl dress, laughter bubbling as Eleni—who had, in time, wholeheartedly welcomed Calista into the family—clapped along with her.

He slipped his arm around her waist and pulled her close. "Finally," he murmured against her temple, "I have you to myself."

She melted into his embrace, her head finding his chest as naturally as breath. "Cassia and Henry look so happy."

"Almost as happy as us," he said, gently brushing his knuckles along her cheek. "How are you feeling? I don't want you overdoing it. You've got precious cargo."

Calista laughed, her hands settling protectively over her belly. "Cargo? Am I that big?"

Nickolas grinned; eyes filled with that familiar blend of awe and adoration. "You're radiant. Glowing. And yes… maybe just a little round."

She playfully swatted his shoulder, then rose onto her toes to kiss him, her lips soft with laughter. "Well, round and radiant, you're still stuck with me."

"Forever," he vowed, his voice low and sure. He rested a protective hand over hers, where the faint thump of their unborn child stirred beneath her palm.

A smile tugged at his mouth. "Our son is quite the dancer tonight."

She laughed, eyes bright. "He's been doing somersaults since dessert. I think he's going to be just like his sister—impossible to keep still."

Nickolas twirled her gently onto the dance floor, one hand at the small of her back, the other cradling her hand as though it were the most precious thing in the world.

"Well, then we're in for a very lively household," he murmured, brushing a kiss to her forehead as they swayed together in the golden light. "And I wouldn't have it any other way."

Calista looked up at him, her heart full. "You've made me so happy, Nickolas. Sometimes I have to pinch myself just to believe this is real."

He smiled, his eyes soft with emotion. "I know exactly what you mean. Every morning, I wake up and see you beside me, and I think… how did I get this lucky?"

She rested her head against his chest, the rhythm of his heartbeat steady beneath her cheek. "We deserve this," she whispered. "All of it."

"And we're just getting started," he said, his hand gently caressing the curve of her belly. "Our forever is only beginning."

And as they danced, the night shimmered around them—full of beginnings, memories, and the quiet certainty of a love that had already built a home and would keep growing with every heartbeat.

The End

Thank you for reading Final Surrender!

If you enjoyed this collection of irresistible alpha heroes, keep an eye out for more upcoming romance collections by Alison Reid, including:

Alpha Kings - *A Billionaire Alpha Male Romance Collection*

Cautious Hearts - *A Trust-After-Heartbreak Romance Collection*

Dark & Dangerous - *Brooding Heroes Romance Collection*

Forbidden Hearts - *A Forbidden Love Romance Collection*

Forever Mine - *A Longing-for-Love Romance Collection*

Guarded Hearts - *A Surrender to Love Romance Collection*

Hearts & Secrets - *Small Town Romance Collection*

Hearts in Peril - *A Suspenseful Romance Collection*

Hidden Truths - *A Secret Identity Romance Collection*

Lies & Hearts - *A Lies, Secrets & Betrayal Romance Collection*

Love After Regret - *A Second-Chance Redemption Romance Collection*

Misjudged Hearts - *A Love After Judgement Romance Collection*

Torn Between Hearts - *A Love Triangle Romance Collection*

All of Alison Reid's books feature standalone stories, swoon-worthy heroes, and guaranteed happily-ever-afters.

Books by Alison Reid

A Billionaire for Christmas

A Heart in Florence

After The Storm

Always You

Before I Fell

Before the Thaw

Beneath the Lies

Billionaire Bodyguard

Billionaire Rancher

Blueprints of the Heart

Branlow

Collide

Echoes of Deception

Falling for the Billionaire

Forever Yours

Heart of the Outback

Hearts on the Line

Hidden Gem

Kept Promises

Mended Hearts

Mistaken Hearts

New Year's Eve Kiss

Quiet Danger

Reckless Hearts

Reflections of Deception

Second Glance

Shadows of the Past

Shattered Dreams

Shattered Hope, Stolen Kisses

Still Yours

The Billionaire's Accidental Legacy

The Billionaire's Bargain

The Billionaire's Mistake

The Billionaire's Regret

The Billionaire's Secret Baby

The Billionaire's Unexpected Heir

The Blood Debt

The Playboy's Surrender

The Wrong Sister

Trust in Time

Undercover Billionaire

Until you Loved Me

Vows of Vengeance

Wife in Name Only

Find all my books on Amazon:

https://www.amazon.com/author/alisonreid1970

About the Author

Alison Reid writes contemporary and small-town romance filled with heart, passion, and second-chance love stories. Her novels often feature strong heroines, irresistible heroes, and the happily-ever-afters readers adore. When she's not writing, Alison enjoys reading, spending time with her family, and imagining new love stories. She hopes her books give readers a few hours of escape, joy, and swoon-worthy romance they won't forget.